The Wild Mother

The Wild Mother

Elizabeth Cunningham

Station Hill Press

Published by Station Hill Literary Editions, under the Institute for Publishing Arts, Inc., Barrytown, New York 12507. Station Hill Literary Editions is supported in part by grants from the National Endowment for the Arts, a Federal Agency in Washington, D.C., and by the New York State Council on the Arts.

Distributed by the Talman Company, 131 Spring Street, Suite 201E-N, New York, New York 10012.

Jacket art and images used in the book as printer's ornaments by Johanne Renbeck.
Jacket and book design by Susan Quasha, assisted by Vicki Hickman.
Photography on end papers by Megan Hastie used in a design by George Quasha.

Library of Congress Cataloging-in-Publication Data

Cunningham, Elizabeth, 1953-
    The wild mother / Elizabeth Cunningham.
      p. cm.
    ISBN 0-88268-147-8 : $20.95
    1. Wild women—Fiction. 2. Mothers—Fiction.　I. Title.
PS3553.U473W55　1993
813' .54—dc20   93-2998
                                                CIP

Manufactured in the United States of America.

To Larry, Betty, and Lois
the fairy godparents
of this fairytale

❦ Contents ❦

BOOK THREE

Spring: The Escape of the Wild Mother

BOOK FOUR

Summer: The Return of the Wild Mother

The Wild Mother

Book One

Autumn
The Approach of
the Wild Mother

1
Behind the Wall

SUMMER would end; Mrs. Ursula Underwood knew it, though the day was deceptively mild. She could hear wild geese calling beyond the wall. Soon they would fly away, and the autumn winds and rains would come, gathering strength and bitterness as they swept over the bare hills of the Empty Land. Then winter would besiege the house, its cold infiltrating the cracks, its damp and drafts undaunted by hardwood fires or the feeble furnace. So on this end-of-summer afternoon, Ursula Underwood flung wide the windows and doors of the house she kept for her son and grandchildren at the edge of the Empty Land, as if to lure summer's warmth and light inside and trap them there until spring.

Out the door she swept the dust of the summer along with her grandson Fred and his dog, Lion, who had tracked the dust inside with their careless feet. As she stood in the doorway, broom in hand, watching Fred and Lion roll and wrestle on a frayed patch of lawn, it occurred to Grammar, as the children called her, that she must see to the state of the children's winter clothes and hang them out to air along with her own woolens. She worried whether the children's clothes would even fit. Fred had grown wantonly as a weed that summer; she would have to take a measuring stick to him. Ionia, Fred's older sister, had also grown taller, though thinner.

Where was Ionia? Grammar scanned the yard. No, she was not outside. Why didn't she ever play with her little brother? Why didn't she ever play? She was probably just sitting in that round window of hers doing nothing; for hours nothing! Grammar felt the mingled anxiety and irritation that always accompanied thoughts of Ionia. In contrast, the sight of Fred getting filthy was comforting. At least Fred was an ordinary little boy, exasperating only in ordinary ways. He, at least, seemed to have escaped harm from his parentage, but Ionia. . . . Grammar shook the image of that Creature, the children's mother, from her as she might have shaken dust kittens from her broom.

"Fred!" she called, taking refuge, as always, in practical action. "Come here and wait for me on these steps. I'm coming right down with your winter clothes. I want to measure you to see if you'll fit."

With that, she propped her broom against the wall and headed into the house, up the stairs, and down the hall. When she reached the small winding staircase to the tower room, her son's study, which she must pass on the way to the attic, she paused to listen. She could hear no pacing, but he must be in the tower room; that was where he always was, except at meals. His pacing sometimes drove her frantic, especially during the evenings, which she spent, after the children were in bed, in her private parlor directly below the tower room. For hours he would pace, and she would listen, too distracted to concentrate on who-done-it as she read a mystery novel or forgetting to cheat at solitaire or dropping stitches as she knitted.

But silence coming from the tower room unnerved her even more. What did he do up there? Oh, yes, she knew; he wrote scholarly articles and books; he composed lectures: Adam Underwood, renowned professor of alchemy at the University. But that was all she knew about what he did: what anyone could know who read his books or attended his lectures, and she was his mother. Yet it seemed to her that she did not know him, at least not since that summer he had disappeared in the Empty Land and returned with that Creature.

She did not trust him.

Cautiously, as if she feared something might suddenly pop out at her or grab her from behind, Grammar climbed the stairs. She hesitated before the door to the tower room, unable to resist the impulse to sniff. As she sniffed her face contorted into an expression of disgust, and she sniffed again, savoring her disgust.

Certainly a peculiar smell came from the tower room, and it lingered about Adam Underwood's person wherever he went. Women wondered if he wore musk; men assumed it must be his brand of tobacco. Ionia suspected stale magic. Grammar was convinced of mold.

Ursula Underwood had not cleaned the tower room in over a decade. It had been her husband's study then. Her son, however, kept the room locked, and no one went inside it but him. Adam, though very particular about his personal appearance, was oblivious to his surroundings and the mess he made of them. Knowing how his bedroom looked after a week, she could imagine the state of the tower room after ten years: litter everywhere, layers on layers of dust, books crawling with mold, mouse droppings on the floor, cobwebs dripping from the ceiling, and bats in the chimney. It affronted Mrs. Ursula Underwood to know that in a house she kept there was a room she could not clean.

She had ransacked the house many times for the key to the tower room, and she always carefully checked the pockets of his suits before they went to the dry-cleaners, but with no success. If she could have laid hands on the key, she would not have hesitated to enter the room and clean it without his permission. Her respect for cleanliness was far stronger than her respect for privacy.

Sometimes, when Adam was away at the University and she had run out of closets to sort and corners to scour and she had lost more than three games of solitaire in a row, Grammar would go to the door of the tower room and pick at the lock with a hairpin. But this afternoon she must content herself with a sniff and perhaps a peek at the keyhole. Just as she bent to steal a look, there was a commotion within the room: a chair scraped; something fell to the floor. Grammar's heart leapt, and before Adam could catch her at the keyhole, she scurried away to the attic.

🦶🦶🦶

Inside the tower room, Adam Underwood rose from his desk and crossed the room to shelve his latest work of scholarship, which he had just read over, with his other manuscripts. He had already contracted to publish this latest book on the Egyptian Alchemists; all that remained now was for the footnotes to be compiled, and he could set some graduate student to work on those. The book would rightly win him scholarly acclaim: his research had been thorough, his exposition compelling. That acclaim would afford him some satisfaction. Yet, in spite of distinction in his field and even some broader fame, scholarship remained an intellectual exercise, dry bones for a man who had once nearly mastered the secret of immortal flesh. And he would not even write about Her, his intimate knowledge of her secrets. A fairy story she would seem without the substantiation of her flesh. His colleagues would laugh him to scorn.

Yet he was not the only one who had encountered the race of Lilith, descended from the primordial Lilith, whom She claimed still lived, for whom She had been named. There were the ancient Babylonian tales. If only he could get his hands on those, maybe he could find a way to win her back, lure her inside the trap he had made. For two years Simeon Reid's agents had searched the Middle East for those tales. He ought to go look for them himself. That would be a summer's work more worthy than scholarship. But he could not take the chance. She might just appear while he was gone. He did not want to be far away from where he had first seen her that summer. Ten years ago was it?

Sighing and suddenly feeling old, Adam returned to his desk. His flesh had not become immortal through contact with hers. He had not possessed her ultimate secret. She had taught him only the trappings of immortality; then she had left him to a ritual existence made up of empty gestures. Yes, left him, but not left him alone, damn her. Six years since her desertion and still her image haunted him, making all his intellectual work acts of sheer will power.

The power of his will. It had always been his will against hers: that was their dance, their struggle and delight. Not love but war was between them, making their mating tonic with danger. Hers was the power of nature: of moon and tide and catastrophe, the haphazard power of a hurricane. But his was the power of man: deliberate, chosen, and his would triumph. Almost he had succeeded in subduing her; almost harnessed her power for his own purpose. Then she had fled, fled because, yes, she knew he was winning.

But it was not over. She might think it was, if she ever thought at all, and he was never sure she did. She might believe herself beyond his grasp, back among her people in the strange, boundless Empty Land. No man's land. He knew he could not seek her there again, as he had that summer ten years ago. Her people, those savage, two-breasted amazons, would tear him limb from limb like the wild animals they were. But there had to be other ways to get her back. He would have her again on his own territory, on his own terms. He must. It could not be over while her image still taunted him, flaunting itself. Somewhere she must still be playing their game, laughing at him, priding herself that she had eluded him forever. Never. His body might have aged, but the strength of his will was undiminished. She had always underestimated the power of his mind. Even now, if her image hovered, he would conquer it by consciously calling it forth.

There she stood before his mind's eye, a wisp of smoke, as he had first seen her on that distant hill, her black hair floating on the wind. As he sat at his desk, he felt his limbs stiffen, taut and ready, at the memory of the chase. It had lasted for days; tireless and swift, he pursued her over the bare hills until one evening at that indeterminate time between dark and light, he found her waiting by one of the pools that lay between the hills of the Empty Land.

She stood, still as the unbroken water; her skin had the same silver gleam. For a moment he felt disappointed. Like a little boy in a game of tag, he had wanted to catch her and wrestle her to the ground. But as he slowed his steps and stilled his own breathing, the man Adam knew that she was wilder in this motionlessness than in flight. Every fibre of his being told him that here was the challenge.

Keeping a rein on his excitement, he approached her and stood before her, staring, willing her to look at him. He could feel her compliance. She raised her eyes and met his. He could not see their color then, the purple that never ceased to startle, but he could feel their strangeness, the subtle lack of recognition they never quite lost, that made her eyes seem other than human. That strangeness stirred him as nothing ever had before.

He reached out his hand to touch her. She wore no garment of any kind. The surface of her naked body was cool and smooth as water, but beneath her skin he could feel a heat. She let his hands explore her, but she did not touch him. Always he could feel her eyes on him; he could sense their wariness. He would not have been surprised if, without warning, she had turned on him and torn him with her teeth and nails. He would not have cared.

When he was ready, he lifted her and laid her on the ground. He could smell the wild thyme crushed beneath her weight. He could smell the dampness of the night earth. He stripped himself and covered the small frame that somehow contained the power of all elements: earth and wind, water and fire in one. She opened the way to the deep, the heart, the secret of the universe. Through her, he, Adam Underwood, possessed it all.

At his desk, Adam sighed and his body slacked. There was some small victory in forcing her image to submit, but whether he made love to her in his mind or in the flesh, he was left unsatisfied. Some part of her evaded him. Afterwards he would search her eyes and find them unchanged. It maddened him and made him want her more. But she must not be allowed to distract him, either with her presence or her absence. He was in control. He would thrust her aside, lock her away in some dark chamber of his mind until he was ready to let her out again into the light of his consciousness.

He had opening-day lectures to prepare. He would fill his mind with those alone. Concentration had always been one of his powers, and he still possessed it, despite Her, and exercised it at will. He opened a drawer and delved into it, drawing out a set of lecture notes on: *Alchemy, Ancient and Modern; an Historic Approach to a Scientific Phenomenon*. These were skeleton notes, undecayed by time. The flesh of his lectures decomposed at the end of each year to be recomposed at the beginning of the next. He never taught any new courses. Professor Adam Underwood's courses had become a tradition. Neither the administration nor the students would tolerate any change in his curriculum; nor did he desire to make any changes. He found tradition a convenience.

Arranging his notes as best he could on a desk cluttered with pipes, pens and papers, rocks and bones, and one crystal ball, Adam began to pace round and round the tower room, following a path years of such pacing had worn in the once thick carpet. Absorbed in his mental oration, he did not hear the wild geese beyond the wall calling to one another. He did not look out the window to see them practice their formation in the sky. Nor did he notice the dust particles he disturbed forming galaxies in shafts of sunlight. Unnoticed, a spider spun down from the ceiling and crawled on the crystal ball. In the passage way outside the door, Adam's mother paused, unsuspected, to take one more surreptitious sniff on her way downstairs.

Outdoors Fred Underwood and his dog, Lion, were hiding behind the rhododendron bushes. Fred did not want to be measured, and he did not want to fit. It was all part of going to school for the first time, and he did not want to go. Grammar had told him that he would have to be clean every day when he went to school, which meant having a bath every night. He probably couldn't get out of a bath by hiding, but at least he could play a little longer. So he stayed still, watching and waiting behind the rhododendron bushes.

There was Grammar now, standing on the back steps, her arms piled high with clothes. "Drat the boy," he heard her mutter, "I told him to wait right here on these steps." Grammar set the clothes down on the doorsill and went back inside. Still Fred and Lion did not dare move, and a good thing, too. A moment later Grammar emerged with some small rugs, which she carried to the clothes-line grumbling, "Dog hair everywhere. All over the rugs. Drat the dog." When she had hung the rugs on the clothesline, she fetched her broom and began to beat them, repeating, "Drat the dog! Drat the boy!" with every stroke.

Fred and Lion watched until they were sure Grammar would go on beating the rugs in their name for a long time. Now they could go on safari to the far flower bed where they might capture worms, woolly bears, spiders, toads, and snakes for Fred's zoo. But they must be careful or Grammar would catch them and throw them into the dungeon and feed them fried slime for supper. Grammar was really a witch, Fred knew.

Without rattling a leaf or snapping a twig, Fred and Lion crawled out from behind the rhododendron bushes. Then, with their bellies brushing the ground, they crept across the lawn, quietly as shadows. The jungle loomed before them, glowing in the afternoon light. Sunflower giants glared down at them. Holly-hock dragons swayed in the sky. Even the chrysanthemums bristled fiercely, but Fred and Lion were not afraid. Was that a diamond-backed snake curled around that rock? Stealthily, stealthily, they stalked. And then the pounce! Too late. That snake was lost.

An hour, two woolly bears, and a toad later, Fred and Lion still hunted for wild beasts. The jungle shadows had grown longer and their shapes more mysterious. When Fred raised his hand to lift a rock that looked as though it might have worms beneath it, he noticed that his hand was barred and crossed with curious shadows. Holding it still in the air, he stared at his hand as another shadow crawled into the pattern, a large shadow with lots of legs creeping across his hand. Fascinated, Fred watched until he thought to turn around to see what was making the shadows. There, suspended between two hollyhock stalks, hung a huge spider's web. At its center sat an enormous black and yellow spider, the biggest, brightest, most ferocious spider Fred had ever seen. In his excitement over his discovery, Fred forgot that he was in the jungle on safari; he forgot he must keep quiet for fear of the witch.

"Ionia! Ionia!" he shouted. "Come and see the spider!"

Ionia Underwood, sitting curled in her round bedroom window, heard Fred call her, but she did not answer or even move. It was not that she did not want to see the spider; Ionia liked spiders, but she had different ideas about them than some people. She thought they ought to be left alone to weave their webs in peace, and so she admired them from a respectful distance. The most she had ever done to disturb a spider was to draw its picture, and that spider was living in her room in a corner obscured by her desk. So far she had been able to keep it a secret from Grammar and Fred. Grammar believed all spiders ought to be cleaned to death, while Fred's idea was to capture and cage them alive. Ionia hated Fred's zoo, a conglomeration of old jars and milk cartons on his window-sill. His zoo animals never lived long, and Fred always cried when they died. Over and over she had told him, "Things can't live in cages." But Fred never learned.

"It's big and yellow and black, Ionia! Come and see!"

Still Ionia neither answered nor moved. She was watching the wild geese. Only from her round window could she look over the high wall that surrounded the house and into the Empty Land. She envied the wild geese their wings. She had never even walked beyond the wall. She and Fred were not allowed to. Their father kept the gate locked, and in the late afternoon light, Ionia could see bright colored pieces of jagged glass glinting and sparkling along the top of the wall. When she was younger, maybe Fred's age, she had thought the glass pretty, but now she understood that it was meant to shred the hands of anyone who managed to climb that high. Why they might not walk beyond the wall she had long ago given up asking. "People have disappeared in the Empty Land" was the only answer she ever received, and that, she knew, was supposed to frighten her into silence. But no one could keep her from wondering about the world beyond the wall. She often spent a summer after-noon sitting in her round window staring out at the bare hills that rose higher than the walls.

On the crown of the closest hill grew three twisted trees. In the winter, with their branches bare and black against the sky, they looked like three huge spiders crawling over the hill. In spring they softened and seemed golden and fleecy until they deepened to a summer green. In autumn they were best of all.

Then their leaves turned a brilliant purple. Just today Ionia had noticed that the tree at the far left was beginning to catch color. Soon they would all burn in a purple blaze.

From behind this tree-crowned hill, the wild geese rose and fell. Each time they rose again her spirit rose with them. "What do you see? What do you see?" she whispered to the wild geese. There must be some kind of water, she guessed, for the wild geese to land on. Was it a little pond or a great lake? So she had spent her life: wondering what lay beyond that wall.

Sometimes at night Ionia dreamed of a woman who crested the hill to dance beneath the trees by moonlight. The woman's hair was darker than the night and wilder than the wind. Her dance would begin gently and then slowly grow stronger until even the trees and the hills seemed to dance with her. Then she would stretch out her arms to the house. "Ionia, Ionia," she seemed to sing, but her voice might have been the wind's. Yet Ionia always felt certain that if only she knew how, she could fly out the window, fly over the wall, fly to the hilltop to dance with the woman with the wild black hair. Just as she was about to open the window to try, she would wake and find herself on the floor beside the window-sill. When she looked out at the hill, the woman was never there.

Whenever she had this dream, Ionia tried to draw a picture of it. She would draw the hill first, then the trees, then the moon, and last the woman dancing. One day when Ionia had been drawing at the kitchen table, Grammar had peered over her shoulder. When she had seen what the picture was, she had snatched it away and torn it to pieces. Not content that the damage was sufficient, she had thrown the bits into the fireplace, muttering over and over to herself, "What if her father had seen it! Just think if her father had seen it!" She had ordered Ionia never to draw again.

Ionia had never bothered to ask why; Grammar never explained anything, especially about her father. But she had not stopped drawing either. She drew pictures at night after she had seen Grammar retire to her private parlor with a hot water bottle and a mystery novel. She kept her pictures and drawing supplies locked in a drawer of her desk to which Grammar did not have a key. Maybe tonight she would draw a picture of the wild geese and the purple trees.

"Ionia! Hurry up and see the spider!"

"Only if you promise not to capture it for your zoo," she called, but still she did not move.

Once again the wild geese rose, catching the last light of day on their wings. This time they did not dip down. Their formation perfect, they flew away into the Empty Land. Ionia watched them until they disappeared. Summer had ended; Ionia knew it.

2
Secret Counsel

FRED! I saw that, Fred!" shouted Grammar from her end of the dinner table. "I saw you sneak your brussels sprouts to Lion," she continued, waving the brussels sprout she had speared at the end of her fork through the air. "I'm warning you, Fred," she concluded, and she bit the brussels sprout off her fork and went back to sawing her liver.

Fred giggled into his napkin, then choked when he tried to drink his milk. Lion skulked further under Fred's chair. To avoid looking at Fred and catching his giggles, Ionia began to unfold a brussels sprout leaf by leaf. Their father, at the other extremity of the table, said nothing; he had noticed nothing. He was engaged, as he always was at the dinner table, in philosophical contemplation. So the meal continued in silence that was broken only by the sounds of silverware scraping plates, of mouths chewing, of throats swallowing.

Grammar had long ago given up trying to conduct conversation at the dinner table. Her son's response to her earlier efforts had been, at best, polite boredom, at worst, downright rudeness. It had become apparent to her several years ago that her son did not wish to deal with her as a person or even a mother. He wished to think of her as a household fixture; or rather he wished not to think of her. One did not think of household fixtures so long as they worked.

Her grandchildren were not much more responsive than her son. If she tried to speak with them, except to reprimand them or correct their table manners, they looked as surprised as if she had laid an egg. She supposed it was not their fault; they had never heard ordinary human conversation. If she could have gotten legal custody over them, she would have taken them away to live among decent human beings. As it was, she found living with her family was not like living with human beings at all.

Once again a slight movement, which she had accustomed herself to see even when she was not looking, caught Grammar's attention.

"Fred! Not your liver too!" she protested. "For shame! Wasting good meat!"

Fred had indeed slithered his liver off his plate into the waiting jaws of Lion, but it was not good meat, and it was not wasted either. Lion liked liver; Fred did not.

"If I catch you feeding that dog one more time at the dinner table, you'll both eat out of a bowl on the kitchen floor."

Fred looked pleased with the proposal. Lion thumped his tail in approval. The Professor, who had not touched his own brussels sprouts, leaned back in his chair and lit a pipe. Ionia discreetly dropped a napkin, concealing her liver, onto the floor.

Grammar sensed a general indifference to her authority.

"Just you wait!" she threatened no one in particular as she rose from the table to clear the dishes. "Just you wait!"

When Grammar had left the room, Fred and Ionia glanced first at their father and then at each other. As usual, their father seemed unaware of their presence, as he sat smoking his pipe and gazing at some distant point on the wall far above their heads. Ionia and Fred preferred to be ignored by their father; for whenever he focused his attention on them, he frightened them by staring at them as if he could see their insides and by asking strange questions they did not understand or could not answer about their dreams and memories. Even when he appeared to have forgotten them, they were careful not to remind him of themselves. So they sat still in cautious silence, regarding their father as they might have a sleeping dragon. Indeed, with his eyes half closed and with the smoke trickling out of his nose, he resembled one.

After some moments had passed, and with her father still staring at the wall, Ionia, as casually and quietly as she could, reached for the butter dish and smeared what remained of the butter over the surface. Then, as if she were idly amusing herself, she began to draw in the butter with a prong of her fork. Glancing furtively at her father to make sure he had noticed nothing so far, she slid the plate across the table to Fred. He examined the drawing of two squares connected by a smaller square with an X at its center and nodded. He understood that Ionia had called a secret counsel.

Stealing another look at her father, Ionia reached for the plate again. Rubbing the first picture out, she began to draw a picture of an old woman in bed with a hot water bottle on her feet and a book in her hands. This was meant to indicate to Fred, who could not read a clock, when the counsel was to be held. Before she could finish and hand the plate back to Fred, Grammar re-entered the dining room to clear the rest of the table. Unlike their father, Grammar noticed everything.

"What are you doing with that butter dish, Ionia?" she demanded.

Before Ionia could erase the picture, Grammar had snatched the dish away and was staring at it. Fortunately, Grammar did not recognize her portrait.

In the small walled world, ruled by their mysterious father and run by their dictating Grammar, Fred and Ionia were like two tiny countries: remote in times of quiet because of different customs, but close in times of crisis because of common need. Especially for Fred, who was going to school for the first time, the end of summer qualified as a time of crisis, and whenever there was a crisis there had to be a secret counsel.

The counsel chamber was a crawl space, accessible on two sides by way of trap doors in the backs of Ionia and Fred's bedroom closets. That night Ionia arrived first, as usual, with matches and a half-burned candle she had pilfered from the pantry drawer. She crouched in the low space, lit the candle, dripped enough wax on the floor to stand it in, then knocked on Fred's wall to let him know it was all right to come in. Fred was afraid both of the dark and of lighting matches. In a moment Ionia heard his trap door creak, and in crawled Fred, followed by Lion.

For a time all three sat in silence gazing at the candle flame, listening to the quiet of the night house, feeling the awful solemnity of a secret counsel. Finally, Fred spoke.

"Tell me the story of school, Ionia."

Ionia began by describing the journey there, making it sound as exciting as possible. They would drive through the gate sitting in the back seat of their father's car. On the way to the train station they would pass a rickety gray farm that always looked as if it were about to blow away with the wind. If Fred looked quickly, he would be able to see pigs rooting in the mud and two cows waiting to be milked. Further off he would see some sheep and goats munching a meadow.

At the idea of really seeing all these animals he had only seen in picture books before, Fred became excited. Joy ran through his fingertips and communicated itself to Lion, who began to thump his tail frantically, and Fred was reminded of his gravest concern.

"Is Lion going to school, too?"

Ionia shook her head.

"I won't go to school without Lion."

"You have to."

"Why?"

"Dogs aren't allowed in school. No one can have a dog in school." Seeing that Fred was about to wail in protest, Ionia tried to distract him by telling him about the train ride and about Albert, the train conductor, who always slipped her a piece of candy when her father wasn't looking.

"Will he give me candy, too?"

Candy was something Fred had only eaten a few times when Ionia smuggled it to him. Grammar did not believe in sweets.

"When he knows you're coming every day he will," Ionia assured him. "And tomorrow," she added, "you can have the window seat. After that we have to take turns, because sitting next to the window is the best part."

Fred considered these new adventures; then he asked again:

"Are you sure Lion can't go with me?"

"Positive."

"I'm not going then."

"You have to. Besides, Fred, school isn't very scary. All you have to do is sit still with a lot of other kids and listen to the teacher talk. It's mostly boring."

"Why do you have to sit still?"

"That's how they make you learn."

"What's learning like?"

"It's all right sometimes. In your grade they teach you letters, and then you learn words, and then you learn reading. It's good to know how to read, because when you're as old as I am and they try to teach you things you don't want to learn, you can keep a book hidden in your desk and read it when the teacher isn't looking."

Fred thought for a moment.

"If I learn reading, I want Lion to learn it, too."

"Well, you can teach him yourself after school."

"But school lasts all day until night, doesn't it?"

"No, it gets out in the afternoon, but then we have to go to Jason Brooke's house until our father is ready to go home."

"Jason Brooke! You mean we get to go to Jason Brooke's house every day!"

"Every day." Ionia sighed.

The idea of seeing the place where Jason Brooke lived and slept and even ate silenced Fred and made him momentarily forget the horrors of school and separation from Lion. Last spring Jason and his mother had come to the house for an evening, and after dinner Jason had visited Fred's zoo. When he had examined each animal and questioned Fred about its capture, care, and feeding, Jason had announced, "You seem to have some very fine specimens here. I congratulate you." For weeks afterwards, Fred had pestered Ionia to come and see his "specimoons" until he had forgotten the word, though never the man.

Ionia did not share Fred's feelings for Jason Brooke. But she said nothing to disillusion him. All summer she had dreaded the recommencement of those long afternoons spent with Jason in his mother's cramped city apartment. If Jason and Fred amused each other, so much the better for her. Maybe then they'd both leave her alone to read or draw in peace.

Jason Brooke was only eleven, one year older than she was, but he liked to act as if he were a grownup. He had made it clear to her that since he was ahead of her in school and obviously knew more besides, having more of what he called "native intelligence" than she did, it was he who ought to talk, and she who ought to listen. Jason Brooke had no lack of subject matter. He was a collector; he collected everything: stamps, bottles, beetles, coins, maps, butterflies, bones, doorknobs, stones, buttons, buckles, arrowheads, knots, teeth. He was always dragging Ionia off to his bedroom to lecture to her on what he called his "items of interest." The walls of Jason's bedroom were papered with pictures of the constellations, and Ionia rather liked to look at them, but whenever Jason caught her gaze wandering towards his walls, he would get out his pointer and go on for hours telling Ionia millions of detailed facts she had never asked to know. Jason Brooke was a person who could make the stars seem boring.

Jason's mother was different. Ionia liked her better than anyone she knew. Although Mrs. Brooke was tall, almost tall enough to be a giant, and big boned, she seemed more like a child than a grownup. Her hair, which she tried to keep tied in a bun, kept coming undone and falling in her face, making her seem shyer than she was. Her clothes often looked as if she had just gotten up from somersaulting in the grass. But it was the way she treated children that made her most unlike other grownups. For one thing, she didn't ask questions, neither strange ones, like Ionia's father asked, nor stupid ones like the teachers at school. Yet she was not like Grammar, who did not ask questions because she was not interested so long as you ate properly, dressed properly, and behaved properly. Mrs. Brooke was interested. She let you know by the way she looked at you.

For a long time Mrs. Brooke had just looked at Ionia and let her be. Then, one day, Ionia had given Mrs. Brooke a picture, drawn on the school scrap paper that she hoarded, as a present. Ever since, Mrs. Brooke had kept Ionia supplied with paper and colored pencils and pens. She had even made one wall of her bedroom a gallery for Ionia's pictures.

Ionia imagined that it must be because Mrs. Brooke was a professor of fairytales that she liked the pictures so much. Mrs. Brooke collected fairytales, Ionia knew; only her collecting was not at all like Jason's collections. She did not store her fairytales in dusty cabinets, then take them out and demand that you admire them. Instead, every once in a while, when you were least expecting it, she would tell you one or give you one, bound in a book with beautiful pictures, when it wasn't even your birthday. The worst thing about Jason's collections—his beetles, his doorknobs, his bones—was that they were all dead, dead, dead. Fairytales were not. Ionia would have liked to spend an afternoon listening to them.

Unfortunately, Ionia only saw Mrs. Brooke in the evening, and then only for a few moments, unless Mrs. Brooke had persuaded her father to stay for supper. Even though it meant more of Jason's company, Ionia enjoyed supper there. Mrs. Brooke liked to cook. She did not just serve meat and vegetables and potatoes, the way Grammar did. She made soup and rolls and gooey dishes with everything all mixed up together, and there was always something for dessert. As they ate, sitting crowded around the kitchen table, Ionia would watch in amazement as her father laughed and talked and looked almost human. Mrs. Brooke would undergo a transformation as well. After soup, her pale cheeks would begin to glow; during the main dish, her soft eyes would start to shine; by dessert and coffee, she would be radiant.

During these meals, Jason, for once, stopped talking, probably, Ionia thought, because he was afraid of her father or because he knew her father knew more than he did. The most Jason dared to do was glower. He would glower defiantly at all of them, but his mother and her father never seemed to notice. Ionia tried not to. She did not want Mrs. Brooke to suspect how much she hated Jason. For Mrs. Brooke's sake she might have tried to like Jason. For her sake she might have forgiven his collections and his endless lectures on the stars. There was one thing she would never forgive Jason, not even for Mrs. Brooke.

"You don't have a mother, you don't have a mother," Jason would begin time and again.

"Well, you don't have a father either," she would say when she could stand it no longer.

"Yes, but at least I know who my father was, and I know where he is. Captain William Brooke: killed in action. One of our glorious dead. Valiant man. A leader of men. May he rest in peace. Heroes' National Cemetery. We visit him twice a year."

"So what good is a dead father."

"A dead father is far more useful than no mother. No one knows who your mother was or where she is. Maybe you never had a mother. Maybe you weren't born at all. Maybe you were made in a test tube. You might have been one of their early experiments."

"Not me. That's how your mother got you, and I bet she's sorry."

"Or maybe you did have a mother," Jason would reconsider, "and she ran away. Ran away because she couldn't stand you. You and your little brother."

For some time Ionia and Fred had been silent watching the flame flicker, their eyelids growing thicker as drop after drop of hot wax dripped down the side of the candle to enlarge the pool on the floor. Lion, lying next to Fred, snored loudly and did not stir at the sound of mice scrambling in the walls. Finally, Fred, in a dream-laden voice, asked what he never failed to ask at a secret counsel no matter what it had been about.

"Ionia, tell me the story of my mother. Does she see me when I'm sleeping?"

Softly, Ionia began to croon the story of the mother with the long black hair, who sang with a voice like the wind's and wandered through their windows in the night to watch them while they slept.

Since Grammar refused to speak of her, and since their father kept secret counsel only with himself, Ionia and Fred had only each other to ask about their mother. What they did not know, they imagined. They had often spent a rainy afternoon in the counsel chamber telling each other stories of their mother: who she was and where she was. There was the story of the mother at the circus riding the elephants. Fred made that one up. There was one about the mother with the traveling stage show who danced every night in spangles and purple tights: one of Ionia's. They had made one up together about the mother with wings who lived in the top of the tallest tree in the world. But the one Fred liked best before bed was the one Ionia had woven of her own dreams and dimmest memories about the black-haired mother who wandered through their windows and watched them in the night.

When she had finished the story, Ionia saw that Fred had fallen asleep. Gently she woke him.

"I don't want to go to school without Lion," he mumbled through his dreams.

Ionia helped him back to his room, tucked him into bed with Lion, then crawled back to her own room, stopping to blow out the candle on the way.

3
Peculiarities

JASON," called Eva Brooke in a gentle voice as she knocked even more gently on his bedroom door. "It's time to get up."

"Don't you think I know that, Mother," answered Jason, who was already dressed and sitting at his desk constructing an intricate series of circles with his new compass, "I got up an hour ago."

"Oh," said Eva. "Do you want breakfast?"

"Of course. Two eggs, scrambled, sausage, toast, and coffee, black."

"We don't have any sausage."

"Bacon, then."

"Jason?"

"What?" he demanded impatiently.

"Are you sure you want coffee?"

"Just call me when it's ready."

Jason could hear his mother sigh as she turned away from his door. The sigh was followed by the sound of his mother's over-sized bedroom slippers slapping against the linoleum. The sound irritated him, but he did his best to ignore it while he went on making circles until he was satisfied that he had invented an entirely new geometric shape. Then, after admiring his work for several moments, he folded the paper and tucked it away in the pocket of a notebook he had labeled "Advanced Mathematics." This course was a new one the school was offering to only the most brilliant of the fifth- and sixth-grade students. Jason had received notice two weeks ago that he was one of the fifteen students chosen to take the course. He was eager to discover if Ionia Underwood had been admitted to the class, especially as he was almost sure she had not. The thought of this new proof of his superiority pleased Jason, and he smiled to himself as he opened his briefcase and began to arrange its contents.

Jason was glad that school was beginning again. Summer had been long and boring. He had no friends from school or in the neighborhood, so there had been only his mother for company. This summer they had not gone traveling as they had the past two years when his mother had been collecting fairytales. Her research grant had run out. Why the foundation had ever paid his mother to listen to stories, Jason did not know. It seemed to him a pointless occupation, but at least it had kept her busy and left him free to make scientific explorations in search of insects and rocks and other items to add to his own collections.

This summer, however, his mother had tried to make up for the disappointment of staying in the city by "spending more time with him" and "going on outings." These attempts at "enjoying each other's company" had mostly failed. They tried going to the beach several times, but Jason was embarrassed to be seen with his mother when she was wearing a bathing suit. Fortunately, as he could not quite bring himself to express his feelings on this subject, neither of them could swim very well, and both of them burned easily, so these outings soon ended. Next they had tried museums, but Jason was not interested in art galleries or costume exhibits, and his mother was not really interested in outer space exploration, though she pretended to be. Jason had felt relieved when they ran out of museums and retreated to their own rooms: she to transcribe the stories she had collected, he to organize and reorganize his collections.

Yet the weeks alone in his room had also proved trying. He did not enjoy his mother's company, but he found his own was not much better. What was the use of knowing all that he knew when there was no one to whom he could communicate his knowledge? His mother, he felt certain, never understood half of what he said, though she always looked impressed.

"Jason, your breakfast is ready."

Jason did not bother to answer, but he carefully laid his ruler, his compass, his calculator, and his slide rule on top of the mathematics notebook inside his briefcase. Soon, he reflected, he would be able to gauge the distance of any star from the earth at any given moment. That was one of the things he would learn how to do in this new class. Such a skill ought to impress Ionia. It would impress anyone. Only the problem with Ionia was that she was not like anyone. She was not normal. You never knew what she cared about or whether she cared about anything at all. Half the time she acted as if she couldn't see what was in front of her eyes. What puzzled him most about Ionia was his suspicion that she was not dumb; she deliberately did not want to know things. That he could not understand.

"Jason. Breakfast."

"All right," he called. "I heard you the first time."

Methodically, Jason checked to make sure he had everything he needed and that everything was in its exact place. Then he snapped shut his briefcase, rose from his desk, tucking the chair neatly beneath it, and left the room, locking the door behind him.

When her son entered the kitchen, Eva Brooke looked up from pouring the coffee and tried not to smile. Jason looked like a miniature professor carrying his briefcase and wearing his white shirt buttoned all the way up to his neck. His dark jacket was surely too warm for a sultry September day. She was about to tell him so when Jason caught her looking at him and frowned.

"You are still in your bathrobe, Mother," he observed critically as he seated himself before his bacon and eggs.

"I don't have to be at school as early as you do," she defended herself, "and, if I want to have your breakfast ready on time, I have to leave dressing 'til later."

Jason made no further comment but began to eat his breakfast. Eva watched him discreetly as she sipped her coffee. He cut his bacon with a knife and fork instead of picking it up in his fingers, and he used one piece of unbuttered toast as an aid to arranging his eggs on his fork.

Eva found Jason's tidiness intimidating at times. She felt it as an indirect criticism of her general carelessness in housekeeping. Jason was critical of her, she knew, and not only of her housekeeping but of her appearance, her opinions, even her occupation. She told herself that it was part of his growing up, this need to differentiate himself from her. She knew it was only natural for an eleven-year-old to be self-conscious. Jason was easily embarrassed. Mothers in general were an embarrassment to their sons, she supposed. Yet all her knowledge of the general rules could not keep her from feeling particularly hurt by his attitude towards her. She knew it was childish of her to mind, but in the last year or two she had often felt that she was the child in their relationship. It was she who was anxious to please and eager for approval. Jason took advantage of it, but that was her own fault, she suspected. She gave way to him too easily. She always had. Allowing him to drink coffee was only a small example.

As Jason finished his eggs and reached for his coffee, Eva looked away. She knew he did not like coffee; he only liked the idea of it. If she watched him trying to drink it without making faces, she would laugh, and Jason would never forgive her. Nor did she dare offer him cream and sugar; it would offend his dignity. Eva did wish that Jason had not so much dignity of which she had to be careful. It made her nervous. She could not relax in his presence.

"Will you go to your new math class today, Jason?" Eva inquired in order to relieve the silence between them.

"I don't know, Mother," answered Jason with an air of tried patience. "The notice only said that I was accepted. Not much happens on the first day of school anyway."

"You know, Jason, this will be Fred Underwood's first day of school."

"I know, Mother. You told me that already."

"He may be a little homesick," Eva continued, ignoring Jason's lack of interest. "I want you to be especially kind to him. Buy him an ice cream after school, and you might show him your collections."

This second idea appealed to Jason.

"Fred is not unintelligent for a child of his age," Jason considered. "I may be able to encourage his interest in science. At least Fred knows how to talk."

"Well, naturally he does. After all, he's six years old," Eva began; then, realizing what Jason had meant, she altered her tone, "Jason, I hope you will try to get along better with Ionia this year."

Jason stared into his cup as if he were contemplating his coffee. He wondered if Ionia had told his mother anything. It would be just like her sneaky, secretive self not to say anything to his face but to go behind his back to his mother.

"How do you know that I don't?" he asked cautiously.

"Just from things you say," answered Eva. "From remarks like the one you made just now."

So Ionia hadn't told his mother anything. Jason felt relieved and then annoyed. She'd have a nerve if she had. If he and Ionia didn't get along, it was more than half Ionia's fault, ignoring him the way she did.

"You must admit that Ionia is a little peculiar, Mother," Jason defended himself. "If you want my opinion, I think Ionia's got a mental problem."

Eva hesitated for a moment, considering how to answer Jason; for it was true, as he said, Ionia was peculiar. A more self-contained child Eva had never met. She seldom spoke unless she had to and never betrayed her feelings by word or look or gesture. There were times when she seemed, not less than human, but other than human. She reminded Eva then of a timid, wild creature, ready to bolt at the first sudden movement made towards her. Eva had never made that movement. She supposed that was why Ionia had finally come to trust her with the drawings that were the sole expression of her carefully guarded self. Ionia's trust made Eva feel protective of her, more protective than she had ever felt of Jason who denied his need of her.

"If you are right, Jason," Eva spoke at last, "then that is all the more reason not to make fun of her. You know that Ionia has lost her mother," Eva continued earnestly. "That can have an effect on a child. You ought to be able to sympathize with Ionia, Jason, having lost your own father."

Jason felt his face grow warm. He took a gulp of coffee to cover his embarrassment.

"Well, at least I'm not peculiar, Mother, even if I did lose my father," Jason pointed out when he had regained his composure. "And neither is Fred," he added, "not the way Ionia is."

Eva sighed and took a sip of her own coffee, feeling that Jason had missed her point and that it was useless to pursue the conversation further. She might only make things worse for Ionia by nagging him.

Jason, however, took advantage of his mother's retreat and attacked.

"What did happen to Ionia's mother anyway?"

Now it was Eva's turn to blush.

"I assume she's dead," said Eva shortly.

"But you don't know," commented Jason. "Do you, Mother?"

Eva was silent for a moment.

"No," she answered.

"Why not?" persisted Jason. "Why doesn't anyone know what happened to Ionia's mother?"

"Professor Underwood has made it clear that he does not like to be asked," said Eva sharply. "You must learn respect for other people's privacy, Jason."

"Well," said Jason triumphantly; for he knew he had gained the upper hand, "if you ask me the whole business is very peculiar, Mother."

Jason drained his coffee cup.

"Very peculiar," he repeated.

Briefcase in hand, Jason rose from the table.

"Good-bye Mother," he said.

For once it was he who smiled and she who did not smile back.

"Good-bye, Jason," she said as coldly as she could; then she relented and added more gently, "Have a good day at school."

Jason's only response was to close the door behind him.

Alone in the kitchen, Eva remained at the table pretending to finish her coffee. She knew she ought to clear the table, wash the dishes, dress, look over her lecture notes, and generally prepare for the day, but Jason's remarks had robbed her day of its goodness. She had lost the enthusiasm with which she had awoken. She knew it was foolish of her to mind what Jason said. He was, after all, only a child. He could not be expected to understand what he considered her peculiar relationship with Ionia's father.

Only here was the difficulty; she did not understand it either. She did wish Adam would tell her more about himself, not because she desired the knowledge for its own sake, but because she longed for evidence that he trusted her. There were times when she, like others, thought it very peculiar that she knew nothing of Adam's wife. Unlike others, she had never attempted to force a confidence. She had confided in him herself, so that he might feel free to reciprocate. Though he had never taken the opportunities she offered him nor said much in response to her story, he had looked at her with such warmth and understanding as he listened, she felt sure that he had suffered, too, perhaps more deeply than she had.

Rising from her chair to clear the table, Eva reminded herself that she had no right to think of Adam as other people might. She was not other people; she was his friend, the only one he had chosen from among his colleagues. She ought to feel honored. She did feel honored. What other people thought was of no consequence. They did not know what it was like to be alone with Adam and to have his undivided attention. Filling the sink with water, she left the dirty dishes to soak and hurried to her bedroom to dress.

There she opened the door to her closet and gazed in consternation at her clothes, trying to imagine what would please Adam. He was a deliberate dresser. Yet she could not recall that he had ever remarked on what she was wearing, perhaps out of politeness. Several times he had stared at a place where a button was missing or frowned at a torn lining when he helped her on with a coat. Often he appeared to be resisting an impulse to brush the hair from her face. Adam disliked personal untidiness; that she knew. Unfortunately, most of her clothes were in a state of disrepair as she could never remember to mend them in her spare moments. After sifting hopelessly through her clothing half a dozen times and finding something askew in each article of it, Eva finally chose a simple green dress. The hem was coming undone in one place, but that could be easily repaired with a discreet safety pin or two. Also, the secretary of her department had once told her that green became her.

When she was dressed, Eva stood before the mirror brushing her hair. Regarding her reflection with an objective curiosity, she decided that the secretary was right. The dress brought out the green in her eyes, which were otherwise a muddy brown, not that Adam would notice her eyes in the murky light of the Pearls and Swine. Eva sighed and began to tightly braid her hair in hopes that a braid would keep it in place better than a bun. She wished that she and Adam could meet somewhere else besides that tavern, but, in the five years they had known one another, Adam had made a tradition of meeting there on the first day of school.

Adam was fond of traditions; he was always establishing them. Eva had hoped that this summer, since she had not gone away, they might have broken with some of these traditions or at least have established new ones. She had looked forward to more traffic between Adam's household and hers, but Adam had met this suggestion with a gentle rebuff. Summer was the time for serious scholarship, he had told her. Adam was a serious scholar. She sometimes had doubts about herself. Yet she had worked hard this summer. She had finished those fairytales and prepared a copy for Adam. She was anxious to read his new book about the Egyptian alchemists. Their work, she told herself, as she wound the braid around her head, had always been a strong bond between them.

When the last hairpin was momentarily in place, Eva turned from the mirror, without further inspection, and crossed the room to her desk. There, instead of collecting her books and notes, Eva found herself staring at Ionia's pictures, which decorated the wall above her desk. It was not a good place to have displayed them. They often distracted her. There was something eerie about them, other-worldly. Eva glanced at one of a spider weaving a web among the stars and the one next to it of a blue lion drinking at the edge of a golden lake. There were several portraits of dragons. Here and there were drawings that consisted of nothing but curved lines, which might have meant the desert or the sea. Over all of these Eva's eyes traveled swiftly until they came to rest, as they always did, on the picture of a woman dancing beneath three trees, drawn in silhouette against a sky that was as purple as Ionia's eyes. Ionia's eyes had always disturbed her, just as this picture did. She could not help feeling that in both she was seeing something of Ionia's mother, Adam's wife, the woman of whom she knew nothing. . . .

All at once, the pain Jason's remarks had caused her flooded back. Abruptly she turned her face from the picture as she might have from a blow. Glancing down at her watch, she saw that she had lingered too long over dressing. There was no time now to wash the dishes. Annoyed with herself, she stuffed her books and papers indiscriminately into her bag; then she hurried from her bedroom without bothering to close the door behind her.

4
Formalities

"THAT was Professor Underwood," Esther Sharp, the manager of the faculty cafeteria, informed Margery Pierce, the new cashier, for Esther had observed that Margery had turned to stare after the tall, well-dressed man whose money she had just taken. "You may have heard of him. He's very famous."

Margery had not heard of him. She had only sold him a cup of black coffee and a french roll, but his eyes had startled her. She had never seen eyes so black that the pupil could not be distinguished from the iris. Their effect was similar to the effect of dark glasses. She felt as though he were hidden behind them, observing yet unobserved. The way he looked at her when he pressed the five dollar bill into her hand made her feel as though her secrets were showing as her slip might have. She felt decidedly at a disadvantage as she fumbled for change under his relentless gaze. But when he smiled at her as she handed him his change, she felt that she did not mind being at his mercy. She would have liked him to know everything about her, and if he had asked, she would have told him. He said nothing, however, as he accepted his change, but he bowed ever so slightly from the waist, and then walked away; or rather he glided away. He was extraordinarily graceful.

"I can see he's cast his spell on you, too," commented Esther Sharp, for Margery had made no response to her remark except to turn back to her cash register and stare at her reflection in the stainless steel. "He looks at all women that way," Esther continued. "I advise you to think nothing of it, my girl."

Margery blushed and tried to think of a sharp retort that would not jeopardize her job, but Esther had not finished.

"He even tried it with me once," confided Esther folding her arms across her large bosom in a protective gesture, "and I can assure you he didn't try it again. I'm a married woman," she added. "My husband is the conductor on the train Professor Underwood rides. Mr. Sharp wouldn't stand for any nonsense."

Margery resisted an impulse to snicker.

"Professor Underwood is not a nice man where women are concerned," said Esther, and she leaned closer to Margery as if she intended to tell her something more.

"Is that why he's so famous, then?" interrupted Margery, not wanting to lower herself to Esther's level.

"Well, there are his lectures on alchemy," conceded Esther in a grudging tone.

"Alchemy," said Margery. "I didn't know they taught that in school. Isn't that when they try to make gold out of metal that's not?"

"That's right," said Esther, straightening up. "It's a kind of counterfeiting."

In the dining room, Professor Underwood had seated himself at his usual table in the far corner. There, his face partially obscured by his open briefcase, he perused his lecture notes while he sipped his coffee and ate his roll. Whenever a crumb fell on his black suit, he automatically swept it away with a small ivory-handled brush he carried with him for that purpose. Now and then he looked up from his notes, but only to rest his eyes. He did not greet anyone by word or glance; nor did anyone approach his table, although several tables away he was the subject of at least one conversation.

"There's old Underwood priming himself for the great performance," remarked Professor Bates.

"Don't knock it," said Professor Beeferman. "I don't see students in line to listen to you lecture on chemistry."

"You're not such hot stuff yourself, Mr. Nuclear Physicist," returned Professor Bates.

"But seriously," continued Professor Beeferman, "what's he got that we haven't got? Do you suppose it has a chemical base? Could it be his electromagnetic field is supercharged? Or is it his aftershave?"

"Nothing so complex," replied Professor Bates. "The man is a damned good actor; that's all. Look at that get-up he's wearing today. It might seem like an ordinary suit, but he comes off looking like the black knight in all the romantic legends. Combine his appearance with the fact that he teaches alchemy, which you and I know is a lot of medieval mumbo jumbo."

"Hell," Professor Beeferman broke in, "the man's not an actor; he's a magician. How can a scientist hope to compete?"

"If you want my opinion," said Professor Bates confidentially, "I think he ought to be eliminated from the science faculty. I mean alchemy is simply not a living science. It's a dead. . . ."

Just then, Professor Underwood rose from his table, closed his briefcase, and began his progression across the dining room. As he neared their table, Professors Bates and Beeferman fell silent. Professor Beeferman even nodded to Professor Underwood, though his greeting was barely acknowledged.

After his first lecture of the season was over, it took Professor Underwood half an hour to disengage himself from students and visiting scholars who surrounded him pressing him with compliments and questions. Even when he had left the hall, they followed him. Only at the entrance to his office building did he finally escape his followers by explaining to them that he had another lecture for which to prepare. Bowing to them formally, he entered the building. When he reached the second floor, he paused to look through the window and saw that the crowd had not yet dispersed. He frowned as he climbed the stairs to the third floor. Before he gained his office, he encountered the department secretary who smiled at him eagerly and offered him his mail as if it were a bouquet of flowers she had picked for him. He lingered at her desk just long enough to make her feel flattered. Then he took his mail into his office and locked the door.

Tossing his mail onto the desk, Adam seated himself before it. He made no motion to open his mail, however. Instead he stared at it dully, not seeing anything or even thinking anything in particular. The muscles of his face and body went slack, and he let himself slide into a semi-conscious state. There he rested, or tried to. Soon the irritation he had suppressed all morning began to surface. He found himself thinking that people were fools. They allowed themselves to be led by the nose like donkeys. He could have lectured to them on the probability of the sun rising tomorrow, and still they would have been all over him afterwards, fawning on him like dogs, acclaiming his brilliance.

Of course his lectures were brilliant; he was no slouch as a scholar. Sir Algernon Riddler, the one authentic scholar present in the audience, had recognized that. Most people, however, were incapable of recognizing brilliance or appreciating scholarship. They lacked understanding and discrimination. Their admiration of him did not prove that he was a great man, but only that they were weak and willing to admire. The weak always worshipped power, and he was powerful; there was no doubt of that. People's response to him, not only in the lecture hall, but everywhere, was proof of his power. Yet what sort of power was his power, this power over cashiers and secretaries, undergraduates and even his colleagues. It seemed to Adam that it was an easy, empty power, a petty pointless power. No one challenged it. He had no need to struggle for mastery. His power was all form; his whole life was form, form for the sake of fools. Over the years the form had hardened. It was rigid in its perfection like an Egyptian mask for the dead.

A knock on his door roused Adam from his thoughts. Instinctively he stiffened, straightening his back and composing his face to form an expression of appropriate severity. Yet he had no intention of admitting this person who dared to intrude on his solitude.

"I am not in," he said in his deepest tones.

A moment later he could hear the sound of feet scuttling away as if they belonged to a frightened mouse. Taking some pleasure in the thought of his fearsomeness, Adam smiled and began to sort through his mail. It consisted mainly of notices about meetings and letters of congratulation on his latest article. After making a note of the meeting or reading a line or two of the letter, he tossed the piece of mail into his wastebasket. About halfway through the pile, he discovered an envelope that arrested his full attention. It was smaller than the others and pale brown in color as if it were intended to resemble faded parchment. The writing on the envelope was italic and the return address read: "Rare Books and Manuscripts, Ltd." His hands trembled as he held it, and he stared at it for a while, both savoring it and preparing himself for disappointment before he opened it. When his hands had stopped shaking and he had gained control over his excitement, he reached into a drawer of his desk for a letter opener and sliced the envelope open. Inside he found a note written in the same italic letters on the same imitation parchment.

Dear Professor Underwood,

We are pleased to inform you that a Persian copy of the ancient Babylonian tales concerning the mythic Race of Lilith has been discovered. Our most trusted employee has brought it secretly into the country. It awaits you now at our address in this city. As we dare not entrust it to the mails, we request you please to come and receive it in person at your earliest convenience.

Your respectful servant,
Simeon Reid

When he had read it over three times, once rapidly, once carefully, and once for pleasure, Adam folded the letter and put it back into the envelope. Then, unbuttoning his waistcoat, he slipped the letter inside a secret inner pocket where he kept the tower room key. Sweeping the rest of his mail, unopened, into the waste basket, he began to consider when his earliest convenience would be. He would go at once if he had his way, but he must do nothing to rouse suspicion or raise questions. In ten minutes he had another lecture to give. Then he had agreed to lunch with Sir Algernon Riddler. After that there were two meetings he must attend. He would not be free until nearly five. If he traveled across the city to Simeon Reid's shop, then he would be late for his date with Eva, but Eva, no doubt, would wait for as long as she must. Patience was one of Eva Brooke's many virtues, too many virtues for his taste. Yet, although Eva's virtues could be tedious, he had to admit they were also convenient, as they included reticence, tact, and a general desire to please. He could count on Eva not to make a fuss or ask questions. He would call Simeon Reid and tell him to expect him.

Just as he rose to his feet, Adam heard the university bell begin to strike the hour. Startled, he stared at his watch and realized that for the first time in his career, Professor Adam Underwood would be late for a lecture. Blood rushed to his cheeks as he rushed to the door. He was fumbling hurriedly with the lock when he suddenly stopped himself. What did it matter if he were late? What did all the dead forms matter? Let the fools wait. Let them wonder. He would be late if he liked. With deliberate slowness, Adam turned and walked back to his desk. Opening the drawer, he put the letter opener away. Then he straightened the chair and tucked it under the desk. At last he left his office, locking the door behind him.

The secretary looked at Professor Underwood questioningly as he passed her desk, but he did not answer her look except with a bare, mysterious smile that was not directed at her. Taking his time, savoring each step, he made his way down the stairs, out the door, across the campus. For once he walked alone, as everyone awaited him already in the great hall. For once he did not think of the crowd assembled there nor of his opening words to them. He scarcely thought at all. Instead, he concentrated on the sensation of his blood moving swiftly through his body as if his veins and arteries were underground rivers whose existence no one suspected. Not in six years had he felt so alive. She was within his reach.

🌴🌴🌴

At five o'clock Eva Brooke stood in the entrance of the Pearls and Swine peering into the green-tinted darkness. She hoped Adam had arrived ahead of her; she disliked walking in alone and looking for a table, expecially as the bar and lounge began to be crowded at this hour. As the day outside had been bright, she had difficulty accustoming herself to the darkness. All she could see were black shapes, some moving, some not. Reminding herself that Adam was a punctual person who would not keep her waiting long if he were not there already, Eva took the plunge. The tables in the lounge were so close together, and the chairs, occupied by people, stood at such random angles that she had to keep standing on tiptoe and holding her breath to squeeze through small spaces. She felt like a big fish in a little aquarium. When she had made her way past all the tables twice without bumping into Adam, although she had nearly knocked a waiter over, she decided to look for a place to sit down. She finally found one uncomfortably close to the men's room but with a view of the front entrance. As soon as Adam arrived, she would see his figure framed in light. Perching herself on the edge of her seat so that she could rise in a moment to meet him, Eva began to wait.

When Adam entered the Pearls and Swine almost an hour later, his first awareness of Eva was a commotion in the corner. She had gotten clumsily to her feet and stood waving at him as a man tried to walk past her to the men's room. Adam hoped she would not rush forward to meet him. To prevent such an incident, Adam crossed the lounge at a swift and purposeful pace, deftly avoiding the tables and chairs as if with some sixth sense. His hand was raised in a gesture that might have been a greeting but was also a command. Obedient, Eva stayed where she was, although she did not sit down until he had taken both her hands.

"Please excuse my lateness, Eva," said Adam, letting go of Eva's hands and signaling to a waiter. "I received an important notice in the mail and had to attend to it this afternoon."

"That's all right, Adam," said Eva, her anxiety turning to contentment under his gaze. "I was just worried. You're not usually late. But you're here now. That's all that matters. I'm glad to see you, Adam."

Adam smiled, rewarding her for her restraint. That was the closest she would come to questioning or complaint.

"I'm glad to see you, Eva," he returned.

Yet when he considered, Adam was not sure he was glad to see her. There was something dog-like in Eva Brooke's devotion that disturbed him. He believed that even if he slapped her face it would still wear that adoring, irritatingly maternal look. But then, he reminded himself, one could not expect domestic creatures to be anything but tame; they were born with their spirits broken. Adam smiled again, this time to himself.

"What would you like to drink, Eva?" Adam inquired, seeing a waiter approaching their table.

"Adam," Eva hesitated, "I wonder if we shouldn't just forget the drink and buy something on the way home. It's getting late, and the children. . . ."

"Oh, come, Eva," he cut her off. "We must celebrate."

He must celebrate.

"Two glasses and a bottle of champagne," Adam ordered; then turning to Eva, he added, "It will do you good; give you some color. You don't look particularly well."

Eva blushed to think that Adam found her complexion too pale.

"I haven't had much time to sunbathe this summer, Adam," she explained. "I've been busy transcribing those stories."

"I'm glad to hear you've had a productive summer, Eva. I've had a productive summer, too, as a matter of fact. I've finished my book on alchemy in ancient Egypt."

"That's wonderful, Adam," said Eva reaching across the table and touching his hand. "Did you bring me a copy?"

"I am still working on the footnotes," Adam explained. "I haven't made copies yet. Even my editor has not read the whole book. Are you interested in having a copy before the book is published?"

"I am always interested in your work, Adam," said Eva warmly.

"So is Sir Algernon Riddler," said Adam. "I had lunch with him today. He and I agreed that this latest book of mine is a pioneering achievement."

The waiter interrupted by arriving with the champagne. When Adam had opened the bottle himself and tested it to make sure it was satisfactory, he sent the waiter away and filled Eva's glass and his own. They raised their glasses in a silent toast to nothing in particular. Then Adam lit a pipe and continued to talk.

As she listened, Eva cradled her glass in her hands, and sipped her champagne until it was gone, but when Adam refilled her glass, she set it down and did not touch it again. The wine was making her warm and dizzy. She focused her eyes on Adam and tried to follow his conversation, but as his talk became increasingly scholarly and technical, she found it difficult to concentrate on his words. Instead she became absorbed in studying his face. It was rich in color, even in these dim surroundings, and perfect in form and proportion. Its every expression was precise. The lines that appeared with a smile or a frown or an arched eyebrow erased themselves when he was done. His eyes were more than perfect; they were magnetic. Their darkness seemed to draw the light. Though that light, at the moment, shone mainly from the sign above the men's room door, the effect of his eyes was, nonetheless, dazzling. Eva had forgotten how warm and vital Adam's presence was.

"You haven't been drinking your champagne, Eva."

The sound of her name startled Eva, and she realized she hadn't been listening. She wondered if he had been waiting for a response from her.

"I really don't want any more, Adam," said Eva, smiling apologetically.

"Well, you warned me," returned Adam. "I should have heeded you. We ought to be going now."

"Yes," agreed Eva. "The children must be getting hungry enough to eat each other, and it will take a while for the casserole to heat."

"I do hope you haven't gone to any trouble about supper, Eva," cautioned Adam as they stood up to leave, "because I'm afraid we can't stay."

"Can't stay," repeated Eva, unable to hide her disappointment. "Oh, Adam, I was so looking forward to supper with you and the children."

"Come, come, Eva," said Adam in a warning tone. "There'll be plenty of other suppers."

When Eva and Adam reached her apartment, Eva went directly to the kitchen while Adam waited in the living room. There she found Ionia, sitting at a table already set for supper, and reading a book. In a glance, Eva realized that the breakfast dishes had been washed and put away.

"Ionia," said Eva softly.

Ionia looked up and almost smiled. "Mrs. Brooke," she answered.

Ionia rose from the table and walked slowly towards her. Eva waited, letting Ionia take her own time. When she was near enough, Eva bent and kissed her. Ionia did not return the caress, but she leaned against Eva and allowed herself to be held.

"What took you so long?"

Eva looked up and saw Jason frowning in the doorway of his bedroom. A moment later, Fred shot past him and hurled himself at Ionia and Eva, throwing one arm around Eva's legs and the other around Ionia's waist. Releasing Ionia, Eva picked Fred up in her arms as if he were a smaller child than he was.

We must be going if we're to catch the seven-thirty train, Eva," said Adam entering from the living room. "Come along, children."

"I want to stay for supper," said Fred, scrambling down from Eva's arms and facing his father defiantly. "Jason said I could and there's cake."

"You can have some tomorrow as soon as you get back from school, Fred," consoled Eva.

Fred opened his mouth to protest again but closed it when his father took a step towards him and grabbed him by the wrist.

"Wait, Adam, just a minute," said Eva. "I have something for you."

Adam looked impatient while Eva stooped and reached into her bag.

"Here," she said. "It's a copy of the fairytales."

"Thank you, Eva. I will read them as soon as I have some spare time."

Tucking the manuscript under his arm, he turned to go.

"If you're too busy to read them right now, Adam, you might let Ionia read them first," Eva suggested, putting her arm around Ionia and following Adam to the door. "She's so good at drawing, she might like to illustrate them."

Adam, who had his hand on the door knob, suddenly turned around and looked at Ionia.

"I did not know that you draw pictures, Ionia," he said. "Why have you never shown me your drawings? What do you draw pictures of, may I ask?"

Was there some secret communion between mother and daughter of which he had been unaware?

Ionia did not answer but pressed closer to Eva,

"I have a number of her pictures in my bedroom, Adam," said Eva, telling herself it was only right to encourage Adam to take more of an interest in Ionia. "I don't think Ionia would mind if you looked at them, would you Ionia?"

"Perhaps I shall look at them," said Adam, still staring at Ionia. "But tomorrow. Now we must go. Good-bye, Eva. Come along, Ionia."

Adam, still holding Fred by the wrist, opened the door and strode out. Before Ionia followed him, she turned to look at Eva. Eva had never seen such an intense look on Ionia's face, a mixture of fear and reproach and pleading. Before Eva could ask what was wrong, Ionia was gone.

Closing the door, Eva sighed and turned towards the kitchen. At least she knew what to expect there, and she found it: Jason sitting at the table looking angry and hungry. At the moment, she appreciated his predictability very much.

5
Left in Charge

THE day was dark November gray; it blustered and blew; Grammar watched it through the window over the kitchen sink as she washed the breakfast dishes. The wind tore the leaves from the garden trees, and though the rain had not yet begun to fall, Grammar knew in her knees that it soon would. Tomorrow, if the weather behaved itself better, she would have to go outside and pick up after it. The leaves the wind wantonly scattered over the yard must be raked into piles and then used to blanket her gardens. The twigs and branches the storm recklessly snapped must be gathered and dried for kindling. Summer or winter, there was no end to this elemental play and the mess it made; there was no end to the reordering of a random creation.

Grammar sighed, feeling the weight of her responsibilities. She had an unworded conviction that she, alone, had been left in charge. She could not have said precisely by whom, nor exactly of what, nor what, specifically, her responsibilities required of her. Grammar, however, did not question her convictions, she acted on them. Reaching for Fred's dishes, she scowled. Fred had barely touched his breakfast that morning, for it had been his intention to sneak out of the house without the rubbers she had told him he must wear. Still, he had managed to make a hole in the middle of his toast and to excavate the raisins from his porridge, and there was no use in saving the remains. As she turned to scrape them into the compost, she caught sight of Lion lying a few feet away and staring up at her with the whites of his eyes just showing beneath the brown.

"Here," she said with a magnanimous gesture. "You may finish his breakfast."

Grammar plopped the porridge and the crusts into Lion's bowl and shoved it towards him with her foot. Lion did not so much as sniff at his bowl. He never moved a muscle but continued to stare steadily at Grammar.

"Still sulking, eh?" she observed. "Well, suit yourself."

Grammar turned back to the sink and scrubbed Fred's bowl more vigorously than she needed to. She was uncomfortably aware of Lion's eyes on her back. For more than a month, ever since Fred had started school, his silent scrutiny had persisted. Whenever Lion was inside or she was outside, Lion followed her. He followed her now with his eyes as she crossed the kitchen to fetch the oatmeal pot from the stove. He was getting on her nerves. On her way back, wooden spoon in one hand, oatmeal pot in the other, she paused to confront him.

"Is it my fault?" she demanded. "Did I make the law that says all little boys have to go to school? Without their dogs?"

No answer.

"Well, did I?"

Clearly she was unnerved.

"I don't like it any better than you do," she declared. "So there."

This great admission, which she had never made before, even to herself, did not seem to satisfy Lion of Grammar's innocence. Still he sat motionless. Still he stared. Exasperated, Grammar plunged the pot into the sink. Then she turned to Lion and grabbed his collar.

"You're going out," she announced.

As she hauled his passive hulk across the floor, his toenails scraped the wax along the way.

"Go on," she said, shoving Lion out the back door. "Go catch moles."

Lion looked bewildered.

"I don't care if they're hibernating. Wake them up!"

She slammed the door in his face.

"Look at me," she said aloud, her hand still gripping the doorknob, "talking to a dog."

She considered for a moment.

"And now I'm talking to myself. This is nonsense," she said firmly. "It has got to stop."

When she was quiet, she could hear the house. Its shutters banged, and its windows rattled with the wind. Its walls scuffled with mice. Now and then it creaked for what Grammar considered no good reason at all.

Releasing the doorknob, Grammar returned to the sink and made as much clatter as she could washing the pots. When the dishes were all done, she scrubbed and rewaxed the floor although she knew it was a foolish thing to do on a wet, muddy day. The children would come home and forget to take off their rubbers in the back hall. Later, Lion would lie on the floor and leave a puddle. But just then, Grammar did not care; while she worked, she did not think.

By midmorning the post-breakfast bustle was over. Grammar stood still in her shining kitchen trying to remember all the things she had to do next. None came to mind. For the past few weeks she had kept frantically busy, taking advantage of having Fred out from underfoot for the first time since he could walk. She had sorted all closets and drawers. She had gone through her old trunks in the attic, and when she had discovered a family of mice nesting among the gowns of her dancing clays, she had searched the house inside and out for their holes and plugged them up wherever she could. She would have had exterminators come to rid the house of all its illegal aliens—squirrels, bats, and insects as well as mice—but the children had overheard her discussing the matter with their father, and they had protested so violently, Fred by kicking, screaming, and biting, Ionia by refusing to eat, comb her hair, and clean her room, that Grammar had given up the idea and had contented herself with having people come to clean the gutters, the chimneys, and the drains.

These early days of excitement were over. Grammar had only ordinary housekeeping with which to occupy herself now, and that was all too easy without Fred to undermine her efforts. Even when Fred had not been in her way, she had accustomed herself to worrying about where he was and what mischief he was making. She had learned to be alert at all times, to listen for the crash of a lamp or for a cry for help, and to wonder, when there was no noise at all, what the silence meant. She listened now out of long habit. There came a lull in the storm, and silence fell on the house, settled on it like a fine film of dust. It was not the silence of a little boy keeping quiet. It was an inhuman silence; the silence of floors that made no resistance to sweeping, of furniture that submitted to polishing, of inanimate objects waiting for the duster, the dead silence that came when all the work was done.

Then the wind picked up again, and the house quivered in response. Grammar shook herself, as if from some sleep, and the rain began to fall.

"I must do something," she remarked aloud. "Something must be done."

Grammar set off for the cleaning closet to fetch her feather duster. Only yesterday she had dusted and vacuumed the whole house, but her mother had told her long ago that in a well-kept house the dusting is done every day. Her son's pipe tobacco and ashes, of which he left a trail everywhere he went, made daily dusting necessary. So she wandered from room to room with her feather duster, lighting lamps and leaving them on, as she would never have allowed Fred and Ionia to do, dusting books and busts, windowsills and coats of arms, table-tops and picture frames, knick-knacks and heirlooms. She might have been a fairy with a wand, but she wasn't. She could not bring to life the objects that her duster touched.

While she worked, the rain fell, softly on the bare flower beds, clamorously in the clean gutters, with a distant roar on the attic roof. Lion howled to be let in, but, over the rain, Grammar did not hear until she returned to the kitchen to find that it was time for lunch.

Letting Lion drip in the kitchen, Grammar took her lunch of artichoke hearts, anchovies, cottage cheese, and toast into the dining room, closing the door behind her. The long polished table seemed longer as she ate there alone, and the gleam of its surface, colder. In less time than she might have liked, lunch was over and her single plate washed and put away. The afternoon stretched out before her like a road without landmarks. She looked at Lion asleep on the floor, for once not watching her, and she debated whether or not she wanted his company. His muddy feet discouraged her, however, and so she let the sleeping dog lie. She might like a nap herself, Grammar considered, and since she had nowhere else to go, and nothing else in particular to do, she let her feet lead her to her private parlor.

She found her private parlor rather damp and dreary. At least there would be no pacing that afternoon making it impossible for her to rest; only the sound of falling rain. For that she was grateful. She did wish she could have a fire, though. The room was chilly, especially with the easterly wind from the Empty Land seeping through the cracks in the windows. The furnace was on, but it was old and cantankerous and generated about as much heat as her own old body. During the winter, fire was necessary as a supplementary source of heat, but Adam had not yet arranged for the delivery of this winter's supply of firewood. She had used the rest of last winter's during two cold, damp weeks of summer. Silently Grammar cursed Adam. If only she had a telephone she could have arranged all such matters herself. Adam took little interest in the house and its maintenance; it infuriated her to have to go through Adam for everything she needed.

Seating herself at her desk, Grammar opened a drawer and drew out her favorite deck of cards, the ones with tea roses on the backs that reminded her of summertime and of some fine china belonging to a favorite aunt, the aunt who had long ago taught her to play cards. She felt a little solitaire might divert her, and so she dealt herself a game and began to play, now and then lifting a pile and looking beneath it so discreetly that she hardly knew she was doing it. In spite of these unacknowledged attempts at cheating, she lost the game. By the time she had lost two more, her fingers were stiff with cold.

"Bah," she said aloud, and, gathering the cards together, she rapped them sharply against the table, as if to show them who was boss, and put them away in their drawer.

Grammar rose from her desk and walked to her work chair by the window where she gathered up her shawl. As she wrapped it around her, she gazed out the window. The rain still fell, but the wind was quieter now; it had finished stripping the garden trees of their leaves. If Grammar had been given to fancy, she might have thought that the trees looked cold and wet and naked. She was fanciful enough to feel annoyed at the brazen purple of the three trees on the hill. Even though they were more exposed than the garden trees, the three trees had somehow defied the wind and clung to their leaves. In a gray world, they alone had color, and they flaunted it; or so Grammar felt without putting her feelings into words. She had never liked those trees. Bright purple was an unnatural color for leaves even in Autumn. Though Grammar had not a very high opinion of nature and considered herself at war with it, she felt that nature ought to at least obey its own laws if it would not obey hers.

Retreating from the window, Grammar went to lie down on the daybed beside the empty fireplace. When she had covered her legs with a heavy blanket, she reached for her current mystery novel, *The Secret Room*. After a few sentences, however, she realized that she had ruined the story for herself by peeking ahead last night. So she cast the book aside and closed her eyes, but she had not done enough that day to tire herself. As she lay fidgeting, unable to sleep, an impulse took hold of her. Why should she read about secret rooms when there was one in her very own house just begging to be exposed? She had told herself she wouldn't try to pick that lock anymore. Now that Fred was gone she worried that her habit might get out of control, and she'd end up fussing with the lock all day. But she couldn't help it. The impulse was becoming compulsion. Her lust to fool with that lock was like an itch screaming to be scratched, a scab ripe for picking.

"This is absurd," she sighed.

Nevertheless, she rose from her daybed and followed her impulse up the stairs to the tower room. Removing a pin from her tidy hair, she began to pick at the lock. She had tried so many times before that she hardly hoped to achieve results. The habitual action was in itself satisfying. Mindlessly she picked. Then, suddenly, an almost musical twang pierced the silence, and Grammar knew she had touched the spring. In awe of what she had done, Grammar stood still for a moment before the door. Then, gathering her loose strand of hair, she pinned it back in place. At last, she gripped the knob and opened the door.

6

 # The Tower Room

THE tower room was all Grammar had anticipated. Even in the dim light of a rainy dusk she could see cobwebs dripping from the ceiling. The windows were all but opaque with dirt, and the dust on the windowsill lay half an inch deep. She cast a glance at his book shelves, but her nose had already told her the story there. The fireplace was full of ashes and other things she did not wish to identify. Before her lay the path in the carpet she had heard being worn. Nothing surprised Grammar except her response; she felt afraid. She knew now that she had been a fool to think that she could simply march right in with dustpan, broom, and disinfectant, throw open the windows, and clear the debris. The tower room needed no lock to make it seem forbidden. It had never seemed more so than at this moment when she stood in its doorway. Adam must never discover that she had been here. She knew that she ought to turn away at once and close the door behind her, hoping that it would lock itself, and then never, never come back.

Yet Grammar did not turn away. There was a fascination in her fear and in the forbiddenness of the room. Gazing into the semidarkness, she perceived a faint glow emanating from something on Adam's desk. As the light of day lessened, the glow grew stronger. Compelled by her curiosity, Grammar took a step forward and then another and another until she stood over Adam's desk staring down at a sphere about the size of a cantaloupe. The glow came from its surface; at its center was darkness. Grammar peered into the darkness, and her head began to swim. She felt as though the darkness was trying to suck her into itself as if it were a whirlpool. Frightened, she tried to look away and found she could not. Then an image appeared. Grammar closed her eyes, not wishing to see what the darkness held. When she opened them again, in spite of herself, she recognized the image of her own face turned upside-down.

"Pooh," she said aloud, "so it's just a bit of glass after all, and that glow is just a trick of the light."

Not entirely convinced by her words, but at least freed by them from the hold of that darkness, Grammar turned her face away, and her eyes fell on a small leather-bound volume. Decorating the cover were strange designs etched in faded gold, and lettering in a language Grammar failed to recognize. But then, Grammar knew nothing of foreign languages except a little French. Adam, she knew, had studied all kinds of heathen tongues. Curious, Grammar picked up the volume and opened it. Inside was more of the same incomprehensible scrawl and also pictures drawn in minute detail with colored ink. Some were of plants and animals, others of men with weapons on foot and on horseback involved in what appeared to be a chase. The most vivid and frequent drawings were of naked women with cruel expressions on their faces, depicted in a variety of obscene poses. So this was the kind of scholarship in which Adam engaged. Disgusted, Grammar closed the book and tried to set it down in the exact spot from which she had picked it up. It was then that she noticed, close by, a manuscript written in Adam's own small, precise hand. Bending over so that she could distinguish the words, she read: "The Race of Lilith." Grammar closed her eyes as if to repudiate what she had just seen. Then gripping the back of the desk chair for support, she opened her eyes and forced herself to read on.

In the Empty places of the earth dwells the race of Lilith: rebellious first wife of the Father of all, consort of the Evil One, grandmother of jinns and giants. Beware, O Man, of the Empty Land. Many have entered into it, but few have returned. Beware, O Man, of the woman that is not woman. Once you have partaken of her evil treasure, no mortal woman will satisfy you. Seek her if you must, O Man, but not in her own land unless you desire to be destroyed by her wild, man-devouring race. Your only hope is to lure her to your own land and then to keep her forever in a cage. How this may be done is an ancient. . . .

Unaware that she did so, Grammar drew Adam's chair from beneath his desk and sank into it. She continued to stare at the manuscript, but she read no further. The crystal ball cast only shadows; it did not shed its light. Darkness had swallowed all but its glow. Grammar could no longer see. Instead, against her will, she found herself remembering what she had tried for more than ten years to forget.

The day had been dark gray, like this one, when Ursula Underwood had driven out to the house with a lawyer and realtor to assess its market value. Her husband had died that summer, and Adam was as good as dead. He had never returned from a camping trip in the Empty Land he had taken early in the summer. Though helicopters had combed the Empty Land for weeks, no trace of him had been discovered. After her husband's death, Ursula Underwood had remained only as long as it took her to set the house and grounds in order. Then she had closed the house, leaving Adam a note of explanation just in case he should return, and she had gone to stay with a cousin of her husband until she could find a small place of her own. The house was too large for a woman alone. She wanted to be rid of it and all its emptiness.

When she had come back with the lawyer and the realtor only a month later, Ursula Underwood was shocked to discover that the wild thyme, which covered the Empty Land, had overgrown the driveway and the lawn. There was no wall in those days to prevent it from growing up to the doorstep, and that was exactly what it had done. She stepped out of the realtor's car and stared about her in dismay, aware that the lawyer and realtor were doing the same. Her gardens had all gone to weed and to seed. The gray, wispy heads of the bygone flowers swayed in the wind, making her gardens look like ghosts of themselves.

A rasping sound startled her. She turned towards the house just in time to see a shingle slide from the roof and fall to rot in a clump of weeds. Eyeing the roof, she saw that it was green with moss. Vines had crawled up the sides of the house, concealing the windows. She glanced uneasily at the lawyer and realtor who had begun to pace about her in circles while they waited for her to give the signal to proceed to the house for closer inspection. What must they think of her, she wondered, leaving the house in such a condition? How could she persuade them that a month ago it had been in perfect repair.

Catching her glance, the realtor stopped pacing.

"The house and the grounds will require some mending before they go on the market, Mrs. Underwood," he informed her, and he reached into his pocket for a large cigar, which he licked thoroughly before he lit it.

"Yes, of course," she answered sharply, "but I assure you, when I left a month ago everything was in perfect order. I don't understand what's happened."

"We understand that you've been under a great deal of strain lately, Mrs. Underwood," said the lawyer soothingly, putting his hand on her shoulder.

Ursula Underwood glared at the man and had all she could do to keep from removing the man's hand from her shoulder. Obviously, they both thought she was crazy or worse. Well, she was not crazy, even if all the rest of the world was.

"I will go on ahead and open the house myself," she announced. "I want to see what damage has been done inside. There may have been vandals."

And she was not about to add cigar smoke to the damage done to the house. If there was anything she could not abide, it was a man who smoked a cigar.

"I thought vandals generally smashed windows; I didn't know they covered them with vines," muttered the realtor with the cigar between his teeth.

Ursula Underwood ignored the realtor's remark, and, without a backward glance, she crossed what had become of the lawn, gripping her keys as she went to steady herself. When she reached the front door, she discovered, to her astonishment, that it stood slightly ajar, and one of its hinges had come loose. Someone must have broken in. No doubt, they were hiding in the house right now. Apprehensive as she was, Ursula Underwood did not for one moment consider calling the lawyer and the realtor, and because she knew they were watching, she went through the motions of unlocking and opening the door.

Once inside and out of sight, she paused to listen. She heard nothing, but she noticed that there were leaves scattered about the floor. These must have blown in through the open door, she told herself, but she did not believe it. Cautiously, trying not to step on any of the leaves, Ursula Underwood tiptoed across the hall towards the dining room. Soft as they were, her steps had a curious open-air sound, as if she were walking in the stillness of the morning on frozen ground. Instead of fewer leaves, there were more as she went on. When she entered the dining room, she stopped dead and found that she was standing ankle deep in leaves. Then, a shrill whistle made her jump. Looking up, she saw a bluejay nesting on the mantle piece. To see a bird nesting where she had dusted such a little while ago was too much. She wanted to turn and run away, away from this house, away from this craziness, away from these things that could not, ought not, be.

As so often happens in nightmares, she could not move. She stood, rooted to the floor, as if she had turned into a tree and had no choice but to remain in this forest of a house forever. Then she heard a rustling in the leaves and felt something alive run over her feet. Fear loosened her lungs, and she screamed. A startled squirrel looked up at her, then scurried on its way to the fireplace where it disappeared up the chimney. She was still staring after it when she heard a voice.

"Adam, Son of Ursula, a new animal has come into the house."

At the sound of her name spoken by this strange, earthy, unearthly voice, Ursula Underwood turned her face from the fireplace and saw, standing in the doorway to her kitchen, what appeared to be a woman. The woman's nakedness was only partially covered by coarse black hair, which fell below her waist. This hair looked as though it had never been combed. It was full of leaves and here and there a wildflower. Most startling of all were the woman's eyes. They were purple in color, and in expression they were as wild and wary as any animal's.

"And it has a strange kind of fur that is blacker than crow feathers," the creature continued, "and it does not speak, although it stands upright as if it were Woman."

"Of course I'm a woman," snapped Grammar, recovering her voice. "Now suppose you tell me what you are, why you are here, and just what you mean by turning my house into a national park."

Before the creature could answer, Adam Underwood appeared beside her in the doorway. He was as naked as the woman herself and, what shocked Ursula Underwood even more, as unashamed.

"Mother," he said, glancing at her briefly and then turning to gaze at the creature. "This is my wife. She is called Lilith."

"Your what?" the creature laughed, and she nipped his shoulder playfully.

"My wife," he repeated. "Yes, you are, my darling. Don't you remember when I wrapped you in that sheet and took you to see that man and he said those words over us and you answered what he told you to? That made you my wife. You're mine. You're bound to me."

The creature only laughed and bit him again, this time a little harder. Adam did not react, except by tightening his grip on her waist. Still staring at Lilith, he addressed his mother again.

"Sometimes she bites, but don't worry, Mother, I'm going to tame her. This is only the honeymoon. She'll do very well as my wife, once I've trained her. Won't you, my darling?"

Ursula Underwood was not sure if the creature's response was another laugh or a snarl. Though she was afraid of this creature, more animal than woman, and afraid of what her son had become, Ursula Underwood knew she must speak.

"Adam," she said, "you are mad. Come to your senses. Look at this house. Look at this creature you call your wife. Look at yourself. How can you behave in this way, now of all times. If you have no respect for me, then think of your father. Turn this creature out. Restore yourself and the house to order. Behave as becomes your father's son."

For a long while Adam did not respond, so intent was he on holding the creature still with his eyes. Ursula Underwood began to doubt that he had even heard her. She was about to leave when he suddenly turned towards her, looking at her directly for the first time.

"My father is dead."

Before she had time to search his face for a sign of feeling, he turned back to the Creature.

"You may live here if you like," Adam said to his mother. "It is a matter of indifference to me. The house was left to me, and I shall live here. I find it convenient. If you wish to live here as well, I am sure my wife will not mind." He took the creature by the shoulders. "You do not mind if Ursula stays with us, my darling. This is Ursula."

"Ursula," she repeated. "Your mother."

For a moment Ursula Underwood remained staring at the naked man and woman who were staring at each other as if no one else existed. She needed no more time to decide what she would do.

"Good-bye, Adam," she said. "I shall not see you again "

Ursula Underwood did not wait for her son to acknowledge her parting but turned at once and walked through the littered hall out the unhinged door and across the thyme-grown lawn as swiftly as possible. She found the lawyer and the realtor sitting on the hood of the car looking bored and annoyed.

"Except that you should drive me to the station, I shall not require either of your services further," she announced in a tone that warned them to ask no questions. "My son has returned."

More than four years passed before Ursula Underwood saw the house or her son again. During that time she heard from Adam only twice. On the first occasion he wrote to announce the birth of a daughter to whom he or, as Ursula Underwood suspected, the creature had given the unheard of name of Ionia. In spite of the name and the circumstances of the child's birth, Ursula Underwood had almost given in to a desire to see her granddaughter, but the memory of that creature and what she had done to the house and to Adam proved stronger than any grandmotherly feeling. Besides, Ursula Underwood half doubted that the child could be wholly human. Adam's second communication announced the birth of a son and the loss of a wife. He would not say how he had lost her, but Ursula Underwood had always had her suspicions. It did not surprise her that a woman like that would abandon house, husband, and children. It was only to be expected. Obviously the creature had no sense of decency or duty and no more natural feeling than an animal. In fact, she had less. Even a wild animal would care for its own young. No, she was not surprised that the creature had left Adam in the lurch. What outraged Ursula Underwood was that Adam should have involved himself with the creature in the first place. Now that it had turned out badly, Adam expected his mother to come and take care of the mess he had made. For that was the essence of the note: not so much a request as a command that she come and take the children off his hands. She had a strong impulse to refuse, and if there had been only the one child, she might have. But Ursula Underwood knew that she could not leave an infant in a man's charge, particularly not in her son's. And this particular infant had been given her husband's name. The name might only have been a ploy to win her over, but it worked. She wrote to Adam saying that she would come, but adding as a condition that the house and grounds be restored to order before she arrived.

On a damp day in early spring, Adam met Ursula Underwood at the station. As they drove to the house they did not speak, although Ursula Underwood had it on the tip of her tongue to ask Adam where the children were and if he had left them alone. She was not sure, however, that she wanted to hear the answer, and, in any case, she would find out soon enough for herself. When they crested the last hill before the house, Ursula Underwood was startled by the sight of a wall under construction. She glanced sharply at Adam.

Do you mean to hold me prisoner?" she demanded.

"The walls are not being built for your benefit," he replied.

When they had driven through the empty space where the gates would be, Ursula Underwood got out of the car without waiting for Adam to open the door for her, and inspected her surroundings. There was no trace of the wild thyme. The ground was covered with short brown winter grass showing here and there a blade of green. Of her flower beds and gardens, nothing remained. The house had been stripped of vines, and the roof appeared to be free of moss and in good repair. Adam, it seemed, had met her conditions. Taking heart, she proceeded up the path to the house, followed by Adam.

Inside, Ursula Underwood found no sign of the fearful chaos the creature had carried in her wake, but the house was not as she had kept it either. Dust had settled on its every surface and it echoed as if it were empty. If she had not known otherwise, Ursula Underwood would have believed that no one had lived in the house for a long, long time.

"Where are the children?" she asked.

Adam led her up the stairs to her private parlor where he had left the children locked; for their safety, he explained. Where he kept the children locked for his convenience, Ursula Underwood added silently. As soon as Adam had unlocked the door and presented Ursula Underwood with a ring of household keys, he left her alone with her grandchildren.

Ursula Underwood stood still, taking stock of the situation before she made a move. A tiny baby with a tuft of shocking red hair on his head that he could not have inherited from anyone in her family lay sleeping in the cradle that had been Adam's and before that her husband's. Crouching beside the cradle staring up at her with eyes unmistakably like her mother's both in color and expression was the girl-child, Ionia. For a second, seeing those eyes again, Ursula Underwood wished she had not come. Then the baby woke up and began to cry. Ursula Underwood forgot her misgivings and was across the room in a moment.

"I am your grandmother," she announced to Ionia as she lifted Fred out of the cradle and laid him against her breast.

Since then Ursula Underwood had scarcely had time for reflection. That spring had been one of the busiest of her life. She had not only had the work and worry of caring for two small children, but she had felt obliged to turn the house inside out, cleaning it and polishing it until it shone with its own light. Then, without help from Adam, she had chopped up the earth with a hoe and put in flowerbeds and vegetable gardens where she had always had them. By the end of that summer the house and grounds looked almost themselves again, although she found the wall a nuisance because it blocked so much of the light. If her vegetables did not grow as they might have, Fred made up for the disappointment. He had prospered under her care and feeding and had grown into a fat and happy baby. Even Adam had been impressed with his development and had bought him a dog by way of a reward. Ionia did not change as much as Fred, but little by little she began to speak as she would not for weeks after her Grandmother's arrival. It was Ionia who gave the name that finally affected Ursula Underwood's transformation. Before the year was out she was decidedly Grammar.

Six years had passed, six years in which Grammar had lived from day to day doing the best that she could. Most of the time she was too busy to brood over the past and too practical to concern herself with anything but the task immediately before her. Slowly she had come to feel that the house and the children belonged to no one but herself. It did not matter that the house was held in Adam's name. It did not matter how the children had come into the world. It was she who cared for the house and children and they were hers.

She would simply not allow it, Grammar told herself. She would not allow Adam to lure that creature back to undermine the order she had established, to steal the children she had raised. Sitting alone in the dark room, Grammar clenched her fist and resolved to fight. The next moment a feeling of helplessness overcame her. What could she do, a lone woman against the powers of evil and chaos? Tears of rage stung her eyes, and she pounded her fist on Adam's desk. Just then she heard the gate clank open and the sound of the car driving through. With her fist raised in mid-air, she froze. All at once the fear she had felt earlier flooded back, and she felt sick with it. She listened as the gate clanked shut and the motor died. In the silence that followed she admitted to herself for the first time that she was afraid of Adam. This thought made her furious. A car door slammed, and Grammar rose from the chair and shoved it beneath the desk. She had all she could do to keep from spitting on the crystal ball. Refusing to give in to the impulse to run, she walked out of the room and closed the door behind her. She could not help the sigh of relief that came when she felt it lock. Pausing for a moment to quiet her breathing and still her trembling hands, she then descended the stairs, neither swiftly nor slowly, but at the dignified pace that became a woman of her years.

In the dining room she encountered Fred, still in his rubbers, wet with the rain and muddy from cuddling Lion, running towards her with a yellow paper clutched in his hand.

"Grammar! Grammar!" he shouted. "Look! I made letters!"

Then Grammar did a thing she had rarely done since Fred was in diapers. She knelt down, reached out her arms, caught Fred to her, and held him close.

7

 The State of Confusion

FOR a week the rain fell. On the day that it ended, Jason, Ionia, and Fred walked the long way home from school that led down by the river and then up through the park. The air was mild and thick with the smell of wet leaves drying in the warmth. The children had taken off their jackets and tied them around their waists. They walked more slowly than usual. The days of solitary confinement had been difficult for them all, and they were glad to be outdoors again.

Ionia walked even more slowly than the others because she wanted to walk alone. Jason would never allow her to get ahead of him unless she ran. He considered running an undignified activity, suitable only for a child of Fred's age. He disliked dawdling, because he could not do it. Even when he was not in a hurry, his feet, accustomed to direction and purpose, kept an even pace. So as the children walked by the river, Ionia managed, bit by bit, to drop some distance behind. Fred, who could dawdle as well as anyone when he wanted to, walked beside Jason, trailing a stick through puddles and leaves, and stumbling now and then; for he was not watching his feet or the way ahead. Instead he stared up at Jason. From his gestures and from his voice, Ionia could tell that Jason was explaining something. She did not care to know what, so she stopped and looked down at a puddle.

Dead leaves lined the bottom of the puddle; its surface reflected the bare branches of a tree and the brightness of the sky. Ionia stood still, gazing at the double image until the sound as well as the sense of Jason's words passed beyond her hearing. Then, still more slowly, she began to move again. Once she had stepped over the puddle, she did not lift her feet but pushed them along through the leaves as if the leaves were an atmosphere that required a different sort of motion. The dry sound the leaves made as her feet parted them, the warmth of the sun on her shoulders and hair, the changing patterns of light and shadow that lay along the ground before her gradually filled her whole awareness, and she forgot everything else, all thought, all fear, even herself.

When Jason and Fred reached the crossing to the park, they stopped to wait for Ionia. Turning to look back, Jason was annoyed to discover that Ionia was almost beyond shouting distance. She was walking so slowly, he could not be sure she was moving at all. If she didn't hurry up, they'd be waiting for her another half hour at least. It was downright inconsiderate of Ionia to lag behind like that, but he wasn't about to make a fool of himself by shouting for her on a public street corner. He turned to Fred, who was incapable of standing still for more than two minutes and had begun to hop, first on one foot, then the other.

"Call your recalcitrant sibling," commanded Jason.

"My what?" asked Fred, pausing on one foot to stare at Jason.

"Your sister," he translated. "Ionia. Call Ionia."

"Oh," said Fred, and standing on both feet, he shouted, "Ionia! Ionia!"

Jason moved away from Fred and stared at the ground, hoping that passers-by would not associate him with the noise. When Fred had stopped shouting, Jason looked up again. Ionia did not appear to have heard Fred call. Now she was plainly standing still, facing not in their direction but towards a tree that was surrounded with fresh-fallen leaves. Cautiously, as if she were a cat stalking a bird, Ionia approached the tree. Then she knelt down and bent over, pressing her face to the earth.

"What is Ionia doing?" wondered Fred.

"How should I know?" asked Jason. "I'm not your sister's keeper, much as she might need one."

"I'm going to go see," announced Fred, and he took off at a lop-sided gallop.

"Tell Ionia to hurry up!" Jason called after him.

Sighing, Jason turned towards the traffic light in time to watch it change from red to green once again. He had hoped they would get back in time to finish the game of Economy they had started yesterday. He was winning, but that was easy with Fred and Ionia for opponents. Neither of them had even the most elementary understanding of basic economic principles. They had failed to learn the rules of the game: Ionia because she didn't listen when he explained them, Fred because he couldn't understand them. Fred played enthusiastically, but he had no business sense. His decisions were based on personal desire rather than practical calculation. He bought candy factories, ice cream emporiums, dog kennels, zoos, toy companies and was on the verge of bankruptcy. Ionia invested her interest in remote islands and unexplored continents, but she refused to develop the natural resources and open up trade.

"They eat fruit and sleep in caves," she argued. "They don't need imports and exports."

"But, Ionia," he reasoned, "no island or country can be self-sufficient, not in these times. Besides, it's against the rules."

"Then the rules are silly," she said. "People don't need rules to live."

"Ionia," said Jason, "do you realize that what you just said borders on anarchy?"

Ionia did not indicate with word or look whether she understood or not but continued to stare at her lost islands.

"What's an archy?" Fred wanted to know.

"Anarchy is the state of confusion," answered Jason, "and an anarchist is someone like Ionia who doesn't believe in laws."

Jason wondered to himself if he would ever be obliged to turn Ionia over to the government. Someday she might be dangerous. Perhaps under torture she would talk.

"Ionia," said Jason, taking a different approach, "if you don't open up trade, you won't get any returns on your investments, and I'll buy you out."

"Go ahead" was all she said.

And he very nearly had bought her out. No doubt that was why she was dawdling today. She knew she was losing, and she didn't want to finish the game. If there was anything worse than an anarchist, it was a spoil sport.

As the traffic light changed to red, Jason turned and saw Ionia and Fred. Fred had hold of Ionia's hand and walked slightly faster than she did, apparently urging her along. Ionia, faintly resistant, allowed herself to be led. Jason studied her as she drew closer. She was not looking ahead or at her feet. She did not look at Fred nor did she acknowledge Jason. Her eyes had that empty look, as if there was no mind behind them. If he had not known otherwise, he might have guessed she was blind.

The way Ionia pretended not to see infuriated Jason. This unseeing was an old trick of Ionia's, but lately she had been practicing it more and more. Before when there had been just the two of them, he had always been able to force her to look at him. Now, whenever he focused his attention on Fred, she slipped away as she had today. And she was becoming stranger and stranger. If someone did not do something soon, she might end up in a mental institution. Jason supposed it was his duty to do what he could to bring Ionia back to reality.

"You do have some very peculiar habits, Ionia," said Jason as Ionia and Fred stopped beside him. "Why on earth were you crawling around under that tree sniffing those leaves? You must think you're an animal."

"What kind of an animal?" asked Fred.

Jason considered for a moment as he regarded Ionia, who steadfastly ignored him.

"Genus: mammal; kind: myrmecophagidae."

"A what?"

Fred's eyes widened at the length of the word.

"An anteater," Jason translated. "Anteaters have long ugly snouts, just like Ionia's nose, and they grub in the dirt looking for ants, and when they find them, they eat them. That's why they're called anteaters."

Fred gaped at Ionia.

"Ionia, did you eat ants? Are they crawling in your belly now? Do they bite you inside?"

Ionia did not answer. Instead she flared the nostrils of what was really a small well-shaped nose and tossed her head. Just then the light changed. Ionia sprinted across the street and began to gallop through the park, leaving a wake of whirling leaves.

"Look at her," disparaged Jason. "Now she thinks she's a horse."

Jason's sarcasm was lost on Fred, who ran after Ionia trying to whinny like a horse but sounding more like a rooster after each attempt.

"Infantile," muttered Jason as he crossed the street. "At best. At worst: insane. The case of the Underwood siblings. Thought they were horses. Ran away in the park. Never seen again," another rooster whinny pierced the air, "or heard from either."

As Jason proceeded through the park at a decorous pace, he projected himself into the future. He was a world famous analyst at the mental institution to which Ionia had been committed. After he had examined her thoroughly and probed the depths of her delusions, he ordered a straitjacket for her. "The patient is unpredictable," he explained to the attendants. "Use every precaution in handling."

Almost to the other end of the park, Ionia still ran. Instead of losing her breath and slowing down, she had found her second wind. She had become the wind and, like the wind, she moved because it was the law of her being. She wished she might never stop. Then, before her, she saw a mountainous pile of leaves looming larger and larger. She knew at once what she would do. Accelerating her speed, she made a flying leap and landed in the leaves.

Stillness after such motion fell around her in folds. She lay back in the leaves and listened to them breathe with her every breath. Gradually her breathing quieted until she stirred only the leaves closest to her mouth. Nestling deeper into the pile, she buried herself in the leaves. Then she drew her arms back close to her body and closed her eyes. She wished Jason and Fred might never find her. She wished they would let her lie there until she turned brown and dry and brittle, like the leaves, ready to crumble at the breath of the wind.

"Ionia! Ionia!"

It was Fred. Ionia could hear him panting in time with his running. Why couldn't he let her be or not be, as she chose? She did not want to respond; she did not want to get up and go on.

"Ionia! Are you in the leaves?" he shouted.

Her only response was to roll over on her side, bring her knees up against her chest, and put her arms over her head. In another moment Fred landed beside her in the leaves.

"Ionia?" he asked uncertainly, and he reached out his hands and felt for her, "Ionia," he laughed when he found her. "You are in the leaves! Are you hiding, Ionia?"

"I was hiding," said Ionia, sitting up, "but you found me."

"You can still hide," consoled Fred. "We can both hide from Jason."

It was too late. Just then, Jason sauntered up to the leaf pile and stopped before it, smirking. Ionia, whose hair was covered with leaves, turned her face away.

"You two look like a couple of eggs that just hatched. Cracked eggs," he added. "The kind that hatch loony birds."

"Why don't you jump in the leaves, too, Jason?" invited Fred. "Then we could all pretend that this is a nest like the one my bird-mother lives in."

Jason said nothing to Fred. Instead he walked around the pile until he stood in Ionia's view, although she still refused to see him.

"What is the child talking about, Ionia?" asked Jason. "What does he mean by his bird-mother?"

Ionia kept quiet and hoped Fred would have enough sense to drop the subject. So far, this year, Jason had not teased her about her mother. Not only for her own sake, but for Fred's, she prayed he would not start now. She was afraid, too, of what she might do if he did.

"Our bird-mother," Fred answered for her. "She lives in a nest at the top of the tallest tree in the world."

"It's just a story," said Ionia still without looking at Jason.

"You and my mother," Jason sneered. "Always telling stories."

"And sometimes our mother rides elephants," Fred continued happily, "and sometimes she wears purple tights and dances in a show."

"Your mother," repeated Jason. "Ah, yes, your mother, your nonexistent mother," he concluded knowingly.

"Shut up, Jason," said Ionia through her teeth.

"And every night she sees me when I'm asleep."

"No, Fred," corrected Jason. "I'm afraid she doesn't. It's scientifically impossible."

"Jason, stop it!" shouted Ionia.

"Yes, she does," insisted Fred. "She does in the night. And Grammar told my father to marry your mother, too. So then we'll have a mother in the daytime. We'll have two mothers."

"No, you won't," said Jason. "You can't have two mothers, because you don't even have one. And just because you don't have a mother of your own doesn't mean. . . ."

"I do so have a mother," yelled Fred, and he began to cry.

". . .doesn't mean you can have my mother. It's just too bad for you, if you don't have a mother. . . ."

"Jason!" Ionia screamed.

"I don't even blame your mother one bit for running away from a couple of crazy kids like you. . . ."

Ionia moved so swiftly and so suddenly that before Jason realized what was happening her teeth were sunk in his arm. He gave a frightened yelp and yanked his arm away from her. Then he skipped back a few steps and stopped to stare at Ionia, who had collapsed as suddenly as she had lunged and lay curled up on the ground breathing unevenly. Fred crept up beside Ionia and began to pat her as if she were Lion. When Jason was sure she was not going to attack again, he looked down at his arm. It was bleeding, and he could see the marks of Ionia's teeth. No doubt, he would be scarred for life.

"You're a wild animal, Ionia," he said in a half-jeering, half-shaken tone. "You ought to be put in a zoo. You're dangerous."

No one answered Jason.

The light of day had begun to diminish and all forms seemed shadows of themselves. Jason gazed at the still figure of Ionia lying on the ground, and he began to feel uneasy. Things had gone farther than he had meant them to. There was bound to be trouble at home.

"Come on," he said gruffly. "It's getting dark. We've got to get back." Without a word, Fred and Ionia got up from the ground and started to walk together. After a few steps, Fred took Ionia's hand; he would not look at Jason. Jason felt badly. He had never intended to taunt Fred. Fred was only a kid, and he was a good kid. He liked Fred. And Fred liked him. There had never been anyone before who just plain liked him. His mother had to love him, because she was his mother, and the teachers at school knew he was smart. But Fred liked him.

It was all Ionia's fault that he had teased Fred. She made him do it by refusing to talk to him, refusing even to look at him. If Fred started acting as if he didn't exist, Jason didn't know how he could stand it.

"Hey, Fred," he said, moving up to walk beside him, and then he forced himself to add, "Ionia. I'm sorry about what I said. I didn't mean it."

"I do so have a mother, Jason Brooke," said Fred.

"I know."

There, that ought to satisfy Ionia. He had even told a lie for her sake. Ionia said nothing; nor did Fred. Jason walked beside them in silence until he could tolerate it no longer.

"Don't you think you ought to apologize to me now, Ionia?" demanded Jason. "After all, you bit my arm. And it's still bleeding," he added.

For a moment there was more silence. Then Ionia spoke. "I'm not sorry."

When they reached the apartment, there was no talk of finishing the game of Economy. There was no talk at all. Ionia sat at the kitchen table with her head cradled in her arms and her face turned toward the wall. Out of loyalty, Fred imitated her. Jason stood by watching them, feeling awkward and angry and helpless until, in exasperation, he retreated to his own room.

After a little while, Fred began to feel fidgety. He raised his head and looked at Ionia. He was tired of sitting still and being miserable. He hoped Ionia was, too, but Ionia had not moved.

"Ionia," he said in a loud whisper.

She did not look up. Fred sighed and laid his head down again, but this time he faced in the direction of Jason's room. He wondered what Jason was doing and if he had put a bandaid on his bite. Fred wished he could see the bite; he had never seen a real bite before. He knew Jason had been mean and that he must have made Ionia very mad. Jason had made him mad, too. But it was hard to stay mad, and he was tired of sitting still. Fred glanced at Ionia again and wondered if she would notice if he got up quietly and went into Jason's room.

While Fred was debating, Jason appeared in the doorway. On his arm was a big bandage, and in his hands he held a large book with pictures of dinosaurs on the cover. Before Jason even said a word, Fred slipped out of his chair and followed Jason into his room.

In spite of the care he took to be quiet, Ionia did notice Fred's desertion, but it did not surprise her. She knew she could not trust anyone, not even Fred. That was why she liked to be alone as she had been when they were outside today. She was alone, no matter how many people surrounded her. It was better to know it, to be it, than to pretend it was not so. Outside and alone she felt free and unafraid. Sunlight and shadow could not hurt her; nor sky nor trees and leaves nor dirt. No bird or animal or fish or even insect could hurt her. An insect might bite, the sun might make her hot, rain make her wet, and cold make her shiver. She could die outside, she supposed, but it wouldn't matter. It would not be cruelty.

Jason was cruel; people were cruel, and she was afraid: not of Jason, not of Jason himself, but just afraid. When she was inside, her fear seemed to intensify.

It bounced off the walls and came back at her, and there was nowhere to hide. Her father frightened her. Ever since he had seen the pictures she had given Mrs. Brooke, he had been watching her. At dinner, she would look up from her plate and there would be his eyes. On the train, she would turn from the window and find that instead of reading his lecture notes he would be looking at her. She did not like his eyes. They were black; they were empty. When she looked at them, she could not see anything else.

Grammar had been behaving strangely, too. She was angry, even angrier than she usually was. She walked around the house muttering under her breath, talking to the furniture. She had started to make Fred and Ionia take a bath every night instead of just three times a week, and she scrubbed them until they were red. At first Ionia had thought Grammar was angry with them, and especially with her. Often Grammar would scold her for no reason, and sometimes she would take her by the shoulders and shake her. Other times, just as unreasonably, Grammar would suddenly grab her and cover her face with hard dry kisses. And Grammar had begun to make desserts.

After awhile, Ionia had understood that her father was at the bottom of Grammar's strangeness. Every evening she scowled at him during dinner, and every morning she deliberately undercooked his eggs. Ionia had seen her do it. One night, after they had been sent upstairs to bed, Grammar had even talked to her father. The sound of voices was so unusual that she and Fred had sneaked downstairs to listen. That was when they had heard Grammar telling their father that he ought to marry Mrs. Brooke.

"You seem to forget that I am married already," their father had said.

"Not to a woman."

"To what else, then, if not to a woman?"

"What else? A wildcat, a creature, a female hurricane, a. . . ."

Then their father had started to laugh, drowning out the rest of Grammar's words. The sound of his laughter was so terrible that Ionia had grabbed Fred's hand and dragged him back upstairs.

Since then, Ionia had scarcely stopped thinking of her mother, except when she managed to lose herself as she had that day in her surroundings. Never before had she heard anyone speak of her mother. Now she knew two things: that her mother was still alive and that Grammar did not like her. But this knowledge did no good; it was not enough. It gave her nothing while it took away what little of her mother had been hers. Before her mother had seemed a dream; she had been a dream, the dream of the woman who danced on the hill and called her to come to her. And the dream of her mother had been all her own, just her own to share with no one unless she chose.

Now she never dreamed the dream anymore, not since that night. Grammar's anger, her father's laughter had driven the dream away. Instead she had started to remember things she had never remembered before. She remembered a dark room; she was locked inside, alone, crying and crying for her mother. Her mother had called her name over and over, just like the woman in the dream, but she did not come to let her out of the dark. She never came. She stopped calling, and she never came back. So it was true, what Jason said: her mother had left her, left her alone to be frightened by her father and bossed by Grammar and taunted by Jason; left her alone without even knowledge of who and where she was.

As Ionia sat staring at Mrs. Brooke's bright kitchen wall, hot, angry tears began to trickle down her cheeks and over her clenched fingers. She bit her lip and held her breath to keep from making any sound. She did not want to lose control in Mrs. Brooke's kitchen. She did not want anyone to know about the anger or the pain. If the others knew, they would use their knowledge to hurt her. The only way she could protect herself was to make sure no one knew anything about her.

Ionia heard the front door open. Wiping her tears with her fist, she sat up, but she did not move from the table. In a moment Fred and Jason emerged from Jason's room. Fred ran to greet Mrs. Brooke as he always did. Jason hesitated, unsure of what he meant to do. He did not want to tell on Ionia, because he did not want her to tell on him. It would be better if they could agree on what to tell his mother.

"Ionia?" he began tentatively.

Ionia did not answer, and, as usual, she would not look at him.

"Ionia, we should decide what to tell my mother. We'll have to tell her something."

"I don't care what you tell her."

Well, if she was going to be that way about it, the decision was his. Sighing loudly and shaking his head, Jason went out to the hall to meet his mother.

"Mother," Ionia heard him say, "I think someone ought to try and find out what's wrong with Ionia. She's been behaving strangely lately. Today she bit me. I think she might have rabies."

"Bit you!" exclaimed Mrs. Brooke. "Where? Come in the bathroom and let me have a look. What did you do to provoke her, Jason? You must have done something."

"Can I see the bite, too?" came Fred's voice.

Ionia heard the sound of the bathroom door opening followed by the sound of running water. Then, a moment later, although she heard no footsteps, she became aware that someone had come into the kitchen. She turned toward the door and found her father watching her with an odd smile on his face, a greedy smile. Ionia felt terrified, but there was nothing she could do or say. She was trapped.

Then, to Ionia's relief, Mrs. Brooke pushed past her father and crossed the kitchen towards her. Ionia knew Mrs. Brooke must be angry with her for biting Jason, but anything was better than being alone with her father. Ionia lowered her eyes and waited. She could feel Mrs. Brooke standing over her. Then she heard Mrs. Brooke's knees crack as she knelt beside her. Still Mrs. Brooke did not speak. Then Mrs. Brooke's warm hands touched her cheeks. Ionia had to look at Mrs. Brooke's face. Amazingly, she found no anger there; only bewilderment, concern.

"What is it, Ionia?" she asked gently. "What has been making you so unhappy lately?"

Mrs. Brooke's inexplicable tenderness overwhelmed Ionia. All the tears she had not cried pressed behind her eyes. For a moment she felt a great longing to hide her face in Mrs. Brooke's shoulder and sob out all the fear and all the loneliness. The moment passed. She fought back her tears and turned her face away. She could not trust Mrs. Brooke. Mrs. Brooke had betrayed her to her father.

She was alone.

8

 ## Inside the Crystal Ball

LATE that night, inside the tower room, in complete darkness, save for the glow of the crystal ball, Adam Underwood stood over his desk. Tonight, he felt sure, after years of empty gazing, he would find what he sought in the crystal ball. First, in order to sharpen his inner vision, Adam selected a memory. Remembering, for Adam, was never random activity but always a deliberate process, an invocation of a power kept strictly under his control.

Now he chose to remember a morning in spring three days after Fred was born when he had awoken to find Her, not in bed with him, but across the room, leaning against the window, staring out. Her face in profile, against the brightness of the sky beyond, was pale as a daytime moon.

"I have been up all night with the man-child," she said without turning towards him. "He will sleep now."

"That milk is probably giving him colic. I told you that you ought to nurse him yourself."

She made no answer. He had already tried to persuade her, to force her to feed the baby, but it was no use.

"You might at least give him a name," he said. "You named the girl before she was born.

"This child is for you to name. I have no name for him. Not one of my race has ever given birth to a male child before."

"Very well, I will. He shall be called Frederick, after my father. See to it that from now on you call him by name."

She said nothing and continued to gaze out the window. As quietly as he could he rose from the bed. He meant to stalk her and startle her into response. This was their dance: this intricate pattern of advance and avoidance, attack and retreat. Now, deliberately, she refused her part and turned to face him.

"It is time for me to go, Adam. I have stayed too long. I should never have come with you to your own country."

Taken by surprise, Adam stopped mid-step.

"Ionia should have been born among my people according to our law. I was wrong to let her be born here and wrong to believe you when you told me that because she was, she is as much yours as mine."

Both were silent for a moment as they stared at each other across the room.

"Now I have given you a man-child," she said. "I have given you your Frederick. I will take Ionia and go back to my people, her people."

"You are forgetting. . . ," he said, taking a step towards her.

"No," she cut him off, her expression suddenly savage, "I am remembering. It is you who have made me forget, you with your snake eyes, it is you who have made me forget again and again what I am. I will not forget anymore. I know. I am."

"You are forgetting," he continued evenly, moving steadily towards her, "that what you are is my wife. I am your husband. The bond between us is not to be easily broken."

"Fool," she laughed. "Mortal fool. The bond between us cannot be broken because there is no bond. Do you think your human laws can bind me? I am a direct descendent of the First Woman, the ninth to bear her name, a member by blood and water and fire of her immortal race, subject to her laws alone. I have amused myself with you. That is all. My life with you has been a game for me, a dangerous game, a foolish game, but a game. I am not playing anymore."

"And what makes you think you can go back," he asked softly, taking another step towards her so that the two stood facing each other inches apart. "What makes you think that your people will accept you back? Have you not said yourself that you have broken their laws? Do you imagine that you are unchanged? Perhaps my mortality has rubbed off on you. Look at yourself. Look around you. What has become of your power, the power that could make herbs grow beneath your feet and vines climb the walls that surrounded you? What has become of that power? By whose laws have we been living: yours or mine?"

She stared down at her feet; he could feel her tremble.

"I have been a fool," she whispered, "a fool to think that I could let you touch me without changing me."

He smiled and laid a hand on her cheek; her cheek was cold.

"You are right," she continued. "My power is gone. I have been losing it all along. Every time I have looked at you. You have drawn my power out of me with your eyes. You have drawn a man-child out of my body. You have drawn the very life out of me."

He laid his other hand on her shoulder; her shoulder was rigid.

"But I will go back," she said, looking up at him suddenly, her nostrils flared and her pupils dilated so that just a rim of purple showed. "Perhaps my people will punish me. Perhaps they will put me to death, but I would rather die at their hands than live at yours."

She wrenched herself from his grip and turned toward the window once again.

"And I will take Ionia," she said, speaking more to herself than to him. "They will not blame her. They will raise her as one of themselves."

She turned from the window, but not to look at him.

"I must sleep now," she said.

She brushed past him. Beside the bed she let fall the silk robe that he had given her. He expected her to climb into the bed. She did not. Instead, utterly naked, she left the room.

He did not follow. There was no danger of her leaving immediately. She would sleep as she said she would. She was incapable of even the slightest deception. Nor was there any point in arguing with her further. She was not a reasonable creature. He needed time, time to himself to decide what he would do.

Gathering up the robe, he went to stand beside the window. He now saw what she had been watching. Ionia was playing in the yard below. What she was playing he could not quite make out. She had a pile of pebbles, a spoon, and his mother's silver teapot. With the spoon, she dug a hole; then she dropped pebbles into it and poured water over them. Was she planting them, he wondered, or trying to make a miniature lake? Before he could watch to see if she repeated the process, Ionia got up and ran to greet her mother. She did not seem to notice or care that her mother was naked. Together the two sat down in a patch of sun. For a little while they talked; for longer they sat in silence. Then, she lay down to sleep. After a time Ionia went back to her play.

All that day she slept in the sun while Ionia played close by. He watched them from various windows, oblivious to the baby's crying. Towards dusk, Ionia went to sit beside her mother again. It was then that he left the house and crept up silently behind Ionia. Clapping his hand over her mouth, he lifted her and carried her inside where he locked her in the private parlor.

When night fell, She woke. He heard her come into the house. He heard her calling Ionia's name. Ionia began to cry and beat against the locked door. Soon she was crying and beating against the door from the other side. She did not even attempt to look for him or importune him. She remained howling and scratching at the door like an animal until she fell into an exhausted sleep.

Then he descended from the tower room where he had listened to the uproar. Lifting her as easily as he had Ionia, he carried her to their bed and fell asleep beside her. When he woke, she was gone.

✿✿✿

Adam opened his eyes and sank into his chair. The memory had tired him. He had never chosen to remember it before. He disliked memories that made him wonder what would have happened if he had acted otherwise. What would have happened, for example, if he had locked her up instead of Ionia? At the time, of course, he had never imagined she would leave without Ionia. He felt that locking her up would be too crude, too reactionary. He had believed that an indirect demonstration of power would be sufficient. He had been wrong. He had made a mistake. That was why, for so long, he had avoided that memory.

Perhaps that was also why he had failed to realize Ionia's usefulness as a point of contact. It had occurred to him to question the girl about her dreams, but he could never get anything out of her. Ionia's drawings had alerted him, her drawings and the Babylonian tales. It was obvious to him now: if he meant to trap Her, he must bait the trap. What better bait than Ionia, the one thing in his possession that she wanted. She did not want him; he had no illusions about that. It did not even matter except that it meant he could never pursue her again. Now he must use cunning to capture her.

Adam smiled. He felt his energy returning to him. He would need it. Entering the crystal ball absorbed all his energy, even when nothing happened. Rising from his chair, Adam stood over his desk, gripping it with his hands for support. He looked out the window. The moon had begun to rise behind the hill of the three trees. It was full. He gazed at it for a moment as if to draw its power into himself. Then he lowered his eyes to the crystal ball, holding an image of Ionia in his mind: Ionia as she might be at that moment, asleep, with moonlight lying on her face, dreaming of her mother.

For a time he remained outside the crystal ball, aware only of the shine of its surface. Then the darkness opened and drew him in. Only this time the darkness was not still; he could sense it moving, taking shape. Then he recognized Her form. Only half of her was visible; the rest was in shadow. She had a dark side, like the moon. He did not attempt to touch her or even speak. He did not know where he was in relation to her or whether they occupied the same space at all. He did not know whether he had a visible form in this empty place or whether her appearance had any reality. So he watched and waited. It seemed to him that she was watching and waiting, too. Then he saw her stretch out her arms; she lifted both arms into whatever light it was that gave her form.

"Ionia! Ionia!" she called.

Silence followed. No voice that he could hear answered her; nor did she appear to have received an answer. She lowered her arms and turned her face to darkness. Afraid that she would disappear, he spoke.

"Lilith."

Her face came back into view. For a moment she looked startled, confused. Then he knew she saw him. He had, somehow, become visible to her.

"You," she said.

It was an accusation.

"You were expecting someone else?"

"You have her locked up still," she said. "She does not come to me though I call and call."

Adam did not answer. It was not yet the time to speak. They stared at each other across an unknown expanse of space.

"Why are you here?" she demanded. "I thought it was Ionia. I thought she had come."

"Ionia is the reason I am here," he answered. "The reason I have called you."

"You called me?"

"Yes. "

"What do you want, then?"

"I want you to take Ionia."

She looked wary.

"I was unwise not to let you take her before," he explained. "I should have known I could not raise her any more than I could keep you."

Still she remained silent, waiting.

"She has gone wild," he said. "She is wild. She has bitten another child and drawn blood. I cannot keep her much longer."

"Why have you not brought her to me, then?" she said at last. "Why is she not here tonight?"

"She is here. As much as I am, as much as you are. But you must understand: none of us is here. Here is nowhere. I cannot bring Ionia to you by magic unless you desire only the illusion of Ionia. I will not enter your country again."

"Let her come to me, then. She hears me calling. I know."

He laughed. Laughter in the emptiness sounded strange. It had no substance; it was only the echo of laughter.

"Perhaps it is because your race gives birth so rarely that you understand nothing of child development. Ionia is still very young, too young to come to you by herself. Her grandmother would never permit it. If you want her, you must come and get her yourself. If you do not, I cannot say what will become of her in human society. We will try to control her for as long as we can at home.

When we can control her no longer we will be forced to hand her over to authorities who can. She is one of your race, not one of ours. If you want her, come and claim her."

He waited for her to speak, but she did not. After a time as immeasurable as the space between them, she turned toward the light and disappeared, leaving the darkness complete. For yet awhile he waited, probing the darkness for the answer she had not given him, the certainty he desired, but the darkness yielded nothing. He felt his energy flagging. It became difficult to remember where he was or why he was there. He knew he was in danger of losing control. With what strength remained to him, he willed to surface. The tower room surrounded him again. He was back inside his body, and it ached with tiredness. Glancing out the window, he saw that the moon had risen out of sight.

9
By Mistake

THOUGH it was only mid-afternoon, Eva Brooke switched on the lights in her kitchen. Outside snow was falling, and it was almost dark on this shortest day of the year. She had finished grading term papers in time to make Christmas cookies. She had promised Adam's mother that she would do most of the baking for their joint celebration at the Underwood's house. This invitation from the Underwoods was unprecedented, and Eva anticipated the Christmas holiday with more excitement than she had ever felt as a child.

The breakfast and lunch dishes, Eva noted, were still in the sink. She debated for a moment whether or not she ought to wash them first. She decided not and began to wander around the kitchen gathering her ingredients and her cooking equipment. When everything was assembled, she continued to feel that she had forgotten something. She remembered the oven and went to turn it on, but that was not it. Then she realized what it was: she wanted someone to make Christmas cookies with her. Knowing it was foolish, she went to Jason's door. Before she knocked she knew he would say *no*, but she felt bound to ask, nevertheless. She was the mother, and he was the child. There were rituals to be observed, even if they were empty.

"Jason," she called as she knocked.

There was no answer.

Eva wondered if he had left the apartment without telling her. She hated it when he did that. She had all but forbidden him to. She had forbidden him, but he refused to recognize her authority. He insisted that he was old enough to come and go without giving her notice. She had failed to make him understand that it was not a matter of age but of courtesy.

"Jason. "

"What?" came a voice from behind her.

Eva turned and saw Jason standing in the doorway to the kitchen wearing his hat and coat and holding a large paper bag in his arms. His face showed a mixture of guilt and defiance. She had not heard him come in. He must have meant to slip in quietly so that she would not even know he had been gone. This attempt at sneakiness hurt her more than open disobedience.

"You might have let me know you were going out," she said. "I wouldn't have stopped you."

"I was on a secret mission," Jason explained and he started across the room.

Eva recognized that he was using her own tactics. She smiled in spite of herself and stepped aside. Not until after Jason had closed the door to his room behind him did she remember what she had been going to ask.

"Jason," she said.

In a moment the door opened.

"What do you want now?"

"Would you like to help me make Christmas cookies?"

Eva thought the look on his face was almost pitying. He sighed as if he were a tired adult and she an over-eager child.

"I'm very busy right now, Mother," he said, and he shut the door firmly in her face.

"Oh," she said, and she turned away.

When Eva had finished mixing the dough, she rolled it out so that she could cut it into shapes. As she set to work choosing the shapes and cutting them out, she found herself thinking of Ionia. She would enjoy forming dough into recognizable shapes. There was magic in making cookies in the image of moon and stars, trees and animals that no one would understand better than Ionia. She wished Ionia were with her now. She wished Ionia were her daughter.

But Ionia was not her daughter, Eva reminded herself as she set the first star on the baking sheet, nor was she ever likely to be. She must not allow her fantasies to deceive her about her closeness to Ionia. She used to believe that she was closer to Ionia than anyone else, and maybe that was still true, but closeness was relative, not absolute. Lately Ionia would not let anyone near her. She behaved, as Jason repeatedly pointed out, like a sick animal. Although Eva discounted Jason's theories about rabies and distemper, she had tried to persuade Adam to take Ionia to a doctor, not because Ionia had bitten Jason, but because she seemed so pale and listless.

Adam had insisted that there was nothing wrong with Ionia, and he had offered to pay Jason's doctor's bill. Of course, she had refused. She was sure Ionia had been seriously provoked, although violence in anyone as quiet and passive as Ionia was disturbing. Ionia's grandmother was worried, too. She had said so in her letter after apologizing profusely for Ionia's behavior and assuring Eva that she had taken steps to see that Ionia would not misbehave again. She seemed to think that over Christmas, Eva might be able to find out what was wrong with Ionia. "Ionia will talk to you," her grandmother had concluded.

Was that why she and Jason had been invited? Had it not been Adam's idea at all?

Eva pushed that thought aside as she arranged some crescent moons over a hill of Christmas trees, but she could not stop thinking of Ionia. Contrary to what Mrs. Underwood believed, Ionia did not talk to her; she had never talked much. The drawings had been her means of expression, and those had stopped. Eva wasn't sure why, but she sensed it had something to do with her having shown Adam the pictures. But how was she to have known that the drawings were not only gifts but secrets, gifts because they were secrets? She still didn't know; she only guessed. Ionia had never told her.

Eva set a reindeer too hastily among the trees; its antlers broke. As she pieced the reindeer back together, she realized that she was evading something; or it was evading her, for she could not place what it was that was making her so uncomfortable. She thought back to the moment when she had told Adam about the pictures, and then she knew her fault had not been a simple failure to understand. She had acted impulsively, but where had the impulse originated: out of concern for Ionia or for herself? Perhaps, as she had told herself at the time, she had wanted Adam to recognize his daughter's talents, but she had wanted even more to have him recognize the picture of the woman. She had, in effect, used Ionia's drawings to trick Adam into revealing what she was afraid to ask him. She had watched him as he studied the pictures. His jaw had tightened; his color had deepened. Other than that, he had betrayed nothing. She had betrayed Ionia.

How to repair the damage, Eva wondered as she cut out a camel. How to explain to a child that adults, too, suffered pain, pain that made them behave in incomprehensible ways. Surely it was pain that had made Ionia bite Jason, and perhaps pain that made Jason torment her. It must be pain that made Adam so forbidding as to seem frightening to his children. It was pain that kept them all apart from each other. It puzzled Eva that pain should work that way. Whatever forms it took, it seemed to Eva that all pain had its source in loss, in longing. Why could they not ease it for one another? Perhaps the time for that was coming, Eva thought as she arranged the camels on what she thought of as a desert plain. Christmas time.

When all the cookies were in place, Eva stepped back to survey the world she had made. Each shape existed in relation to every other. It seemed a pity that when the cookies were baked, she would have to take them off the baking sheet and pile them indiscriminately into a tin. No one who ate the cookies would realize that each tree was part of a forest, each reindeer, camel, and sheep part of a herd or flock, each star part of a galaxy, each moon the satellite of a world. As she gazed at the shapes, she reflected that nothing could be understood separately. By itself, nothing was whole. Moving one camel deeper into the desert, she picked up the cookie sheet and carried it to the oven.

In his room Jason was wrapping Ionia and Fred's Christmas presents. He did not want his mother to know what they were, because she would not approve of them. He had no intention of letting his mother spoil his fun by taking them away from him: not that she had any right to. He had bought the presents with his own money.

Fred's present was a trap, large enough to catch mice and squirrels alive. Jason knew Fred would appreciate the trap, even if no one else appreciated his giving it to him. During the winter, Fred's zoo population dwindled as it consisted mainly of creatures that could be caught outdoors during the summer. Fred would be thrilled to keep his zoo going all year round and to add mammals to his collection.

Ionia's present was a book called: *The Inferiority of Women; Or Why Little Girls Grow Up to Be Like Their Mothers.* He knew the book would make Ionia angry. He was still angry with her for never apologizing to him; in fact, hardly speaking to him since she had bitten him. He was also angry with his mother for taking Ionia's side, so he didn't care if his present to Ionia embarrassed her. He doubted the book would get him into serious trouble as a more obvious reference to her biting might have. He had considered for awhile giving her a muzzle.

With some difficulty, Jason tied the ribbon on Ionia's package; Fred's present was wrapped already. He disliked fussing with wrapping paper and ribbons. They seemed silly, especially if you knew what you were getting as he knew about the telescope his mother was giving him. He had asked her to let him have it early, but his mother, usually so easy to manage, had balked at that. He hoped Christmas would be worth the trouble he was taking over it. Usually Christmas was not, but this year it might be different. He had not liked the idea of spending Christmas at the Underwood's at first. It seemed to him that they saw far too much of the Underwoods as it was. Upon reconsideration, he realized that Christmas there might offer some distinct advantages. For one thing his mother's enthusiasm would be diffused among five people instead of concentrated upon him alone. For another, he would be able to take his telescope up to the Underwood's roof, which would provide conditions far superior to the ones on the fire escape of the apartment. He only wished his mother would let him assemble the telescope now so that he could use it as soon as they arrived. His mother was such a child with her obvious secrets.

Sighing, Jason picked up Ionia and Fred's Christmas presents and carried them to his closet where he meant to hide them. As soon as he opened the door, a loud crash from the kitchen startled him. He paused for a moment to listen. Then, hearing nothing more, he hid the presents behind a false panel in the back of his closet. Mission accomplished, Jason supposed he had better go and see what his mother had done now. He found her in the kitchen, on her knees, picking up the fragments of what appeared to have been some cookies.

"What happened this time."

It was more a comment than a question.

"I grabbed the potholder that has a hole in it, by mistake," she said without looking up. "I burned my hand and dropped the cookie sheet."

"Why don't you throw that potholder away?" he demanded.

"I don't know," she said shortly. "There's not always a reason for what people do or don't do."

"There ought to be," said Jason; then, realizing that his mother was upset, however unreasonable it seemed to him, he added. "It doesn't matter, Mother, they'll taste the same."

"There's more to a cookie than its taste, Jason."

She picked up the cookie sheet and turned her back towards him as she set it on the counter.

"Fred and Ionia know the difference between a whole cookie and a broken one if you don't."

She was at it again: comparing him unfavorably with Ionia and Fred. It made him furious.

"I'll have to start all over again," she said.

"Not now!" protested Jason. "It's time for supper."

"All right, Jason," she sighed. "It's time for supper. Just give me a moment, will you? Will you just please give me one moment?"

Then, without warning, his mother walked out of the kitchen. A moment later he heard her bedroom door opening and closing. For awhile he stood still. He didn't get it. His mother was not only infantile, she was insane. How could anyone with all her marbles make such a fuss over a batch of broken cookies?

Jason shrugged his shoulders. Then, because he was hungry, he went to the counter and started to eat the crumbs.

BOOK TWO

Winter
The Captivity of
the Wild Mother

10
Like a Thief in the Night

IT was near midnight. From the window in the tower room, Adam Underwood kept watch; for if She came in the night, as he suspected she would, he must be awake or she would take Ionia and be gone before the light.

The night was clear and still. By the light of the waning moon, he could see the three trees. When she appeared beneath the trees he would see her: a small shadow against the stars. He would not rush outside to meet her. He was not a boy, eager and undisciplined in his desires. He was a man, and he knew how to take pleasure in taking time.

Because the snow was bright, even in that weary light, he would be able to watch her walking down the hill. Before she came close enough to see the gate, he would reach into his pocket for the touchstone. At his touch, the gates would open wide. Then, as she drew nearer, he would lose sight of her, beyond the wall, until she came to stand in the empty space. He wondered: would she hesitate before the open gate? Would she guess the meaning of the wall? There was a chance that she might. There was a chance that, in that moment of hesitation, he might lose what he had waited for; but he thought not. Even if she recognized the risk, he reckoned on her daring.

She would look about her, like an animal sniffing for danger, but she would not see him in the shadows of the tower room. Then she would dart across the lawn, into the shadow of the house, into the house itself. Softly, she would steal from room to room, searching for Ionia. The silence of the house would match the silence of her movements, and she would imagine that no one was awake. When she found Ionia, she would lift the child, still asleep, and carry her out of the house without waking her. Then he would see her again, hurrying towards the gate with her treasure in her arms. He would wait until the last moment; then he would touch the stone and seal the trap.

Over and over, as he stood by the window keeping watch, Adam Underwood rehearsed this scene. Only the tension of anticipation kept him awake, worn out, as he was, with long nights of watching. Only her image gave coherence to thoughts that had grown distorted and confused. Yet there were times when he wondered: cold and stiff and aching at dawn, he wondered; he wondered, when he fell into bed for a small morning sleep and wondered when he woke again before noon, if that was all she was, an image of his own making. She seemed so wildly improbable. Perhaps she did not exist independently of his mind. Perhaps it was the power of his mind that had once given her form, and he had begotten children on a creature of his imagination.

When he watched at night, these thoughts did not disquiet him. Under the stars that stretched out into unknown space, the improbable was the only probability. If he had imagined her, then he might have imagined it all; all that he saw and touched and took to be real emanated from himself. As he watched, hour after hour, night after night, it seemed to him that even the stars were his creation, and that if he closed his eyes, their light would go out.

Although it was late at night, much later than she customarily went to bed, Grammar, in her private parlor, still knitted beside the fire. She was determined to finish Mrs. Brooke's shawl before Christmas, and tomorrow was Christmas Eve. All the necessities—scarves, hats, mittens, socks, and sweaters for the children—were wrapped and hidden away, and she had only the shawl to complete. She had meant the shawl to be a warm solid brown that Mrs. Brooke might wear with anything, but when she set out to make it, she discovered that she had not enough brown wool left, nor enough of any one color. So, in a moment of wild inspiration, she had decided to use all the colors.

Grammar had just finished a blue stripe. She held the shawl up to the firelight in order to determine what color the next stripe should be. By firelight, the colors looked deeper and richer than by daylight. They seemed to have a glow of their own. She ran her fingers over the fabric; they lingered on an orange stripe, and she knew that orange was the color she wanted next to the blue. She laid the shawl in her lap, then reached into her bag for the skein of orange wool. Breaking off the blue wool, she tied it to the orange in a neat, indiscernible knot and began to knit again.

The uneven sputtering of the fire and the rhythmic clicking of the needles combined to soothe Grammar. Though she was tired, she felt that she could knit all night. Knitting rested her as much as sleep did, perhaps more; for it eased her mind as well as her body. Knitting gave her a center of calm, a sense of control; it kept the unknown at bay. She watched the loose wool pass through her fingers, over the needle, into strong fabric. Because of its color, it seemed of one substance with the fire. The whole room was warmed with orange light. The cold and dark beyond the wall of her private parlor scarcely seemed real. They could not touch the warm round world she had created with firewood and orange wool.

Asleep in his bed, with Lion lying across his feet, Fred dreamed. He dreamed that he and Lion got out of bed in the middle of the night when everyone else was asleep. Cautiously, they tiptoed down the dark hall, and monsters watched them through the cracks in the wall, but they didn't reach out their slimy fingers to catch him, because they were afraid of Lion biting.

When Fred and Lion reached the landing above the hall, they saw a light. The light came from the living room, and Fred thought that Christmas must have come. Grammar said it would come in the night. Fred wanted to see Christmas when it had just come, when it didn't know anyone was looking. So he and Lion crept downstairs, across the hall, and came to stand in the living room door.

There was the Christmas tree, shining; only not with the electric lights he had helped Grammar string, but with real lights: lights, all different colors, that sizzled and burned and blazed as if they were about to explode. Afraid, but yet more curious, Fred came closer to the tree to see if the lights were hot.

In the room next to Fred's, Ionia woke suddenly from sound sleep. If she had been dreaming, she did not remember her dreams, and she did not know why she was awake, so very awake, in the middle of the night. She made no attempt to go back to sleep. Instead, she lay still, with her eyes opened wide, and listened. The house was silent. No wind rocked it; no night creatures stirred beneath its floors or behind the walls. Even its clankings and creakings had ceased. Ionia thought that this was what people must mean when they spoke of the dead of the night.

Quietly, so as not to disturb the stillness, Ionia slipped out of bed. Her bare feet made no sound as she crossed the cold floor to the round window. Cold crept in through the cracks in the window, but Ionia, sitting with her knees drawn up against her chest, did not mind the cold. Cold was part of being awake in the dead of night, part of the three trees bare and black against the sky, part of the stars, part of the snow, part of the dark side of the waning moon. Ionia lost her own coldness in the coldness of night.

The moon's bright side shone on the snow. Here and there a crystal of snow caught that distant light in such a way that it glittered as if it were an earthbound star. Ionia felt that she was seeing a secret: all that was, without her; beauty that would have been, whether she was awake or asleep. That there should be stars and moon and shining snow when she wasn't looking was an awesome thought. Ionia lifted her eyes from the snow to the three trees. She thought of them, standing still on the hill night after day, winter after summer, in snow and rain, wind and light. She wondered if they knew, in some unseeing way, what she did not. She gazed at the three trees and tried to imagine herself inside them, tried to imagine herself not herself, but something else altogether.

Then, a figure appeared beneath the three trees, the figure of a woman. Ionia forgot the trees and began to tremble all over. She pressed her hand against the window pane. The pane was cold and hard. Ionia knew she was awake, more awake than she had ever been in her life. The woman was not a dream. Nor did she dance as she always did in the dream. For a time she stood as still as the trees. Then she started down the hill. Ionia could see her moving over the snow, swiftly, smoothly, as if she were her own shadow. Ionia watched only a moment longer. Then she sprang from her window and ran out of her room.

As Ionia sped down the stairs, Lion woke and cocked his head to listen. He began to whimper with excitement. Pulling himself up to the head of the bed, he pressed his cold, wet nose against Fred's face. Fred woke and sat up in bed. It was the middle of the night, and he and Lion were awake.

"Christmas," he whispered, and he tumbled out of bed and tiptoed towards the door, following Lion's lead.

In the private parlor, Grammar stopped knitting in the middle of a row. She thought she had heard the front gate open. Only she and Adam had keys, and Adam was asleep; or so she had believed. She had not heard him climb the stairs to the tower room, and she had turned out all the lights when she went up. If Adam had gotten up in the middle of the night to open the gate, it meant no good.

Grammar rose from her chair, laid her knitting aside, and went to peer out the window. The gate was open, wide open, but she could see no one outside. Then she heard the front door opening, and there was Ionia, running barefoot in the snow towards the gate. For a moment, panic paralyzed Grammar; then it propelled her into action. She ran to the chair and seized her knitting bag. Then, armed with a spare needle, she hurried down the hall.

Before Grammar reached the landing, she saw Fred and Lion approaching from the other direction.

"Go back to bed at once," commanded Grammar without slowing her steps.

Fred stopped still, but Lion bounded ahead, nearly losing his balance on the stairs. Grammar paused and glared at Fred who still stared at her.

"I said go to bed," she shouted, and she waved her knitting needle at him.

Fred made as if to turn around, and Grammar headed down the stairs, unaware that as soon as she turned her back, Fred began to follow her.

Grammar made straight for the open door. Before she reached it, the cold hit her. Cold had penetrated the hall; it was filling the whole house, it served to enrage her even more. Unmindful of her slippered feet, Grammar marched out to meet the night.

She never got farther than the front steps. There she was arrested by the sight of Ionia and a woman, that woman, standing in the open gate gazing on one another. It had come to pass: the thing she had dreaded for so long. But now that it had, it hardly seemed real. The look that passed between those two excluded, not only her, but all that was hers, all that she knew. She felt as though Ionia had passed beyond her reach already. In a moment she might be gone from sight, gone with the thief into the night. Helpless, frightened, Grammar would have cried if she could have, but numbness, beginning in her toes, had overspread her body and her mind. She could not think what to do. She could not think.

Then she became aware of Fred by her side, clutching her bathrobe. "Grammar," he whispered, "who is that lady?"

Grammar looked down at Fred. Even darkness could not dim the orange of his hair. Then she looked again at the woman. At that distance, the woman seemed no more than a shadow against the snow. She must not give in so easily. She must not allow that creature to come out of nowhere to snatch the children away from her care. What was the creature thinking, to let Ionia stand out in the snow in her bare feet. Outrage restored Grammar to her senses.

"I told you to go to bed," she said to Fred, but she grabbed him and held him tight, belying her command. Then, raising her voice, she shouted, "Ionia, come here at once."

Startled, both Ionia and the woman turned toward Grammar, but neither answered.

"I said come here at once."

Ionia looked at the woman. At a sign from her, Ionia obeyed and began to walk slowly up the path. To Grammar's dismay, the woman followed, with Lion at her heels. Grimly, Grammar waited, holding her ground and holding Fred.

✦✦✦

Still standing by the window in the tower room, Adam waited, too. Bewildered, he watched her follow Ionia up the path to the house, away from the open gate. It did not make sense. It did not make sense that she should walk so trustingly into the trap. He wanted her to take Ionia and make for the gate. He wanted to witness her rage and humiliation when the gate closed in her face. He did not want her to dare walk freely and calmly into his house, as if she had never left it, as if she had never betrayed him.

The two disappeared from sight. Adam stared at the empty yard and the open gate. For a moment his hand hovered over his pocket; then he lowered it. He had waited so long, he would wait a little longer. He would not cheat himself of that supreme moment. It would come; it must come. Meanwhile, she was here, here in his house. He need wait no longer to see her. Perhaps, if he chose, he would have her tonight in his bed. Then, just let her try to steal away, as she had before, by morning light. Just let her.

Clenching his hands to still their trembling, he turned from the window and left the tower room.

11
Ionia's Mother

ON the landing, Adam paused. She was there in the hall. Someone had turned on all the lights; it must have been his mother; for she was there, too, with the boy. Why were they all there? He had not reckoned on their being awake. What had they to do with Her, with what was between him and Her? They were in the way; it was their fault that things had not gone according to plan. His mother was making a fuss. She was waving something in the air and shouting, but her words had no more meaning in his ears than the barking of the dog. He shut his mother's voice out of his consciousness. He shut out everything except Her.

She stood straight and still. Her bearing suggested attention, but on her face was that uncomprehending animal look he knew so well. Something about her was not quite right. He puzzled over what it was. The light, he decided; the overhead light was too bright. It made everything seem unnatural and harsh. He did not remember the starkness of her face, the sharpness of the bones and shadows. Nor did he remember the matted roughness of her hair or the hardness of her body. Her beauty had been wild but delicate. Her body had been strong but soft. What he saw under the electric light was a cruder version of the woman he remembered.

Her clothes, too, added to the effect of crudeness, and he reminded himself that he had never seen what she wore when it was winter in her own country. With distaste he examined the outlandish garment made of dried mosses and fastened with vines and feathers. He would have it burned, and he would have her washed. Apparently, she remembered or, at any rate, chose to practice nothing of what he had taught her. He would have to begin all over again with her. If she had reverted entirely to her wild ways, there would be a great struggle between them. But then, a struggle was exactly what he wanted. Smiling, Adam started down the stairs. Before he was halfway down, she sensed his approach and turned towards him.

Her eyes. For the first time in over six years her eyes met his directly. They were just as he remembered them, only more: more beautiful, more mysterious.

Overcome, Adam's steps almost faltered, but he controlled them. He could never hope to master her unless he was master of himself.

"Welcome, Lilith," he said.

He crossed the hall, silencing his mother with a look, and came to stand before Her, near enough to touch her, though he did not. From her clothes came an earthy smell, which he found at once disgusting and exciting.

Adam and Lilith stared at one another in silence.

Unnoticed by her father, Ionia moved nearer to the woman. Lion rose from where he was lying at Lilith's feet and growled softly. Everyone waited.

Then, abruptly, Lilith turned her face from Adam.

"No, Adam, Son of Ursula, it seems I am not well come," she said, and she gestured in Grammar's direction. "Why did you not tell me that Ursula is unwilling?"

Released from the silence Adam had imposed on her, Grammar stepped forward, still holding Fred with one hand and her knitting needle with the other.

"What is the meaning of this, Adam!" Grammar demanded. "Have you made some pact with this Creature? Well, it won't stand up in a law court. It. . . ."

"What does it matter whether or not Ursula is willing?" Adam asked, ignoring his mother and focusing on Lilith, trying to draw her eyes back to his.

Lilith would not look at him.

"It matters," she stated. "If Ursula is unwilling to let Ionia go, perhaps Ionia is unwilling to come. I do not know. I have not yet had a chance to speak alone with my daughter."

"Your daughter, is it!" sputtered Grammar. "And where were you all her life? Who raised her? You have no right to call yourself a mother, you. . . ."

"Quiet, Mother," commanded Adam. "This does not concern you."

"Adam, Son of Ursula, I cannot speak with you unless Ursula is also free to speak. You only live because this woman suffered you to."

"That is as may be," said Adam. "Nevertheless, what becomes of Ionia is not her concern. I, alone, make that decision."

"No, Adam. According to the law of my people, the choice is Ionia's. I cannot take her to my people unless she chooses to come freely."

"According to our law," broke in Grammar, "there's no such thing as free choice for a minor."

"That's right, Mother, and I have legal custody."

"Don't be so sure, Adam," cried Grammar. "I'll take you to court. I'll prove you're no more fit than this, this. . . ."

Grammar and Adam continued to argue.

Fred, his arm aching from the tightness of Grammar's grip, did not listen. He was staring at the lady who was Ionia's mother and maybe his mother, too. He hoped she was. He wanted to ask her, but he was afraid; not afraid as he was afraid of monsters and the dark. It was a good kind of afraid, like when he saw real lions at the zoo. Then, he had wanted to touch the lions' manes. Now, he wished he could touch the lady's hair. He had never seen hair like that before: long and loose and snarly like no one ever made her comb it. Her clothes were funny, but he liked the way she smelled, like playing outdoors in the dirt. Lion liked her, too. He hoped she would stay and play with him. He hoped she really was his mother. He wished she would look at him, just once. But she was looking at Ionia again, and Ionia was looking at her. Then the lady took Ionia's hand, and they turned away.

"Just where do you think you're going!" said Grammar.

Lilith turned to face her.

"I am taking Ionia to some silence so that she can discover what she wants to do. "

"No, you are not," returned Grammar. "I am taking her to bed where a child of her age belongs at this hour of the night."

"Take yourself to bed, Mother," suggested Adam. "You're too old to stand arguing all night in a drafty hall."

An image of the knitting needle sinking into Adam's flesh flashed through Grammar's mind. Outwardly, she ignored him.

"Ionia, come with me."

Ionia only stared. Never had Grammar found her eyes so unsettling.

"Ionia, come with me this instant."

"No."

It was the eyes more than the answer that defeated Grammar. In them there was no recognition, no recognition of her authority, no recognition of herself, Grammar. Grammar felt her face contort. Tears burned her eyes. She knew she must do something quickly. She refused to humiliate herself before the Creature.

"Adam, bring me that chair," she said in a low, barely controlled voice, and she gestured towards a chair in the corner of the hall.

"Whatever for, Mother?"

"So that I can sit in it, in front of the door. All night."

"Don't be silly, Mother."

"Adam, Son of Ursula, obey your mother."

Adam looked from Lilith to his mother. Both were standing with their feet planted apart in a posture of defiance. Suddenly Adam began to laugh softly to himself, for it was his own private joke: the absurdity, the irrationality of women. There was no point in reasoning with women, wild or human. That was not how to handle them. He ought to know that better than anyone. Still chuckling, Adam went to fetch the chair.

"Now," said Grammar when she had seated herself calmly and with dignity, as if she were about to pour tea. "Take this child up to bed and see to it that he stays there."

As Grammar released his arm, and as his father approached him, Fred let out a howl. But it was cut short. His father picked him up roughly, knocking most of the wind out of him, and carried him under his arm up the stairs. Lion cast one look at Lilith, as if for permission. Then he ran after Fred, barking and nipping at Adam's heels.

In a little while the house was silent.

Grammar sat straight and stiff in the old horsehair chair, and she strained her ears to catch whatever conversation passed between the two in the other room but she could hear nothing. By the light of the hall, she could see them sitting cross-legged beneath the Christmas tree, not quite facing one another. Both pairs of eyes were cast down. If they communicated at all, it was by some means unknown to Grammar. Perhaps the Creature had meant it when she said she was taking Ionia to some silence, but Grammar did not trust her not to try to influence Ionia, not to try to trick her. Perhaps the silence was itself a trick. Perhaps, even now, that Creature was working magic on Ionia. How could she expect Ionia to make a decision like that? Ionia was a child. For that matter, why would anyone choose to leave what he knew, for what he did not, unless someone deceived him?

Grammar watched and waited, wishing that something would happen, something that she could see. But nothing did. Unseen, the cold crept in through the cracks of the door, undermining her concentration. Soon, that she was cold was all she could think. Though she stared at them, the two figures under the tree began to lose their meaning. She forgot why they were there, why she was. Unaware that she did so, she curled her legs up under her body and leaned back against the chair. It did not occur to her that she could fall asleep. She hardly knew she was awake. The scene that had just taken place in the hall played itself over and over again with all the vivid unreality of a dream. Sometimes her eyes were open, sometimes closed. At last she gave up the struggle. The needle slipped from her hand and rolled across the floor.

The sound broke the silence, a silence that had enveloped Ionia even before the woman had led her away. While they argued—her father, Grammar, the woman—Ionia had wrapped silence around her until what she heard was no more than a muffled roaring. In silence, she had suspended all thought, all feeling. Now this protective silence fell away from her, and she began to perceive again.

Her first perception was of a smell, a smell of leaves, of earth. If she had closed her eyes, she might have imagined that she was outdoors in autumn. She did not close her eyes. Without moving her head, she lifted her eyes so that she could see the woman's legs and feet. Her dress fell just below her knees. Her legs and feet were bound with vines, and on the soles of her feet was more moss. Through the vines, her legs showed strong and hard. They were covered with curling hair; so were her toes. Ionia would have liked to touch the hair to feel how soft or tough it was, but she did not want to draw attention to herself. She wanted time to look at the woman, get used to her, without the woman looking at her.

Slowly, Ionia raised her head to take in more of the woman. The woman's hands, resting on her knees, were large and strong but slender. The veins and bones showed through: her arms, like her legs, were muscular, but the hair that covered them seemed finer. Beneath the strange stuff of her dress, the woman's breasts were just visible. Ionia studied them curiously. She had never seen a grown woman's breasts. The woman's were small, but they looked soft, surprisingly soft, compared with the rest of her body. Ionia watched the breasts rise and fall as the woman breathed deeply and evenly. She watched for what seemed like a long time, and still the woman gave no sign that she noticed Ionia's scrutiny.

At last Ionia dared to look at her face. The woman's hair swept away from her face as if the wind had blown it back. Her face made Ionia think of the hills under the moonlight as she had seen them that night from her window. It was bare and open, like the hills, yet, at the same time, like them, mysterious and unknowable. Her eyes seemed to see nothing; it was impossible to tell what she was thinking or if she was thinking. All at once, Ionia felt afraid, not afraid as she was of her father, but afraid as she had been when she thought of the night and the stars existing without her.

"Ionia."

Ionia saw the woman's lips move, but it took her a moment to realize that the woman had spoken to her. Then the woman turned towards her and looked at her directly.

"Ionia, what have you discovered?"

Ionia did not understand; she shook her head. The woman waited, looking at her as if she did not understand either.

"Do you know anything about your people, Ionia?"

Ionia shook her head again.

"Have they, Ursula and your father, told you nothing about me?"

"No," said Ionia, speaking to the woman for the first time. "They never told us anything."

"Us?" the woman questioned.

"Me and Fred."

"Oh, yes," the woman said.

She was quiet again for a time.

"Ionia, do you know who I am?"

Ionia hesitated, afraid that if she named the woman, she might lose her.

"Yes," she said at last. "You are my mother."

"And you are my daughter," she answered. "The youngest of our race. Now, Ionia, I will tell you of our people."

Her mother sat up straighter and folded her hands. Although her mother still looked at her, Ionia sensed that she had ceased to see her.

"The story begins when Lilith, the First Woman, for whom I am named, chose to leave the Garden to wander in the Wilderness where no man has dominion."

Her mother spoke in a sing-song voice. After a while Ionia no longer heard the words. Instead she saw pictures. She saw the First Woman, who looked in her mind like her own mother, leaving the garden, a garden like Grammar's vegetable garden. She saw the First Woman walking beyond the wall that surrounded her own house and over the hill of the three trees. Then she saw a sea of hills rising and falling without end. She saw the clear pools that lay between the hills. She saw the First Woman walking and walking, with the wild she-animals following. She saw the First Woman drinking milk from wolves and deer, lions and goats. She saw the wild animals watching over the First Woman as she gave birth to the first child.

"And now," her mother was saying, "there are almost one hundred of us, all mothers and daughters, born over hundreds of years. Men do not often come into our country, and we do not let them stay. Most men, in this time of their world, do not even know we exist; or so I understand from your father. They say we are," she paused again, "a myth."

Suddenly, Ionia's mother threw back her head and laughed. Ionia did not understand what her mother had just said about men or what they had to do with the first woman and the wild beasts. But there was such delight in her mother's laughter that Ionia began to laugh, too. They laughed and laughed.

And it occurred to Ionia that all her life she had been waiting to laugh like this with her mother.

"And so, Ionia," said her mother, stopping the laughter and looking at her again, "you are the youngest, the last. I have come to take you, if you want to go, to your people. Only remember, Ionia, if you leave here, you must leave as freely as the First Woman left the garden. She was not cast out of the Garden as the Man and the Second Woman were when they ate of the tree of knowledge. She chose the Wilderness, and the Wilderness welcomed her as it has never welcomed Man, who tried to subdue the Wilderness as he tried to subdue the First Woman."

Ionia and her mother continued to gaze at one another. Her mother's eyes were so like her own that Ionia might have been looking into a mirror that reflected an older, stronger version of herself, except that she could never be so beautiful, and her hair was brown and soft and would have fallen into her face like Mrs. Brooke's if Grammar had not kept it cut short.

"Do you understand the choice you must make, Ionia?"

"To go with you or to stay here?" Ionia asked uncertainly.

"That is not all of it," said her mother gently. "It is not just a choice between me and Ursula and your father. You have to decide what you are. Your father told me there is no question that you are wild. But your father knows very little for one who knows so much. It is not for him to decide what you are; nor for me. Only you can know for certain."

Ionia looked down at her own hands, clasping and unclasping themselves in her lap. She could not think when she looked at her mother, and she knew nothing for certain, but that her mother was here, now, beside her, and that everything was different than it had been when she went to bed. And more difficult. She did not know what she was, and she didn't understand how she was supposed to decide. Why didn't her mother just take her if she wanted her? If her mother wanted her, why had she ever left her? That was what she wanted to ask, but she was afraid.

Ionia glanced at her mother. She had turned her face away. She sat quietly, and, Ionia thought, peacefully, as if she were not at all anxious about Ionia's answer, as if she would wait forever if she had to. Ionia wished she would just stay and not go away. Then Ionia would not have to decide what she was. She could just be Ionia, not the Ionia Jason made fun of, but Ionia, who had a real mother who was there all the time like other mothers, like Jason's mother.

Only her mother was not like other mothers. Ionia had only to look at her to know that. She had gone away before without Ionia, and she would go away again, but this time Ionia might go with her if she wanted to. She pictured herself walking with her mother beyond the wall, over the hill of the three trees, and on and on into what her mother's people called the Wilderness. She would see what the wild geese had seen. She would know all she had ever wondered when she looked out her window. And if she did not go, the wondering would be unbearable now that she knew her mother was real, now that she knew her mother lived in the Empty Land.

"I want to go with you, Mother," she said; then, prompted by her mother's searching look, she remembered the rest of the question and added, "I am what you are."

Still her mother gazed on her. Ionia met her gaze, content not to think anymore, content to lose herself in her mother's eyes.

"Good," said her mother at length, "then let us be gone. Have you warm things for your feet or shall I carry you? What about food? Are you hungry? Shall we eat before we go? You do not look over-strong, Ionia. But the water of our country will soon heal you, and I have brought some herbs," she indicated a small pouch slung over her shoulder. "I will make an herb tea for you to drink before we go. It will strengthen you for the journey."

While she had been speaking, Ionia's mother had gotten to her feet. Ionia remained sitting; she felt unable to move. It was all too sudden, too real: the boots for her feet, the food for the journey. It was not like the picture in her mind. The picture had not included getting ready to go or leaving the house or saying good-bye. In the picture it had not been night, and there had been no snow.

"What is it, Ionia?" her mother asked.

"Are we going," Ionia whispered, "right now?"

"I thought it might be best to leave before the others wake."

"But Grammar. . . ."

"There are other ways to leave a house than through the front door."

Still Ionia did not move. Her mother watched and waited.

"But we can't go without telling them, without saying good-bye."

"Why not?" asked her mother. "If we wait to tell them, Ursula will squawk, and the man-child will wail. It would be better to leave quietly."

Ionia did not answer. She thought of Fred waking up and finding her gone, too, never knowing where she had gone or why, just as she had never known about her mother.

"You don't know," Ionia said slowly. "You don't know what it's like to be left."

"No," agreed her mother, "I don't."

She sat down again beside Ionia.

"Ionia, are you sure you know what you are?"

All at once Ionia felt angry. She would not answer that question. She would not answer any more questions, not until her mother had answered some. She looked at her mother.

"Why did you leave me? Why didn't you take me with you before?"

Ionia expected her mother to look hurt or angry like other grown-ups did when you asked them something they didn't want to tell you, but her mother's expression had not changed.

"When I lived with your father," she began, "I lost my powers and broke the laws of my people. I had almost forgotten what I am. Yet, when I listened, I could sometimes hear my people calling me. Often, at night, I dreamed of them. After the man-child was born, I told your father I was going back to my people. I told him I was taking you with me. That night he locked you up so that I couldn't get at you. I understood, for the first time, that he meant to keep me against my will. I did not know to what lengths he would go to keep me. I did not wait to find out."

Ionia stared at her mother. The memory of the dark room and of the fear and the longing came back to her.

"So you just left me. Alone. With him."

"Yes."

Ionia waited. She waited for her mother to say something more, to excuse or explain what she had done; or better, to say how sorry she was and that she knew now that she had been wrong to leave Ionia.

Her mother said nothing. She continued to look at Ionia as calmly and steadily as she had before.

Slowly, Ionia began to realize that her mother was not going to defend or blame herself. Her mother had told her the truth, and that was all she was going to do. She would say nothing to soften it or make it easier to understand. Her mother had left her. Ionia had to accept that or she could not accept her mother, the real mother, who sat before her now, who had come back to find her.

"I have had dreams of you." Ionia said.

"Have you, Ionia?" asked her mother, smiling. "That is because I have been calling you ever since I left."

"I didn't know how to answer," said Ionia. "I didn't know how to come to you. I didn't know where you were. I thought you were out there under the trees, but every time I woke up you were gone."

"Well," said her mother, "I am here now. How soon can you be ready to go?"

Ionia looked down at her hands. They had been lying quiet, but now they began to clutch one another.

"I guess as soon as I'm dressed, but. . . ."

She hesitated.

"But what, Ionia?"

Before Ionia could go on, she was interrupted by Lion, who trotted across the living room, lay down at her mother's feet, and began to lick her mother's toes. Looking up, Ionia saw Fred standing in the doorway, holding a quilt that trailed behind him into the hall. Ionia glanced at her mother. She was returning Fred's stare. Ionia thought she looked as wary and uncertain as Fred did.

"What is it that you want, man-child?"

"Are you my mother, too?"

For a long time, Ionia's mother did not answer.

"Yes," she said at last.

"Oh," said Fred.

For another moment Fred stood in the doorway. Then he crossed the room, dragging the quilt with him. Without another word, he lay down, with his head in his mother's lap, and closed his eyes.

His mother looked down at him. Ionia could not guess from her mother's expression what she thought. Although Ionia felt a little resentful of Fred walking in and taking over her mother's lap, she also felt relieved. Now she would not have to explain to her mother about Fred, and how hard it would be to leave him.

"I will tell you something else, man-child," their mother said gingerly touching Fred's hair as if she feared it might be hot. "You have your grandmother's hair."

Ionia looked at her questioningly. Grammar's hair had been brown, like her own, before it turned gray; or so Grammar claimed.

"Your wild grandmother's," she clarified.

Fred had not heard what his mother said. He was asleep.

"Mother," said Ionia, "the day after tomorrow is Christmas."

"Ah, yes," she said, "the New Man's birthday."

"I was wondering, could we stay until then? Fred wouldn't have a very good Christmas if I were gone," she paused, "and if you were gone."

Her mother said nothing.

"See, Fred wanted you to come back, too. He believed in you as much as I did. Maybe more," she added, "because he didn't have the dreams, and he doesn't remember when you were here before, like I do."

Still her mother did not respond.

"So I thought if Fred could have a mother for one Christmas, and then if he could understand why you're going away, why we're going away," Ionia corrected herself, "it might be better than just leaving now without telling him."

Feeling that she had said all she could say, Ionia waited.

"I don't know, Ionia," her mother said, shaking her head. "I don't know. I don't understand these things, these human things."

Ionia and her mother sat in silence. Fred and Lion, both asleep, breathed in unison. In the hall, with her head tilted back and her mouth open, Grammar snored. Ionia noticed that the room had grown lighter. She looked at her mother in the early light and held her breath because she was so beautiful. Ionia decided then that whatever her mother willed she would do.

"Ionia," said her mother, turning towards her. "I want you to be sure of what you are. We will do as you say. We will wait until Christmas. Then we will see. Now let us sleep."

Her mother lay down with Fred's head still in her lap; then she reached out an arm for Ionia and drew her close. Ionia fell asleep, breathing her mother's scent and dreaming of leaves.

Upstairs in the tower room, Adam watched the sky turn pale. He had waited all night for her to leave. And now, at dawn, she seemed as unreal as she had after all the other nights he had waited for her to come. Yet she was real; she was here. He thought of her dark, earthy odor, and his desire for her stirred, but he was too tired to satisfy it. Perhaps if he could just go downstairs, rip those garments from her body, and take her then and there, swiftly, wordlessly. . . . But his mother, the troublesome old woman, might wake up. The girl, if she was still with her mother, would cling. All the noise and commotion would begin again. It would not be worth it. What he wanted now was to forget them all and go to sleep, dreamless sleep. He wondered if he could risk leaving the gate open while he slept. Everyone else would be waking soon. Surely if She tried to escape with Ionia, his mother's ruckus would raise the dead.

A ray of light shot through the three trees and hit the glass along the top of the wall. Adam turned from the window and headed for bed.

12
Eva and Lilith

AT nightfall on Christmas Eve, the Empty Land train unloaded the last passengers of the day. Albert Sharp, the conductor, helped the tall woman with the grumpy son carry her too many bundles to the bench on the station platform. "You look like a female version of Santa Claus," had been her son's snide comment. Albert would have liked to cuff the boy, yet there was some truth to his observation. There was a jolliness, a generosity about the woman. Albert had taken a shine to her. She was one of those rare customers who made him feel like himself, Albert, instead of a mere function, a human ticket-taking machine. He could not imagine how she came to be friends with that cold fish Underwood or why anyone would want to spend Christmas with the old Scrooge. But Esther, Albert's wife, who managed the University's cafeteria, assured him that women went mad for Underwood, herself always excepted, of course.

"Are you sure you'll be all right?" Albert asked when he had installed the woman and her bundles on the bench.

The station was already deserted, and he did not like leaving this woman beside the unbroken darkness of the Empty Land. It was beginning to snow again, too.

"Quite sure," she said. "Professor Underwood will be along any minute. Thank you so much, and Merry Christmas."

"Merry Christmas to you ma'am."

As the train pulled away, Albert watched from the back window. It was none of his business what became of the woman, Esther would tell him, though she would no doubt be furious that he had not found out the name of a woman visiting Underwood and would make a point of finding out herself as soon as the cafeteria reopened. But Albert could not quell his disquiet as the pair began to fade from view: the boy standing and kicking at the snow; the woman, cradling her wicker basket—full of pies, she'd told him—as if it were a baby, and gazing into nowhere.

Alone at last, in her kitchen, Grammar sat down to drink a cup of tea while the potatoes were boiling. She had decided not to bake the potatoes in the oven with that mess the Creature had made. Nor would she eat whatever it was, and neither would the children if she could help it. The ground nuts and cheese were all very well, but she did not trust the unidentified herbs the Creature had taken from the pouch she wore and added to the mixture. Grammar had thawed pork chops for the rest of them to eat. She did not care if the Creature refused meat, but it enraged Grammar that she was attempting to make vegetarians of the children.

That morning, while Grammar had been cleaning the Christmas goose, the Creature, the children, and the dog had crept up behind her so quietly that she had been unaware of them until suddenly all four of them began to howl, startling her so that she nearly fell off her stool. Recovering herself she whirled around to face them, and they stopped their noise.

"What are you doing with that dead bird, Ursula?" the Creature asked.

The children just stared at her, making her feel that she had become something ugly and frightening in their eyes.

"This is not a dead bird," she replied as calmly as she could. "It's Christmas dinner."

Grammar turned back to the bird. She would not be intimidated.

"Christmas dinner?" the Creature repeated. "You mean you eat dead bird to celebrate the New Man's birthday?"

Grammar ignored her.

"Ionia, Fred," said the Creature, "are you going to eat dead bird for Christmas dinner?"

"They had better," said Grammar without turning from her work, "or starve instead."

"We always have goose on Christmas," explained Fred. "The kind of gooses you eat aren't the kind that fly."

"Yes, they are, Fred," said Ionia.

"Are you going to eat dead bird?" the Creature persisted.

Still the children didn't answer.

"How would you like it if I were to eat you for my Christmas dinner?"

Grammar heard a commotion behind her. She turned to see the three of them rolling about on the floor while the Creature pretended to be eating the children up. Both children were laughing and screeching.

"Or," the Creature said, letting go of the children and sitting up, "how would you like it if I were to call the wild geese and tell them they could come and carry you away? Would that be a fair trade?"

Ionia looked thoughtful; Fred looked worried.

"Now you listen here," said Grammar. "Don't you go frightening the children by telling them things that just aren't true. Geese don't eat people, Fred."

"Then why do people eat geese?" asked the Creature.

Before Grammar could think of an answer, Ionia spoke.

"We won't," she said. "We won't eat geese anymore or any kind of meat ever again."

"Not never," added Fred. "And Lion won't either, he likes vegetables."

"Just a moment, you two," said Grammar. "And you."

The Creature rose from the floor to face Grammar.

"This is my house," she continued, "and these are my grandchildren. You might be their mother, but who is it that raised them these last six years? Answer me that! Where were you when they had the measles? Where were you when they had the mumps and the chicken pox, for that matter? Who is it that's washed them, fed them, clothed them, kept them warm and safe and alive? You might be their mother, but you never mothered them a day in your life. Mothering is hard work. So is grandmothering. As long as I am in charge of this house and these children, they will eat what I prepare for them, and we're having goose for Christmas dinner."

To be fair, Grammar had to admit that the Creature had listened, and she had looked her straight in the eye the whole time. When Grammar had finished speaking, the Creature had bowed her head before she looked up again and made her answer.

"You speak the truth, Ursula, Grandmother of Ionia and Fred. You have given these children what I have not: your own life. But I have given them life itself. I do not like to see what I have given life taking life from any other living creature. Will you let me prepare some of the food my people eat and let them try it?"

Out of fairness, for the sake of peace, Grammar had agreed, but she soon regretted it. The afternoon that followed was anything but peaceful. With the Creature in charge and the children helping, the kitchen was a shambles. By the time they had finished their concoction, they had smeared cheese from one end of the table to the other, and the floor was covered with nutshells. They did help to clean up, but not without some protest. The Creature liked the floor better with nutshells.

Grammar shook her head and took a large, bracing gulp of tea. She could hear the four of them, Creature, children, and dog, chasing about the house, playing some wild game. Later, she would survey the damage that had been done and do what she could to repair it; there was nothing she could do to prevent it. The Creature had but to walk through a room and the room was in disarray as if some sudden wind had torn through it. It seemed to Grammar that the house, as well as the children, was coming under that Creature's influence, just as it had before. Grammar felt as though it was she who was the stranger, a stranger to her own grandchildren, an exile in her own house.

Grammar stared down into her tea cup. The tea reflected her face, but she failed to recognize it. She saw only varied light and dark, shape without meaning. She tried to think, but thought seemed inadequate to the situation at hand. How could she think what to do when she did not know anything? She did not know how long the Creature meant to stay; she did not know what Adam intended to do; she did not know when she might turn around and find the children gone, everything gone. All she knew was that in a little while the potatoes would boil and she would mash them.

Then, from the general direction of the living room, came a crash. Without needing to think, Grammar sat down her teacup and went to see what had fallen.

When she reached the living room, Grammar paused in the doorway. The Creature had dragged the Christmas tree into the center of the room. In the process, she had apparently knocked the bust of Paracelcus onto the floor, where it lay prostrate, as if in homage to the tree. The Creature was leading the children and the dog round and round the tree in a frenzied dance. While she danced, she sang a wordless song, which to Grammar's ears had no more tune than the cry of a wild bird. The children added their own shrill voices to hers, and Lion howled. Grammar felt like a lone missionary lost among the savages.

Then, through the branches of the Christmas tree, she spied Adam. He was sitting in the easy chair in the corner, smoking a pipe and reading a book as if he were unaware of what was happening, as if he did not care. Rage seized Grammar. It was all Adam's fault, all his fault from the beginning. He must be made to do something.

"Adam," she screamed. "Adam!"

Her voice was lost in the din. Adam never looked up. The dance went on and on.

Then, all at once, without warning, the Creature stopped midstep. The children and Lion, who could not come to a halt so quickly and gracefully, tumbled about her feet and looked up at the Creature, who remained poised with one foot about to fall and a look of intense concentration on her face. While she was still no one spoke.

"Adam, Son of Ursula, there is someone at your door."

She lowered her foot and turned to look at him.

"There is no one, Lilith. You heard nothing."

He spoke smoothly, soothingly, as if to a child. Grammar felt the effect of his voice and could not remember for a moment what the Creature had said. The Creature turned her face from Adam and looked confused. Then her face cleared, and she spoke again.

"There is," she said, "and if you do not open your door, I will."

"You heard nothing, Lilith, there is no one."

Then came a knock, so timid that, if not for the silence, it would have been inaudible.

"Mrs. Eva Brooke," Grammar gasped. "The train. We forgot. Adam get up. Get up at once and answer the door."

Grammar turned and fled to the kitchen to take more pork chops out of the freezer.

Adam knocked the coals from his pipe and rose from his chair. Slowly he crossed the room, pausing to fix Lilith with a stare on the way. She stood rigid until he was gone from the room. Then she sank down beside the children on the floor.

"What is Mrs. Eva Brooke?" she whispered.

"She's Jason's mother." Fred whispered back.

"What is Jason?"

"Jason's a boy." Ionia explained. "Mrs. Brooke's son. We go to their house after school."

"Mrs. Brooke is a woman? A human woman?"

"Yes," said Ionia.

"Is she," her mother paused as if searching for a word, "friend to your father?"

"Yes."

"Is she friend to you?"

Ionia hesitated.

"Yes," she said at last.

"And Jason is too," added Fred.

Ionia looked doubtful, but she said nothing.

"Why did you forget them then, if they are friends?"

Before Ionia or Fred could think of an answer, they saw Mrs. Brooke and Jason standing in the doorway with their father behind them. Their mother rose from the floor, raising them with her. Then Fred let go of his mother's hand and went to hug Mrs. Brooke even though she was covered with snow.

Ionia remained with her mother. The expressions on Mrs. Brooke's face and on Jason's made her remember how strange her mother must seem, for she had forgotten. Her impulse was to protect her mother, to shield her from these stranger's eyes. She wished Jason and Mrs. Brooke had not come. Yet, when she looked at Mrs. Brooke, she could not help feeling sorry for her. She seemed so awkward, standing in the doorway, not knowing what to say or do. Her wet hair had fallen in her face and her eyes were hiding behind it like two frightened fawns in a thicket. In her shapeless coat and buckle boots, she might have been an old woman or a little girl. She was shivering with cold or shock or both.

Without intending to, Ionia took a step towards Mrs. Brooke. Then she paused and turned to look back at her mother. Seeing her mother standing straight and still, her face beautiful and stern, her body balanced and graceful, Ionia realized that her mother needed no protection. She was strong the way rocks and trees were strong. She was gazing at Mrs. Brooke, calmly and curiously, as if she herself had never been cold or lonely or frightened in her life.

"Eva, this is my wife, Lilith."

For a moment Mrs. Brooke said nothing. Then she spoke, softly but distinctly. "I am so glad to meet you, Mrs. Underwood."

"Oh," said Ionia's mother moving towards Mrs. Brooke, "but I am not Mrs. Underwood. I am Lilith. I believe Ursula calls herself Mrs. Underwood. Have you not met Ursula, Grandmother of Ionia and Fred, who mothers them? I am only their mother who does not. But come, Mrs. Eva Brooke," she said taking Eva's mittened hands. "Your clothes are making you cold. Let me take you before the fire and undress you."

Dazed, Eva allowed Lilith to lead her to the fire.

"Mrs. Eva Brooke," said Lilith unbuttoning Eva's coat, "my children tell me you are friend to them, so I am friend to you."

Eva stood passively as Lilith removed her coat and began to unfasten her dress. All at once Lilith turned to Ionia and Fred, who were watching the procedure in silence.

"Where is the man-child of Mrs. Eva Brooke?"

Fred pointed to the doorway where Jason skulked in the Professor's shadow.

"I suppose he is cold, too. Go, then, Ionia, and bring him likewise before the fire and undress him."

Ionia, though reluctant, would have obeyed, but Jason turned around, ducked under her father's arm, and ran. In the hall he encountered Grammar. Ionia could hear her exclaiming.

"Jason Brooke, where is your mother! What have they done with your mother!"

A moment later, Grammar pushed past Adam into the living room just in time to see Lilith slip Eva's dress from her shoulders and let it fall to the floor.

"Adam Underwood!" shouted Grammar, turning on him. "What kind of a human being are you? How dare you let this Creature undress a decent woman while you stand by watching as if you were at a circus. Oh, Mrs. Brooke, can you ever forgive us?"

Grammar crossed the room and put her arms around Mrs. Brooke's now naked shoulders.

"Come, Mrs. Brooke. Your room is all ready. I've drawn a hot bath. When you're ready, I'll bring you your supper on a tray."

"That won't be necessary, Mrs. Underwood. I'll be fine once I've changed into some dry clothes."

Ionia was surprised by the calmness, the ordinariness of Mrs. Brooke's voice.

"Ionia," called Grammar over her shoulder, "bring Mrs. Brooke's things to her room."

Ionia looked once at her mother, who was staring after Grammar and Mrs. Brooke with her head cocked to one side, the way Lion cocked his when he didn't understand. Then she left the room, shrinking from her father as she passed him.

In the hall she stood before the bundles, pondering over which one was most likely to contain Mrs. Brooke's clothes, unaware that, from his hiding place behind the coat rack, Jason watched her.

13
☘ Confrontation and Confusion ☘

AFTER Ionia had slipped past him, Adam remained in the doorway looking at Lilith. She stood perfectly still with her eyes cast down; she might have been a statue of herself. As he studied her, he tried to imagine what it might be like for an unprepared person to see her for the first time. He had received unexpected enjoyment from witnessing Eva's bewilderment. When Lilith had lived with him before, he had never let anyone else near her for fear other people might upset the delicate, often precarious, balance between himself and her. Now, of course, conditions were different. They could no longer be always alone together, playmates in a private wilderness, as they once had been. The time for that was past. To compensate, there were new possibilities, new pleasures he might contemplate.

Why should he keep his discovery to himself, a discovery that defied the limit of scientific knowledge and human understanding? What good was a discovery unless others were made to acknowledge it? Of course, before she appeared in public, she must be refined. That would be his triumph: the restraints of civilization, imposed by him, holding in check her natural wildness. Let archeologists and paleontologists dig up ruins and old bones. Let scholars and critics write dry treatises and dull books. He was an alchemist, a magician. She would be his masterpiece, his living work of art.

Fred, crouching on the floor beside Lion, looked from one parent to the other and wondered how long they were going to just stand there without saying anything. He sensed they had both forgotten him, and he felt uncomfortable, but he didn't want to leave his mother alone with his father. He didn't like the way his father looked at his mother, like he wanted to eat her. And his mother's stillness scared him. Except that she was standing up, she hardly seemed alive. He wanted to touch her to make sure she was, but he was afraid to move. His father might see him and be angry because he was there. He wished Ionia would come back—or Jason.

Jason. Jason was here. Remembering Jason's presence, Fred suddenly felt better, braver. Jason was older. Jason was bigger. Jason was never afraid of anything, and he always knew what to do. Jason knew everything. He would go find Jason, Fred decided. Then he wouldn't be scared anymore, and he would fight his father. Whispering to Lion to stay and guard his mother, Fred tiptoed from the room as quietly as he could.

Adam, who had not been aware of his son's presence before, did notice his movement, and he glanced down at the boy as he sidled past him, vaguely surprised and displeased that his son should exhibit fear. But he forgot the child when he looked up at Lilith and realized that, for the first time since she had come back, he was alone with her. All at once, he wanted to do more than look.

"So, Lilith," he said, advancing towards her, "you grace us yet with your presence. I had not expected so long a visit from you."

"I am only waiting, Adam," she said without looking up.

"Waiting for what?" he asked stopping before her.

"For Ionia to decide."

She raised her eyes.

"You were wrong, Adam, to decide for her, wrong to tell me to come and take her when there was any question."

"We see these matters differently, you and I," he said. "I must think of the good of everyone, not just of Ionia's good."

"I do not know about good."

"Nor evil, eh, my wild innocent? You don't need to tell me again of how your race never ate the apple. It's an old story. But answer me this: if you had not come back, how would Ionia have been able to choose? She would not have known what to choose between."

"Ionia knows; she has always known. It is not the kind of knowing you know."

They stared at one another. Staring at Lilith was like staring at a cat. It was a contest of will, of nerve. He won; Lilith lowered her eyes first. Yet it was a dubious victory; he had severed the connection between them. To re-establish contact, he put his hands lightly on her shoulders, touching her for the first time in six years. He felt the heat of her flesh. And his own.

"Will you come and say good-bye to me before you go," he said more softly, running his hands down the length of her bare arms, then up again from her waist, bringing them to rest on either side of her breasts, "no matter what time of the night or day?"

"Ionia, if she chooses to come, will say good-bye to you if she thinks it right. As for me, I owe you nothing."

"Are you still so hard against me?" he asked, tightening his grip.

She raised her eyes and met his.

"I am what I will be."

Still behind the coat rack in the hall, Jason heard Fred calling him and saw Fred searching for him. He would have liked to answer and be found. He was bursting with indignation and curiosity, but he did not want Fred to know he had been hiding. So he waited until Fred left the hall on his way to the kitchen; then he slipped out of his hiding place and began to saunter in the direction Fred had gone, pretending he had just come from somewhere else. In the dining room he collided with Fred, who had just taken a quick survey of the kitchen and turned tail before Grammar could catch him and make him do something helpful.

"Jason," said Fred breathlessly, "I've been looking for you. You've got to help me fight my father!"

"Why on earth should I do that?"

"He's looking at my mother," explained Fred, still breathless.

"Well," said Jason, "if that woman, whoever she is, whatever she is, is your mother, then I suppose your father's got every right to look at her. Where did she come from, anyway? She looks like an escaped lunatic to me."

"She's not," said Fred, though he hadn't understood the word lunatic. "She's my mother."

"Well, where did she come from?"

"I don't know."

"Then how do you know she's your mother?"

"Because," said Fred, "she said so."

"All right, all right," said Jason, realizing that Fred was about to cry. "She's your mother. I'm not sure I'd be so happy about that if I were you."

"You're not my friend," accused Fred.

"Yes, I am," insisted Jason, "but I still don't understand what you want me to do about your father."

"Just make him stop."

"Stop what?"

"Stop him looking at my mother like that. Stop him making my mother like she's not alive."

Jason sighed. The child was not making sense. Perhaps he was a little delirious. No doubt he had suffered a great shock, discovering that that thing in the other room was his mother. He must try to think of a way to soothe the child if he could not reason with him.

"Now listen, Fred, your father's a grown-up. Right?"

Fred nodded.

"And he's bigger than us. Right?"

Fred nodded again.

"So we can't just go and fight him. What we have to do is outsmart him. To do that we have to watch him for a while, find out his weak spots. The way you do that is by keeping your eyes open and your mouth shut. Understand?"

Fred looked solemn.

"Will you come with me now and watch in the living room?" he whispered.

Jason thought fast. The last thing he wanted was to be anywhere near that woman again.

"Not now, Fred. I haven't changed my wet clothes yet. That's why I was looking for you."

"Oh," said Fred, "in my room. You're going to be sleeping in my room, Jason. Come on. I'll show you."

For a moment, the pleasure of showing Jason his room again made Fred forget everything else. He took Jason by the hand and led him out of the dining room, up the stairs. On the landing, they passed Ionia, who did not acknowledge them, but kept right on going.

"You could at least say *hello*, Ionia," said Jason angrily, turning to look after her.

"Hello," she said, barely pausing.

"We're going to my room so Jason can change his clothes," announced Fred.

"Oh," said Ionia, stopping on the stairs and looking up at Fred, "I carried all the bags to Mrs. Brooke's room. I didn't know which ones were Jason's. You could at least have helped me carry them up, Jason."

Jason could contain himself no longer; his rage exploded.

"I? Help you carry them up? Serves you right if you had to carry them up by yourself! I hope your back aches all night! My mother and I had to carry them by ourselves two miles in the snow."

"I'm sorry about that," said Ionia with an effort.

Jason was not finished.

"And then you let that crazy woman you call your mother undress my mother in front of your father!"

"Who let her?" demanded Ionia, angry now herself. "I didn't see you trying to stop her."

"She might have been dangerous," Jason defended himself. "Maniacs are supposed to have superhuman strength, you know. I didn't want to do anything that might excite her."

"My mother is not a maniac," shouted Ionia. "She wouldn't hurt a fly! She doesn't even eat meat!"

"Well, how was I supposed to know that?"

"All right," said Ionia. "So you didn't know. So suppose my mother was a maniac? Then how come you ran away and left your own mother alone with her?"

Jason suddenly felt himself near tears.

"That's not fair, Ionia, and you know it!"

But it was fair, and he knew it.

"You're nothing but a coward, Jason Brooke," said Ionia. "A coward and a bully."

Ionia turned and ran the rest of the way down the stairs.

"Our father's in the living room," Fred called after her, "alone with our mother." Ionia did not stop to answer. Fred watched, marveling at her bravery, as she crossed the hall and disappeared into the living room.

When Jason knocked on her door, Eva Brooke was still in the bathtub. She had been there for a long time; the steaming water had grown tepid, yet, although she was beginning to feel chilly, she made no motion to get out of the tub. She did not feel ready to face whatever was going to happen next; she had hardly comprehended what had happened already. While she lay in the bathtub, she did not try.

She gazed down at her body floating in the water. It was white, almost as white as the bathtub, and soft, soft as a baby. She did not feel related to the arms and legs, breasts and belly that she saw. They might have belonged to anyone. She laid her hand on her stomach as if to feel that it was hers. In contrast to the white anonymity of her body, her hands looked dark, experienced, as though they belonged to a particular person, with a particular history. But who? Who was this person?

Eva tried to conjure an image, a memory, a moment that expressed herself, herself alone, but she failed. All that she was, she was in relation to other people. Now, suddenly her relation to Adam had shifted, leaving her uncertain of where she was, who she was. It would take her a while to get her bearings. Right now, she felt too tired to care. She wanted to lie in the water, in limbo, indefinitely.

Down the hall, Jason was growing anxious because his mother had not answered his knock. Had he been calmer, he might have concluded that she was in the bathroom, but Ionia's words had shaken him. He began to feel afraid that something had happened to his mother and it was all his fault. Or maybe she was angry with him and did not want to see him or speak to him. Maybe she thought he was a coward, too.

"Why don't you open the door?" Fred asked.

But Jason did not want to open the door his mother had closed. He did not want to see her standing there, still half-naked, with that dazed look on her face, or lying in a faint on the floor. But he knew that if she did not answer soon, he would have to open the door.

"Mother," he shouted. "Mother! Are you all right? Answer me!"

Jason, Eva realized; Jason was calling her. She climbed out of the bathtub and pulled the plug. Feeling dizzy, she gripped the sink to steady herself until she became accustomed to her own weight again. Then, without bothering to dry herself, she wrapped her robe around her and hurried down the hall to Jason.

"Mother," he said, "where were you? I was worried about you."

"I'm all right, Jason," she assured him, touched by his concern. "I was just taking a bath."

"Mother," he went on, "I didn't mean to run away before. I'm not a. . . ."

"Ssh," she said. "It's all right. There's no harm done."

So his mother was not angry. How could he have thought she would be? His mother was never angry, not really.

"I should have stayed with you," he said.

"Jason," she said, "you're still in your wet things."

She was still his mother.

"Jason's going to change his clothes," Fred explained, "in my room."

"But Ionia brought everything here," Jason added.

"Oh," said his mother, "well, let's not stand shivering in the hall any longer. Come and find your things."

She opened the door.

When Jason and Fred had gone, Eva rummaged through her suitcase for socks, sweater, and woolen slacks. This was a cold, drafty country house, and she wanted to be warm. Mrs. Underwood had hung the dress she had worn on the back of the door. As she pulled on her clothes, Eva shook her head at her own foolishness. It didn't matter what she looked like; it had never mattered.

"Adam has a wife," she said out loud, trying out the words for the first time, trying to absorb their meaning.

Yet the words "Adam's wife" seemed inadequate to describe the woman she had just seen. That woman seemed no more Adam's wife or any man's wife than the woman in the moon was. In spite of her heavy sweater, Eva shivered at the memory of the woman's eyes. There could be no doubt that the woman was Ionia's mother. But where had she come from with hair like that, clothes like that, a face like that? Who was she? What was she? For it was more than her appearance that was different. It was her whole manner, her bearing, her being. Eva would have found it difficult to explain to another why she had allowed the woman, Adam's wife, to take her before the fire and undress her. She found it difficult to explain to herself. She supposed she had been in a state of shock; so she must have seemed to the others. Yet there was more to the story than that. Something inside her had given assent to Lilith. That part of her had wanted Lilith to go on talking to her, touching her, as if she were a child, as if they both were children.

A knock on the door interrupted Eva's musing.

"Mrs. Brooke."

"Yes, Mrs. Underwood," she answered, recognizing Grammar's voice.

"I shall be serving supper in about ten minutes. Will you be ready or shall I keep yours warm or would you like it in your room after all?"

"I'll be ready, Mrs. Underwood. Thank you."

"Mrs. Brooke?"

"Yes?"

"I'm terribly sorry about this afternoon. It is inexcusable that we forgot to pick you up. But perhaps after seeing what has happened to us here you can understand that we have been discombobulated."

"I understand, Mrs. Underwood."

But she did not. She did not understand anything.

While Grammar served the food, there was silence. She put two pork chops on Adam's, Eva's, and Jason's plates and one on Ionia's, Fred's, and her own. Beside the pork chops, she heaped mashed potatoes and boiled cabbage. Ionia eyed the plates as she passed them and thought that, for one thing, the colors were all wrong. No one could look at all that white and off-white without feeling sick. She thought of telling Grammar that she didn't want any but decided it would be best to say nothing and just not eat.

When everyone else had been served, including herself, Grammar passed Lilith an empty plate.

"Take what you want," she said.

Lilith helped herself to a large slab of the nut-cheese roast that had sat, until now, untouched in the center of the table. Then, Ionia was sure it was out of politeness, she added a spoonful of potatoes and cabbage to her plate and began at once to eat. Everyone except Grammar watched her, envious of the melted orange cheese, the golden brown nuts, the green of the celery and peas.

"Please begin," Grammar prompted the others. "Don't mind the...," Grammar paused, trying to think of how to refer to the Creature, "ah, my daughter-in-law. She's a vegetarian."

Grammar cut herself a piece of meat and began to chew.

"Are you, Lilith?" asked Eva, turning towards Lilith who sat on her left. "I have often thought of becoming one myself. What made you decide?"

"I did not have to decide," answered Lilith. "I have always been what Ursula calls a vegetarian. I have never eaten dead animal in my life."

Lilith glanced across the table at Ionia and Fred's plates. Neither of them had touched their pork chops.

"What kind of dead animal is pork chops?" Fred wanted to know.

"Fred," said Grammar, "I will not have that kind of talk at the dinner table."

"I don't know," said Lilith. "I never met a pork chop when it was alive."

"Pig," supplied Jason in a low voice.

Fred looked down at his pork chops.

"I like pigs better alive," announced Fred; then he asked, "Grammar, can I have some of what me and Ionia and my mother made?"

"No," said Grammar shortly. "Eat what's on your plate."

"But Grammar," protested Ionia, "you promised that we could at least try it."

"Well, I changed my mind," said Grammar. "I don't know what's in it."

"You saw what we put in it, Ursula," Lilith pointed out.

"Yes," said Grammar, growing excited, "I saw you open that little pouch of yours and sprinkle God knows what into the mishmash. . . ."

"Herbs," said Lilith, "from my own country."

"Herbs," mimicked Grammar. "How do I know they're not dangerous?"

"I'm eating them myself."

"That makes no difference," insisted Grammar. "What's good for you might be poisonous for the rest of us."

"Do you really believe I would poison my children, Ursula?"

"How should I know what you would do? You abandoned them once. You're an unnatural woman, you. . . ."

"I would prefer that my mother and my wife did not bicker at the dinner table before our guests."

There was silence for a moment.

"Please," said Eva, "Mrs. Underwood, if you don't mind, I would like to try what the children and their mother have made. I am always looking for new recipes. I use herbs for seasoning myself. I can't believe the herbs are harmful."

"They are not," said Lilith. "My people use only healing herbs."

"You know, I think you may be right about not eating meat," said Eva to Lilith. "If I knew I had to slaughter the animal myself in order to eat meat, I'm not sure I could do it."

"Of course you could, Mother," said Jason, who did not approve of his mother's pending conversion, nor of her friendliness to that crazy woman; craziness might be catching, and his mother was highly susceptible. "You could do it if you had to, to survive."

"As far as I'm concerned," said Adam," the question is academic. Man, because he is the only animal who walks upright, uses his hands to make tools, and has the power of intelligent speech, has dominion over the earth and all its creatures. He has the right to take what he wants."

"To take and take and take without giving anything back is death," said Lilith softly.

"But as for these particular pork chops," Adam went on, "they are tough. Eva, when you have helped yourself, will you please pass some of that intriguing dish to me."

Grammar watched as that Creature's conglomeration made its way around the table and listened to the murmurs of: "This is delicious." She wanted to say something. She wanted to say she hoped they all choked on it. She wanted to tell them they could find another cook. She was resigning. Let someone else get up at the crack of dawn to fix Christmas dinner. Let someone else have the work and worry of trying to nourish growing children. But she didn't trust herself to speak.

When Ionia had helped herself and Fred, she started to set the platter back into the middle of the table.

"Pass it to me," Grammar commanded. "If you all die, I don't intend to be left alone to bury you."

Grammar took a spoonful. She meant to swallow it without tasting it. Against her will, it tasted good.

14

 Christmas Presents

LONG after Fred had gone to sleep, Jason lay awake listening to the house grow quiet, counting each bedroom door as he heard it close. As soon as he was certain that everyone had retired for the night, he meant to sneak downstairs and remove his presents to Ionia and Fred. Before he could prevent her, his mother had put all the presents under the tree. There were so many that no one would notice that two were missing. As his mother was giving more than one present each to Ionia and Fred, he could easily change the tags to make it look as though two of his mother's gifts were from him. That would solve everything. He had only to explain to his mother what he had done so that she wouldn't ask any stupid questions at the wrong time. His mother might be angry or pretend to be angry when she found out what the presents had been, but he could handle her.

Ionia's mother was another matter. He wasn't going to risk a run-in with her. Despite Ionia's claims that her mother was harmless, Jason did not trust that woman. Being a vegetarian, she would no doubt object to the trap he had planned to give Fred. He might still give Fred the trap secretly. As for the book on the inferiority of women he had meant to give Ionia, that he would hide in his suitcase and take back with him to the city. Jason shuddered to think of the form Ionia's mother's vengeance would take if she ever found out about that book. Of course, he did not believe in witchcraft—it was at best a pseudo-science—but he wouldn't be surprised if Ionia's mother fancied herself a witch. That would explain her superstitious sympathy with animals and also her bizarre appearance. As Jason pondered Ionia's mother, he concluded that inferiority did not adequately describe the position of women in relation to men. They were not only inferior but alien, some other kind of species altogether.

Another door closed. According to Jason's calculations, everyone ought to be in bed. He waited another few minutes; then, reaching under the pillow for his flashlight, he got up and tiptoed out of Fred's room and down the hall. On the landing, satisfied that no one had heard him, he switched on his flashlight and made his way down the stairs, keeping close to the bannister so that the stairs wouldn't squeak. Once downstairs, he sighed with relief. Confidently, he crossed the hall to the living room. In the doorway, he froze.

His light fell not on the presents but on that woman sleeping beneath the tree. Or she had been asleep. Before Jason could think what to do, she opened her eyes. They glowed like an animal's. She watched him for what seemed to Jason a long time. He stood still, unable to speak, unable to move.

"What do you want, Jason, son of Mrs. Eva Brooke?" she said at last.

"Nothing," he tried to say, but no sound came out.

"Why do you shine your light on my sleep?"

"It was the presents," Jason managed to mumble. "I wanted to see that the presents were all right."

"Well," she said, moving aside, "Come and look."

Jason remained where he was. He did not want to take one step nearer that woman. He shone the light on the presents, but he could not distinguish the ones to Ionia and Fred without coming closer. He took a couple of steps, trying to ignore the woman who was watching him. He wondered if he could just snatch the presents and run away, but then, he considered, if he ran, she might run after him.

"I. . .there's two presents I need to fix."

Jason crouched down and began to search among the presents. When he found the ones he wanted, he picked them up and walked away as swiftly as he could without seeming to run, forgetting, in his haste, that he had meant to change the name tags.

On Christmas morning, Jason found no opportunity to speak alone with his mother. After breakfast, old Mrs. Underwood shoved him outdoors along with Ionia, Fred, the woman, and the dog.

"Go play in the snow," she ordered them, "and don't come back indoors until dinner is ready."

She slammed the door in their faces, and Jason heard it lock.

During the night, several inches of new snow had fallen—heavy, wet snow, easy to pack. Jason could have made some mean snowballs and started a fight, but he had no intention of fighting or playing with the others. He had been forced out into the snow with them, and he would not participate in any games. While the others tore about the yard playing games or falling down on the ground to make snow angels, Jason wandered slowly towards the gate. It was open now, as it had been last night, but when he and his mother visited last spring, the gate had been closed. "It's always locked," Fred and Ionia had explained to him when he questioned them. "They're afraid we'll get lost in the Empty Land." Why was it open now, he wondered?

Jason stood in the open gate and looked out at the Empty Land. One day, he thought, he would like to explore it. There were no maps of the Empty Land, so far as he knew, no detailed maps, anyway, none that showed the altitudes of the hills or named the lakes and rivers. On large maps, the Empty Land was always depicted as an unfilled space. He had asked a number of his teachers why this was so, and they had answered him with stories about quicksand and sudden storms, but these stories only explained why the Empty Land was uninhabited, not why it was uncharted.

Jason had a theory of his own. He believed that the Empty Land was a landing base for extra-terrestrial spacecraft and that beings from other planets controlled the area. That would account for the alleged disappearance of previous explorers and also for the lack of maps. He, Jason, might succeed where others had failed. He would get to the heart of the mystery. It would be a dangerous mission, but someone must accomplish it. He would go to the government and volunteer himself for the job. Then, just let Ionia try to call him a coward.

"Jason," Fred shouted, "do you want to help build a snow man?"

"Not right now," called Jason over his shoulder.

"No, not a snowman," came the woman's voice. "A snow woman. We'll build a snow woman."

Then, in spite of himself, Jason turned to watch.

Inside, Grammar and Eva worked together in the kitchen. Eva was mixing batter for some biscuits, and Grammar was washing, peeling, and chopping vegetables. Both had steaming mugs of tea close at hand, which Grammar kept refilling. During her days of anticipation, Eva had imagined a scene like this, a cozy kitchen scene, but now that it was being enacted, it was not quite right, perhaps because nothing else was. Instead of easy, intimate talk about the children, there was constrained silence with intermittent attempts at neutral conversation. Neither knew what to say or how much to say. Eva sensed that if only she asked the right question, Mrs. Underwood would break down and tell her everything, but Eva was not sure she wanted to know everything. She did not want to be responsible for eliciting any ill-advised confessions. It would be better to know nothing. Besides, she felt rather distant from the situation. Adam had scarcely spoken to her last night, and the children were totally absorbed in their mother. She and Jason did not belong. It would be best to leave as soon as they politely could. Her throat was sore and her head felt fuzzy. Undoubtedly she had caught cold. That would provide her with an excuse.

Eva reached for her tea and gazed through the steam towards the window over the sink. Through the window, she caught a glimpse of Ionia and Fred pushing a large and growing snowball over the ground. Jason was close by, gesturing with his hands, apparently directing the operation. Eva smiled.

"The children are having fun," she commented.

Grammar sniffed and wiped her eyes. She was slicing an onion.

"So long as they have it outside," she said. "They tore up the house yesterday. There's no controlling them when they're with Her."

Eva said nothing; she did not know what to say to Mrs. Underwood's obvious dislike of her daughter-in-law.

"Mrs. Brooke," began Grammar in a confidential tone, "what do you think of Her?"

"I have hardly had time to think, Mrs. Underwood," said Eva cautiously. "It's all been so sudden."

"Yes," said Grammar, "suddenly she's here. After all these years, she appears out of nowhere."

"How many years?"

"Six," answered Grammar. "Six years I've raised the children myself. Now she comes back and wants to take Ionia."

"Take her," repeated Eva. "Take her where?"

"That's just it. I don't know where. Nowhere. I don't know where she comes from or what she is. Only Adam knows, if he does, and he's going to let her."

Grammar stopped trying to control her tears. She sobbed as she diced the onion. Eva, though her hands were covered with flour, went to Mrs. Underwood and put her arms around her.

"Help me, Mrs. Brooke. Talk to Adam. Maybe he'll listen to you. Ionia must not be allowed to go with that Creature."

"But Mrs. Underwood," protested Eva, lowering her arms, "I can't interfere in something like this. I'm not a member of the family. I'm an outsider. I can't. . . ."

"That's exactly why you can. He doesn't give two hoots about his family."

Eva was shocked into silence.

"Please, Mrs. Brooke, Just talk to him. Now. Before it's too late."

Forgetting to wash her hands, Eva left the kitchen and went to look for Adam, more to prove to herself that Mrs. Underwood was wrong about Adam than for any other reason. She found him in the living room, standing by the window, looking out. She paused for a moment to study him before she spoke.

Daylight made his face seem paler than it had last night. He looked tired. Perhaps his wife's return was as much a surprise to him as to his mother.

"Adam," she said timidly.

He turned towards her, startled. He must have been absorbed in what he was watching not to have heard her enter the room.

"Well, what is it, Eva?" he asked. "Is something wrong in the kitchen? You're all covered with flour."

Eva looked down at her arms and blushed.

"No, Adam," she said. "Everything's fine in the kitchen. It's just that your mother is upset."

"That is not at all unusual. My mother is frequently upset, generally over nothing."

"She's upset about Ionia," Eva explained. "She's afraid your wife has come to take her away with her."

"My mother told you that?"

Eva nodded.

"My mother does not know everything, although she thinks she does. My advice to you is that you pay her no attention. She's an old woman who talks too much."

Again Eva was shocked. She had never heard Adam speak discourteously of anyone. He must be, she concluded, under a great deal of strain.

"What is to become of Ionia?" she forced herself to ask.

"Let that be my concern, Eva."

He stared at her for a moment, then smiled reassuringly and turned back to the window. Eva stood awkwardly, unsure of whether she had been dismissed or whether she ought to say something more.

"By the way, Eva," said Adam without turning from the window, "what do you think of my wife?"

There was that question again. Though Eva sensed that the answer Adam wanted was different than the one his mother wanted, she was just as reluctant to supply it.

"I don't know," she said. "I have never met anyone like her before."

"No," mused Adam. "I don't suppose anyone ever has. Now," he said, turning abruptly from the window, "if you will excuse me, Eva, I have some work I would like to do before dinner."

"It's Christmas, Adam," she said, but he was already gone.

It did not feel like Christmas. Eva crossed the room to the window where Adam had stood. Outside she saw the children and Lilith clustered around an enormous snow figure, the figure of a woman, a massive naked woman with legs like tree trunks and a waterfall of hair tumbling down her back. Lilith, with what looked like Jason's pocket knife, was working at some of the details. Ionia and Fred were making necklaces or crowns of ivy. Jason was just watching. She wondered what he was thinking. She wished she could go outside, too. She wanted to see the snow woman's face. She wanted to crown her with a wreath. She wanted to be with the children, be one of them, the way Lilith was.

Then she remembered Mrs. Underwood, alone in the kitchen, weeping over the onions. Reluctantly she turned away from the window and headed for the kitchen. Mrs. Underwood needed her; the children did not.

After dinner, everyone gathered in the living room to exchange gifts. All of them watched one another open the presents, exclaiming over not only what he had received but what the others received as well. Eva was proclaimed a gifted gift-giver. Grammar tore off her shoes and at once put on the fleece-lined slippers that Eva had embroidered with touching lack of skill. When Grammar had opened the book of herb lore that Eva had given her, she called the Creature to come and identify the herbs she carried in her pouch.

Fred laughed with delight when he discovered the miniature farm that looked almost exactly like the one he passed on the way to the train. Eva had also given Fred a book of letters, each one featuring a different animal. Soon Fred was engaged in teaching Lion the alphabet. Lion, however, was more interested in the rawhide bone that was his present from Eva.

Jason, in a corner by himself, was reading the directions for assembling his telescope. So far no one had noticed the absence of his gifts, but he felt bad. Fred had given him a box, which he had made himself of popsicle sticks. The box was full of what Jason knew Fred considered to be treasures: stones, feathers, hits of broken glass, all intended to enlarge Jason's collections. Jason had hidden the trap in Fred's closet, and he would tell him about it as soon as he got the chance, but there was nothing to give Ionia. She had given him a handsome present, a book on early theories of universal order. Perhaps he would tell her that he had ordered her something that hadn't arrived on time.

Ionia was not wondering where Jason's present was. She was lost in a history of storybook illustrations that Mrs. Brooke had given her. Then Mrs. Brooke, wrapped in her new multi-colored shawl, sat down on the floor beside her and began to whisper to her about an easel that she had for Ionia back at the apartment.

In his easy chair, Adam sat reading the footnotes of the book Eva had given him, Sir Algernon Riddler's latest work. He was pleased to find several of his own works cited there. To enhance his enjoyment, he was about to light a pipe.

Then he remembered Eva's other gift to him, and he decided to open that first. He was so startled by what it was that he called to the others.

"Look."

They all obeyed. In Adam's hand they saw a dagger. Its ivory handle was carved in the shape of the upper half of a woman's body. The hair swept back from the woman's face as if she belonged on the prow of a ship. Most remarkable about the carved face was its resemblance to Lilith's. Everyone saw it, though no one said anything about it.

"An exquisite gift, Eva," said Adam, lightly fingering the handle. "Wherever did you find it?"

"In that rare book shop of yours, Adam. It was just sitting in the window for decoration. Mr. Reid had not intended to sell it, but when I told him I wanted it for you, he changed his mind. He thinks very highly of you, Adam. He says the dagger is very old, perhaps made by the ancient Persians. I thought perhaps you might find it useful as a letter opener."

While Eva was speaking, Lilith had slipped down from her perch on the arm of Grammar's chair and approached the dagger.

"The Persians," she repeated. "Yes, that is what they called themselves, the men, the hordes of men who came and tried to conquer my people."

"Too bad they didn't succeed," commented Grammar.

"They captured your image," Adam reminded her, "and then they forgot that you even existed. Men believe in what they make."

"Then men believe in nothing," Lilith said, and she turned away and went to look out the window. "And they are fools," she added, "if they do not know how dangerous it is to steal the image of one of my race."

Confused, Jason glanced from Ionia's father to Ionia's mother. He had not understood this exchange between Professor Underwood and his wife, and it irritated him. He did not like secret conversations being carried on right in front of him. He did not like what did not make sense. What did this woman mean when she said she remembered the ancient Persians? Who did she mean by her people, and why would anyone want to conquer them? How had she traveled all the way from Iran or wherever in that get-up? He meant to find out.

"Are you from the Middle East, Mrs. Underwood?" he began cautiously.

"Certainly not," snapped Ionia's grandmother.

"Excuse me, Mrs. Underwood. I didn't mean you, I meant. . ." he paused unsure of what to call her.

"Me?" asked the woman turning towards him. "I am called Lilith."

"Well, are you from the Middle East?"

Even though she was not like other grown-ups, he hesitated to call her by her first name.

"Yes," she said. "I am from the middle east and the middle west and the middle south and the middle north."

Jason thought she was making fun of him.

"Sounds like the middle of nowhere to me," he said angrily.

"Jason," warned his mother.

"The Middle of Nowhere," mused Lilith. "Yes, that is where men say my people live. Do you not, yourselves, call it the Empty Land?"

"The Empty Land," said Jason. "No one lives in the Empty Land."

"No man lives in the Empty Land," said Lilith in a sing-song voice.

"It is scientifically proven that the Empty Land is unfit for human habitation."

"No man drinks from the stone," she sang.

"And if it were inhabited, I mean by human beings, the government would know about it."

"No man lives in the Empty Land," she repeated.

"There aren't even any maps of the Empty Land."

"No man knows the unknown."

All at once, without warning, Ionia's father began to laugh. Jason turned red. He was sure Professor Underwood was laughing at him, laughing, with that woman, at him. She had begun to sing her song again. In his ears it sounded like a playground taunt.

> No man lives in the Empty Land.
> No man drinks from the stone.
> No man lives in the Empty Land.
> No man knows the unknown.

She sang it over and over until he could stand it no longer.

"Stop it," he shouted. "Stop it!"

Then there was silence, and everyone was looking at him instead of at Ionia's mother. He felt like he did in dreams where he found himself in school, naked or in his pajamas. More than anything, he wished he could just disappear.

"Jason," said his mother.

The gentleness of her voice drew a sob from his stomach. It caught in his throat, and he managed to swallow it.

"Where are your presents to Ionia and Fred?"

"I don't know," mumbled Jason. "I must have forgotten them on the train."

"That's funny," his mother blundered on. "I was almost sure I saw them last night."

"Where are the ones you fixed, Jason, Son of Mrs. Eva Brooke?"

"What did you fix, Jason?" Fred wanted to know.

Jason was cornered, and he knew it. Suddenly, he did not care. He lost all impulse to protect himself.

"I'll go and get them," he said.

When Jason returned to the living room with the presents, he ignored his mother's anxious, questioning look. Without a word, he handed Ionia and Fred their packages and then sat down again.

"What is it, Jason?" wondered Fred, when he had torn the wrapping paper away.

"A trap," answered Jason. "For capturing squirrels and mice alive."

Jason glanced at Ionia to see if she had opened her present yet. She had. The book was lying in her lap, but she was not looking at it. Her eyes were on her mother. Her face showed nothing: no surprise, no hurt, no anger. Jason realized that his present hadn't affected her one way or another. Ionia did not even care enough to hate him anymore.

"Why do you want to capture squirrels and mice, Man-child?"

Fred only stared at his mother. Jason wondered whether Fred understood the connection between the trap and his zoo. He thought of explaining it, but he did not want to appear to be excusing himself.

"Fred has a zoo," Ionia spoke for him.

"A zoo," her mother repeated. "What is a zoo?"

"It's a place where foolish people keep wild creatures in cages so that they can gawk at them," said Fred's grandmother. "And I'll tell you one thing right now, young man, you're not adding squirrels and mice to your menagerie. It's bad enough having them in the walls without your making pets of them."

"Let the Man-child speak for himself. Why do you want to capture squirrels and mice?"

"Because I like them." Fred answered at last.

"I do not understand. Man-child. Why do you put what you like in cages?"

"It's really very elementary," interrupted Fred's father. "Of course, the boy wants to keep what he likes. It's perfectly understandable. I kept animals myself, as a boy, until one day, without my permission, my mother let them all go. What is incomprehensible to me is not that small boys should desire to keep pets, but that their mothers should fail to understand this desire as a natural part of their development."

Fred looked at his father, then at his mother, and finally at the trap. Then, without a word, he turned away from the trap and began playing with his farm animals again.

Jason watched him, feeling puzzled and hurt. He hadn't expected any of the grown-ups to approve, but he had hoped that Fred would be pleased. It was all the fault of that woman. Jason glanced at her, wondering if she meant to damage the trap or take it away from Fred, but she appeared to have lost interest in the trap, too. She had moved to the fireplace and was pacing small circles as if she were a dog about to lie down for a nap.

"And what did Jason Brooke give to you, Ionia?" asked her father.

Jason looked at Ionia's father. The expression on the Professor's face startled him. He had thought, when the Professor defended the trap, that he was on his side, another man against all these silly women. Now Jason saw that the Professor was actually enjoying his humiliation. Jason's stomach turned over.

"Well?" persisted Ionia's father, for Ionia had not yet answered.

"It's just a book."

Jason turned towards Ionia in bewilderment. Could it be that she was protecting him? Nothing was predictable anymore.

"There is no such thing as `just a book.' What is it called?"

"It's about women," Ionia stalled.

"I asked: 'what is it called?'"

"*The Inferiority of Women*," Ionia said at last, "*Or Why Little Girls Grow Up to Be Like Their Mothers*."

"Jason!" gasped his mother.

"An intriguing question," commented the Professor. "I have often pondered it myself."

"It's no mystery to me," muttered Grammar, "considering their fathers."

"What does that word mean?" asked Lilith, ceasing her circles. "Inferiority. My people do not have that word."

"Inferiority," repeated Adam. "The condition of being inferior, that is: situated under or beneath; low or lower in order, degree, or rank; low or lower in quality, status, or estimation; from the Latin *inferus*, meaning low."

"Oh," murmured Lilith. "One of the words men made up when they started making things."

Lilith yawned, circled one more time, and lay down on the carpet beside Lion to sleep.

The Professor went back to reading footnotes. Jason's mother got up to look at the herb book with old Mrs. Underwood. Ionia, laying his book aside, stretched out on her stomach to study illustrations. Fred, murmuring happily, played farm. Jason found himself and his offenses ignored, utterly ignored. His face hot with shame and humiliation, Jason picked up the book Ionia had given him and attempted to take comfort in the order of the universe.

15

The Trap

ALONE in her room, Ionia considered what she ought to take with her. Christmas was almost over; Mrs. Brooke and Jason were getting ready to go, in spite of Grammar's insisting that they should not. While they argued, Ionia had slipped away as unobtrusively as she could, thinking it best to make her own preparations while Grammar was busy with the Brookes.

Standing in the middle of her room, gazing at her possessions, Ionia realized that she had few preparations to make. She could not picture herself walking over the hill of the three trees with a suitcase in her hand. What could she possibly need in her mother's country that a suitcase could contain? Clothes she would need only for the journey. When she lived with her mother's people she would wear what they wore and those were not what Grammar considered clothes. When it was warm, they didn't wear anything, her mother said. Books would not withstand the snow and rain nor the earth floors of the houses under the hills where her mother said her people lived. Drawing paper would weather no better, and her pencils would soon wear down to nothing. Anything she tried to take with her would come to nothing in the Empty Land. She would enter the Empty Land empty-handed.

All she had to do was to put on her warmest clothes. Would it make Grammar feel better to know that Ionia was wearing the new sweater Grammar had made for her? But she did not want to think of Grammar or of Fred, of their being without her. It was one thing to imagine going, another to imagine being gone.

When she had finished dressing, Ionia still lingered in her room. She did not feel ready yet. She wandered about her room as if she were a nosy stranger exploring it for the first time. Finally she sat down at her desk, bent, and reached under the small rug where she hid the key to her drawer. There was the spider still alive. No one would protect it now from Grammar, though she did not think Fred would want to capture it for his zoo anymore.

Straightening up, Ionia opened the drawer and began to leaf through her pictures. There was picture after picture of the woman dancing beneath the trees. There were pictures of the wild geese and of what they might see spread out beneath their wings. All the pictures were of that other country, her mother's country. Now it had all become real. She didn't need to draw the woman dancing anymore; she didn't need to wonder what lay beyond the hill of the three trees. She was going there, with her mother, to live in that country always. Trembling, Ionia put the pictures away, locked the drawer, and replaced the key. Then she rose, turned out the lights, and went to sit in her round window for the last time.

Night had come to the eastern sky, and the first pale stars appeared. The snow held the afterglow of day and seemed, not white, but dim blue, a softer shade of night. Under the snow, in that light, the shape of the hills seemed less certain, as though, at any moment, the hills might fall, then rise again, like sea swells. Only the three trees were definite, darker than earth and sky, partaking of both, marking the boundary between them.

Ionia fixed her gaze on the three trees, as she had so many times before, and she imagined herself beneath the three trees, looking back at the round window. For a moment she was outside herself, and she saw her own face in the window staring out at the night. Then she shivered and shook the image from her. Turning her face from the window, she looked into the enclosed darkness of her room. She wished she might crawl under the covers of her bed and sleep, just for a little while. Perhaps she would, just for a little while.

"Ionia."

It was Grammar's voice, half-anxious, half-angry.

"Ionia, are you in there?"

"Yes," she answered, slipping down from the window; Grammar did not like her to sit in the window.

"What are you doing in there?" demanded Grammar, pushing the door open with more force than necessary.

"Nothing."

The two stood facing one another in the dark room, Grammar framed by the light from the hall, Ionia by the light from the window.

"What do you mean disappearing like that? Where are your manners? Why have you changed into your old clothes? Christmas isn't over yet."

Ionia did not answer. She could not tell Grammar, not yet, not when she was alone with her. She needed her mother with her.

"Well," said Grammar giving up, "come downstairs now. The Brookes are leaving. You must say good-bye and thank you."

Grammar turned towards the door, but she waited for Ionia to go out first. Then, casting a suspicious glance over the room, Grammar hastened after her.

When Eva Brooke and Jason had closed the door behind them, Grammar went to the kitchen to see to supper. Fred, unable to interest his mother in the farm, trailed after Grammar, with two cows and some sheep clutched in his hand. Lion followed, sensing Fred's sadness. Ionia remained in the hall with her mother, who stood perfectly still, her eyes not focused on Ionia or anything else that Ionia could see. She seemed, again, to be waiting, waiting without question or impatience, as if waiting were not simply a passage of time between one event and another, but a way of being.

"I am ready," Ionia said.

Her own voice sounded strange to her, as if she had spoken alone to someone who was not there. But her mother responded at once, turning to look at her with a mixture of intentness and detachment.

"Are you sure?" her mother asked.

"Yes."

Outside, the car doors slammed. Ionia's ears registered the sound; a moment later the meaning followed. It occurred to Ionia, as it had not when she was saying good-bye, that she would never see Jason or Mrs. Brooke again. She repeated the words in her mind and tried to feel something, but she could not, not even for Mrs. Brooke, who had looked at her anxiously and held her closer than usual when she said good-bye, almost as if she knew. Yet, somehow, Mrs. Brooke's tenderness failed to touch her. Ionia thought of Jason, his embarrassment, his awkwardness as he mumbled his apology about the book, but she was unmoved. It didn't matter anymore; it didn't matter that Jason had teased her or that he was sorry. Nothing that had happened before mattered anymore.

"I just have to put on another sweater and my boots and my coat and hat," she said.

Swiftly she went about the business of getting dressed for the outdoors. Then she returned to her mother, bundled up and somewhat breathless.

"And now, Ionia, last of our race, youngest daughter of the Grand Mother, do we say good-bye to Ursula and the man-child or not?"

Inside her mittens, Ionia's fingers curled up and dug their nails into her palm. Her teeth bit her lip, and her stomach tightened. Furious, she demanded of herself why she had to feel now, at the last minute. Why did she have to feel about Grammar and Fred? Why didn't they seem as distant, as unreal and unrelated to her as Jason and Mrs. Brooke had? Why did she have to feel at all? Yet as her feelings for Grammar and Fred rose in her, uncontrolled, so did her feelings for Mrs. Brooke. Suddenly she remembered Mrs. Brooke whispering to her about the easel, and tears spilled over the rim of her eyes.

"Let's go now," she said. "I don't want to say good-bye."

"Very well," agreed her mother. "But first, while we have light, let me look at your eyes. I think there is something wrong with them. They are watering."

Ionia's astonishment that her mother did not know what tears were stopped them, and she stared at her mother as her mother bent to examine her, unaware that Grammar had just entered the hall from the dining room.

"Ionia! What are you doing in your outdoor clothes!"

Ionia whirled around to face Grammar. If only Grammar's face had been as angry as her voice, Ionia would not have been so unnerved. She was used to Grammar being angry, but now Grammar looked frightened, as frightened as Fred did when he came to crawl into her bed after a nightmare.

"Take off your coat, Ionia, and your hat and boots," commanded Grammar. "And set the table for supper. Now!"

Ionia saw that Grammar was fighting for control. So was she. Not trusting herself to speak, Ionia shook her head. Then, she looked to her mother, but her mother offered no help. When she looked back, Fred was beside Grammar, his eyes and mouth wide open. For a moment he stared; then he shouted:

"I'm going, too!" and he ran towards the closet.

"No one is going anywhere," said Grammar, the authority of her tone contrasting with the look of helplessness on her face. "Except you." She turned towards Lilith. "You, get out! Get out and leave my children alone."

Fred, one boot on and one boot in his hand, looked up at Grammar, startled by the savageness of her tone. Ionia looked from Grammar to her mother, waiting for her mother to respond, to say something that would settle everything.

"Get out," Grammar repeated, her voice a snarl.

Still Lilith said nothing.

Slowly, Ionia understood that her mother was waiting for her. Her mother would go with her or without her, but Ionia must decide.

"I'm going, Grammar," said Ionia in a low voice.

Before Grammar could realize what was happening, Ionia darted at her and kissed her. Then Ionia turned to look at Fred across the hall. Fred looked back, bewildered, about to burst into tears. Without a word or gesture, Ionia turned and ran out the door. More slowly, her head slightly bowed, Lilith followed.

"I'm going, too," Fred wailed, and one boot on, one boot off, he stumbled after his mother with Lion at his heels.

Stunned, Grammar stared after them, blinking as if a sudden light had blinded her. Then she, too, ran for the door.

Not until she was all the way down the front steps did Grammar realize that the gate was closed. Pausing for breath, she clutched the railing and watched while the creature and Ionia took turns trying to open the gate. As the breath she had lost began to come more easily, Grammar began to think more clearly than she had in days, perhaps months, maybe years. One by one the pieces came together: the gates, the wall, Adam's secretiveness, the tower room, the crystal ball, the book, and she wondered how she had failed to understand before that Adam's whole purpose had been to capture the Creature. Ionia was a side issue, a distraction, a decoy.

"Fool," she whispered to herself. "Fool."

Angry as she was that Adam had made a fool of her, her primary feeling was one of relief, relief so great that it was almost triumph. Now, no matter how trying the presence of the Creature was, the children were safe. She would not lose them. The calm, the sense of control that deserted her these past few days returned, and she descended the path to the gate.

"It's no use," she said coming up behind them.

Ionia and Fred turned towards her, but the Creature did not seem to hear. "It's no use," Grammar repeated.

This time the Creature let fall the ring and slowly turned around.

"Of course, it is locked," said Grammar. "I should have known all along. We all should have known."

Still the Creature stared at her, silent, uncomprehending.

"Don't you see?" Grammar went on. "This is a trap and you walked into it."

Then fear came into the Creature's face, not in any discernible change of expression, no widening of the eyes, no drop of the jaw. It was like a sudden coldness, a stiffening as when the fur rises along the backbone of an animal. For a moment the Creature stood rigid, and Grammar felt the cold of the Creature's fear creeping into herself, hollowing her bones. Then, without warning, the Creature wrenched herself from that stillness and hurled herself at the gate, throwing her whole weight against it. Then she began to leap at the gate again and again, making high, frightened yelping sounds.

Grammar instinctively reached for Fred's hand and backed away. She tried to take hold of Ionia's hand, but Ionia resisted. Torn, she wanted to go to her mother, grab hold of her, make her stop. At the same time she wanted to turn and run away, away from the fear that made her mother like an animal. Without realizing it, she took a step back, a step closer to Grammar and Fred. All three watched, not wanting to see, not able to look away. Only Lion crept nearer, whining softly.

After what seemed like a long time, Lilith's frantic assault on the gate ceased as suddenly as it had started. She crumpled to the ground and lay there, her black hair spread out over the snow. Cautiously, Ionia, Fred, and Grammar approached her. Lion was already beside her, licking her hands, nosing her hair, trying to find her face. Grammar bent over her, and Ionia and Fred crouched down beside her, softly, tentatively laying their hands on her body. In spite of the snow and the cold, her body was warm and she breathed. Ionia lifted her hair and uncovered her face. Her eyes were closed, and she seemed, at first, to be asleep. Slowly she opened her eyes. For a moment they showed no recognition. Then she murmured, "Ionia," and closed her eyes again.

"We must take her inside," decided Grammar. "She must not lie like this in the snow. Ionia and Fred, you take her legs, and I'll lift her under the arms." Grammar bent down, about to carry out her plan, when the Creature opened her eyes again and raised herself on her elbow.

"No, Ursula," she said looking up at her. "If I wanted to come inside, I would walk there myself. But I would be alone, Ursula. Go."

Grammar opened her mouth to protest, but then closed it again. Something in the Creature's face silenced all her reasonable arguments.

"As you wish," Grammar said. "I will leave the back door open until I go to bed. I have made soup, vegetable soup. I'll leave it on the stove. You're welcome to it if you want it."

The Creature bowed her head.

"Come, children," said Grammar. "It is time for your supper and you must have baths tonight."

"No," said Ionia.

And she looked at her mother, begging her to say "stay," but her mother said nothing; only looked at her once and then away, laying her head on the ground. Ionia sensed that her mother didn't want her; worse, it did not matter whether Ionia was there or not. Either way her mother was alone.

"Let her be, Ionia," said Grammar, almost gently. "You cannot help her now."

Tears filled Ionia's eyes, blinding her, and she did not resist when Grammar took her hand and raised her to her feet. Passive, she was prepared to follow Grammar, but Grammar hesitated.

"Lilith," Grammar said, and the awkward silence after the name betrayed what it cost her to speak it, "don't let him see you like that. It's what he wants."

Tightening her grip on the children's hands, Grammar led them up the path to the house. Lion remained with Lilith, indifferent to whether or not he was wanted.

Back from the train station, Adam drove through the gate, hesitating a moment before he closed it again. He wanted to maintain the illusion that she was free to come and go for as long as he could. Yet if she had tried the gate and found it locked while he was gone, she might be lurking in the shadows now, waiting for her chance to escape. Curse having to take Eva Brooke to the train station; Eva, with her polite bewilderment and her oppressive innocence. He could not risk leaving the gate open.

Adam reached into his pocket for the touchstone. In the rear view mirror, he watched the two sides swing shut. They came together quickly, so that unless she were able to leap the length of the car, she would never get out while he was driving through the gate; the gate was only just wider than the car. He doubted she would even come near the car. As he had discovered before, she was afraid of machinery. Nor could she climb the walls; they were high, and the cement was smooth and free of vines. Naturally, he had made sure there was no ladder on the premises that was tall enough to come near the top of the wall. Nor was there even a hammer or nails. When he needed such equipment, he rented it along with the men to do the labor.

There was no doubt: his trap was well made, and yet it seemed crude, a mere mechanical device. He wanted some subtler means of control. The wall was only a beginning, a visible symbol of what must become a psychological condition. That was why the moment she discovered her physical captivity was crucial to him.

Adam got out of the car and surveyed the yard. Though the moon was on the wane, it shed enough light by which to see. Light, too, came from the kitchen, casting the shadow of a tree so that it met with the deeper, less distinct shadow of the wall cast by the moon. Adam searched the shadows, but so far as he could see, they concealed nothing. He listened, but the night was still, as only a winter's night can be. Adam broke the stillness and began walking up the path, unable to control the squeaking of his shoes in the new snow. Then suddenly he stopped.

Some hundred yards away he saw her, massive and pale, unmoving in the moonlight, seeming twice her usual size. Against his will, Adam felt a prickle of fear on the back of his neck, which turned to a flush of shame when he realized that what he had seen was not her, but the snow figure she and the children had made. Adam continued up the path, looking neither to the right nor to the left until her voice arrested him.

"Adam, Son of Ursula, you have betrayed me."

Adam turned towards her voice and saw that she had come out of hiding to stand beside the snow figure. Though smaller and darker, she was so similar to the snow woman in shape and bearing that she might have been its shadow. Her face was as white as the snow woman's and as cold and expressionless, as if it, too, were carved of snow. He wondered how she could be so still, so silent, so seemingly calm. Then he heard a sound that could only be called a growl. He smiled, thinking that the sound came from her and that she would now display her true nature. Yet, though the growling continued, her face changed not at all, and she made no move towards him. Then Adam saw the dog beside her. The fur on its back was raised, and its lip curled. She placed a hand on the dog's back, and the dog quieted.

Adam frowned, annoyed that she should restrain the dog, as though she and not he was the master here. It further disconcerted Adam that she should check the dog, knowing of her captivity. Briefly Adam thought of denying the betrayal, of saying that he had only closed the gate for the night, and then opening it again so that he could watch her walking towards it; but in the next moment, Adam knew he could not. To attempt to deceive her twice would be petty, on the level of a prankster. She knew. She was confronting him with her knowledge. He must match her austerity with his own.

"Yes," he said. "You were a fool to think I would not."

He stood, regarding her, waiting for her calm to give way, waiting for her to plead or to loose the dog or to attack him herself, caged animal that she was. She did nothing, except to stare at him in that same unseeing way she always had. Just as he was about to reach out and claim her, she turned and moved away, the dog at her heels.

Adam remained, gazing after her, but he made no motion to follow. Of course, he could; it would be easy, too easy. She was in an enclosed space, his space. He could do what he liked. An image came into his mind of forcing her to receive him in the snow, the heat of their loins contrasting with the cold surrounding them, but he rejected it. He did not want to hunt her down in his back yard. Compared with the chase in the Empty Land, the idea seemed ludicrous, on the level of a bedroom farce.

The fact was, he did not know what he wanted. He felt confused by her behavior. Nothing was as he imagined it would be. But then, he had imagined nothing beyond the moment of her capture. Now, cheated of that moment, he began to construct another.

16
Consultations

ALONE in the kitchen on New Year's morning, Grammar stuck cloves, one by one, into the ham she would roast for New Year's dinner; never mind who would or would not eat it. Ham on New Year's day was traditional, and Grammar felt strongly that tradition, any tradition, ought to be maintained, if not for its own sake, then simply as a measure against mayhem.

The small but distinct plopping sound of the cloves penetrating the ham emphasized the silence of the house. Grammar thought she almost preferred the riotous play of the day before Christmas to the unnatural stillness that had pervaded the house since then. She seldom knew where the others were or what they were doing. When she went to look for them, she usually found them doing nothing, just nothing, and that disturbed her most of all.

The Creature slept most of the day, and when she was not sleeping, she wandered aimlessly around the house and yard. The children followed, never minding that she did not seem to notice them. While she slept, they sat beside her and watched, resisting all Grammar's attempts to distract them. Grammar wished it was time for school to begin again. Then, at least, they would leave the house every day and be away from their mother.

Adam's behavior worried Grammar, too, although in a different way. The children's motives were simple; they wanted a mother, or rather the overgrown playmate she had been a few days ago. Much as Grammar disliked the Creature, she could understand that. But Adam, what did he want now that he had succeeded in trapping her here? He did not treat the Creature as Grammar considered a man ought to treat a wife. He seldom talked to her, touched her, or spent time with her, though sometimes, like the children, he watched while she slept. More often, he was nowhere in sight, which meant, most likely, that he was in the tower room. But doing what? What more could he do? What was he waiting for? For Grammar sensed he was waiting. His waiting weighed on her; it was heavy, like the atmosphere before a storm. Grammar wished whatever was going to happen next would happen. The silence and the suspense were getting on her nerves.

Grammar reached for the honey with which she meant to glaze the ham. "Bother," she muttered, for the jar was sticky. Crossing the kitchen to fetch a sponge, Grammar concluded that the condition of the jar was the Creature's fault. That morning she had been eating honey straight out of the jar with her fingers. Grammar hoped that the Creature had thought to wash her hands before she stickied the rest of the house. "Drat the Creature," said Grammar as she soaked the sponge.

Turning from the sink, Grammar was startled by the sight of Adam standing in the doorway, smiling a smile that could only be called insolent. That Adam should sneak up on her and catch her talking to herself so enraged Grammar that she almost threw the sponge at him. Only out of curiosity as to why he had come to the kitchen to find her did Grammar restrain herself.

"Well?" she demanded. "What do you want?"

"I have come to consult with you, Mother," he said entering the kitchen. "I have decided to give a banquet."

"A banquet," Grammar repeated; Adam had never so much as given a dinner party.

"Yes, a banquet, on the occasion of Twelfth Night. Here is the guest list: fifteen people, colleagues of mine, and their spouses. I've written the invitations. I'm going to town to have them printed and mailed tomorrow. I will also shop for suitable clothes for my wife. I would appreciate it if, before then, you would give me a list of the supplies you will need. Here is the menu I have planned."

Appreciate. Grammar repeated the word in her mind with rancor, as she studied the menu, which included several kinds of meats, numerous salads, exotic *hors d'oeuvres*, and side dishes. Appreciation had nothing to do with it. Adam was not consulting her; he was issuing her an order.

"Adam, you are mad," she said. "Do you have any idea how old I am?"

"Old enough to be my mother?" he ventured.

"Old enough that I ought not to be asked or expected to prepare a feast of these proportions."

"Not feeling equal to it, Mother? I suppose you're not as energetic as you used to be. I keep forgetting that."

Grammar bristled.

"It's not a question of stamina. It is a question of decency, propriety, respect. I am your mother, not your servant or your wife."

"Then I shall hire you some help. You shall simply oversee the operation. I will also ask Eva Brooke to come early. I'm sure she will be glad to help."

"You will do no such thing," shouted Grammar, incensed, and this time she did throw the sponge at him, hitting him full in the face. "You may be able to get away with treating me like a galley slave, but you will not treat Mrs. Brooke that way. Have you no shame, Adam? How can you ask anything of that woman after the way you treated her at Christmas, and now that you have that Creature you call your wife living under your roof!"

Adam remained silent for a moment after his mother's outburst, his face reddening with anger and embarrassment at his mother's lack of emotional control.

"My relations with Eva Brooke have never been other than those of intellectual friendship. Our relations have not altered with the return of my wife. Of course, Eva Brooke is free to refuse her help, or even to refuse to come to the banquet if she wishes. But I don't think she will. Not everyone is so ungenerous as you, Mother; nor is everyone's view of human relations so narrow."

With that, Adam turned and left the kitchen.

"What if I refuse?" Grammar shouted after him.

But he made no answer.

After a moment, Grammar bent and picked up the sponge.

Upstairs in the secret counsel chamber, wearing their winter coats and huddled together for warmth, Ionia and Fred were having their own consultation; or rather they intended to. So far, neither one had spoken. The sputtering of the candle and the rhythmic softness of their breathing were the only sounds. Earlier that morning their mother had asked them to go away from her for a while. Both children felt the weight of their misery too great for words. Fred had suffered a double loss since Lion would not follow him. Ionia's sense of loss was mixed with guilt. If only, if only, if only, her mind kept repeating, you had gone right away when she wanted to. At last it was Ionia who broke the silence.

"We have to help her escape, Fred."

"But I don't want her to go away."

"Neither do I, but she's not happy here."

"How come?"

"Because she can't get out."

"Why does she want to?"

"Well, don't you sometimes?"

"No," said Fred stubbornly.

"How would you like it if you knew you could never get out ever again?"

"I would like it," insisted Fred, "because then I wouldn't have to go to school anymore."

"And you wouldn't see the animals on the farm anymore, either, or Jason or Mrs. Brooke."

Fred considered.

"I would like all the animals and Jason Brooke and Jason's mother to come and live here, too. Then everyone would stay, and my mother would play again like she did before."

"She's not going to play anymore, Fred."

"How come?" he asked automatically.

"Don't you understand?" said Ionia exasperated. "She's unhappy. She's trapped. She's in a cage."

"You mean like my zoo animals?" asked Fred slowly.

"Yes."

"But, Ionia, where is the cage? I don't see it."

"What do you think the wall is?"

"Oh," said Fred.

They were silent for a moment. Ionia picked up the candle and poured out the wax that had almost quenched the flame. Then she settled the candle in the new puddle of wax.

"Ionia," said Fred, "is that why my animals died, because they were in cages?"

"One reason, I think."

"Is my mother going to die?"

Ionia's stomach turned to ice; she had not thought of that before.

"I don't know."

"I don't want her to be dead."

"Then will you help her get away?"

"Where does she want to go, Ionia? Does she want to go to Jason's house?"

"No. She wants to go back to her own country."

"Where is Own country. Ionia?"

"I don't know, exactly. Somewhere way over that hill where the three trees grow. "

"I'm going, too," said Fred.

"No, you're not, Fred."

"How come?"

"You don't belong there. You belong here. You said yourself that you didn't care if you could never go out again."

"But, Ionia, you were going to go."

"That's different," she said. "I don't belong here. I never have. I've always wanted to get out."

"Do you belong in Own country, Ionia?"

"Yes," she said with more certainty than she felt.

"Ionia," said Fred, "I don't want you to go."

Ionia could hear the tears in his voice. They'd never get anywhere if Fred started crying.

"Look," she said gruffly, "no one's going anywhere if we don't do something. So just stop asking questions and think."

Fred obeyed, and they were silent again for a time. As Ionia watched the candle's flame leap and fall, she realized that she hadn't an idea in her head; only half-formed images of impossible flight. Nothing practical presented itself. She wondered desperately if there was something that she or her mother could do that was so terrible her father would never want to see them again, but her mind stopped short of imagining the deed. She was stuck as she might have been if she was trying to walk, surrounded by darkness, afraid to take a step forward for fear of falling.

"We could lock our father in the dungeon," suggested Fred. "Then we could let our mother out."

"How could we do that when he has the keys and we don't?"

"Grammar has keys," said Fred.

"Yes," said Ionia. "And we could steal them. All we have to do is find out where she keeps them."

"In her apron pocket," supplied Fred.

"No, I mean at night, when she's asleep. Listen, Fred, I've got an idea. One of us could pretend to be sick, so she'd have to get her keys to open the medicine cabinet."

"You, Ionia. I don't want to take medicine."

"All right, me. And the next night, I'd go back to steal them while you keep watch."

"Then could we put my father in the dungeon?"

"No, Fred, listen. . . ."

While Fred and Ionia plotted, Grammar sat at the kitchen table, writing her list of supplies. Although she had begun her work muttering maledictions against Adam, she was now deeply absorbed in imagining all she would need for the feast, and, without knowing it, she was deeply content. This banquet gave her a focus for her anxiety, an outlet for her nervous energy. Never mind that it was more work than she could manage; she was equal to super-human effort; she always had been; that was the story of her life. She had no intention of letting Adam hire strangers to work in her kitchen. She would do everything herself or nothing at all. She would show him; she would show them. So involved was she in visions of the heroic feats that would fill the days to come that, until a lock of black, matted hair swept across her list, she did not notice the Creature standing over her.

"What do you want?" she demanded, angry that she had been taken by surprise a second time that morning.

"I am watching the little black lines come out of that stick," explained the Creature, straightening up.

Grammar studied the Creature and thought again that Adam was mad. How did he expect to make the Creature presentable to human society in six days? Her hair was so matted it might not have been combed in a century, and there were dried grass and flowers tangled in it. If that hair were hacked off, it could well be used as a doormat. Beneath those strange garments, Grammar could see a layer of dirt that would need to be scraped off. She hoped Adam did not expect her to take part in those preparations.

"The little black lines are not coming out of this stick. I am making them." She paused embarrassed to hear herself using the Creature's words. "I mean, I am writing; or I was until you interrupted me. Where are the children?"

"I asked them to leave me. I do not know where they have gone."

"Good. They spend too much time moping after you."

"Yes," said the Creature simply.

Grammar wondered for a moment if it were possible that the Creature shared her concern for the children. But the Creature offered no more information about her motives or emotions, and Grammar could not read her face. Grammar returned to her list, but she found it impossible to concentrate with the Creature still standing over her.

"Well, what is it?" she asked irritably, refusing to look up. "Or do you have nothing better to do than to stand there and gawk at me. Because if you don't, I do, more than I can manage, and it's all your fault."

"What is my fault, Ursula?"

"You mean he hasn't told you about this blasted banquet?"

"What is a blasted banquet?"

"A fancy name for a lot of people eating a lot of food and making a lot of work for me."

"Do you mean a feast, Ursula? But I do not understand, why is a feast my fault?"

"Adam has never given banquets," Grammar said. "He has never given anything. If he's giving one now, you're to blame."

"To blame for a banquet?" wondered the Creature. "Among my people, a feast is a celebration. We celebrate the waxing moon and the moving water, the healing wind and the yielding earth. We do not blame what we celebrate."

"Celebrate, blame; it makes no difference. It's all how you look at it. I'm blaming you, and he's celebrating you. Only I wouldn't call it a celebration; I'd call it an exhibition."

"What is that, an exhibition?"

"An exhibition is a show, and you're the exhibit."

"Me?"

"Is there no end to your innocence?" marvelled Grammar. "Of course *you.* Now that he's got you here, he's going to show you off. You'll be even more of a sight than you are now when he's done with you."

"Done with me?" echoed Lilith. "Do you mean he will be done with me and let me go after this banquet?"

"Don't I wish he would," sighed Grammar. "No. I mean he's going to make you over. He's going to wash you and comb you and deck you out in fine clothes and show all his friends—I mean his associates; he hasn't got any friends, except Mrs. Brooke, so far as I know—what a rare creature he's captured for a wife."

"Ah," said Lilith. "I remember. He did that to me before. One day after the first frost, I covered myself with dirt for the winter. He washed it off. I covered myself again. He washed me again. Then the ground became too frozen. I could not cover myself again. I had to wear clothes to keep warm."

"I never before heard of the insulating properties of dirt," muttered Grammar, reluctant to abandon her theory that the Creature was simply slovenly.

"But he did not make me exhibit then," she continued. "I never saw any other human beings."

"Wanted to keep you to himself, I suppose."

"That is what he said, Ursula. But I never did understand. I never did understand the way human beings use the belonging words. Among my people they only mean kinship. Among human beings they mean something else. Another kind of ship."

"Ownership?" suggested Grammar.

"Yes, ownership. And I wanted to see other human beings then. Most of all I wanted to see human women. But Adam told me that human women were all alike."

"Hmph," snorted Grammar. "A lot Adam knows about women. A lot Adam knows about anything."

"So I thought he meant they were all like you, Ursula, because you were the only human woman I had ever seen. But now I have seen Mrs. Brooke, too. Adam was wrong. You and Mrs. Brooke are not alike."

"Indeed, we are not," said Grammar; then, curious in spite of herself, she asked, "Do your people wash in the summer?"

"I do not know if you would call it washing, Ursula. Everywhere in my country there is water. We are often in it. We do not need dirt to keep warm in the summer. I never understood why Adam wore clothes in the summer, and why he made me and Ionia wear them."

"Civilized human beings do not wear clothes merely for warmth," said Grammar. "Come to think of it, even savages understand that. Even in tropical countries people cover their private parts. You must come from the middle of Nowhere. Have you never heard of decency? Do you know no shame?"

"I do not understand, Ursula. What are the private parts?"

Grammar blushed.

"If you don't know, I'm not going to tell you."

The Creature stared at her with her head cocked to one side, the way Lion cocked his when he was puzzled. Grammar decided that it might be best to explain these matters to her now to avoid further embarrassment and to prevent her asking the children.

"All right," she said. "The private parts are the parts of a man's body that are different from a woman's and the parts of a woman's body that are different from a man's. Now do you understand?"

"I understand the parts, but not why they are private."

"Well, if you don't understand that, I can't make you. All I can tell you is that decent human beings keep those parts covered, and they have ever since Adam and Eve ate the apple."

"Ah," said Lilith. "And would it be shame for the parts to be uncovered?"

"Certainly it would, in public."

"Ah," murmured the Creature, and without another word she wandered away as inexplicably as she had come.

Grammar went back to writing her list, but she gave it only half her mind. With the other half she ruminated over the Creature's ignorance. She seemed untouched by thousands of years of civilization, and, in Grammar's opinion, thousands more might not be sufficient to civilize the Creature, and here Adam meant to do it in six days. In six days, Adam might alter the Creature's appearance, but he could not hope to reconstruct her entire being. The Creature was bound to disgrace him at the banquet by doing or saying something outrageous that would seem to her to be perfectly natural.

Well, Grammar concluded, let that be Adam's worry as the whole affair was his folly. She would prepare the feast and serve it, and no one would be able to say a word against her work. Beyond that, she was not responsible for anything that might happen. In fact, she almost hoped something dreadful did happen. Adam deserved it, and perhaps a disaster would bring him to his senses, make him see that he could not keep the Creature here.

Grammar stopped writing to give that possibility her full consideration. The more she thought, the more convinced she became that social embarrassment might be the solution. Adam was so conscious of appearances. What better occasion for a catastrophe than a Twelfth Night Banquet? Why should she not help the worst, and therefore from her own perspective, the best, to happen? She had charge over the Twelfth Night cake. It would not be impossible to arrange that the Creature find the bean, and if she could make the Creature understand the power of a Twelfth Night Queen to command. . . . Half-frightened of her daring and half-pleased, Grammar went back to her list with renewed interest.

When the list was finished, it was five pages long. Grammar folded it and put it in her apron pocket. Then, since it was not yet time to start the vegetables for dinner, she decided to go to the good china closet to count plates and cups and silverware to make sure that she had enough. Rattling her keys, she left the kitchen and entered the dining room. By the light of the long window, she searched among her keys for the key that opened the china closet. The dozen or so keys, which she knew by touch as well as sight, did not feel right to her. She paused in her search and stared at the keys lying in her hand. Then she knew what was wrong: the key that opened the gate was gone.

Frantically she tried to remember the last time she had seen it, but, because she could lock the doors on the inside without them, she had not used her keys in days. She almost never opened the gate; she had no reason to, and it was difficult to push open by hand. The last time she had opened it herself had been to let in the repairman who had come in the autumn. But surely the key had not been missing all that time or she would have noticed before now.

The truth quickly became apparent to her: someone had stolen the key, and she knew who it was. Whose movements were more stealthy and cat-like than the Creature's? Who had stronger motivation? Grammar stood still for a moment, rigid with fear and fury. Here she had been planning to help the Creature and the Creature had gone behind her back. She had stolen the key and she intended to steal the children. But she wasn't going to get away with it, not while Grammar had breath and blood and bones.

Glancing out the window, Grammar saw that the gate was still closed. They could not have left already in broad daylight. No doubt they meant to wait for nightfall. Grammar had time. She would find the children and lock them in their rooms. Then she would hunt down the Creature and tear the key out of her. Once she had the key in her possession, she would let the Creature out herself, on the condition that she never come back, never, never come near the children again.

"Ionia!" she shouted, making for the hall. "Fred!"

As Grammar climbed the stairs, Ionia and Fred heard her calling their names. They blew out the candle and held their breaths. When they were sure she had gone down the hall to search the attic, they crept out of the council chamber into their rooms. Meeting in the hall, they paused for a moment to make sure the coast was clear; then they ran down the stairs and burst into the living room, where they found their mother sitting cross-legged beneath the Christmas tree. To their joy, she smiled when she saw them.

"We're going to help," they said breathlessly as they tumbled down beside her. "We have a plan."

"So have I," she said.

The three bent their heads together and began to whisper.

It was just so that Grammar discovered them after her fruitless search of the attic. It seemed she had not come a moment too soon. The children were wearing their outdoor clothes, and they were so absorbed in their plotting that they didn't notice her presence. Grammar waited until she had caught her breath and gained command of herself before she spoke.

"Give me the key," she said.

The conspirators looked up. Fred and Ionia looked guilty. The Creature only looked puzzled.

"What key, Ursula?" asked the Creature. "We have not even taken it from you yet."

Both the children and Grammar were startled by this answer. The Creature seemed to have no conception of what stealing meant.

"What are you talking about?" asked Grammar sharply. "I know you have my key. Give it back at once."

"We don't have the key, Grammar," said Ionia.

"We were going to steal it," admitted Fred, "but we didn't know where you keep it at night when. . . ."

"Fred!" Ionia cut him short.

"Stop all this nonsense," said Grammar. "The key to the front gate is missing. One of you has it. You, Lilith, give me the key, and I will let you out myself, but you will not steal my children. If you don't give me the key now, I shall be forced to tell Adam."

For a moment no one spoke. Then Lilith rose from the floor and approached Grammar.

"I do not have the key, Ursula, and neither do the children."

Grammar remained silent, unconvinced.

"Do you not understand, Ursula? We are all prisoners here."

Before Grammar could register the meaning of Lilith's words, she heard Adam's voice behind her, and she saw the Creature stiffen.

"I hate to disturb this intimate family gathering, but I need to consult with my wife about her clothes for the banquet. Come, Lilith."

To Grammar's surprise, the Creature did not resist. Instead she bowed her head and followed him, leaving Grammar alone with the children.

17

Backstage

AT the dawn of Twelfth Night Day, Grammar rose and crept downstairs. She wanted to wash and wax the hall and dining room floors before the children got out of bed and underfoot. She had been unable to wax them yesterday because Adam had been arranging and rearranging the tables in order to discover how best to accommodate his guests.

First, he had tried to fit all three of the tables into the hall, but the effect had been to make them seem cramped. He would not listen to her when she pointed out that he could manage with only two tables if he had the guests seated all around them. He insisted on having three tables pushed together so that they formed an open-ended square with the guests seated only on the outside. His solution had been to arrange them around the entrance of the dining room to the hall, with the sliding doors open as wide as possible so that the dining room and the hall formed a more or less continuous space. Musicians would sit on the railed landing above the hall, and the guests would dance in and out of the dining room.

At the end of the hall nearest the living room, Grammar began her own dance with the mop. Glancing under the Christmas tree as she leaned forward and back taking a small step with each stroke, Grammar was relieved to see that the Creature was not sleeping there. She need not worry about waking her or watching to make sure that the Creature did not step on the newly waxed floor. Yet the idea of where the Creature was sleeping made her uncomfortable. Ever since the cleaning and combing process had begun, Adam had taken the Creature to bed; or so Grammar assumed. She supposed it was legitimate since, technically, they were married, but she did not like to think about it. It seemed somehow a violation, although she could not have said of what; nor did she try. Dismissing that thought and all others, Grammar abandoned herself to the dance.

When Eva Brooke entered the hall a few hours later, she found the hall transformed. Everywhere were evergreen boughs and vines bright with berries. The floor, which she had never noticed before, had a shine that made it look like black ice. The hall, perhaps because the greenery obscured its boundaries, seemed larger than she remembered. She felt as though she had walked into a winter forest or at least a stage-setting for one. She might have guessed that any entertainment Adam Underwood offered would be lavish, theatrical, but Adam had never given a banquet before. This party had no precedent, and nothing he had said had prepared her for this whole other world she had stepped inside.

Then Eva saw Lilith, whom she had failed to notice at first. In the far corner of the hall, Lilith stood poised on a step ladder. Her arms reached as high as they could, and her whole body was one suspended stretch, except for her hands, which moved as if with independent life as they wound a vine around a bough.

So Adam was not responsible for these decorations. It was Lilith who had arranged the vines and boughs so that they looked as if they had grown there of their own accord. Fascinated, Eva forgot herself and watched the deftness of the hands and the balance of the body whose very stillness seemed a dance.

A blast of cold air coming from behind her recalled Eva to herself. A moment later Adam stood beside her.

"Well, how do you like it?" he inquired.

"Adam," she said, "it's magical."

"Yes," he agreed. "That's the intended effect. My wife is quite skillful, don't you think?"

"More than skillful," Eva said.

But Adam was not listening anymore.

"Lilith," he called, "come and greet Eva Brooke who has been kind enough to bring you the gown and shoes you will wear."

Lilith continued to twist the vine as though she had not heard. When she was done, she turned towards them and, without warning, leapt from the ladder, landing on her feet as softly as a cat. As she made her way across the hall, Eva studied her, aware that something was wrong, or, at any rate, different about Lilith. It was not only the shift she wore, nor that her hair was combed and her legs clean. The very way she walked seemed awkward in contrast to the ease with which she had perched on the ladder. Though the grace was not altogether gone, something impeded it. She walked slowly and stiffly, as if she were self-conscious in the way a dog is when it's had its fur shaved. Her greeting, too, was guarded; no word or gesture, only a look that made Eva think of Ionia.

"Say thank you to Eva, Lilith."

Adam spoke to Lilith as if she were a child, Eva noted with some irritation. Then she rebuked herself. She also had thought of Lilith as a child. Yet today she reminded Eva more of an animal one would not dare pet for fear of being bitten.

"There is no need to thank me," said Eva. "It was no trouble to pick up the dress. I pass the costumer's on the way to the train."

She smiled at Lilith and held out the package. Lilith received it gingerly, as though it were something she were afraid to touch.

"Come, Lilith. We must have a fitting now in case any alterations need to be made. Eva, I expect you will find my mother in the kitchen. It is very good of you to come and be with her, especially since she has refused any hired help."

Smiling at Eva, Adam took Lilith by the arm and led her to the stairs.

Eva remained for a moment looking after them and wishing she knew what she felt: about Lilith, about Adam and Lilith, about herself in relation to them. What was she doing here? Helping Mrs. Underwood prepare the feast was the ostensible reason. But why was she doing that? Since she did not know the answer, she dismissed the question and turned towards the kitchen, telling herself that she ought to be glad to be here, a friend of the family, not merely a guest, not a member of the audience, but someone who belonged backstage.

Outdoors, Jason lingered by the gate wondering why it was closed today when it had been open on Christmas. Even more, he wanted to know how Professor Underwood operated those gates. He guessed there might be some remote control device, but he had examined the instrument panel of the car and discovered nothing there. He supposed the Professor might keep the device somewhere on his person, but if he did, he used it discreetly. He toyed with the idea that the Professor might use mind control, but he rejected that solution as being too unscientific. If only he could take the lock apart, he might understand how it worked. There was little he could discern by peering into the keyhole. Come to think of it, why should there even be a keyhole if no key was needed to open the gate? None of these questions could be answered without further investigation. Finally, compelled by cold and curiosity, he headed towards the house, averting his eyes from the snow woman who stood, solid and undiminished, dominating the yard.

Inside the hall, Jason paused and stared at the artificial forest. Though the craftsmanship was impressive, Jason was not impressed. He considered it as silly to pretend that a hall is a forest as to make believe that a forest is a hall. But then he had suspected all along that this banquet would be silly; or at least he had since he had seen his mother's evening gown: a lot of grownups playing dress-up. He had debated not coming, but his mother had insisted on hiring a baby-sitter if he didn't. The banquet seemed the lesser of two evils.

Besides, he was here not as a participant but as an observer. He and Ionia and Fred could amuse themselves by making fun of the grownups, that is, if they were still on speaking terms. About that he felt apprehensive.

Glancing towards the dining room, he saw Ionia and Fred apparently setting tables. When he had made sure there were no mothers around, his own or theirs, he sauntered towards them, attempting to think of something friendly but sufficiently sarcastic to say, so that they would know he had not been intimidated.

"Hello, Jason," said Ionia, looking up when Jason entered the dining room.

"Hello," he said.

Surprised by her greeting, Jason found that he had nothing at all to say.

"Jason, we're setting tables," Fred announced.

"So I see," said Jason. "And you're doing it wrong. Look, Fred, the knife and the spoons go on the right and the forks go on the left."

Fred looked puzzled. Grammar had marked his hands with an R and an L, but he had forgotten what they meant.

"Oh," said Fred. "But, Jason, I want the forks and the spoons to be together."

"They can't be," insisted Jason.

"How come?"

"Because if you arranged the silverware any differently than they're used to, the grown-ups wouldn't know what to do. They probably wouldn't be able to eat."

Ionia laughed. Jason was startled. He had never made Ionia laugh before.

Fred laughed, too. Pleased with himself, Jason began to correct Fred's settings.

"Ionia," said Fred, "Jason's helping me. "

Ionia glanced at Jason and almost smiled to see him arranging the silverware with mathematical precision. It occurred to her that Jason might be able to help with the secret plan, which she was not at all sure could work the way they had it set up now. Yet how could she trust Jason enough to let him in on it?

"Ionia," said Jason, interrupting her thoughts, "I was just curious: how does your father operate those gates? By remote control?"

"I don't know," she answered.

"Magic," said Fred.

"That's impossible. There's no such thing as magic. There's got to be some scientific explanation."

"I wish I knew what it was," sighed Ionia before she realized that she might be revealing something.

Jason looked at her sharply.

"Why?" he asked.

"Oh, just curiosity, like you."

Jason did not believe her. Ionia had never before evinced the slightest scientific curiosity in anything. Something was up, and he meant to find out what it was.

"Ionia," said Jason, making his voice sound as casual as possible, "why is the gate sometimes opened and sometimes closed?"

"What do you mean?" she asked guardedly. "It's always closed."

"It was open on Christmas," Jason reminded her.

"It's because of my mother," said Fred.

"Fred," warned Ionia.

Jason heard the warning in her voice and realized that he was on to something. "What do you mean because of your mother, Fred?"

Puzzled, Fred looked at Ionia, but she gave him no sign, so he blundered on. "So she can't get out. My father doesn't want her to."

Jason began to grow excited.

"Do you mean you father is holding your mother prisoner? Is that true, Ionia?"

"Keep your voice down, Jason," said Ionia, as she took a longer time than she needed folding a napkin.

Then she looked up, looked at him directly for perhaps the first time "Yes, it is true."

"And, Jason," said Fred, eager to include him, "we have a secret plan. We're going to. . . ."

"Fred!" Ionia silenced him.

"But, can't we tell Jason?" Fred appealed.

"No."

"How come?"

"Yes, how come, Ionia?" said Jason. "It's hardly fair to start to tell a secret and then stop."

"It's not my fault Fred doesn't know how to keep his mouth shut."

"But, Ionia, how come we can't tell him? Maybe he could help."

"Because we can't trust him. That's how come. Now keep quiet."

Bewildered, hurt, Fred looked from Ionia to Jason. Then, sadly, he went back to setting silver backwards. Jason followed him around the table, methodically correcting each setting, considering what his next move should be. It would be easy enough, he knew, to get Fred to spill the secret plan. Too easy, in fact. Any bully could do it. The difficult thing was to win Ionia's trust. He had no idea how to go about it. When he had finished Fred's table, he approached hers at the opposite side of the room. Fred followed him.

"Ionia," he began, "why don't you trust me?"

"Why should I trust you?"

Jason blushed. It was all those times he had teased her. She was holding those against him; he was sure.

"I've apologized to you twice," he reminded her. "I'll apologize again if it makes any difference."

"What makes you want to know so badly?"

Jason almost said he was curious, but he realized in time that that would be the wrong answer.

"Well, as Fred says, I might be able to help."

"Yeah, Ionia," Fred said, glad to be included in the conversation. "We could try it out on Jason first to see if it works."

Jason bit his lip to keep from saying: if what works?

"Why do you want to help us, Jason?" asked Ionia, looking up at him again. "You don't care about my mother."

"Listen, Ionia," said Jason, forcing himself to sustain her gaze, "I may not love your mother. I mean, I don't even know her, but I'm not on your father's side, I can assure you of that."

Ionia scrutinized Jason. His face was a deep red, and Ionia realized that he was embarrassed. To her surprise, Ionia found that she wanted to trust him, not only because she needed help, but for his own sake. Still, she was not sure she dared.

"It is not enough for you not to be on my father's side. You have to be on our side."

Now Jason hesitated. No one had asked for his allegiance before; nor had he ever given it. He had made decisions based on what would be to his advantage. It would be to his advantage now to offer Ionia his allegiance; he would find out the secret plan. Yet, if he gave his allegiance, he felt that he would have to mean it or come to mean it. There would be no going back on it. Suddenly, the whole matter seemed more serious than it had a few minutes ago. He did not know the nature of the secret plan. He might be getting himself into something he couldn't get out of for the sake of a woman he didn't even like. Yet, here was his chance to prove to Ionia that he was not a coward.

"I am on your side, Ionia," he said at last. "I want to help."

Ionia searched Jason's face for signs of falsehood. Jason had always been her enemy; it was hard to imagine an alliance with him. Yet, if she didn't take the chance, if she didn't trust him. . . .

"Fred," she said, "run and get the fishing rod and tackle box and a blanket. We'll test the plan right away, so if it doesn't work, we can think of something else."

Overjoyed that Jason was to be included, Fred bounced away. Lion, who had been asleep under one of the tables, woke and raced after him. When Fred returned with the equipment, which he and Ionia had fished from the attic and hidden in his closet, he found Jason and Ionia sitting at the bottom of the hall stairs, their heads bent over a napkin on which Jason was drawing a revised version of the secret plan.

"We won't need that rod, Fred," said Jason. "But leave me the tackle box and all the line. We're going to build a pulley and lower the hook from the chandelier. After you put the rod away, go stand watch by your father's door, near enough so you can hear, but not near enough so that he can see you if he steps out. If he even opens the door, run here as fast as you can and warn us."

"But, Jason," protested Fred, "I want to help build the pulley."

"No," said Jason shortly, "Someone's got to stand on the ladder, and Ionia's taller. "

"Besides, Fred," consoled Ionia, "keeping watch is the most important part. You know what happens if we're caught."

"The dungeon?" whispered Fred.

"No doubt," said Jason. "Here. Take this knife." Jason took a knife out of the tackle box. "I've got my own. You might need it. Remember, don't make a sound."

Satisfied that his part was sufficiently heroic, Fred tiptoed up the stairs, turning every few steps to signal Lion to be quiet.

"What about your grandmother, Ionia?" asked Jason as they set to work. "Whose side is she on? She doesn't know anything about this, does she?"

"She knows we're up to something, but she doesn't know what. She wants to get rid of my mother, so she's making sure my mother gets the Twelfth Night bean. She doesn't know what's going to happen after that. She says she doesn't want to know."

At dusk, Grammar and Eva sat down at the kitchen table to rest and drink a cup of tea. All day long they had labored. Now the roasts and casseroles that were to be served hot were safely in the oven. Other dishes simmered on top of the stove. Cold meats and salads crowded each other in the refrigerator. Baskets of bread and platters of fruit and cheese were already arranged on the tables. A whole vat of wine sat on the kitchen counter, and on the table, where Grammar and Eva could admire it while they sipped their tea, was the Twelfth Night cake, decorated with chess pieces made of marchpane.

"I never could have done this without you, Mrs. Brooke," said Grammar. "I want you to know I'm grateful for your help, though I don't understand why you offered it under the circumstances."

"Oh, I'm glad to help," said Eva lightly. "I always enjoy the preparations for parties more than the parties themselves."

"Well, I'll be glad when this one is over, I can tell you that."

"Yes," sympathized Eva, "you must be worn out. I'd be glad to stay and help you clean up afterwards, Mrs. Underwood."

"You've done enough, Mrs. Brooke," said Grammar firmly. "It's not only myself I'm thinking of; it's Adam. He's pushing his luck, don't you agree?"

"How do you mean?" asked Eva guardedly.

"You must have noticed that my," Grammar paused, "my daughter-in-law is lacking in certain social graces."

"Perhaps she is not quite used to people," Eva admitted, "but I suppose it is only natural for Adam to want to celebrate the return of his wife. What does it matter if she doesn't know the correct things to do or say? Some people may find that refreshing. And if Adam doesn't mind, why should they?"

Grammar sighed. All day she had been dropping hints as to how matters really stood between Adam and Lilith, but Mrs. Brooke refused to pick them up. She resisted all criticism, open or implied, of Adam, all suggestions that the Creature was other than a little unusual. Mrs. Brooke's innocence irritated Grammar more than the Creature's, because it seemed willful, false. Perhaps it was not innocence at all—Mrs. Brooke could not be as stupid as she pretended to be—but rather loyalty to Adam, misguided loyalty, in Grammar's opinion. She was disappointed in Mrs. Brooke. In Mrs. Brooke she had hoped to find an ally, an accomplice, someone to share the responsibility for the dubious action she meant to take, but, at last, Grammar accepted that she would have to act alone.

"You had better go bathe and change your clothes," said Grammar. "I hope the bathtub is clean. My daughter-in-law has had so many baths this week, I am surprised she has not dissolved altogether."

"What about you, Mrs. Underwood? Wouldn't you like a bath first?"

"Oh, I am not changing for the party. I'll put on a clean apron. That's all. I'm not a guest; I only work here."

Mrs. Brooke looked shocked at last.

"If you are not going to be with the guests, then I'm not either."

Grammar was touched, but she shook her head.

"Adam would be offended if you were not among the guests," she pointed out, "and embarrassed. His colleagues are your colleagues, too. Think how it would look if you were waiting tables at a dinner party given in honor of his wife."

Eva blushed.

"But you are his mother," she said. "And who will help you carry things back and forth?"

"They don't know I'm his mother, and I don't mind pretending I'm not. Sometimes I'm none too proud of the connection."

Again, Eva looked shocked.

"And the children are quite capable of clearing the table," she concluded. "So run along and make yourself beautiful."

When Eva Brooke had passed through the dining room, into the hall, and out of sight, Grammar reached into her apron pocket for the small, hard bean she had only pretended to mix into the batter. Checking once again to make sure no one was looking, she lifted one particular pawn and buried the bean in the cake beneath it. When she replaced the pawn, there was no evidence of her handiwork. No one would suspect what she had done. It was not getting caught that worried her. She knew that rigging a Twelfth Night cake was questionable from a moral point of view, her own point of view. But the deed was done; she would not undo it, though she could not predict the consequences of her action. She would take them, whatever they were. To calm her nerves and to quiet her conscience, Grammar emptied her teacup and made her way to the wine vat.

Upstairs in the tower room, Adam Underwood put the final touches on Lilith. He had chosen the tower room rather than his bedroom as a dressing chamber because of its remoteness. Here his concentration would be unbroken by the comings and goings of others, and no one would dare disturb him, not even his mother. The tower room had no electricity, but he was accustomed to working by candlelight, and by candlelight, Lilith would appear before the guests.

To make space, Adam had moved his desk out of the room onto the landing. Lilith, sometimes sitting on a stool, sometimes standing, occupied the center of the room. Against the walls, he had propped four full-length mirrors, one before her, one behind her, and one on either side, so that he could see her at once from several angles as she would be seen that night by his guests. On either side of each mirror burned candles, giving the mirror the aspect of an altar. As Adam labored over Lilith, he worshipped the image that he created.

A woman wearing a dark purple dress held still in the mirror. If her eyes had been raised, their proximity in color to the color of the dress would have been startling, but they were cast down, and the smooth lids gave the effect of stone. The dress, made of velvet, clung to the woman's body until just above her hips. There it fell away in folds, hinting a fullness only revealed by motion. The woman's feet were as yet bare, and her black hair still coarse and thick after interminable combings, tumbled down her back below her waist.

The man, having examined the woman from all sides, came to stand behind her. His body framed hers in the mirror. As if to smooth her dress, he slipped his hands beneath her arms and ran his hands over her breasts and down the front of her body. Except that he could feel her warmth, he might have touched stone. The image in the mirror gave no response, no indication of sensate life. Yet she was pliable. Increasing the pressure of his hand around her waist, he caused her to sit. Then he picked up a brush and some ebony pins and began to dress her hair. Higher and higher it rose as he gathered coil after coil and wrapped it around her head. The loose strands that refused to be incorporated he wet with his own spit and fashioned into deliberate curls. Satisfied that each hair was in harmony with every other, he bent and picked up a box that lay at her feet. From it he withdrew a silver diadem, which he placed at the base of the construction. From the same box, he took a black diamond necklace that lay, when he had fastened it, against her bare skin. Finally, he knelt before her and fitted her feet into slippers woven of silver thread. He was finished; she was complete.

Adam stood up and left Lilith sitting on the stool while he fetched from behind the door the cape he would wear, a black velvet cape, lined with purple silk. Donning the cape, he came to stand beside her. With one hand he raised her.

"Look," he commanded.

Lilith lifted her eyes; like an animal, she showed no recognition of her image. But when their eyes met in the mirror, he felt her tremble. A trembling of his own answered hers. He let go her eyes and looked at himself, himself and her in the mirror. Their splendor among men and women could not be equaled. They were as gods. For this had he waited. This he had created.

"Come," he whispered. "It is time to go down and light the candles in the hall."

Letting go of her arm, he went to blow out the candles beside the mirrors. Then, searching for her in the dark, he found she had already left the room and was waiting for him on the landing beside the desk. He took her arm again, and together they went downstairs.

18

❦ Twelfth Night ❦

ALBERT Sharp, the train conductor, watched curiously as a company of uncommon passengers boarded the seven o'clock train to the Empty Land. If he was not mistaken, these passengers had something to do with the unprecedented midnight run a private party had requested. Ordinarily, only half a dozen regulars on their way home from work rode this train. They were eclipsed by the unknown travelers as pigeons might have been by birds of paradise. The ladies and gentlemen, boarding the train two by two as if it were an ark, appeared in elaborate evening dress. The women wore fur coats or stoles over heavy jewelry and flimsy gowns. Beneath the various capes and greatcoats of the men, Albert could see ruffled shirts and tails. Yet, in spite of the brilliant costumes, the actors, on closer inspection, appeared to be ordinary middle-aged men and women. As they filled the seats, murmuring together in low voices as though they were in a theatre waiting for curtain rise rather than on a one car commuter train, they looked, in Albert's opinion, more silly than splendid.

Amused, Albert surveyed the coach and tried to single out the individual who would be most inclined to talk. Since he had to work the midnight run, he intended to find out what this business was all about. He was debating between a large woman in pink and diamonds, who kept turning in her seat and craning her neck, presumably to see who else was there and what they wore, and a hearty, red-faced man, who looked as though he had already begun to celebrate whatever was the occasion, when a young man dressed from head to toe in green, much of the expanse being taken up by green tights, dashed onto the train as though fearing he were late. Gasping for breath, he stood in the aisle gazing, dismayed, on the others in their formal attire. They looked back at him with cool recognition and obvious disapproval. The young man blushed, then searched for a seat and sat down, much abashed. Albert knew he had found his man.

The train began to move, and Albert made his way up the aisle towards the young man in green. The other passengers handed him their tickets without looking at him. They seemed partly embarrassed, partly defiant, as though they dared him to ask any questions. Robin Hood, as Albert had begun to think of the young man, was more deeply embarrassed that the others. He blushed again as he offered his ticket.

"I thought it was a costume party," he mumbled, as if in apology.

"Perhaps it is," said Albert. "Are you all going to the same party?" he asked, indicating the others with a nod. Then he winked and leaned closer to Robin Hood, "You don't look any more ridiculous than the rest of them do."

Encouraged, Robin Hood smiled.

"Yes, we are going to the same party," he said. "Or at least I think so."

Growing bolder, Robin Hood turned in his seat.

"Aren't all of you going to Professor Underwood's Twelfth Night banquet?" he addressed the company. "I thought it was supposed to be a costume party."

Relieved at having explained himself, Robin Hood sat back.

Then talk, confined before to couples, broke out among the company. To make themselves heard over the racket of the train, people raised themselves in their seats and shouted to one another like school children. Albert listened.

Isn't it strange, they all exclaimed. Yes, we got the invitation on the purple card, too. Who could pass it up, they agreed. It was an unprecedented event, a party given by Adam Underwood. No, no one had ever seen his house before, they concurred. He kept to himself pretty much, didn't he? No one really knew him, except Eva Brooke, maybe. And where was she, they wondered. Wasn't it odd that she should not be among the guests?

"Oh, that's easily explained," said the woman in pink and diamonds. "The party is being given by Professor and Mrs. Underwood."

"I never knew he had a wife," commented one man.

"It seems he hasn't until recently," said another woman.

"No, he's had one all along," corrected a man. "I heard she's been mentally ill, though. Perhaps she's been released from the hospital."

Insanity had always been Esther's theory.

"No," protested a woman, "I heard she left him for another man."

A rumor Esther refused to credit.

"Well, if she did, she's back now," said the red-faced man. "And we'll all have a chance to see her and decide for ourselves whether it was insanity or infidelity. There's something else that puzzles me more. That is all this business about `take the seven o'clock train and transportation will be provided at the station.' Why couldn't he have included a map with the invitation and let us find our own way?"

"Who knows?" said someone. "Maybe there isn't a banquet after all. Maybe he's making fools of us."

"He'd better not be," said the red-faced man.

"He wouldn't," said a woman. "There must be a reason why he wanted to do it this way. Perhaps he was afraid we might take a wrong turn and get lost in the Empty Land."

"Most likely he wants to show off," said Pink and Diamonds' husband. "Transportation probably means a flying carpet."

"That's right," agreed another man. "Alchemists can do anything."

"Maybe he's transformed Eva Brooke into Mrs. Underwood. Maybe that's the secret to the whole affair."

"Impossible," said Pink and Diamonds.

"Well, we're in for an adventure. That's for sure," said Robin Hood.

After that, conversation lapsed into companionable silence. Each person felt closer to all the others, even the ones whom he disliked. They were journeying together towards an unknown end. It made them comrades.

Albert wished that he might share this adventure. When he considered, he didn't see why he shouldn't. The guests did not appear to be friends of Professor Underwood or even to like him very much. They were attending the party out of curiosity. Albert was curious, too. He saw no reason why his curiosity should not be satisfied, especially since he had nothing to do after this run until the run back to town at midnight. Resolved, Albert went to ask the engineer if he would mind calling Esther to tell her he would not be home for supper. Then he returned to the passenger car and sat down beside Robin Hood to make friends.

At the station, no magic carpet awaited the guests. They huddled together on the platform and peered anxiously into the night. Most of them had never traveled to the edge of the Empty Land, and they did not like the look of it. The unrelieved darkness of the land made them uneasy, and some of them wondered whether the old stories about the Empty Land might not be true—a thought that would have been pleasantly exciting had they been sitting before their own fireplaces but was decidedly unpleasant now as they shivered in their evening clothes, feeling as though they had been transported to the dark side of the moon.

Just as the plaintive murmurs and the indignant mutterings were beginning, a bus pulled into the deserted parking lot.

"Hardly a magic carpet," someone commented.

Everyone laughed nervously and then, in silence, they filed towards the bus. Professor Underwood was not the driver. No one had thought he would be, but they wished the driver would at least say something to reassure them. Instead he only nodded curtly in answer to their questions. When they had all boarded the bus, the driver left the parking lot and took the narrow, unlighted road that none of them knew. It crossed more than one mind that Professor Underwood was kidnapping the whole company. More than one person accused himself of being a fool for having played into Underwood's hands. More than one told himself that he had suspected all along that Professor Underwood, though brilliant, was mentally unsound.

When the bus crested the last hill and the passengers were able to see the lights of a large house, a breath of collective relief filled the bus, and everyone began to talk at once.

"That must be it."

"It's like a small-scale castle."

"Yes, it has a wall around it, hasn't it?"

"Why would anyone need a wall in the middle of nowhere?"

"To keep the banshees at bay, I expect."

"I wonder if there's a moat around it, too."

"With crocodiles, I hope."

As the bus descended the hill, the lights disappeared behind the wall, and the passengers fell silent once again. The closer they came, the higher the wall appeared to be. The bus rounded a bend, and there was a gate swinging open as if of its own accord. The bus was barely inside when the gates swung shut again. A few guests glanced nervously over their shoulders and wondered if the gate had locked behind them, but a mood of anticipation predominated. The evening was before them. The house was alight with candles and the path leading to the door was strewn with pine boughs and lit with torches. As soon as the first guest was out of the bus, the door to the house was flung wide. There, framed by the light inside, stood Professor Underwood and the woman who must be his wife.

It was then that Albert quailed. On the train it had been easy enough to make fun of the guests' finery. Their clothing and their surroundings had seemed so comically incongruous. Here, as they processed up the path to greet that imposing pair, their dress, however ridiculous it looked in other lights, was only appropriate. It was he, Albert, who was absurd, his presumption that was out of place. Turning to Robin Hood, who walked beside him at the rear of the procession, clutching his arm as though they were yet another couple, he said: "Look, friend, I've made a mistake. I've got no business going through that front door. I'm going round to the back to see if I can wait it out in the kitchen."

"No," said Robin Hood, and he tightened his grip on Albert's arm. "You can't do that. You've got to come with me. I'm the only junior faculty member here."

Albert thought of pointing out that he was not any kind of a faculty member, only a train conductor, but he saw that Robin Hood was in no condition to listen to reason. Besides, when he turned his head to look for the back door, he caught sight of an enormous, ghostly figure. Though he realized after a few moments that it was made of snow, it gave him second thoughts about prowling around the grounds. No doubt Professor Underwood would direct him to the kitchen himself. Albert sighed and resigned himself to his humiliation.

As he and Robin Hood drew near enough the door so that he could observe his host and hostess in some detail, Albert forgot his social embarrassment in fascination. Professor Underwood, though intimidating, was no surprise to Albert. His costume this evening was a little more elaborate than usual, but no matter what Underwood wore, he always appeared dressed to the teeth, armor-plated, impeccable. It was the smile Albert had never seen before, and he decided at once that he did not like it; perhaps because it was restricted to his mouth; the rest of his face did not participate. It was an alligator smile, full of teeth, but Albert had no time to waste counting them. He would much rather look at Underwood's wife.

Now there was a woman! Not your store-bought variety or your home-grown either. Albert could tell at a glance that this woman was different from all the other women at the party. The other women seemed dominated by their clothes. It was the dress one saw, not the body, the necklace one noticed, not the neck. The hair was lost in the hairstyle, and the face in the makeup. This woman seemed barely contained by her clothes, heavy and ornate as they were. Even in her stillness, she seemed impatient of them, as though at any moment she might shake them from her, as a horse, with a sweep of its tail, rids itself of flies. An image of the woman naked filled Albert's mind, and he let it remain. It was not a lustful image but a respectful one.

Presently, Albert and Robin Hood were near enough to overhear the exchange between host and guests. Albert strained his ears to listen.

"Mr. and Mrs. Bates," Professor Underwood addressed the Pink and Diamonds'. "I am delighted you could come. Allow me to present my wife, Lilith Underwood. Lilith, welcome our guests, Mr. and Mrs. Bates."

"Mr. and Mrs. Bates," the woman repeated, "I am delighted to meet you."

It struck Albert that her voice was like the voice of a child who is reciting something without understanding the meaning of the words.

"But Mrs. Bates," the woman continued, "I do not understand."

Suddenly, her voice came to life, and Albert's skin turned to goose flesh.

"Why are you and all the other human women wearing dead animals?"

Albert almost applauded.

"The woman's got spirit," he whispered to Robin Hood, who looked, if possible, even more frightened than before.

Mrs. Bates gasped, and her husband drew her quickly away, while Underwood turned a look on his wife that would have made Albert quake. She, however, stared boldly back at him. Though she made no more remarks to the women themselves, Albert thought he heard her murmuring under her breath "dead mink, dead bear, dead raccoon," as each woman passed by her into the hall.

At last came Albert and Robin Hood's turn to be presented. Professor Underwood was so taken aback by their appearance that he forgot to be civil and glared at them. But the woman—Albert could not bring himself to think of her as Underwood's wife, though one look at her astonishing eyes assured him she must be the little girl's mother—beamed at them.

"I like these two best," she announced. "Are both of you human men or is one of you a human woman?"

"Cer-certainly not," stammered Robin Hood.

"Oh, it's you, Sherwood," said the professor at last. "I didn't recognize you in that costume. Who is the man you've brought with you, and why is he dressed like a train conductor?"

Before Albert or Sherwood could answer, another woman, who was in charge of taking coats, approached them. Albert recognized her as the kind woman with the nasty son, and he thought she looked very well in the plain, dark green dress she wore.

"I know this man," she said smiling at him. "And so should you, Adam. He is the train conductor. Isn't it fortunate he came along? Now we know the train will wait for the guests."

"Yes, ma'am," said Albert removing his hat. "That's exactly why I came, and also to keep Robin, I mean Sherwood, here, company. Old friends, Sherwood and I."

He patted Robin Hood reassuringly on the back.

"Well," deliberated the Professor, "I suppose he can go into the kitchen, along with the bus driver, and have something to eat."

"No," opposed Underwood's wife. "He will sit beside me at the feast."

Without awaiting Underwood's verdict, she took Albert and Sherwood by an arm each and swept them into the hall.

Since she had no more coats to put away, Eva stayed beside Adam while he closed the door. She guessed he might be angry, but except for a tightness about the mouth that suggested a frown, his face betrayed nothing of his feelings. Without seeming to notice her, Adam turned towards the hall. She watched his eyes following Lilith as she moved in time to the music, Sherwood and the train conductor in tow, in and around the clusters of guests who sipped champagne and murmured in hushed, uneasy tones. Eva felt an impulse to mediate between husband and wife, but she dared not yield to it. Instead, in a gesture meant to indicate affection and support, she took Adam's arm. Beneath the soft material of his shirt, she could feel how rigid it was.

Adam made no response to Eva's touch; he scarcely noticed it, absorbed as he was in considering what he ought to do about Lilith's insistence that the train conductor sit beside her at the banquet table. His inclination was to refuse her, but if he did, she might well make a scene. The passive creature of the past few days whom he had washed and combed and rehearsed had vanished. In its place was this insolent being. Part of him rejoiced: she had flung him a challenge, and the chase was on with all the heat and intensity of the old days; only now it took a different form. No longer was it a simple matter of pursuit and capture, but a subtle one of domination. In this match of will, everything was at stake: his reputation, his career. They were not alone in the Empty Land, but in his house, in the presence of his professional peers. The wisest course, for the moment, might be to appear to indulge his wife's whims.

"Eva," he said, noticing her presence now that he needed her, "go tell my mother to set another place and to rearrange the place cards. The train conductor will sit on Lilith's left."

The seating was not so easily managed, however. When the guests came to the table, the train conductor would not be parted from Sherwood. Lilith, who refused to relinquish the train conductor, loudly insisted that he have his way. So the two men sat beside one another at the center table, upsetting the order of heterosexual seating and offending everyone's idea of symmetry and propriety; for Sherwood was only a junior faculty member. At length everyone found a seat, whether he liked it or not, and the feast began with a toast.

"To my wife," said Professor Underwood, and he raised her to her feet, "in whose honor this banquet is given."

The guests, all except Professor and Mrs. Bates who had lost their seats to Sherwood and the train conductor, lifted their glasses. Albert, under the influence of more than champagne, cheered. Then there was silence while the guests waited for some signal to lower their glasses, but the woman remained standing until she had looked at each guest in turn. Under her gaze most of the guests felt uncomfortable, some affronted. Only a few returned it in full measure. At last the woman resumed her seat, and the feasting began in earnest.

The flickering candlelight gave the room an underwater atmosphere. Laughter and talk washed back and forth across the room. Music, soft and insinuating, drifted in from the hall, affecting the guests without their knowing it, intoxicating them like the wine that flowed freely. Soon the guests began to glow. Men and women reached for each other under the table, and everyone ate with his fingers. After awhile, the periodic singsong of Underwood's wife no longer disconcerted the guests.

Who will have some dead duck?

> *Who will eat a butchered cow?*
> *Who would like a murdered lamb?*
> *Who will eat a slaughtered sow?*

Some of them even shouted back, "Yes, we'll have some defunct duck. Send us a little of that debilitated beef." The cook, who had obviously been imbibing in the kitchen, joined the game, too.

"So you picked the bones of this dead pig," she hiccupped. "Vultures!"

Removing the platter, the cook swayed towards the kitchen, followed by a little boy and a big yellow dog who picked up whatever she dropped. Two older children were in charge of keeping the wine glasses full. One of them was plainly Underwood's daughter; for she had her mother's eyes. When she re-filled Albert's cup, he caught hold of her arm and informed her that she could do no better than to grow up and be exactly like her mother.

"Finest woman in the world, your mother. I'll drink another toast to her."

He drained his glass in time for the child to fill it again before she moved on.

Her Majesty, as Albert had begun to think of Underwood's wife, had been most attentive to him. He had told her all about his sculptured hedges and his flower garden, his cat, Priscilla, and his wife, Esther.

"Is she a human woman?" her Majesty wanted to know.

"Very," sighed Albert.

Eva Brooke, seated on Adam's right, tried again and again to engage him in conversation, but he resisted, responding only with a single word or a nod. He was too tense to lose himself in talk; for he sensed that the situation, which he had created, was getting out of his hand. His silence was an attempt to keep control of the whole company. He could not afford to focus on a particular person. So he watched, expanding his awareness until he was satisfied that not the least gesture or grimace escaped him.

After an hour or two of feasting, there came a lull. The guests had eaten and drunk themselves into a pleasant stupor. They lolled in their chairs or leaned forward to rest themselves against the table. The music from the hall was plainly audible now, soothing music that comforted aching stomachs and suggested sleep. Only Adam and Lilith remained upright in their chairs.

Because of the candlelight and because of the wine-muddled vision of most of the guests, the two dominating the center table no longer appeared as Professor Underwood and his wife. According to the historic or literary period in which each guest was expert, he altered the identity of his host and hostess. Before them the guests saw Arthur and Guinivere, Henry VIII and Anne Boleyn, Caesar and Cleopatra, Heloise and Abelard, Tristan and Iseult, Troilus and Cressida, Theseus and Hippolyta, Mars and Venus, Zeus and Hera. Just as the guests hovered, bleary-eyed, at the indecisive moment between waking and dreaming, they were roused by a loud, unmusical noise.

A moment later, the little boy, blaring a toy trumpet, and the dog entered the space surrounded by the tables. Following him was the cook, bearing what appeared to be an enormous chessboard. Behind the cook came the older boy and girl carrying plates. As they processed towards the center table, they sang between blasts on the trumpet:

> Twelfth Night cake, Twelfth Night cake.
> Who will find the Twelfth Night bean?
> Who will be the king or queen?

When she had placed what was apparently the Twelfth Night cake before the Underwoods, the cook steadied herself against the table and addressed Underwood's wife.

"My dear Mrs. Underwood, 'd you be so good as to cut over the presiding of the Twelfth Night cake?"

"I will," she said, and she picked up a knife.

Adam looked at his mother with distaste, for she was leaning against the table and making faces. As unobtrusively as he could, he motioned to her to go away, but she was in no condition to take subtle hints.

"Serve yourself and your husband first, my dear Mrs. Underwood. Then the children will carry the rest to the vultures."

Albert, who was looking on, urged her to cut herself a piece with a queen.

"No," she said. "Let Adam eat the queen. I will eat this pawn."

When the cake was cut and distributed among the guests, the cook began to sing her song again. Then taking a child by each hand, she did a drunken dance, still chanting:

> Twelfth Night cake, Twelfth Night cake,
> Who will find the Twelfth Night bean?
> Who will be the king or queen?

While the guests ate, they conferred: "I haven't found it, have you?" "No, I haven't, have you?" Suddenly they were all silenced by Adam Underwood's voice.

"Ladies and gentlemen of the court, behold your queen."

All the guests turned to look. There was the woman, standing alone and silent, not giggling or blushing or clowning as most of them would have been. They all sensed that the child's game had become serious. In her royalty there was reality. Even the ones who disliked her felt it. Some, if they had not feared ridicule, would have fallen to their knees. All stopped their titterings and fidgetings and became almost as still as she.

"Yours is to command, Queen," Adam reminded her.

"Oh, command me, your Majesty," pleaded Albert. "I'll do anything."

Her Majesty smiled at Albert and patted him on the head as if he were a dog.

"Your turn will come," she said softly. Then in a voice of queen-like volume, she addressed the court, "My first act as queen will be to make Adam King. My first command will be to ask the King to dance with me."

Eva caught a look of fierce joy on Adam's face as he rose to stand beside Lilith. For her it was an illumination. Suddenly she understood that though she had known this man for five years, she had known him only half alive. The Adam she knew was a shadow compared to this Adam with his flushed face and trembling hands. She had known the form of the man: here was the fire. For the first time, Eva felt jealous of Lilith; for the first time, she admitted desire.

"Musicians," the Queen cried, "give us music for the dance!"

All the guests sat up in their chairs and leaned forward eagerly as the King led the Queen to the floor. Their drunkenness had worn away, but the magic of the wine still worked on them. Or maybe they needed no more magic than the magic that moved before their eyes. Two more beautiful beings never danced together. So attuned were their bodies that they seemed not two but one magnificent creature, what man and woman were meant to be. Her skirt was a purple whirlwind at their feet. His cape billowed behind them like a cloud of smoke. The floor over which they danced shone like a night sky, reflecting the flames of the candles as stars. No longer were they King and Queen, but god and goddess of the night.

When they glided into the hall, the guests who sat at the side tables stood up and crowded near the entrance so that they could see. So entrancing was the dance that no one noticed the girl break away from the cook and make for the stairs, nor did they see the boys creep into a corner of the hall. Not one was aware of a hook being slowly lowered from the chandelier. So when the King's cape suddenly flew up into the air, like a huge black and purple bat, no one knew how it had happened. No one wondered. No one had any wonder to spare.

There, in the center of the hall, stood Professor Underwood, naked from the waist down, his pants and shorts lying in a puddle about his ankles. He stared down at them, unable to move. Beside him, the woman stood as still as he, with a dagger clutched in her hand. For an undetermined space of time, there was no sound, no motion in the hall, save for the gentle flapping of the cape caught in a draft.

Then the woman let out an animal cry, and the music began again, savage, blood-pumping music. With the dagger the woman slashed her dress and leaped out of it naked. Taking the dagger between her teeth, she tore off the crown and jewels, dashing them to the floor. Then she kicked off her shoes, sending them spinning across the room. Last, she loosed her wild black hair and began a frenzied dance that took her out of the hall into the dining room. In one bound she gained the table and continued her dance among the dishes so deftly that she shattered not a single one. In horror, the guests shrank back from her. All except Albert. He rose to his feet and stretched a hand towards her. Tossing the dagger aside, she gave a glad shout, and jumped down beside him.

"Come," she sang, "who will join me in a dance?"

Together she and Albert gathered the guests, compelling them to follow. When they had all joined hands, they danced into the hall.

Adam saw them coming and tried to yell, but though his mouth gaped open, no sound came out. He willed to move, but his legs would not obey. He had lost all control over action and reaction. He had passed from dream to nightmare as helplessly as one who sleeps. The dance surged towards him and surrounded him. He did not recognize the dancers, strangers with twisted faces. Round and round him they danced, blurred images of ugliness. For him they were all aspects of Lilith: Lilith with her naked body gleaming; Lilith with her black hair tumbling over some man's arm; Lilith with her animal exaltation; Lilith whose beauty had become ugliness itself. He looked at her and hated.

Then, suddenly, someone broke the circle and the dance ceased. Eva Brooke, clutching something in her arms and sobbing, stumbled towards him. Falling at his feet, she wrapped her arms around him, covering his nakedness with a blanket.

19
 The Morning After

EXCEPT for the rhythmic repetition of a solitary snore, no sound eased the silence of the dining room and the hall as the grey early light gave form to the devastation of the night. Chairs lay on their backs with their feet in the air as if they had fought one another to the death. Tabletops appeared as battlefields for regiments of glasses, silverware, plates, crumbs, bones, all crowded together in violent disorder. The evergreen boughs had turned brown overnight, and their needles fell to the floor, burying the evidence of scuff-marks and scrapes inflicted on the wax by frantic feet. On the bottom step where she had thought to rest just for a moment before she tried to climb the stairs, Grammar slept.

Upstairs in the tower room, Adam Underwood did not sleep. He had spent what remained of the night moving his valuable books and papers out of his study and into his mother's private parlor. If he could have carried his heavy desk by himself down the narrow stairs, he would have. As he could not, he pushed it back into the tower room. For perhaps the last time, he sat at his desk, now empty of its contents and barren of the objects that once cluttered its surface. In the morning light, his face looked grey, his skin slack. His eyes were like dead water, unmoving, stagnant, too dull to reflect the light.

Dully, he stared at her, asleep on the floor beneath the window where he had hurled her last night, knocking her unconscious. Over her he had thrown a blanket, not to keep her from the cold, but because he could not bear the sight of her body. It disgusted him; she disgusted him. For awhile he hoped he had killed her, but he had not. Beneath the blanket he could see her breathing softly as a baby. He supposed, if he wanted to, he could kill her now. He had the dagger in his pocket. He had thought to take possession of it before she could use it against him again. It was the dagger Eva had given him at Christmas, the dagger whose handle was carved in Her image. She had warned him of the danger. In her hand the dagger must have had magical powers or she could never have accomplished her work so easily. She must have taken it from his desk last night while he blew out the candles and hidden it in her gown. While his arms encircled her in the dance, she had slipped her hand between her breasts. Then, without missing a step, she had done her work so swiftly, so smoothly that the stroke of the blade had felt like a caress. He felt for the dagger now and imagined it gently, soundlessly slitting her throat.

Immortal, she could not die of natural causes, he knew, but she could be killed. Flesh and blood, she was vulnerable to the blade. While she had life that flesh would never decay, as his mother's had, as his own would. But if death came, if he should force death upon her, what then? Her flesh would be no better than anyone's, no better than his. She would rot with the rest. There was some satisfaction in that thought.

Yet, when he considered, he did not want her dead. Dead, the thing that was she, the thing that had always eluded him, even when he possessed her body, that thing would escape him forever. He would never know for certain whether she was or was not, whether he had touched what she was or not. Alive, he knew he could make her suffer, and he meant to. He could not escape the pain of his humiliation, so neither should she. He would make her pay for what she had done to him if it cost her all the days of her endless life. And it would. That was the price of the manhood she had undone.

But how had she accomplished it? How had she done this undoing? She who had no conception of shame, no recognition of nakedness? There was no doubt that she wanted to destroy him, but others must have told her how to do it. Others must have been involved, though he did not know to what extent. His mother had been too drunk to answer him coherently; Eva too hysterical. The guests, cowards that they were, afraid to act except in a crowd, had fled as soon as he had recovered his control. But he would find out who had engineered this disaster. It was too carefully planned, too obviously rigged to have been a spontaneous expression of her rage. There was a conspiracy against him; he would discover it and destroy it. Then those who had plotted against him would know that he was not defeated. Unmanned for a moment, he was still a man.

As the sun rose over the hill of the three trees, Adam's thoughts went round and round, relentlessly as a wheel of torture. With each revolution, the lids of his eyes grew heavier. When the white winter light grew unbearably bright, he covered his eyes to keep it out. Surrounded by his own darkness, Adam slumped over his desk and slept.

In his sleep, the circling thoughts became voices, the voices of a multitude murmuring against him. He stood at a podium in a lecture hall dressed in his evening clothes; only the crowd before him was far larger than any hall at the University could hold. It stretched out for miles and miles, like a sea, until it reached a horizon. Waves of sound rolled through the crowd and broke over him.

"Silence," he shouted over the roar. "Silence. I am about to begin."

All sound ceased; the crowd became motionless. He waited, savoring his power. In his own time, he would begin. Meanwhile, let them be still; let them be what he willed. Just as he was about to end the state of suspension he had imposed, something went wrong. The crowd stirred. Adam looked for the cause of the disturbance and found it: Sherwood, wearing that ridiculous costume, standing on a chair, making an ass of himself as usual. Before Adam could think what to do, Sherwood began to shout:

"It's all right! Don't be afraid! He's naked under his clothes! I saw him myself! He's as naked as the rest of us!"

Sherwood disappeared into the crowd, and the crowd began to murmur and move again as if it were not made up of many people but was one creature, a monster. The breath of the crowd blew towards him, strong as the wind. The murmuring rose and rose, no longer the voices of people speaking but the sounds of sobbing, singing, shouting, moaning, laughing, all the human sounds mingled in one inhuman noise.

Yet, he discovered that when he looked, he could distinguish individuals. There was his mother shouting. What was she doing here with all his students and colleagues? His colleagues: one by one, he recognized them. They were jeering at him, making primitive schoolboy gestures. There was Jason, Eva's boy, mimicking them. And Ionia and Fred, his own flesh, laughing, laughing at him. Then he saw Eva Brooke. At first he thought she was laughing, too, but then he saw the tears. She was weeping, as she had last night, yet, at the same time, smiling, too. He focused on Eva, and the rest of the crowd faded. Sound gave way to silence. There was only Eva, beckoning to him with her arms. Her lips were moving, too, as if she spoke, but he could not hear her. Suddenly, he realized that he wanted to hear very much. He decided to leave the stage and to go stand beside her so that he could hear what she was saying to him. But as soon as he took a step towards her, the rest of the crowd returned. He could see their grimacing faces; he could hear their disgusting noises. Among them, Eva still wept and smiled and beckoned.

"No," he whispered to her. "Never."

Then he lost Eva in the crowd. He could not see her face. The crowd itself became faceless; a vast formlessness rising like a sea to swallow him.

"No," he shouted. "Never!"

He turned to run from the stage, but his cape had grown long and heavy. It tripped him; it entangled him. Helpless, he lay on the floor, waiting for the wave to take him. It was black and huge. He could see it curling over him. Just before it broke, he woke, sweating with terror.

Confused, he looked about him. There was the tower room, bare of his books. There was the woman lying quietly on the floor. All at once, it seemed strange that she should be there. She seemed utterly unrelated to him: a creature from a nightmare brought to life, something that did not belong in the day time. He found it difficult, even when he looked at her, to believe in her existence. Yet there she was and there she would stay until she evaporated into the air or vanished by some magic other than his own. He would never let her go. That was one certainty, one fixed point in the chaos, and he clung to it.

Without looking at the woman again, Adam rose from his desk and left the room, locking the door behind him. Outside the door, he paused, wondering what to do next. It occurred to him that he was hungry; he had not eaten much at the banquet. Perhaps, if he ate, he might go to bed and sleep, really sleep, without dreaming. He needed rest. There was work to be done before the University opened next week. Taking care to silence his steps, Adam headed for the kitchen, barely resisting the impulse to kick his mother, who lay on the bottom step impeding his way.

As her father crossed the hall, Ionia woke. Sunlight poured through her round window and warmed the foot of her bed. She looked around her room amazed by the ordinariness of everything. She would have been less surprised if the house had tumbled down in the night. For a moment she wished it had. Shivering, she curled her body around the cold lump in her stomach, trying to melt it with her warmth. Maybe then she would go back to sleep. She wasn't ready to be awake yet.

Whether her eyes were opened or closed, Ionia could not escape the images of her father's nakedness and her mother's face, more naked in its cruelty than her body could ever be. Ionia could not sleep unless she could forget, and she could never do that. Never before had she known what it meant to do something that cannot be undone. Lying awake in the morning light that was like the light of other mornings, Ionia felt that she was different, changed forever from what she had been, so that she could not even remember what it had been like to be herself before. This feeling made her miserable, almost sick at her stomach. She wished she could go back to before, however bad it had been. At least she had not been wrong then. None of them had been, except her father. Now they all were. That was what was so awful. Worse than fear of her father or fear for her mother was her part in the thing that had happened last night.

As Ionia lay still, in dread of herself as much as of the unknown consequences of what she had done, it came to her that she must make a decision. She did not know what kind of decision, but she knew she could not stay in bed all day, and she couldn't go back to before: she couldn't daydream anymore. She must do something. That was how her life would be from now on: every day deciding what to do. The idea of a whole life of unending deeds and decisions weighed on her, and, in spite of her resolve to act, she pulled the covers over her head and wished again that she might not be at all.

"Ionia."

It was Fred's voice, muffled by the wall but plain enough.

"Ionia!"

Without needing to think what to do, Ionia got up and tiptoed down the hall to Fred's room. Opening the door, she saw Fred sitting up in bed and clinging to Lion.

"Ionia," he said. "I had a bad dream."

"What did you dream?" she asked, sitting down beside him.

Fred didn't answer, but his eyes widened as if he were seeing the dream again.

"Ionia," he asked after a few moments, "where is my mother?"

"I don't know," she said. "Stay here. I'm going to find out."

"I'm coming, too."

"No," she said.

She spoke with such authority that for a time Fred remained obedient.

As Ionia neared the landing, she could hear someone snoring. She stopped to gather courage and then went on. When she reached the stairs, she saw, to her relief, that the sleeper was Grammar, not one of the guests, or worse, her father. She wondered, for a moment, if she ought to wake Grammar and find out what she knew, but Ionia decided against it. She had never seen anyone drunk before, but that was what Grammar must have been last night. If Grammar remembered anything, she would not be pleased, and doubtless she would be angry when she discovered that she had slept in the hall with her clothes on and her hair undone. And when Grammar was angry, she was noisy.

Cautiously, Ionia tiptoed down the stairs. Since her legs were not long enough to allow her to step over Grammar, she leaped, landing almost soundlessly on her feet. When she had made sure that Grammar was still asleep, she crossed the hall into the dining room, where she went to look out the window. The gate was still closed. The snow woman stood melting in the sun. All was as it had been before the party. Ionia lingered at the window, not wanting to look at the mess behind her. Then a sound, coming from the kitchen, startled her. The coldness in her stomach spread out over her whole body, but she knew what she had to do. She made her way to the kitchen. In the doorway, she froze.

There was her father, with his back towards her, reaching for a glass from the cabinet. He did not see her as he turned around. Still unaware, he walked to the table where he poured some orange juice into the glass. It was when he lifted his glass to his lips that he saw her. Without drinking, he lowered the glass and stared at her.

No one had ever looked at Ionia that way before, with pure hatred, not even Jason. Jason had hated her, Ionia. But she sensed that who she was had nothing to do with this hatred of her father's. She was just there, in its way. She wanted to look away from him. She could feel the hate pouring into her through her eyes, poisoning her. But the longer she looked, the stronger the fascination she felt. That was how the poison worked. She was yielding to its effect, but something in her still resisted; it forced her to speak.

"Where is my mother?"

It worked; she felt the hold of his hatred lessen. She had become only Ionia again.

"How dare you spy on me," he said, setting his glass down and taking a step towards her.

"I wasn't spying," she said. "Where is my mother?"

"What part did you play last night? Who else is in the plot? Who told you what to do?" he asked advancing steadily.

"No one told me what to do. Where is my mother?"

"She-devil's whelp. Don't pretend innocence with me. Tell me what I want to know, and it will go easier for you."

He came closer. In a moment he would be close enough to lay hands on her.

"Where is my mother!" she shouted.

Suddenly he stopped and looked at her curiously as though he had never seen her before.

"You're a fearless little monster, aren't you? Where did you get that nerve?"

"Where is my mother?" she repeated.

All at once his body, which had been towering over her, slacked. Shrugging his shoulders, he turned away from her and walked back to the table. Picking up his orange juice, he drained half the glass. Then he looked at her again, this time without intent or intensity.

"You won't be seeing your mother again."

His voice was matter-of-fact, without emotion.

"Have you let her go?"

"I didn't say that, did I?"

His tone became menacing again.

"Then what have you done with her!" Ionia demanded.

Before he could answer or refuse to answer, Grammar entered the kitchen with Fred and Lion at her heels. When she saw Adam, she stopped short.

"Oh, there you are," she said in a voice that betrayed some embarrassment.

"Yes, here I am," mimicked Adam. "And why are you standing there gaping at me instead of crawling to me on your hands and knees begging my pardon. Consider yourself fortunate if I don't put you away in a home for your part in last night's performance. You've obviously lost what few senses you ever had."

"Now, Adam," protested Grammar, "if you're going to blame me. . . ."

"Whom am I to blame, Mother?" he asked. "I want to give credit where it's due. The plan was really ingenious. Tell me, Mother."

"Grammar's not to blame," said Ionia before Grammar could speak. "She didn't know what we were going to do."

"What you were going to do?" he repeated; he hadn't thought of the children as other than pawns in someone else's game. "You and who else?"

"Adam," said Grammar stepping between him and Ionia, "you are not to blame the children either. If you have anyone to blame, it is yourself for keeping that wild creature caged here. I'm sorry you got denuded, but I can't say I think it's any more than you deserve. I hope you've learned your lesson. Has she gone?"

Adam stared at his mother. He could hardly believe what he had heard. She spoke as though what had happened to him was no more serious than a spanking she might have given him as a child. Didn't she understand? His whole career had been put in jeopardy.

"Well," persisted Grammar, "did you let her go?"

"What I have done with her," he said slowly, looking at each one of them in turn, "is no one's business but my own. Is that understood? No one's business but my own."

"She's my mother!" shouted Fred, and he ran towards his father with his fists raised, but Grammar and Ionia caught him and held him back.

"Another little monster," said his father. "Soon I'll have to make cages for you all. Things have come to a pretty pass when a man can't even trust the members of his own family."

"What do you know about your family!" demanded Grammar. "When have you ever treated any of us as your family? She was more family to these children in twelve days than you've been in six years."

Grammar paused, shocked to hear herself defending the Creature.

"Anyway, it's not just your business. You've involved us whether we like it or not, and we have a right to know."

Before Adam could answer, a cry rang through the house and pierced its heart. A brief silence followed, and then a steady wailing.

"My mother," whispered Fred.

Both he and Ionia turned to run in search of the sound.

"Stop," their father commanded. "You won't find her. She's locked away where you can't get at her, and she can't get at me. Any attempts you make to help her will only hurt her. I promise you that."

The children turned to stare at their father."

Adam," gasped Grammar, "you must be mad. You can't lock her up like that. We can't live with that noise, not if we're human we can't."

"Don't worry, Mother. She'll wear herself out in a few hours, and you can forget that she ever existed. Now, if you will excuse me, until I can sleep, I have work to do. And so," he said glancing about the kitchen, then into the dining room, "have you."

Adam finished his orange juice and left the others to the restoration.

20
⚘ New Terms ⚘

AFTER school, on the first day of the new term, Jason waited in the usual place on the far side of the parking lot for Ionia and Fred to meet him; although he wasn't sure they were coming or even if they were alive. Since Twelfth Night, his imagination had been full of rat-infested dungeons and sophisticated torture devices, of which he had ventured to make a few sketches. On these racks of torture, he imagined Fred, and more often Ionia, contorted in pain.

It bothered Jason a bit that he was not sharing Fred and Ionia's sufferings and had only to endure his mother's coldness towards him. He consoled himself by considering that it was just as well that he was free since he could go and rescue them if need be. He would have gone already, but his mother had grounded him until school started. If Ionia and Fred did not show up today, he would go directly to the train station and take the first train to the Empty Land. Just how he intended to rescue them from near death was, as yet, a little vague, but he would think of something. He had to find out what had happened. The suspense was killing him.

While Jason waited for Ionia and Fred, Eva Brooke waited for Adam Underwood's lecture on "Alchemy as an Archetypal Symbol" to begin. She had come early to make sure of getting a seat, and she had found one fairly near the front. Quickly the seats around her were filled, some by members of the faculty who had been present at the Twelfth Night banquet. There were Bates and Beeferman, a few seats to her right, sitting together. She eyed them coldly, then turned her face away, resolving to ignore them if they spoke to her. Adam's mother was right; they were vultures, come to pick at the remains of a man's pride. But as long as she was there, they would never get near him. She would be at his side as soon as the lecture was over. Adam would know he had one true friend. Then the rest wouldn't matter.

But would he even appear at his lecture? That was what worried her. She had no way of knowing what had happened since that night. After she had brought him the blanket, he had mastered himself sufficiently to order the guests out of the house. She had begged to be allowed to stay, but he had sent her away, too, and she had received no word from him since. She only hoped that he had been able to work and to find relief in work as she had not. But then, her lectures did not matter so much; Adam's did. As always, at one of Adam's opening lectures, the hall swelled with people. Possibly the students had not heard the story yet. With luck they might never hear it. But if Adam failed to show up today, the rumors would be rampant. Or worse, if he did lecture, and something went wrong. . . .

Eva stopped herself. She could not bear to imagine anymore. She closed her eyes and tried to shut out the sound of the crowd. Over the noise, Eva heard the University clock strike two. Suddenly, the hall hushed. Eva opened her eyes to see Adam entering from the wings. Wild applause broke out as he crossed the stage with his head held high and his eyes glittering, dangerous. Dear God, he was beautiful. No vulture would dare come near this living man. Eva's eyes filled with tears. He mounted the podium and turned to face the people, silencing them with a glance. Eva's tears overflowed; unashamed, she let them fall. Adam surveyed the waiting crowd, his power undiminished, his command unbroken. Their eyes met. Sure that he recognized her, Eva smiled through her tears and nodded her head to encourage him.

All at once, Adam's face turned gray, and he gripped the podium. He looked as though he might faint or be sick. The crowd began to murmur. Just as Eva was about to get up from her seat and rush to help him, he appeared to recover himself. His color returned, and he stood up straight.

"Silence," he commanded in a voice that destroyed the least whisper. "I am going to begin."

A drop of sleet splattered on Jason's nose. He checked his watch again. They were now fifteen minutes late. Another drop of sleet landed on his neck. Since he had refused to wear the scarf his mother had pleaded with him to wear, the drop slithered down his back. Jason decided that he ought to go home before going rescuing. He would need supplies. It would be foolhardy to go armed with nothing and with nothing to eat. He would take what was left of those brownies and he would load his water pistol with ammonia. Then he would follow Ionia's father to the train, taking care to keep out of sight, of course. Somehow, at the Empty Land station, he would manage to hide in the back of Professor Underwood's car. That way he would make sure of getting through the gate. . . .

Jason was heading out of the parking lot when he saw Ionia walking towards him. For a moment their eyes met. Then Ionia lowered hers. Jason stopped to wait for her, and, with his right foot, he started drawing circles in the slush that was accumulating on the ground. Now that he had seen Ionia, he felt awkward, unsure of himself. He wished she were locked up. His plans for rescue had just been getting organized. Rescue would have been exciting. He didn't mind real danger. After all that had happened, he found the prospect of being alone with Ionia a bit unnerving. He had not seen her since she had signaled to him from the balcony. He wished Fred were with her. He had gotten used to having Fred as a buffer between himself and Ionia. But perhaps Fred was locked up. If he were, then he and Ionia could rescue Fred together. It would give them something to talk about. He had no idea of how to begin talking about what had happened on Twelfth Night.

In a moment another foot was beside Jason's drawing circles in the slush. Jason looked up, and there was Ionia.

"Where's Fred?" he asked.

"Home with a cold," she answered. "That's why I'm late. I had to get his workbooks from his teacher."

Jason and Ionia began to walk side by side, not speaking until they reached the park. It was deserted that day, and the silence of the park, unbroken except by the sound of sleet battering the frozen ground, made them conscious of the silence between them.

"Your mother, Ionia, has she. . . ."

"No," said Ionia.

"Then the plan didn't. . . ."

"No," said Ionia again.

"Then is she. . . . "

"No."

"No, what?" said Jason, exasperated. "Come on, Ionia. I've had enough suspense already."

"No, she isn't dead," clarified Ionia.

"Then what is she?" persisted Jason. "Is she still a prisoner?'

"Yes," said Ionia. "Only it's worse than before."

"What do you mean?" asked Jason growing excited. "Has he locked her in the dungeon?"

"We don't know exactly where she is. He says she'll get hurt if we try to find out, but she's probably in the tower room, because he's moved his study into Grammar's parlor."

"Oh," said Jason, a little disappointed; there were not likely to be rats in the Professor's study. "Has he tortured anyone?"

"What do you think he's doing now?"

The bitterness in Ionia's voice startled Jason. He glanced at her. Her face was pale, and her head was bent forward. Her shoulders were hunched, perhaps only with cold. Yet there was something different about her, her expression maybe. He had seen her scowl before, but that wasn't it. Nor was she frowning exactly. It was a hard look. Suddenly she seemed old, much older than his mother. She looked, at the moment, more like her grandmother than herself. Jason sensed, without knowing how, that she knew something he did not, and he felt a new respect for her.

"Jason, your mother, is she. . . ."

Ionia stopped, unable to formulate her question. Jason relaxed. Ionia was young again, a year younger than he was.

"Is she angry, do you mean?"

"Well, is she?"

"Yes," said Jason. "She is. I tried to tell her why we did it, but she won't listen. She's more goopy about your father than ever. She won't believe he's holding your mother prisoner unless he tells her himself. `And even if he is, Jason, that does not excuse what you did.'"

Jason gave a good imitation of his mother, but Ionia did not laugh, as he had hoped she would. She did not even smile.

"He won't tell her," said Ionia. "He says it's no one's business but his own. Do you think if I wrote her a letter she'd believe me?"

"`Even if it's true, that's no excuse for what you did.'"

"I don't want her to excuse me," said Ionia impatiently. "I just want her to help."

"Help?" repeated Jason; he was accustomed to thinking of his mother as helpless. "What could she do, even if she did believe you?"

"She could talk to him. He might listen to her."

"I doubt she'd do it. She'd say, `It's not my place to interfere.'"

"Well, I want to ask her anyway," said Ionia. "If I write to her when we get to your house, will you give her the note after I'm gone? I can't do anything in front of my father."

"Sure," agreed Jason. "But I doubt it will do any good. I've got a better idea."

"What?"

"We'll rescue her."

"How?"

Jason opened his mouth to explain his plan when he realized that it wasn't as organized as he had thought. It needed further development. He would wait until it was foolproof; then he'd tell her. Or perhaps, he wouldn't involve her at all. He would accomplish the whole thing himself, and then she would only have to be eternally grateful to him.

"Just leave that to me," he said mysteriously.

They walked on in silence. Ionia, her eyes cast down, noticed that they were walking in step. She wondered if Jason was doing it on purpose or if she was or if it had just happened that way. She supposed, if she wanted to, she could skip a step and walk in a different rhythm, but she did not want to. It felt good to walk in time with someone, even Jason.

Since Twelfth Night, she had been alone almost all of the time. Fred had gotten sick, and even though he only had a cold, Grammar nursed him night and day. Her father spent all his time in Grammar's private parlor and did not even take meals with them. Of that she was glad. It was the thought of her mother alone in the tower room that made her most lonely. She dared not tiptoe past her father's new study to sit beside the door and talk to her mother as she longed to do. Her father would be sure to find out. So she spent most of her time alone in her room, sometimes staring out the window, sometimes drawing, but both these things, which had once sustained her, now saddened her.

The three trees twisted against the winter sky looked so old; she could scarcely believe there would be leaves again. The hills, when they weren't snow covered, were cold and grey as a winter sea. Yet she could never forget that she might have walked over the hills with her mother. Always, in her mind, they were purple then with late summer flowers. No matter what she began to draw, her picture always turned into one of herself and her mother standing beneath the three trees that were just turning purple, looking into the Empty Land with the wild geese flying before them.

Now, after days that seemed like years of silence, Ionia found that she wanted to tell Jason something, not just something that had happened, but something that was herself. Yet she was so accustomed to guarding this self that she did not know how to offer it. She wondered if she might tell Jason the story of her mother's people, of how the First Woman left the Garden to wander in the Wilderness, but Jason would never believe it. Even if he did, she was afraid of betraying her mother's people. Jason was, after all, what her mother would call a man-child.

"Ionia," said Jason speaking from his own thoughts, "What your mother said on Christmas about living in the Empty Land and remembering the ancient Persians, that can't be true. Was she joking or is she," he paused trying to think of a tactful way of putting it, "or is she, well, not quite right. I mean, a little confused, perhaps. . . ."

"You still think she's crazy."

For a moment Ionia felt angry. Then she realized that Jason was not making fun of her as he used to. He really wanted to know.

"She's not crazy, and she wasn't joking either," said Ionia.

"But how do you know? Have you ever met a crazy person before?"

"No," Ionia admitted.

"Then how do you know she's not crazy?"

"How do you know she is?" Ionia countered.

"She couldn't have meant those things she said unless she's crazy. If she's not crazy, she must have been joking."

Ionia was perplexed. To her, Jason's logic made no sense, but she did not know how to argue it. If it had been the old days before her mother had come, she wouldn't have bothered. Now she felt she must make Jason see—she didn't know what, exactly—but just see.

"I don't know my mother's not crazy the way you know things," she said slowly. "I mean I don't have any proof. It's not like knowing the answers in arithmetic. It's a feeling."

"What kind of a feeling?"

Ionia puzzled over how to reply. She had only pictures of this feeling, this feeling that her mother was real, more real than anything else.

"I used to dream of her," she began. "You could say that's only because I remembered her from when I was little, and maybe I did, but the dream was different from other dreams."

Ionia paused. Jason waited, without interrupting. He had never heard Ionia speak in this voice before. Except when she was angry, her voice, at least when she spoke to him, had been a monotone. There was a secretness in her voice now that excited him.

"When I dreamed of her, I felt like I was awake. When I woke up, I felt like I was asleep. When I saw her, I was awake when I was awake. And that's what the feeling is."

"I don't get it," said Jason. "What do you mean? I'm always awake when I'm awake."

Ionia felt frustrated. In a moment she'd be angry. Jason wasn't trying to understand, but she was determined that he would. She reconsidered.

"Do you know what it's like to be well after you're sick?"

"Yes," said Jason encouragingly.

"Well, that's the feeling, too. It's like you're more alive, and so is everything else, even things that usually aren't."

They had reached the steps. Ionia turned to look at Jason to see if he had understood. On his face was a wondering expression she had never seen there before. Before he had mostly looked smug. Now, his whole face seemed to be stretching.

"You mean she gives you this feeling?" he asked.

"Yes."

"She made me feel afraid."

Ionia could scarcely believe what she had heard Jason admit.

"That's part of the feeling," she said.

Simultaneously, they turned and began to walk up the steps.

"Maybe she's not crazy," Jason conceded. "But I still don't understand this business about the ancient Persians and the Empty Land."

"I don't either, exactly, but I don't see why it shouldn't be true, anyway. Lots of things might be true that haven't been proved. You believe in flying saucers, Jason."

"Spaceships," corrected Jason, "are within the realm of scientific possibility. Your mother and the ancient Persians. . . ."

Still debating, they entered the building and climbed the stairs to Jason's apartment together.

❦ ❦ ❦

After the lecture, which was a success, Eva Brooke failed in her resolve to be first at Adam's side. Before she even got up from her seat, there were dozens of students and visiting scholars crowding around him, notebooks and pens in hand, shouting their questions and trying to take down every one of his words. Eva decided to wait and catch Adam on his way out. Glancing about her, she saw, to her satisfaction, that Bates and Beeferman were preparing to leave. Beeferman caught her eye and nodded to her respectfully. She nodded back without smiling and turned her face away. She did not know why she had worried. These men were too tiny to touch a man of such magnitude that he was impervious to his own humiliation.

The seats around her had emptied. Everyone except the group that still pressed about the Professor had left the hall. Adam was closing his briefcase. Eva picked up her bag and buttoned her coat, leaning forward eagerly as she watched him descend the stairs, still trailed by students. She waved to him as he walked down the aisle, but he did not see her; nor did he hear her when she called his name. So she got up and followed him, feeling like one more nameless student. The crowd straggled after him through the sleet, and he did not lose them until he had reached his office building. There he excused himself and walked alone up the steps. At the door, Eva caught up with him, catching his arm and his attention.

'Oh, it's you," was all he said, and he turned to open the door.

'Adam, you were wonderful," she said, and she followed him through the door, failing to notice, in her enthusiasm, how deeply embarrassed he was.

"Oh, were you there?" he asked casually, not turning to look at her as he climbed the stairs to his office.

"Yes, of course I was," puffed Eva, still breathless with pursuit. "I thought you saw me. Adam, what happened just before you began? I was afraid you were going to be sick. Are you all right?"

Adam did not answer as he unlocked the door of his office.

"There is nothing the matter. Will you come in?" he asked, but his voice lacked welcome.

Eva hesitated in the doorway, while Adam proceeded to his desk, unsure of what she ought to do, of what Adam wanted her to do. Perhaps seeing her brought back too vividly what had happened, and of course he wanted to forget. Yet it amazed her that this man who was strong enough to stand before a crowd and vindicate himself should dread to be alone with one woman, and a woman, moreover, whose sympathy for him was boundless. Perhaps that was the problem: he feared she would pity him. Well then, she must show him that she did not. She must make him believe that to her he was the same man as before.

"Yes, I will," she said.

Closing the door behind her, Eva went to sit in the chair that was always hers when she visited him. At his desk, Adam opened his briefcase and seemed to be sorting through his papers. The silence between them grew louder. Adam's wife had always been a silence between them, but a small enough silence that Eva had been willing to overlook it. Now this silence seemed to have swallowed everything else, and there was nothing between them but this terrible silence of an unspoken name. She could bear it no longer.

"Lilith," said Eva tentatively.

The name hovered in the air between them. Although Adam made no response, Eva knew that he had heard. With exaggerated care, he stacked his papers, rapping them sharply on the desk to straighten them. She could see that his hands were shaking. It occurred to her that she must not leave the name hanging; she must form a sentence with it.

"Lilith," she repeated, "is she still with you or has she gone?"

Adam laid his papers in his briefcase as carefully as one might lay a sleeping baby in a cradle. Then he closed his briefcase and locked it. At last he turned to face Eva. She almost cried out when she saw his eyes. They were hard and smooth as black marbles. What frightened her was that, though he looked straight at her, he seemed not to see her, not her, herself, Eva. She was not there. His eyes unmade her.

"So you were part of the plot, too."

A shot of pain reassured Eva of her existence.

"Adam," she pleaded, "how can you say that!"

"You seem to understand its purpose well enough."

"Jason explained it to me," she said. "Adam, I would never do anything to hurt you. I. . ."

. . .love you, she concluded silently.

"So it was the children," he said more to himself that to her. "There is no innocence in the world anymore, not even among infants."

"Yes, there is innocence," Eva interrupted. "If the children were not innocent, do you think they could have done what they did? They didn't understand how serious it was. They got carried away. They thought they were helping. Don't blame them, Adam. Don't punish them too severely. Don't. . . ."

"Whom I blame and whom I punish is no one's business but my own."

His voice was soft, but dangerous, like the footfall of a cat before the kill.

"So is what I do with my wife. Is that quite understood? In the future, if you have any regard for me, you will not mention this subject again."

Eva and Adam stared at one another until Eva's soft eyes grew softer with tears, and she turned her face away. Adam continued to watch her. On his face, if Eva could have seen it just then, was a look of curiosity that was almost wonder. Eva Brooke was crying; he had made her cry; he had hurt her. He had always known he could sway a crowd. The effects of his smile and his clever conversation were easy to calculate. He could put his mother in a rage or frighten his children without even trying, but he had never, directly and personally, made anyone cry. Lilith refused to cry, no matter what he did to her. She seemed incapable of tears.

He pictured Lilith as he had seen her that morning, her eyes full of animal hatred, hatred not of him, but of her captor. He sensed that he, himself, Adam Underwood, did not exist for her. It infuriated him. It would drive him to kill her, all without ever really touching her. As he thought of Lilith, his expression hardened again. He gripped the arms of the chair as if to control the rage within him, rage of such frightening force that he believed it could destroy the world if he loosed it. Struggling with his fury, he forgot Eva until her movement made him recall her presence.

Then he saw her: a large, awkward woman, clumsily buttoning her coat while reaching for her bag at the same time; a soft, unprotected woman, so easily wounded by mere words. Her face was full of hurt, human hurt. It touched him.

"Eva," he said gently.

She looked up at him, surprised by his change of tone, a tone she had never heard in his voice before.

"Forgive me. I have been unfair, unkind."

"Forgive me, Adam, for questioning you. It's just that I've been so worried, I. . ." She stopped herself.

"I appreciate your concern, Eva. But you will understand that there are certain matters of which I would rather not speak."

He looked at her steadily.

"Of course, Adam."

"Let's go, then, and have a drink at the Pearls and Swine. We will talk of other things, just as we used to."

Adam picked up his briefcase and went to the door. Holding it open for her, he waited. Eva wished she could say something more before they went to the Pearls and Swine. She wished she could ask how they could possibly go back to before after all that had happened. But the door was open, and, even in the dim light, Eva could see that Adam's face was closed.

21

Choosing Sides

GRAMMAR looked out the window as Adam and the children headed for the car. Against her will, Adam had ordered Fred back to school. She felt alone and tired more than angry. If Adam, with an arbitrary word, could usurp her authority, then that authority was empty, and the territory she had so carefully staked out for herself—children and house—was a captive country in which even the ruler was a slave. If she was beaten before she began, what was the use of fighting?

Yet she kept watch at the window, for the path was icy. Fred, she could see, was deliberately trying to slide, but Ionia would not let him. Midway down the path, Ionia stopped, bent down, and whispered something in Fred's ear. Then both children turned towards the house, their heads tilted back. Grammar guessed where they were looking, and she drew in her breath for fear their father might catch them at it. But Ionia's timing was exact; she allowed only a moment. Before their father reached the car, the children were back on their way down the path.

Grammar let out her breath. Adam opened the door and waited for the children to scramble into the backseat. Then he got in and started the car. Obedient to some command of his, the gate opened, then closed again. They were gone, and she was alone, left alone, a prisoner like the Creature, with the Creature.

Although it was not her custom, Grammar lingered at the window, reluctant to face the house she had scarcely kept since Fred was sick. Yet the sight of the yard depressed her, too. The thin sunlight that managed to seep through the frozen haze did nothing to brighten the dingy snow. Heavy sleet had shot holes through the snow as if a shower of bullets had fallen from the sky. Twigs and branches broken by storms littered the ground. Battered beyond recognition, no more than a graying lump, was the snow woman the children and their mother had made.

"Ugh!" said Grammar aloud.

Wearily she turned towards the house. Its stillness seemed a reproach, as though it had died of her neglect. In her mind, she made a list of the things she must do that day. Besides the daily tasks of washing dishes, sweeping the kitchen floor, making beds, dusting, there was mopping the hall, vacuuming the rugs, polishing the furniture and the silverware, and if she had any time left, there was always mending. Since Adam had taken over her private parlor, she had let the mending go. She had let everything go. She had not even taken the Christmas tree down yet, and here it was almost February. She must take charge again. She must set the house in order. She must. Yet even as she thought of all she must do, she made no motion to begin. Somehow, in the last few weeks, she had lost the will to work. She remained by the window, frozen as the snow figure, as battered and defeated.

Then, in the absence of will, habit, acquired through long years of disciplined willing, came to her rescue. Scarcely aware that she did so, she began to clear the table. As mindlessly, she washed the dishes in the scalding water that, over time, had toughened her hands so that she hardly felt it. Then she went upstairs to make the beds, and, though she took care to arrange wrinkles and lumps in Adam's, she received no malicious satisfaction from the deed.

Downstairs again, she went to the cleaning closet and found her feather duster. When she had finished the dining room and the living room, she started upstairs, dusting the bannister as she went. Then the singing began. As always, it made her uneasy. She stood still, debating whether or not to go back down, so as to be farther away from the singing. A moment later, without realizing she had made a decision, she continued on her way. Little by little, as she made the rounds in the room upstairs, her movements lost their mechanical dullness and took on, once again, the grace of the dance.

By the time she had finished the dusting, Grammar had grown so accustomed to the singing that if it had stopped, the silence would have startled her. Humming tunelessly, like the drone of a bagpipe, Grammar went downstairs to dismantle the Christmas tree.

The tree bare, she put on her old coat and wrapped a shawl around her head, mummy fashion. Then she opened the front door, and, with some puffing and much cursing, managed to get the tree, trailing needles all the way, to the bottom of the steps. There she paused for breath and wondered what to do with it. She remembered the suet she had saved and the strings of popcorn the children had made for the birds, and she decided to prop it in the southeast corner of the yard and decorate it. If ever she sat down in the living room with her mending, she would be able to look up from time to time and watch the birds at their feast.

As Grammar struggled across the yard, stumbling now and then because of the snow, Lion, excited by the sight of Grammar outside playing with a big stick, began to bark and chase around her in joyous circles.

"Why don't you shut up and make yourself useful!" she panted. "Help me carry this thing!"

Lion had his own ideas about usefulness. Grammar left him nosing the tree, wondering whether or not it wanted watering.

When Grammar returned with the suet and the popcorn, Lion appeared to have lost interest in the tree. Instead he was standing beside it, looking up at the house with his head cocked to one side. So intelligent and intent was his expression, that Grammar felt compelled to turn and look where he was looking.

Then she saw: what Lion saw, what the children must have seen: a flash of skin, a sweep of hair. The reflection on the glass made it impossible to see the whole creature, but here was a gesture of a hand, there the curve of an arm. The motion alone was continuous, for it seemed that the Creature danced.

The dancing, like the singing, unnerved Grammar. What cause would anyone imprisoned in such a small space find for dancing? For a moment she wondered if the Creature had gone mad. Then she almost laughed aloud at herself, for to question the Creature's sanity was absurd. The Creature had never been what could be called normal, and it was impossible to judge her behavior by the standards of normality—or morality, for that matter. Yet Grammar remembered the Creature's frenzy when she had encountered the locked gate. She remembered the Creature's sudden collapse onto the snow and then the decline that had lasted for days. How could she dance now, when her condition was all the more desperate?

Yet she did. She danced on and on. Grammar watched, forgetting after a while to wonder why, forgetting everything: the cold, the snow, the suet and popcorn she clutched in her hands, her frozen toes, her aching bones. Then without warning, the dance ceased; the Creature receded into the shadows of the room. Grammar felt strangely bereft. "Come back," she started to cry. Then self-conscious again, she turned to the tree and began tying suet to the branches with fingers clumsy with cold.

When the tree was decorated, Grammar stepped back to survey her work. Already the birds were finding their way to the feast. They hovered about the tree: bluejays, cardinals, chickadees, live ornaments. It occurred to Grammar that the Creature, too, would be able to watch the birds. She glanced up at the tower room to see if the Creature was looking, but the windows were empty as unseeing eyes. Suddenly conscious of how cold she was, Grammar wrapped her arms about herself and hurried back to the house.

Inside the singing had stopped. Grammar decided she did not feel up to vacuuming the needles now. She went to the kitchen to eat lunch. While she perched on a stool, sipping a cup of soup and nibbling anchovy crackers, she fell to worrying over what Adam was feeding the Creature. She never saw him preparing any food; nor had she noticed that her stores were depleted. If he visited the Creature, it must be at night or in the small hours of the morning. During the day he was away, during the evening he occupied her private parlor; she knew, because she had on several occasions spied through the keyhole. If he fed her, he must. . . .

The cup on the way to Grammar's lips stopped and trembled in midair as it dawned on Grammar that Adam might not be feeding the Creature at all. But if he was not, surely by now she would have. . . . But no, there was a water closet in the tower room, and, if she had water to drink, the Creature, being uncommonly tough, might take a long time to. . . .

Grammar could not bring herself to think the word, but she was now thoroughly alarmed for she wouldn't put it past Adam. And if Adam intended to starve the Creature, what could she do to stop him? She had no way to notify the police. Even if she had, the police might not believe her. Adam, with the charm he showed to strangers, could easily persuade them that it was she and not he who was mad. Still, she could at least get the Creature out of the tower room or get food in. She had picked the lock before; she could do it again.

Grammar set her soup, unfinished, on the table and got to her feet. Tearing a pin from her hair, she headed for the tower room and was halfway up the hall stairs before she stopped to consider what might happen if Adam discovered her interference. Replacing the pin, she sank down on the steps. She must not act hastily; she must not be a fool. She did well to be wary of provoking Adam's anger, having encountered its effects before. What was most dangerous about his anger was the deliberateness of its expression. He never struck out blindly. Even as a child he had not been given to temper tantrums. When thwarted, he seldom reacted immediately. He knew how to take his time. Then, when she had forgotten all about an incident, he would take revenge.

She remembered one time in particular. Adam spent one summer capturing animals and keeping them in cages. Exactly how he trapped them, she did not know; his eyes seemed to have an hypnotic effect on them. All she knew was that once he caught them, he did not take care of them, and their cages smelled. One close night, the stench was more than she could stand. She got up, when everyone else was asleep, and let them all go.

When Adam discovered what she had done, he had not cried and carried on, as Fred would have, nor had he sulked. He had simply said: "They were mine. You had no right to let them go." That was all he ever said. For several days, nothing happened. Then one morning, she found every one of her flowers, not wantonly, but carefully uprooted, laid neatly in piles, withering in the sun. Even now, it made her feel sick to think of it.

As Grammar remembered, it occurred to her that her fear of Adam dated to that time. Something had gone wrong, then, that summer of the animals. That was the summer, too, when he had first taken an interest in ancient religions and cults, magic, hypnosis, and alchemy. He had been eleven then, the age of Eva Brooke's boy. His father had encouraged what he called his "budding intellect," hoping that Adam might become the scientist he himself had wished to be. Though she had neither approved nor understood his interests, since his father apparently did, she had let Adam be. Indeed she had little choice. That was the summer he stopped being a little boy, the summer her influence, if she had ever exercised any, had ended.

As she sat on the stairs so many years later, she tried to call to mind what he had been like before that summer. Certainly he was never what one could consider an ordinary child, being always extraordinarily beautiful and quick, both in mind and limb. He always, more so than any other child she had ever known, except perhaps Ionia, had been secretive. But Ionia was so quiet and serious. Adam's secrets, then, had been in fun; or so it had seemed; they were part of the solitary games he endlessly played. But even then, she supposed, she had been a little in awe of him, and there was no doubt that she had adored him, perhaps as blindly and foolishly as Eva Brooke did now.

Over the years, the awe had changed to fear, and in the man, the tyrannical stranger whom she served, she could find no trace of the infant she had held at her mercy, nor even of the child she had fed and washed as she did Fred now, though Fred, on occasion, when he was absorbed in some game or asking a series of seemingly unrelated questions, reminded her of the lost child she had almost forgotten.

Sighing, Grammar stood up and went slowly back downstairs. She did not dare pick the lock of the tower room. If Adam found out, he would know how to punish her. He would send her away from the children. He had more than once hinted that she was living on his charity, as if she did not more than earn her keep. Nothing must separate her from the children: neither the Creature's life, nor, if it came to that, her death. But perhaps, Grammar comforted herself, it would not come to that. Perhaps Adam would lose interest and let the Creature go.

Yet as Grammar made her way back to the kitchen, she felt unsettled. She had resolved nothing; she was stalling for time. But what else could she do, helpless as she was, an old woman tired to the bone, too tired to make decisions anymore? Really, it was not up to her. Nothing was up to her. It was all up to Adam. No longer was she responsible for Adam's actions; what he did was not her fault. She would mind her own business. She could not be held accountable for anyone else's.

The left-over soup put away and the table wiped clean of crumbs, Grammar went to get the vacuum cleaner. She would not take a nap. It was best to be busy. While she vacuumed, the roar of the vacuum cleaner emptied her mind of everything but its din. When she shut if off, the silence was dreadful. It seemed somehow a judgment on her. She put the vacuum cleaner away with as much clatter as possible and cast about in her mind for something to do next. Then she remembered the box of Christmas ornaments. It belonged in the attic and would have to go back sooner or later. On her way to the attic, she would have to pass the tower room. Adam could not blame her for that. Half-fearful, half-excited, she fetched the box of ornaments from the living room and started on her journey.

When she reached the door of her late private parlor, she paused to sniff. The familiar smell of moldiness and must revived her anger against Adam. What right had he to contaminate her private parlor, to spread his filth from room to room? Trembling now with rage, she continued on her way. She hesitated by the door of the tower room, but she did not stop, for she did not yet know what she intended to do. In the attic, she sat down on one of her old trunks and asked herself. As the attic was bitterly cold, the answer was not long in coming. In moments she was on her feet, knowing that she must find out what Adam was up to, even if she could not stop him.

Standing before the door of the tower room, Grammar listened, but she could hear nothing: no movement, no breathing. Out of long habit, she leaned closer to take a whiff. Instead of the usual smell, the smell which now pervaded her private parlor, an altogether different smell greeted her. It seemed to Grammar that she recognized the smell; it made her remember something, but what? She closed her eyes, and an image filled her mind, an image of a huge, airy barn on her grandmother's farm where she played as a child. The barn was clean, but rich with the smell of sweet hay and animals, a smell, to Grammar's way of thinking as a child, not unlike pumpkin pie.

A slight sound from within recalled Grammar from her memory. She opened her eyes and, knees crackling, bent to look through the keyhole. There was the Creature lying on the floor, curled against the wall beneath the window, with only her hair for a cover. She slept; or so it seemed. Grammar watched, trying to discern the rise and fall of breathing, but the Creature was still, so still. . . .

"Lilith," said Grammar able to bear the stillness no longer. "Lilith, wake up!"

Slowly Lilith opened her eyes, long purple slits, the only color in her pale face. Then she sat up, her eyes widening, and looked straight at the keyhole.

"Ursula," she said

It was not a question or a greeting, but a statement, a complete definition.

"Yes," Grammar agreed.

There was silence for a time as the two women eyed what they could of one another. Grammar's back began to ache. She lowered herself to her knees. The floor, she noted, was cold.

"Doesn't he even let you have a blanket?" she demanded.

"There is one," she said indicating the other side of the room. "But I do not mind the cold."

Grammar could not imagine not minding the cold. Just the sight of the Creature's nakedness made her shiver, and the Creature hadn't any excess flesh to insulate her. She was, Grammar decided, definitely thinner. The thought of those sharp bones unprotected from the hard floor pained her own bones.

"What does he feed you? You're scarcely more substantial than a skeleton."

"Honey," the Creature answered. "He forces me to eat."

"Forces you?" Grammar repeated.

"Forces me," she said. "He wants me alive because he knows I would rather die."

Grammar experienced momentary relief on learning that starving the Creature was not part of Adam's plan. Then she grew anxious again. She had not reckoned on the Creature's wanting to die. That, somehow, seemed even worse, though she did not know why; nor did she pause to consider the cause of a growing conviction that the Creature must live whether she liked it or not.

"No," she said firmly as though she were forbidding something to Ionia or Fred. "You must not die. You must not even think of it."

"Why not, Ursula?"

The Creature sounded curious. Grammar was nonplussed. When confronted so directly, she found she hadn't the least idea why not. It had never occurred to her to question whether or not life is preferable to death. Like any sensible mortal being, she had simply assumed so. Now here was the Creature asking why. Why live? Why not die? Indeed why not? What was the point of living, struggling, losing, always losing in the end? Why did she go on living herself? Then suddenly Grammar knew the answer, and she wondered how she could have overlooked it, even for a moment.

"Think of the children," she said.

"What am I to think of them, Ursula?"

Again Grammar was taken aback.

"Think of how it would affect them, having their mother die."

The Creature was silent for a moment; Grammar felt hopeful.

"How does if affect them having their mother live," the Creature paused, "like this?"

Grammar made no answer, but she conceded to herself that the Creature had a point. It did the children no good to have a naked, half-starving mother locked in the tower room. As far as Grammar was concerned, it did the children no good to have a mother at all, or at least not this mother. Why, then, was she arguing that the Creature live for the sake of the children when she wanted nothing more than for the Creature to go away and never come near the children again?

"Why do you want me to live, Ursula?"

The Creature gave emphasis to the word you, and suddenly the question became personal. Grammar had not considered it that way before. She had thought of what the Creature ought to do; it had not occurred to her that what the Creature did might matter to herself, Ursula. Yet it must or she would not be here wearing out her knees. Why should it? It didn't make sense. Wasn't the Creature her natural enemy, like the weeds invading her garden, the squirrels tunneling in the walls, the moss taking over the roof, the mice nesting in her dancing gowns? Wasn't the Creature the very embodiment of the forces she had been fighting all her life? Why should she dread the Creature's death? Wouldn't it be, for her, a victory?

Yet, though it did not make sense, Grammar understood, as she looked through the keyhole at the Creature huddled naked and diminished in the tower room, that the Creature's death would mean defeat, not only for the Creature, but for herself.

"If you die," she began slowly, waiting for the words to come, "Adam will have won."

A look of fear, like the shadow of a swift-moving cloud, swept across the Creature's face, and Grammar knew she had reached her. But then the Creature shook her head.

"No, Ursula, I told you. He wants me alive."

"All the same," said Grammar, "he will have won. His side will have won."

Grammar knew what she meant by Adam's side, but she did not know how to say it, how to name the thing she feared in Adam, the thing that had made him tear up the flowers, that force, that power to which he had given his allegiance and taken for his own.

"Ursula," said the Creature at last, "you are right. And I am wrong to say that Adam wants me alive. He doesn't. He wants me dead alive."

Only a few months ago, Grammar reflected, she would not have understood what the Creature meant by dead alive. Now she did. She had experienced it herself. It was what she had been that morning as she stood by the window and as she had moved mechanically through the house. Yet the Creature's singing had revived her. How was it that the Creature could not help herself?

"That is what I dread," the Creature continued. "I would rather be wholly dead, if I can't be wholly alive."

"But if you can sing, if you can dance. . . ."

"Yes," she agreed, "I have been trying to keep all of me alive as long as I have to live. Every day I lose strength. I cannot live long in captivity. That, alone, will kill me. It doesn't matter that I eat."

"Then we must get you out. I will pick the lock at once!"

Creaking painfully, but relieved to have something to do. Grammar stood up and pulled a pin from her hair.

"No, Ursula," the Creature's voice arrested her. "Unless I can escape beyond the wall, he will lock me up again, and if he finds out you have helped me, he may lock you up, too."

Grammar jabbed the pin back into her hair, feeling annoyed with the Creature for being so uncharacteristically reasonable and with herself for being so uncharacteristically rash. It was not as if she hadn't thought of that argument herself.

"Then I will just have to speak with him. I will make him see that he must let you out. I will threaten him with the police, I will. . . ."

"Peace, Ursula. We need silence."

Grammar stopped talking, feeling as though she had been rebuked. She waited for what seemed to her a long time, unable to hear the silence, because of her impatience. When she was about to break into the silence, the Creature spoke again.

"Eva Brooke," she said. "Eva Brooke must speak with him."

"Eva Brooke?" repeated Grammar, "What good will that do? Haven't you seen the way he disregards her? As for her, she refuses to see anything wrong in what Adam does. She's a good woman, mind you, I'm not saying a word against her. But where Adam's concerned, she's hopeless, like a schoolgirl, a baby, a. . . ."

"Eva Brooke must speak with him," said the Creature again. "That is what the silence told me. There is something she knows which no one else knows."

If Grammar could have seen herself then, she would have seen her own head cocked to one side as she stared at the door and listened, in bewilderment, to the voice behind it.

"You must take your magic stick and make words, Ursula. Ask her to speak with Adam. Can you bend down again? I am going to give you something to give her."

Curious, Grammar obeyed. What had the Creature, naked in that empty room, to give? Peering through the keyhole, Grammar winced as she saw the

Creature tear a lock of hair from her head without flinching. Then she rose, crossed the room, knelt, and slipped the hair through the crack under the door.

As if it were some wild, live thing she did not quite like to touch, Grammar gingerly picked it up. Then, instinctively, she sniffed. As she did, she thought of fresh turned dirt in her spring garden.

"All right, Lilith," she said. "I will do as you say. Meanwhile, you are not to die or even to want to. Is that understood?"

"Yes, Ursula. Don't worry. I will not die while there is hope of living."

Grammar stopped herself from saying that she considered hope in Eva Brooke's effectiveness ill-founded. Instead she said gruffly:

"If you like, I can come and talk to you again."

"I would like, Ursula."

"Just to make sure you aren't getting morbid," she added.

With that, Grammar put the hair in her apron pocket and started downstairs to write the letter.

22

 Intercession

ONE morning after Jason had left for school and before her day at the University had begun, Eva Brooke sat down at her desk. Pushed to one side was a stack of papers she would read during intercession next week, to the other side a new collection of fairytales she had been asked to review. Directly before her lay two letters. One was in Ionia's hand, each letter carefully made, as if it were a picture, like a Chinese character, and not merely an arbitrary symbol. The other letter was in Ursula Underwood's elegant but almost illegible scrawl. On top of the letters lay a lock of black hair, coiled and shining as a snake.

A shaft of sunlight began to stretch across it, and the hair turned from blackness to rainbow. Cautiously, as she might have extended her hand to some strange animal, Eva reached out to touch the hair. It felt warm, as if it were not somebody's dead cells but had its own life. She lifted the hair to her face. Its scent made her think of summer berries, hot and ripe in the sun. Its texture was tough, wiry, more like the mane of a horse than human hair. Experimentally, she held the hair to the top of her head. She felt the strange black hair breathing next to her cheek. Lowering her eyes, she watched it tumbling past her shoulders and over her breast like a black waterfall. For a moment she forgot herself and became Lilith.

Curious, she went to look in the mirror. There she encountered herself, yet with a difference. The black hair made her face new and unknown. She looked on herself as she might have looked on a stranger. She reached for a hairpin and fastened the hair to her head. Then she began to braid Lilith's hair with two thin strands of her own. Against the black hair, her plain brown hair looked almost golden. When she had finished the braid, she held it in her hands. Then, impulsively, she opened a drawer, drew out some scissors, and snipped the braid from her head. Before she could question or regret what she had done, she heard the kettle whistle. She wound the braid into a loose ball and put it away with the scissors in the drawer. Without checking the mirror to inspect the damage she had done to her hair, she went to her desk, gathered her letters, and headed for the kitchen. Because the breakfast table was still cluttered, she spread out the letters on the counter and read standing up while she drank a fresh cup of coffee.

Dear Mrs. Brooke,

We are sorry for what we did. We did it because my father won't let my mother go and she wants to. We thought he would if he saw it was trouble to keep her. But he didn't. Now she's locked up where we can't see her. If you are not too angry about what we did, please talk to my father and ask him to let my mother go.

Ionia

Jason had given her this note from Ionia weeks ago. Failing to find an opportunity to speak alone with Ionia, Eva had written to her, assuring Ionia that she was not angry with her, but making it clear that she could not interfere between Ionia's mother and father. Yet even though she had made up her mind that there was nothing she could do, what Ionia had written continued to disturb her. She did not doubt that Ionia was telling the truth, at least as far as Ionia understood it. But Ionia was a child. How could she understand the complexities of a relationship between a grown man and woman? Eva did not understand them herself. Certainly she did not understand Adam's relationship to his wife. It hardly seemed a relationship between two people at all, but rather between two opposing, attracting forces whose union was explosive. Her impulse had been to stand clear of the rubble, but if other people—Ionia, Fred, Ursula Underwood—were getting hurt, how could she stand back? Wasn't she obliged to help? Ursula Underwood seemed to think so.

Dear Mrs. Brooke,

I know you are fond of my son. (I do not know why.) If he is not fond of you, he ought to be. I do not know if you have any influence over him. (I do not.) If you have, I beg you to use it on behalf of all of us: me, the children, Her. She says that you know something about Adam that the rest of us don't. Only you can talk to him. She told me to ask you to.

She is locked in the tower room. (It used to be his study; now he is using my private parlor.) She is naked (you know how cold it is in this house, Mrs. Brooke) and thin. He force feeds her, but she claims she cannot live long in captivity.

*It is not right, Mrs. Brooke. You must see that. Whatever your feelings for my son—*Here Eva's face reddened—*I beg you not to be willfully blind. Intercede for us. Help us if you can. And do come to dinner again. It is always a pleasure to see you.*

Sincerely,
Ursula Underwood

P.S. She tore this lock of hair from her head. No scissors!
P.S. 2 Please do not reveal your source of information, if you can help it.
There are no more tower rooms. Only attics, cellars, and old age homes.

Eva shook her head again, as she had the first time she read the letter. Attics, cellars, old-age homes. It was all too incredible. Try as she might, she could not reconcile Ursula Underwood's image of Adam with her own. The letter had upset her so that she had put it away after reading it when she received it earlier that week via Ionia and Jason, and she had not taken it out again until this morning, the last day of school before intercession. All that week she had managed to avoid being alone with Adam. She could not go on dodging him or herself indefinitely. She must make a decision. Either she must speak to Adam or she must refuse and inform Ionia and Mrs. Underwood that they had chosen the wrong person to be their intercessor. But that was the strangest part: not only Ionia and her grandmother had chosen her, but so, it seemed, had Lilith. What did Lilith mean when she said that Eva knew something about Adam that no one else did? What did Lilith know about Eva to make her think so? Something, Eva concluded, that she did not know herself.

Noticing that her coffee had grown cold, Eva glanced at the clock. She had only one hour before she was due at the University. Dumping her coffee down the drain, she took the letters and hurried to her bedroom. There she pulled on a sweater and some slacks without bothering to notice whether they matched. Hastily, she did her hair, attempting, without success, to hide the two short tufts of hair.

Outside Eva headed not for the campus but for the river. She needed open air in which to think. The river was frozen in grayish masses of rough ice. Eva found the river's frozen motion eerie. Except for the traffic on the drive, everything around her was still. There were not even any gulls about; they had all flown away to open water. She felt as if she were the only living creature in a dead world.

Then, out of the corner of her eye, she caught sight of movement. She turned to see what it was. There, in a tiny patch of open water, swam a wild goose. Slowly, so as not to startle it, Eva stepped closer. Squatting down, Eva peered into the water. One of the goose's legs was banded. Eva supposed the band might have something to do with an experiment being conducted by the University. Probably the poor thing's wings were clipped.

Checking her watch Eva discovered that she had only twenty minutes left until the meeting. It would take her at least that long to get there. So she stood up and began to walk briskly in the direction of the University, chiding herself that she had accomplished nothing of her purpose. Her pace had an effect on her thoughts. As she had wandered so had they. Now that she had a direction, her thoughts had too. She began to order her thoughts as if she were doing an algebraic equation.

She loved Adam; that was a given. How long this had been so she did not know; perhaps since the beginning, perhaps since Twelfth Night. Only since then had she dared to name her feeling for Adam love. Before then, love would have been presumptuous, out of place, inadmissible. In spite of her speculations about a hidden wound, Adam had always appeared to be invulnerable, self-sufficient, complete. Now she had seen the frailty underlying the superstructure. The vision made her feel responsible for Adam in a way she never had before. How could she have felt responsible for someone who had so little need of her, of anyone. But Adam did need, maybe not her in particular, but he needed, just as Jason did, just as Fred did. He could be hurt; he could be humiliated; he was human and therefore in need of understanding. That she could offer.

For a while Eva had thought her sympathy for Adam would make everything simple; for it would preclude sympathy for anyone else involved in what happened on Twelfth Night. Now Ionia and Ursula Underwood had complicated everything by forcing on her the other side of the equation and demanding that she treat it equally. Whatever she had done to deserve it, Adam was abusing Lilith to the distress of his whole family; that, too, was a given. The unknown quantity was what she should do, given the fact of her love and the fact of Adam's abuse. Up until now, she had never questioned that love meant acceptance. If so, then she must have loved Adam before, because all she had ever wanted to do was accept him, receive him, regretting only that he did not offer more of himself. Yet now she was reluctant to resist him for fear of discovering more than she wanted to know. Yes, that was it: she was afraid of the darker, crueler Adam his mother presented, afraid of the stranger she had encountered that day in his office, afraid that if she opposed him, she would encounter the stranger face to face and lose the Adam she knew.

Though the light at the crossing to the park was green, Eva stood still as this truth emerged from the place where she had kept it hidden. Her orderly equation fell apart. Contemplating the complications of this revelation, she started across the street just as the light turned red, and she narrowly missed being run down by an irate driver.

She made her way across the park, wondering what such a timid love was worth. Was it worthy to be called love at all if it did not embrace the whole of Adam: the known and the unknown? Or was what she called love mere sentiment? It occurred to her that unquestioning acceptance could as easily be called cowardice as love. But how was she to oppose him? On what authority, by what power? "She says you know something about Adam that no one else does," Ursula Underwood wrote. "Only you can talk to him." What did she know? What did Lilith mean?

As Eva left the park, she saw that she was back at the beginning, back to the same questions; only there was a difference: she knew now that no amount of walking and thinking was going to answer them. She would have to act. She could not calculate the effect of her action. That remained an unknown quality. Only by daring that unknown would she learn what Lilith meant.

What Lilith meant. Walking the last few blocks to the University, Eva realized that since she had come outside to think, she had not thought of Lilith, only of Adam. But then, Lilith did not lend herself to rational thought. She belonged to dreams; like them, disturbing and with a meaning difficult to grasp for more than a moment. Yet though Eva had tried to deny it since Twelfth Night out of loyalty to Adam, she felt drawn to Lilith. There was a bond between them; not love, perhaps, but something more primitive.

The University clock began to strike twelve. Eva hurried the rest of the way, but before she entered the gate, she paused and felt beneath her scarf for the two tufts of hair.

Late that afternoon, Eva stood before the door of Adam's office gathering courage. She had spent some time in the women's room doing what she could to fix her hair, but she did not feel confident. Though they were not obtrusive, the tufts of hair would be evident to anyone who looked carefully. She could only hope that Adam would not. While she was in the women's room standing before the mirror, she had noticed that the purple sweater and the brown pants she wore did not become one another. Purple, she knew, was an unfortunate color to have chosen. She should have thought. Drawing her coat closer about her to hide her poor taste, Eva finally knocked.

"I am not in," came Adam's voice, deep and threatening.

If she were a student, Eva thought, she would surely have turned and fled. As it was, she hesitated. Adam had told her about this tactic, and they had laughed over it together. Really, when she considered, it was the sort of thing a schoolboy might have done. She resolved not to be intimidated.

She knocked again. There was no response at all this time. She supposed he was trying to prove his previous statement. As Eva waited before the door, she began to lose her nerve. Perhaps she ought to take the hint and go away. Yet she knew if she waited any longer, she would lose her nerve altogether. It was now or never. As quietly as she could, Eva opened the door.

Adam did not look up; nor did he seem aware of her entrance. He was reading something and seemed to be deeply absorbed. Knowing that it was wrong yet unable to resist the temptation, Eva stole a moment to watch him in unself-consciousness. His brows were drawn together in concentration, but the rest of his face muscles were slack, as she had never seen them before. It occurred to her that he must expend incredible energy keeping his face toned, molding it into its various masks. With all the muscles slacked, his face looked younger, more vulnerable. It was an unformed face: no permanent lines or creases, no lingering expressions, no mark of the suffering there must have been. Yet, if his face looked younger in this unguarded moment, it also looked older. His color was poor, and he looked tired, more than tired. She had never seen such weariness. She wished she could embrace him, revive him, infuse him with her own life.

Then suddenly his face changed; the muscles tensed. He had become aware of her presence. He looked up at her, his face stiff with displeasure.

"You might at least announce yourself when you walk, unbidden, into my office."

"I am sorry, Adam. I know. I should have."

Adam relaxed a little and continued to regard her more curiously than angrily, as if wondering how she had come to be so bold.

"Why are you just standing there without speaking?" he asked. "Are you some ghost come to haunt me?"

"Yes," she said. "I am the ghost of Christmas past."

Adam almost smiled.

"Well, sit down, now that you're here, and stop looming."

"I am disturbing you," she hesitated. "You were reading something."

"Nothing important," he said laying the book aside. "I would much rather be disturbed by you."

He was wearing the mask of charm again, and it was so complete she could scarcely believe in what she had seen before.

"Have you anything particularly disturbing you wish to discuss?"

"Yes. Adam," she said, seating herself and trying to keep calm.

"How very intriguing."

She could hear the wariness in his voice.

"I hope you won't keep me in suspense for long."

"No, Adam," she paused for a moment as if testing the water with her toes before taking the plunge. "I will tell you right now: I know you are keeping your wife locked in the tower room."

"Who told you that?"

"Never mind, Adam. I know." Before he could speak again she rushed on. "I know you have been hurt, Adam, and humiliated, past the endurance of any man, any ordinary man," she added. "But you are not an ordinary man; you are a great one. This action is beneath you."

He remained silent, staring at her. The intensity of his gaze was almost more than she could bear. It was not, like that other look he had turned on her, impersonal. What had alarmed her then was that he had seemed not to see her, Eva, at all. She felt now that he was attempting to see inside her, to penetrate a place so deep that it was unknown even to herself.

"You dare to interfere between me and my wife?"

His words diffused the effect of his eyes; she breathed again and realized that she had been holding her breath.

"Yes."

"What makes you dare?"

There was the question that she had asked herself: on what authority, by what power did she oppose him? Suddenly she knew the answer. It had been there all along.

"I care for you."

He said nothing, but the mask cracked, and the crack expanded until his face was almost naked, not merely unguarded as it had been when she watched him without his knowledge, but naked before her.

"Let her go, Adam."

"Never," he said softly, then louder. "Never!"

Embarrassed by his loss of control, Adam turned his face away, then rested it against his hand so that she could no longer see it.

"This is something you can't understand, Eva. Don't ask me to explain it. I don't understand it myself."

They sat in silence. Eva felt closer to Adam than she ever had, and she was no longer afraid of what she might find out. She no longer believed in the stranger. Adam had admitted to confusion. He was not willfully cruel. He was suffering too.

"Adam," she said at last, "you are making everyone unhappy. Your children, your mother, yourself, me. You are punishing us all, not just her. Don't you see?"

"I can't let her go. I won't let her go."

His tone was petulant. He sounded just like a child. Perhaps she could reason with him as if he were one.

"If you can't, you can't," she said. "But if you're going to keep her at least treat her decently. Let her out of that room. Let her be with the children and walk in the yard. You are right, Adam. I can't understand what you're doing or why. I won't question you anymore. What passes between you and your wife is your business, but if it affects others, others have a right to speak. It affects me to see you suffer and to see that your actions belittle you. It hurts me."

Adam turned to look at her again.

"You care for me," he said.

Eva nodded.

"Very well," he said slowly, "to please you, I will consider letting her out of the tower room."

"Not to please me, Adam. Because it's right."

"Don't ask too much."

The cracked mask congealed. His face was perfect, impassive, but in his eyes, Eva caught a glimpse of the stranger.

BOOK THREE

Spring

The Escape of
the Wild Mother

23

 The Run of the Yard

EARLY one morning, Adam Underwood stood alone in the tower room. The wind that had rocked the house all night had subsided to a sigh that barely stirred the branches of the garden trees and only rustled the dried vines that clung to the house. The warm rain had stopped, and the clouds had gathered themselves into separate shapes, leaving patches of sky where the morning stars shone down on the Empty Land, which seemed black and formless as the sea. In the stillness, Adam could hear Her singing in the yard below.

In the dead of night, perhaps awoken by the heavy rain, Adam had left his bedroom, climbed the stairs to the tower room, and unlocked the door. He did not know what had prompted him to open the door that night; it was some time since Eva had spoken to him, and her words had done more to confuse him than convince him.

What did he want? That used to be clear to him. He wanted to know her, in all senses of the word; he wanted to know what she knew, to possess her secrets, the Secret. He thought that would be possible once he had her here, at his mercy. But everything had gone wrong. She had turned on him viciously. Then for awhile all he had wanted was to punish her. But even in that he had failed. There were signs that her body suffered, but when he looked into her eyes, he could discern nothing.

After he had unlocked the door, he had hesitated with his hand over the knob. Should he let her know the door was open? Should he go in and take her, right there on the tower room floor, humiliate her, and at least momentarily satisfy himself before letting her have the run of the yard? No, he decided. He would leave the door closed and just wait to see what she would do. Maybe she would come to him in his bed: beg, plead, offer herself. . . .

Adam had turned and gone back to his room where, despite efforts to stay awake and listen for her, he dozed uneasily until dawn. Then he had returned to the tower room, finding it empty and himself empty of desire to follow her. What did he want? He did not know. He knew nothing, except that, until he found out, he would never let her go.

As he stood at the window, the sun rose; the hills took their shapes and cast their shadows. The highest stars faded into light. The singing went on and on. He could see her in the yard below where she walked with birds flying after her and squirrels running in circles at her feet. Three times he saw her try the gate: like an animal never learning, like a human hopelessly hoping, yet like neither. She was herself, neither animal nor human, but perverse. A perversion. He wondered why he still wanted her.

The weeks in the tower room had wasted her body; yet her beauty had always been a beauty of bone, of starkness, like winter's beauty: the beauty of leafless trees and treeless hills. She had beauty still, though the shadow she cast was a skeleton's shadow, and her skin was loose like the skin of a snake half-shed. Her hair had lost its once independent life; its blackness was dull and void of light. Only her eyes remained unchanged. They were hauntingly alive, shining from a death-white face, as she paused in her pacing and stared up at the tower room, stared at him standing in the window where she must have stood. He could not sustain her gaze. He looked away beyond the wall where she must have looked.

Then the singing stopped.

Startled, without realizing why, Adam looked down into the yard again. There he saw Lilith holding both Ionia's hands in her own. Mother and daughter appeared to be looking at one another without speaking. Then, slowly, the two began a dance that grew wilder and faster until it whirled over the whole lawn. He could hear Lilith singing again and Ionia laughing.

Then Adam caught sight of his own mother, still in slippers, bathrobe, and nightcap, chasing after them and flapping a strange pink garment in the air. Close after her followed Fred and the dog. The boy stumbled every few feet, because his pajama legs were too long. Each time he fell, the dog stopped to lick his face. When Adam's mother was in reach of Lilith and Ionia, Lilith let go of Ionia's hand, grabbed one of Grammar's, and dragged the old lady along in the dance. Then all three of them swooped down on Fred. His two hands made the circle complete. With Lion barking at their heels, they danced until they all fell down.

Adam watched them gasping on the ground. His mother was the first to get to her feet and brush herself off. Then she raised Lilith. From the gestures and from the sounds of their voices, Adam guessed that there was some disagreement between the two women, he supposed about the pink garment, for his mother was waving it violently in the air. Finally, Lilith bowed her head, apparently in assent, and his mother wrapped her in the garment, covering her frail nakedness, and tied the garment emphatically at the waist. Turning to the children, she issued some order. In response, the children scrambled to their feet, took hold of their mother's hands, and followed their grandmother into the house. The dog took up the rear of the procession, wagging his tail as he went. They all worshipped her, Adam reflected, just as he did. No, not as he did.

They did not suffer.

Adam raised his eyes once more and looked out on the Empty Land. The warm night rain had melted the snow from the tops of the hills, and the bare brown humps, rising from the remaining whiteness, made the Empty Land look like a sea of floating whales. Above the hills loomed large, white clouds, all with such suggestive shapes that it would have been easy to imagine that they were a convocation of giants come to debate about matters below, for they seemed to be looking directly down, as if they had decided on the center of the universe and had gathered themselves about it.

24

 # On a Small Scale

STILL in his pajamas, Jason Brooke stood by his bedroom window admiring the construction he had set in its light. On the table before him was a cardboard model of the Underwood house and grounds. For weeks he had been working in secret on this project. Now he was ready to reveal it to Ionia and Fred. He let his imagination linger over how impressed they must be with his craftsmanship. Locked in a drawer of his desk were pages of calculations and dozens of detailed drawings, which he would show to Ionia and Fred to make sure they appreciated the scientific and mathematic complexity of his undertaking. Though the model was only made of cardboard, his measurements had been so precise that he had needed neither tape nor glue to hold it together, but only a few strategic notches cut with a razor blade.

Jason reached out his hand and lightly touched the model, feeling the tension of perfect construction. Then he fingered the wire that signified the lock of the gate. According to his calculations, this lock must give way under the force of the catapult he had designed. He wished he could test the plan now, but the test must wait until Ionia and Fred were there to witness it. Still, if he aimed the catapult away from the model, he could try it out to make sure of its working order. Everything must run smoothly that afternoon.

Securing a key from beneath a loose flap of linoleum Jason went to his desk and opened the locked drawer. There, on top of his papers, sat a miniature catapult he had made with safety pins and rubber bands. Beside it was a bag of marbles. Jason lifted his weapon and ammunition out of the drawer and set them on the desk. Taking a black marble from the bag, he loaded the catapult and aimed it into the center of the room. He would gauge the force of the bolt by the distance it traveled. Counting down from ten, he released the spring. The black marble hurtled across the room. . . .

A missile moving so fast it was almost on fire smashed the gates into a million pieces. Disregarding the concrete and brick falling all around him, Jason rushed through the rubble, leaping over the corpse of Professor Underwood as he sped towards the house with Fred and Ionia cheering him on and following after him up the stairs where, with his brute force, he burst open the door and released their mother.

The marble landed with a small thud on the other side of the room, then rolled until it stuck in the crack under the door.

"Jason," called his mother from the kitchen, "is that you? Are you awake?"

"Yes," answered Jason, recalled to the present, "I'll be out in a minute. I want two fried eggs over easy and toast. And make sure the eggs aren't runny this time."

Retrieving the marble as quietly as he could from under the door, Jason put it with the others in the bag. Then he locked the bag and the catapult in the drawer and slipped the key back under the linoleum. At last he carried the model to his closet where he concealed it behind the secret panel. Taking what clothes he needed, he closed the closet door. When he was dressed, he glanced around his room to make sure he had left no evidence of his secret activity. Satisfied, he sauntered out of his room humming a tuneless tune.

In the kitchen, Jason was surprised to discover that his mother had begun no preparations for breakfast: no knives, spoons, forks, plates clattering and cluttering the table; no oranges half-squeezed into juice, no eggs frying, no toast popping, no butter melting, no coffee perking, none of the customary commotion of his mother making breakfast.

Instead, Jason found his mother standing before an open window staring outside, utterly unaware of his presence. Though he was not sure in what way, it struck Jason that she looked different this morning, not like his mother at all, but like someone he did not know. She was wearing one of her old shapeless nightgowns and her hair was loose and uncombed. A breeze blowing through the window made both the nightgown and her hair seem to float. It was the expression on her face that discomforted him most. She seemed to be smiling at something he could not have seen even if he had looked out the window with her. For the first time in his life, it occurred to Jason that there had been a time when she had been alive, and he had not.

"Mother!" Jason commanded.

Jason's voice recalled Eva from her wanderings. She had been searching for the dreams she had dreamed last night. She could not remember them in sequence or detail; she only knew that Lilith had been there. She had said something to Eva, something important. Eva stood still at the window and listened for the voice again. "You must enter the shadow. Yours is the power, Eva, daughter of the Second Woman. Yours alone is the power." She did not understand the words. She knew she was not powerful. Yet, when she heard the voice, she felt, somehow, that she was.

"Mother?"

Now another voice called her back, demanding that she be the ordinary woman she'd always supposed she was. She turned from the window, and the kitchen closed around her as if welcoming her back with an embrace, for she felt as though she had been away for a long time, and everything looked new to her in a way only familiar things can. Jason looked new to her also, and the sight of him standing there eyeing her so suspiciously brought to her mind the first time she had seen him, when she realized that he was a stranger living outside of herself.

"Breakfast?" she asked.

"Yes, breakfast."

"I forgot."

"I noticed."

"Well I'll tell you what," said Eva pushing her hair away from her face, "why don't you squeeze the orange juice while I cook the eggs or we'll both be late?"

Jason thought of protesting, but there was reason in what she said, so he went to the refrigerator and found the oranges while Eva got out the eggs and butter and set the kettle on the stove to boil. After rummaging through half a dozen drawers and opening and closing at least that many cabinets as noisily as possible to let his mother know that it was not to his liking to be made a galley slave, Jason found a knife and the squeezer and took them to the kitchen table where he began his operations.

"What were you looking at out the window, Mother?" Jason asked as he sliced an orange in half with one satisfying stroke.

"Oh, nothing in particular," said Eva, and she cracked open an egg.

"Then why were you staring like that?" persisted Jason, carefully picking the seeds out with the point of the knife.

Eva was silent for a moment as she held the two halves of the egg shell suspended in the air and watched the last of the white ease slowly into the pan.

"I was trying to remember what I dreamed last night," she explained, still holding the egg shell although the egg was now sizzling in the pan.

"Well, did you?" Jason asked, examining the seedless half of the orange.

"Not really," she answered, and she threw the egg shell into the garbage and reached for another egg. "Jason," she said as she cracked it, "I wonder about Ionia's mother."

"What about her?"

Jason balanced the orange on the squeezer.

"I don't know," said Eva, not realizing that the egg was dripping onto the stove instead of into the pan. "I have this funny feeling that something has happened."

Jason pressed the orange down onto the squeezer with all his might and watched the pulp gush out. It was not fair. He was going to rescue Ionia's mother. She must be rescued. What did his mother know, anyway? His mother with her funny feelings. Jason looked over at her.

"Mother! You're slopping that egg all over the place. Pay attention to what you're doing!"

Startled, Eva stared down at the egg shell she held in her hand and saw that Jason spoke the truth.

As Jason left the school building, he spotted Ionia and Fred in the parking lot crouching over a puddle. He shook his head; they were as odd as ever. Why would anyone want to stare into a puddle? When he came closer he saw that they were floating bits of paper, crudely constructed to represent boats of some kind. Child's play, he thought, annoyed that they had not acknowledged him yet. Glancing about him, Jason spied a stone. He picked it up; then, stealthily, he walked towards Ionia and Fred until he stood over them. Taking careful aim, he dropped the stone. It hit one of the boats dead center and sank it. The ripples spread out, making giant waves in the small puddle. Fred and Ionia looked up.

"Jason," Fred protested, "You sank my boat!"

"Oh, is that what it was?"

"Jason, you knew it was a boat," said Ionia, "That was mean."

"I'll make you another boat, Fred," cajoled Jason. "A bigger one."

"Can you make it right now, Jason, so we can go play with it in the river?"

"Not right now, Fred," said Jason. "Right now we have to go to my house."

"Why do we have to go to your house?" challenged Ionia. "It's so warm. I want to stay outside."

"No. We have to go to my house."

"But why?"

"You won't find out until we get there."

"Is it a secret?" whispered Fred.

"Follow me and find out."

Jason began to walk swiftly out of the parking lot towards the quickest route home. To keep up with him, Ionia had to take her longest strides, and Fred had to trot.

"We could tell something, too, if we wanted to, couldn't we, Fred?"

"What?" asked Jason, slowing his pace.

"What?" puffed Fred.

"Is it about your mother, Ionia?" demanded Jason.

"Oh," said Fred, "it is about our mother."

"What about your mother? Come on, Ionia, don't tease."

"It might be about our mother, but we won't tell Jason until we find out why we have to go to his house, will we, Fred?"

Fred looked from Ionia to Jason, then from Jason to Ionia and decided to keep quiet.

When they reached Jason's house, Ionia and Fred were ordered to wait in the kitchen while Jason went about some business in his room.

"You may come in!" he announced at last.

Fred went first. When he saw the model, he tiptoed towards it, Ionia close behind, as if he were afraid it might vanish. He stood for a moment in silence, then he whispered:

"It's my house! Jason you made my house!"

"Oh, so you recognize it."

"It's perfect, Jason," Ionia pronounced.

"Yes," Jason cleared his throat, "I tried to be rather careful."

Thinking it an opportune moment, Jason went to his desk drawer for the pages and pages of plans.

"See here," he said, spreading the papers out on the table, "the measurements are all exact. Precision is of the utmost importance."

Fred stared at the figures and drawings on the paper and then at the cardboard model, only vaguely understanding the connection.

"Is it magic?" he asked.

"Science," said Jason firmly. "Pure science."

"Are we going to play with it, Jason?" Fred wanted to know.

"What we are going to do," said Jason slowly, "is far more important than playing."

Jason paused to let silence give weight to his words.

"What are we going to do with it, Jason?" interrupted Ionia.

Jason looked at her with annoyance. She did not seem properly impressed.

"That," said Jason, "is something you will never know unless you tell me what you wouldn't tell me before."

"What?" asked Fred, who had forgotten.

"About your mother," said Jason. "She hasn't escaped, has she?"

"No," said Ionia.

"Oh, good."

"What do you mean good!" demanded Ionia.

"That means the plan must be put into operation."

"What plan?" asked Fred.

"Unless," Jason paused, "well, what is it you were going to tell me about your mother?"

"She's been let out of the tower room," said Ionia.

"Oh," said Jason, somewhat disappointed. "But the gate is still locked?"

"Yes," answered Fred, "my father makes it lock with magic."

"Well, then," said Jason, "the plan is still essential."

"What plan?" asked Ionia angrily, for it seemed to her that Jason cared more about his plans than about her mother.

"Wait," commanded Jason. "I'll show you."

Gathering his papers from the table, Jason took them back to the desk. He returned with the catapult and the bag of marbles. Ionia could see that his hands were trembling.

"What's that?" Fred asked pointing to the safety pins and rubber bands.

"A catapult," said Jason.

"What kind of cat?" wondered Fred.

"An instrument of destruction."

Though he did not understand them, Jason's big words silenced Fred. He and Ionia watched as Jason loaded the catapult and aimed it at the gates of the model. Then, holding his breath and steadying his hand, Jason released the spring. The marble spun through the air, across the table, and crashed open the cardboard gates. The plan worked! Jason stood up straight and let out his breath. Then he turned towards Ionia and Fred to see what effect the brilliance of his plan had made. Fred was staring at the blasted gates.

"How come you wanted to break it, Jason?" wondered Fred. "Are you going to fix it so you can do it again?"

"Don't you understand, Fred?" said Jason. "This is just a model of the plan."

"You mean," said Ionia slowly, "you're going to find big safety pins and rubber bands and marbles and build a big catapult to knock down the real gates?"

"Well, it won't be made of safety pins and rubber bands."

"What will it be made of?" Ionia pressed.

"I haven't decided yet," Jason stalled.

"How are you going to get it there if you do build it?"

Jason didn't answer; he didn't know the answer; he hadn't thought that far. He had simply assumed that if his plan worked on a small scale, it must work on a large scale as well. He wasn't about to give up his assumption.

"Well," he said at last, "I will mount it on wheels and drag it there myself. You two can help if you want to," he added.

Fred and Ionia said nothing. Fred still had not comprehended the magnitude of Jason's plan; nor was he interested. He wanted to play with the model and the marbles. He glanced at Jason, who was gazing at Ionia. Hoping Jason wouldn't notice, he edged closer to the table and began to try to fix the gates.

"Well," said Jason, "what about it? Will you help pull the catapult or not, Ionia?"

Ionia shook her head.

"It won't work, Jason."

"What do you mean it won't work?" demanded Jason. "All my measurements are precise. The proportions are perfect. It's an exact replica of. . . ."

"It's not real."

"Not real," repeated Jason. "Well, of course it's not real. Not yet. It's not supposed to be. It's a model. We have to. . . ."

Jason stopped, suddenly aware that Ionia was watching him rather than listening to him. On her face was not the closed look to which he was so accustomed, but rather a look at once more open and remote, a strange mixture of patience and impatience. Once again he felt that Ionia knew something that he did not.

"What do you mean by real, Ionia?"

Ionia was at a loss. She did not know how to put into words a wordless sense that something was wrong with Jason's plan. She supposed that technically it could work. If Jason could find the materials for building a catapult, if they could find a way to transport the catapult without her father knowing, and if Jason had estimated correctly the amount of force necessary to open the gates, then why shouldn't it work? Perhaps the problem was that he made it all sound so simple, as if to him it were a game or a puzzle that he had solved for the fun of it or to prove how smart he was.

"What do you mean by real, Ionia?" Jason repeated.

This time Ionia did not try to think what she meant. The words just came out: "I mean my mother."

Jason looked at her, puzzled. He didn't understand. How was her mother real and his plans not? Even if this particular plan didn't work—and it did have its drawbacks, he had to admit—he would think of another. He would rescue Ionia's mother. That would show Ionia, he didn't know exactly what, but it would show her.

25
The Sky in a Teacup

GRAMMAR shook her head as she cleared the remains of the children's breakfast from the dining room table so that they would not offend Adam when he came down for his breakfast. Lying beside Fred's plate was a piece of toast with a hole bitten in the middle of it through which a large glob of strawberry jam oozed. He had not touched the rest of his breakfast except to poke a hole in the middle of the egg to see if it would run. It had run, spreading out into a yellow puddle that filled his whole plate. The yolk had hardened, and she would have to scrub to make the plate come clean. The remains of Ionia's breakfast were somewhat tidier. She had carefully eaten the yolk of the egg and left the white. Of her toast she had eaten only the crusts. Both children, after toying with their breakfasts, had run outside to look for their mother, ignoring their grandmother's bribes and threats.

Since their mother had been let out of the tower room, morning play had become a ritual that undermined the routine of breakfast. Lilith slept outdoors—something the children would have liked to try had Grammar not locked them in at night—and every morning before they woke up, she would hide herself somewhere in the yard. Finding their mother each day had become a game Fred and Ionia could not wait to play. They were all but oblivious to breakfast, and Grammar had no means to force them to eat it. She prevented malnutrition as best she could by mixing eggs into the milk they drank at night and mashing vitamin pills into their food, what they would eat of it. Ionia still steadfastly refused to eat meat, but Fred, who found most vegetables distasteful, had given up and gone back to hamburgers.

As she rinsed the dishes and stacked them beside the sink, Grammar glanced out the window and caught sight of Lilith, the children, and Lion playing some sort of tag. Lilith seemed to be it. She chased first after one child, then after the other. Lion bounded back and forth between all three barking in excitement. Once he knocked Fred down. Grammar could see that Fred's pants were spattered with mud; Ionia's knees were far from clean. Grammar sighed. So the children would go to school dirty as well as hungry. What could she do? She was helpless. Besides, Grammar knew that even had she the power to stop the play, she would not have had the heart. After weeks of the children's silence, she welcomed the play, dirt and all.

"Mother," Adam called from the dining room, "is my breakfast going to materialize or must I go to school without it?"

The sound of Adam's voice made Grammar start; being startled irritated her. With deliberate slowness she turned from the sink.

"If you don't mind," came his voice, "I'd like my coffee while I wait."

Grammar went to the stove and turned up the flame under the coffee to let it boil while she fetched a cup. Sniffing to satisfy herself that the coffee had turned bitter, she filled the cup and headed for the dining room. In the doorway, she paused.

At the far end of the table, Adam sat with his lecture notes spread out before him. His head was bent and resting in one hand. In the other hand he held a pencil, and from time to time he made corrections or scribbled comments in the margin. Grammar noticed that his shoulders were hunched, and, in the light, all the gray, in what she still thought of as his black hair, was evident. She had not realized there was so much gray. It occurred to her that her son was middle-aged. Unconsciously, Grammar straightened her own shoulders, and she raised her hand to tuck away a wisp of hair that was straying on her cheek. Just then she caught sight of Lilith whirling past the window. The sound of laughter penetrated the glass.

His concentration broken, Adam turned to look, and Grammar saw his face contort, whether with pain or anger she could not tell. The expression was an involuntary one, almost like a facial tic. In a moment it was gone. Turning back to his lecture notes, he became aware of her standing in the doorway with his coffee. His face reddened, but otherwise he had control of it. Deliberately, he frowned and looked at his watch.

"I have fifteen minutes in which to eat my breakfast."

Without a word, Grammar delivered his coffee and returned to the kitchen to fix his eggs. He liked them poached. To save time, she undercooked them.

When the children and their father left for school, Grammar washed the dishes. Since her hands knew their work so well, her mind was free to wander. It wandered out the window into the yard where the snow had melted, exposing the debris of winter. If the air was mild enough, she meant to do some yard work today: picking up sticks that were scattered over the lawn, uncovering patches of snowdrops and crocuses. And it was high time to give the house a spring airing, especially her private parlor. Though Adam had taken his books and returned to the tower room, the musty odor lingered and no amount of scouring seemed to have any effect.

The dishes washed, dried, and put away, Grammar got out the broom and swept the kitchen floor. Then she opened the door and prepared to whisk away with one swift stroke of the broom the tidy pile of dirt and crumbs, but the sight of crocuses blooming through mulch and melted snow on either side of the doorway arrested her. Carefully, so as not to shower the crocuses with dirt, she nudged the pile onto the doorstep. Then she stepped outside herself and scattered the dirt in the yard. The sun shone warmer than the air. Grammar could feel the rays penetrating the morning chill. Leaning against her broom, she closed her eyes and raised her face to the light. When she opened her eyes again, the edges of everything looked soft.

Grammar scanned the yard for Lilith, but she was nowhere in sight. She only came inside to eat, and that she invariably did when Grammar was in some other part of the house. She might not have been aware of Lilith's eating habits at all if Lilith had not left evidence: a crumb here, a dab of honey there. The evidence did not reassure her that Lilith was eating enough. Though a few months ago the Creature's scarcity would have suited her, Grammar now wished that Lilith would at least have lunch with her. She wouldn't mind having the Creature in the house, so long as she kept to the kitchen. Grammar turned towards the door, resolving to make some strong tea, spread some bread with peanut butter and honey, and take a tray outside to Lilith.

A little while later, Grammar emerged from the house carrying her second-best tea service. As she wandered about the yard looking for Lilith, Grammar felt as though she were walking in a dream. There was something of dream-like incongruity about her second best tea service being out in the open air surrounded by robins plucking worms from fresh melted mud and squirrels cracking nuts and moles waking from winter sleep to tunnel through the lawn again. Grammar had walked halfway around the house, peering under porches, glancing up into trees, before she spotted Lilith sitting in the sun in the south corner of the yard, leaning against the wall with her eyes closed. One hand rested on Lion, who never left her side when Fred was away at school , and the other hand lay in her lap. At Grammar's approach, Lion looked up, but Lilith did not. She seemed to be asleep. Grammar watched the rise and fall of her even breathing, undecided whether to wake her or not.

It worried Grammar that the Creature looked so worn out. She had always thought of Lilith as a young woman, yet in sleep her age was undetermined. Her expression was as vulnerable as a sleeping child's, yet the bone-stretched skin and the shadows under her eyes might have belonged to an old woman. Her body, though still perfect in proportion, had a new fragility that was due to more than loss of weight. All its resilience was gone. Grammar found it difficult to conceive that this woman dozing in the midmorning sun was the same woman who had earlier romped with the children. She must have saved all her strength to play with them, and now it was spent.

The thought of this economy touched Grammar. Without being sure of what she meant to do, Grammar set the tray on the ground, then bent over Lilith. Impulsively she reached out her hand; for a moment it hovered beside Lilith's face. Then, barely touching her, Grammar removed a dry leaf from the tangled hair that lay against Lilith's cheek. At this whisper of a caress, Lilith woke.

"Ursula," she murmured.

Embarrassed to be caught in an act of unaccustomed tenderness, Grammar drew back and reached for the tea tray, upsetting the cups as she jerked it towards her.

"Here," said Grammar, picking up the teapot in one hand and seizing a cup with the other, "I've brought you some tea with lemon, and some honey and peanut butter sandwiches. I don't know if you've ever eaten peanut butter but I want you to try it. It's very nourishing, and you don't get enough nourishment."

"Thank you, Ursula," said Lilith, accepting the cup and the slice of bread. "You are kind to bring me food and drink. You do not usually eat outside, I think?"

"Indeed I do not," said Grammar standing up and looking around for a dry place to sit, "but since you refuse to come inside, I must."

Everywhere Grammar looked, the ground was damp with melted snow. Then, suddenly inspired, Grammar removed the teapot, the second cup, and the plate of sandwiches from the tray, and, taking careful aim, she sat down on the tray herself and poured another cup of tea.

The two women drank in silence. The steam rising from the tea bathed their faces; between sips, a soft breeze dried them. Now and then they paused, balancing the warm cups in their laps and gazing down into the clear brown liquid that rippled with the wind and shimmered with the light. Grammar discovered that, if she held her cup very still and protected it from the breeze with her hand, she could see the sky in her teacup and also two white clouds and the red, bud-swollen tips of a tree branch. It occurred to Grammar, as she studied the reflection, that she had never before seen the sky in her teacup.

"Ursula."

Grammar looked up at Lilith, who was cradling her teacup in both hands and holding it against her chin.

"What does he want of me?"

Grammar opened her mouth, but no answer came cut.

"Have some more tea," she said, at a loss for what else to suggest. "And finish that sandwich."

Lilith held out her cup and obediently took another bite of her sandwich, but she was not to be distracted.

"I do not understand," she went on. "He never touches me. He never speaks to me. He never looks at me. You are human, Ursula. What does he want? What do human beings want?"

Stalling for time, Grammar poured herself more tea. While she sipped, she wondered. It was true, as Lilith said, that Adam never sought her out. Except when Lilith invaded his consciousness, as she had that morning, he acted as if she did not exist; or rather as if she were a ghost: a being whose existence he both doubted and dreaded. Why he continued to keep her, what satisfaction it afforded him, Grammar hadn't a clue.

"As to my being human," she said at last, "or even his mother, I don't see what that's got to do with it. Adam hasn't spoken to me, except to say `Do this!' or `Do that!' in the last ten years. It's my opinion that since he met you, he hasn't been quite right in the head. . . ."

Grammar paused and glanced at Lilith to make sure she was taking no offense. She did not appear to be offended, only puzzled, uncomprehending, in a pathetic, animal way that moved Grammar's pity. She resolved to try harder.

"I suppose, at first, when he locked you in the tower room, he did it to get back at you for what you did to him at the banquet. That's only natural. All human beings want revenge. Or at least most of them do," she amended, "and the ones who don't generally end up getting killed by the ones who do."

She paused, taken aback by her own words. She tried to think of something more to say, not only in explanation of Adam, but in defense of human beings. Nothing came to her.

"I don't know," she sighed. "I can't tell you why he's keeping you now. Only he can tell you that, and maybe he doesn't even know himself."

Grammar fell silent. Lilith leaned back against the wall and closed her eyes again. Grammar scrutinized her anxiously. To prevent her from drifting into sleep, withdrawing into weariness, Grammar pressed her.

"Isn't it any better, now that you're out of the tower room?"

Lilith opened her eyes, but she did not sit up; nor did she look at Grammar.

"Yes, it is better, Ursula. At night, I can see the stars and watch their dance, and, though these stars are not the ones I see in my own country they are part of the same dance, the One Dance. When I lie on the bare ground, I can feel the earth spinning, following its path in the Dance. I can see the moon waxing and waning in time with the Dance. In the melting snow and the greening grass, I see the eternal changes of the Dance, and, in the wind, I hear the music of the Dance. . . ."

Her voice trailed away. Grammar waited, unsure of whether or not Lilith was finished, unsure of what she was talking about.

"So it's all right, then?" said Grammar tentatively. "You'll just go on?"

Slowly Lilith shook her head.

"You do not understand, Ursula. Outside, in the yard, I can watch the Dance but I am not in the Dance. I am out of my place; I am not following my steps. No living thing, mortal or immortal, can live long outside the dance."

Grammar was still bewildered, and being bewildered made her angry.

"I haven't the least idea what you're talking about," she snapped. "I don't know what you mean by this dance. Dancing is a pleasant pastime; I don't deny that; I did a good deal of dancing in my youth, but dancing has nothing to do with life."

"The Dance has everything to do with life."

"Not real life, day in and day out, as it must be lived by those of us who haven't got time to worry about dancing."

"But, Ursula," said Lilith, "you have always been a dancer. Didn't you know? You've never missed a step."

Grammar was now not only confused but flustered.

"All I know," she said, "is that if I'm going to get any work done today, I'd better get to it."

Grammar tried to stand up, first by crossing one leg over the other, then by reversing the procedure. While she struggled Lilith quietly stood up and extended her hand.

"Thank you," said Grammar gruffly, reluctantly accepting help.

Both on their feet, they bent over, picked up the cups, the pot, and the plate, and set them on the tray. Then Lilith reached for the tray.

"No," Grammar stopped her. "No one carries my second best tea-service but myself."

Grammar lifted the tray and headed for the house.

"I will follow you, Ursula," Lilith announced.

Grammar turned to stare at her.

"But I'm going inside to clean!" she protested.

"If you can have tea outside with me, I can clean inside with you."

Grammar considered the proposal dubiously. She was not at all sure she wanted Lilith following her around helping with—or more likely hindering—the housekeeping. Still, the offer was touching, and it might be a good thing for Lilith to do some work, keep her from getting morbid and fanciful. Then Grammar had an idea.

"I'll tell you what," she said. "If you want to help me, you can start by picking up the yard."

"The yard? I did not know that you clean the outside, too?"

"It's not cleaning, exactly," explained Grammar. "It's more like tidying. What I want you to do is pick up all the sticks and pile them in one place. Maybe later you can help me inside. Since you're taller you might be able to sweep the cobwebs more easily than I can."

"Do you keep house for spiders, too, Ursula?"

Grammar sighed.

"Or maybe we'll wash windows. You on the outside, me inside." Grammar started to turn away. "And Lilith," she added, "will you eat lunch with me?"

"I would be honored, Ursula."

"And do you mind if we eat inside? It's not good for my bones to sit on the damp ground."

"I do not mind," said Lilith. "And, Ursula, could we have some more peanut butter for lunch?"

"Anything you like," said Grammar, and she headed for the house, telling herself that a combination of mild labor and lots of peanut butter would be sure to bring Lilith around.

26

An Invitation

WHO was that?" asked Margery Pierce.

She turned from her cash register to watch a rather large woman with rain-soaked hair wearing a shapeless brown raincoat walk away with the cup of plain tea she had purchased.

"Who?" replied Esther Sharp.

Mrs. Sharp left her task of arranging dry cereals on a rack to go stand in the entrance and look into the dining room.

"There!" Margery said, and she pointed. "That woman in the ugly raincoat. I've never seen her here before. She doesn't look very distinguished if she's a faculty member."

Esther Sharp squinted her eyes the better to focus on the figure of the woman crossing the dining room.

"Can't tell much from the back," she commented.

Margery nodded, but she thought to herself that perhaps Esther Sharp did not know everything about everyone on the faculty as she professed to. Margery was about to turn back to the cash register when the woman selected a table on the far side of the swinging doors and sat down so that she faced them. Margery watched as the woman unbuttoned the first three buttons of her raincoat. Then the woman looked up towards the door.

"Well, who'd have thought it!" said Mrs. Sharp.

"Who'd have thought what?" asked Margery half turning towards the cash register.

"That Professor Eva Brooke should come here."

"Oh, so that's who it is," said Margery turning to look again. "Why shouldn't she come here?"

"When she's not been here these three years at least," continued Mrs. Sharp as though she had not been interrupted. "And to meet Him!"

"How do you know that's what she's doing?" demanded Margery.

"Well, what else would she be doing?" countered Mrs. Sharp going back to the cereal rack. "I ask you."

"Having a cup of hot tea on a rainy day?" suggested Margery.

"Not her!" said Mrs. Sharp, "And after all that's happened. Well, some women are bold. Or plain foolish."

"Oh, I don't believe half that story," said Margery, still staring at Professor Eva Brooke, who was sipping her tea and reading something; Margery could not see what it was.

"But I am telling you as I have told you many times before," said Mrs. Sharp rejoining Margery at the cash register, "my husband Albert saw it all with his own eyes."

"Your husband, Albert, couldn't walk when he got home, and you know it," Margery reminded her. "You told me so yourself."

"Mark my words," prophesied Esther Sharp, ignoring Margery's remark, "she's waiting for him."

Shaking her head at Professor Eva Brooke, Mrs. Sharp went to see to the souffle that was to be the luncheon special.

"Well, I suppose she's got a right to," Margery murmured to Mrs. Sharp's broad retreating back. "I'd wait, too, if I were her."

Margery turned back to the cash register, catching a glimpse of herself in the stainless steel. Her curls were tight and tidy; even the dampness could not disarray them.

🌿🌱🌿

As Eva Brooke read over the pamphlet about the World Conference of Professors and Practitioners of Ancient and Magical Arts, a drop of water, which had gathered at the end of a loose strand of hair, fell and spattered the page. Jason had taken the umbrella to school this morning at her insistence. She had felt sure of finding a rain hat in the hall closet. She bought one nearly every time it rained; only she had forgotten that the reason she did was that she always lost the hats as soon as the sun came out. They blew away with the clouds or evaporated with the puddles. This morning she had started out bare headed, and before she reached an appropriate shop, her hair was already soaked.

Unbuttoning another button of her raincoat, Eva reached inside a pocket of her blouse for a handkerchief with which she wiped the drop of water that had beaded on the page. Then, taking another sip of tea, she went on reading about the conference. She had received the notice in yesterday's mail, and she was sure that Adam had, too. The date of the conference was the week after school ended, and she wanted to discuss with Adam the possibility of their going together.

Lately, she never saw Adam, except when he stopped by on his way to the train station to pick up Ionia and Fred. He worked late in his office and avoided walking home with her as he used to. If she suggested lunch the next day, he was always busy; if she asked him to stay to supper, he never had time. The last time they had spoken alone together had been in her office when he had come to tell her that he had let Lilith out of the tower room. He had seemed angry then, as though he held her responsible for making him do it.

Adam had never spoken of Lilith since then. He was closed as the gate, impenetrable as the wall that surrounded his house. Lilith was locked up inside him, and she, Eva, was locked out. She had been tempted to just turn and walk away. Really, Adam left her little alternative. Then the announcement had come, and she had begun to hope that maybe, if she could persuade Adam to go with her to the conference, the change, the distance, might restore his perspective, restore him to himself. So, that morning she had decided impulsively, perhaps foolishly, to come to the cafeteria to find him.

Eva glanced at her watch; Adam should be arriving any minute.

When Adam Underwood swept into the room, looking distinguished in a Scotland Yard style raincoat, he did not notice Eva Brooke at the table beside the door. He did not hear her call his name nor see her half rise from her chair. While he poured his coffee and selected his roll, he was unaware of Margery eyeing him from behind the cash register; nor did he see Esther Sharp peering out at him from the kitchen. If he had, he would have thought nothing of it; he was used to people staring at him. When he had made his purchases, he headed for a table in the far corner of the room. There he arranged himself, setting down his coffee and roll, standing his umbrella against the wall to dry, unbuttoning his raincoat. Finally, he sat down, opened his briefcase, and disappeared behind it.

He began to nibble his roll and sip his coffee, but his tongue did not register the taste. Though he stared at his notes, he did not read them. No matter what he did to engage his senses or occupy his mind, nothing stopped the images. Images of Lilith as he had seen her that morning: peering at him from behind a tree, pink tatters of what was now a rag plastered to her body by dirt and rain; one bare, mud-streaked knee; tangled hair obscuring one thin white arm; animal eyes watching him walk towards the gate. For he had turned suddenly without knowing why, and he had caught her there behind the tree.

Or had he? At times he was not sure whether she was there or not. She seemed, at once, to be everywhere, then nowhere. Now hideous, now beautiful.

Now beckoning, now fleeing. But never there, so that he could see her, know her, fix her, once and for all, in time and space. Unknowable, she unmade all he did know: the daylight world of lectures and books, meetings, classes, students, colleagues, the campus, the great clock tolling the hours. He moved in this world, but it did not touch him. It seemed insubstantial; or was it he who lacked substance? He did not know anymore what was real and what was not. More than once he wondered whether his mind was still his own or if he had lost it.

Possessed by Lilith's image, Adam was unaware of Eva crossing the room. He did not see her hesitate within a few feet of him and almost turn back. Nor did he witness the squaring of the shoulders and the lift of the chin with which she determined to go forward. Only when she had stood beside him for a few minutes summoning the courage to speak did he become aware of her as a presence. He did not see the loose folds of her brown raincoat nor her hands clutching the pamphlet and her bag. He experienced her presence as a hovering warmth. He did not at once look up, for this presence must be made to realize that he was absorbed in his work and that it was intruding. Yet he did not want it to go away. Annoyed as he was that someone dared to interrupt him, he was also curious as to who it was that dared. Curiosity was a welcome distraction. He was about to confront the presence when it spoke:

"Adam."

He raised his head and saw Eva Brooke standing before him. He did not register in particular that her raincoat was shapeless and unbecoming or that her hair was untidy. Instead he received a general impression of haste, impulse, lack of control, all that he most disliked. And what was she doing here anyway? It was not her custom to come to the faculty dining room. He never met Eva Brooke here. Yet here she was, smiling down at him. Her eyes were soft and brown—or was it green—and they had a look of pleading in them. He had the power to crush or elate her. He regarded her for a moment considering.

"Well, Eva, you are a surprise," he smiled deciding to be generous. "I am just going over my notes, as you see," he added, indicating the papers spread out before him.

"Yes," Eva paused still uncertain of her welcome.

She looked so awkward, Adam reflected, standing there squeezing her bag and a pamphlet, all her weight balanced on one foot, while with the other foot she attempted to bury her big toe in the floor as if the floor were made of sand. For all the poise she had she might have been thirteen years old instead of something over thirty.

"Well, sit down now that you've found me," he said, rising to pull a chair out for her. "You must have come for a reason. Nothing wrong at home, I hope?"

"No," answered Eva as he seated her. "It's just this." She handed him the pamphlet as he resumed his seat, thinking she had better state her business as quickly as possible. "I wondered if you've received one, too."

"No, I haven't," said Adam slowly as he studied the pamphlet. "I wonder why that is."

"City delivery is more efficient," she said quickly; for she saw that his vanity had been wounded because she, who was not, properly speaking, a professor or practitioner of any ancient or magical art, had received notice of the conference before he, whose name was well known in scholarly circles. "You'll probably receive yours today," she added. "Or perhaps you're to be personally notified."

"No doubt," he answered absently; he was absorbed in the pamphlet.

Eva fell silent and watched him while he read. He leaned back in his chair with his head inclined to one side. His brows were drawn together. One hand held the pamphlet; the other hand was suspended in the air as if he were about to gesture. Eva was relieved to see him take an interest in the conference. He had seemed so indifferent to everything lately. His display of professional vanity was a healthy sign, she considered.

Eva looked at her watch; there were only fifteen minutes left to the hour. Then she looked back at Adam. Though he still held the pamphlet and stared at it, he no longer seemed to be reading it.

"Adam," she ventured, "do you think you will go?"

He turned towards her, laid the pamphlet on the table, and looked at her vaguely, as if he thought she had spoken but had not heard what she said.

"Because if you're going to go," she continued, "I think I will, too."

"Go to the conference?" he repeated. "Yes, I think I will go. Sir Algernon Riddler is going to be one of the speakers and I'd like to renew our acquaintance."

He paused, and the vague, musing expression overspread his face again.

"Perhaps we can go together," she suggested; her voice sounded strained, as if she were talking in her sleep. Its sound embarrassed her, but Adam's lack of response was worse, so she continued, "Do you think Jason could stay for the week at your house? School's out by then, and I'm sure Jason would like to."

This time she knew he had heard. The vagueness gave way to wariness. He focused his attention on her, and she felt the full force of his eyes for the first time in weeks.

"My house," he repeated. "What do you mean by that?"

"Just what I said," she answered. "I can't leave Jason alone in the apartment all week while I'm at the conference."

"Oh, are you going?"

So he had not been listening at all before.

"I thought I'd like to," she said, her voice as unsteady as her feelings. "If you're worried about Lilith. . . ."

Eva stopped, astonished at the effect of the name. It was almost as if a muscle spasm had seized Adam's face. In a moment it was over, and Eva wondered if she had seen it at all. His face was as controlled as ever, only the look of wariness had turned to one of warning.

"Well you shouldn't be, that's all," said Eva, forcing herself to continue. "I know she exists, Adam. Jason knows she exists. I know you're doing what you feel you have to do. I'm not questioning you. But you don't have to hide her from me, Adam. In fact, I wish you wouldn't."

Feeling that she had said all she could, Eva reached for the pamphlet, stuffed it into her bag, and began to button her coat.

Adam watched her, unaware that the muscles of his face had relaxed. He was conscious of feeling relief. In his mind, Eva's words reverberated: "I know she exists, Adam." He realized that for weeks he had put himself under a great deal of strain by trying to behave as though she did not. Somehow, Eva Brooke's matter-of-fact confirmation of Lilith's existence was comforting. It took Lilith out of the realm of nightmare and exposed her to the light of day. He found himself feeling grateful to Eva for her ordinariness, the plainness of her features, the nondescript color of her hair, even the ugliness of her raincoat. Suddenly, he wished he might look at Lilith beside Eva.

"Come to the house for dinner on Friday, Eva," he said.

Eva looked up from buttoning her coat; her face showed her surprise.

"You and Jason," he continued, enjoying his effect. "We'll talk about the conference then. At the moment I have a lecture to give."

Eva still had not spoken. She stared dumbly at Adam as he collected his notes and laid them in his briefcase. She was pleased with the invitation, but she could not understand what had prompted him to offer it. His internal processes were a mystery to her, but she would not question them.

"You'll save Friday, then," he said, coming to stand beside her.

"Yes, Adam."

Adam placed his hand lightly beneath Eva's elbow and guided her across the cafeteria.

"Will you look at that!" said Mrs. Sharp.

Margery turned obediently from the cash register to stare.

"Didn't I tell you she was meeting Him!" triumphed Mrs. Sharp. "And walking out together arm in arm!"

"Elbow in hand," corrected Margery, and she turned back to the cash register.

27
 Collaboration

As Adam Underwood drove through the gates on Friday evening, he kept a lookout for Lilith. He was anxious about her appearance. Strange that it had not bothered him to have Eva see Lilith in the barbaric costume of her own country, but that it worried him now to think that Eva might see her in that tattered pink robe. He had told his mother to clean Lilith and dress her, but Lilith could easily resist his mother if she chose. He wondered if this inclination to keep Lilith separate from the rest of his life had not been wise after all.

Adam parked the car, and Eva and the children scrambled out at once. More slowly Adam gathered his briefcase and the coat he had not needed to wear. Then he got out. When he turned to slam the door, he saw Lilith. She had appeared as if out of nowhere. To his relief, the pink rag was gone, but its replacement was almost as bad. He vaguely recognized an old black dress of his mother's. Once it might have been respectable; now it had lost its shape. It hung loosely from Lilith's shoulders, but since his mother was so short, it barely covered Lilith's knees, which were still not altogether clean. Except for smudges of dirt, her skin was dead white, and the black dress emphasized the whiteness. Eva, however, did not seem to notice anything strange. She stood holding both Lilith's hands in her own. She was taller than Lilith and heavier. She looked warm and solid in her brown dress. Beside her, Lilith seemed a wraith.

As Adam watched, the two women turned away and began to walk, arm in arm, around the yard. He could hear the murmuring of their voices. Fred raced ahead of them; Ionia walked beside them at a distance; Jason trailed behind, while the dog bounded from one person to another. Then came Grammar around the corner from the back door, making her way towards Eva and Lilith.

Adam, still standing by the car, found himself left alone and unconsidered, baffled. He was the connection between all these people; without him they would not know one another at all. But he did not go after them. That knot of women, the scattered children, were too much for him all at once. Instead he went straight to the house to see to the drinks.

When all the grown-ups and even Lilith had gone inside, the children fell into step with one another. The sun was just setting, and the yard was in a shadow. The air, warm all day, turned chilly, and the grass began to gather dew. In the eastern sky, stars appeared. The night would be fine, a perfect one for watching stars.

"I wish I'd remembered to bring my telescope," said Jason. "I never did get a chance to go up on your roof with it."

"Grammar doesn't like us to go on the roof," Fred said.

"Why not?" asked Jason. "If I had a roof like that, you can bet I'd be up there every night. "

"She's afraid we'll fall off," explained Fred.

"But there's a railing, isn't there?"

Jason paused to look up at the roof. Between the two ends of the house there was a level walkway surrounded by a railing; he could see the railing by the light of the western sky. Satisfied, he let his gaze drop. He saw the grown-ups, or at least his mother and Professor Underwood, sitting in the living room apparently absorbed in talk.

"They wouldn't see us if they looked out, would they?" mused Jason.

"No," said Ionia. "It's getting too dark. We can see them, but they can't see us."

"Are we going to spy on them?" asked Fred.

"No," said Jason.

Motioning Fred and Ionia to follow him, he headed for the gate, keeping close to the wall. When they reached the gate, Jason began to explore the lock with his fingers.

"What are you doing, Jason?" Fred wanted to know.

Jason didn't answer for a moment. He was hoping Ionia would ask as well. She, too, was watching, but she said nothing, so he explained.

"I'm trying to figure out this lock. I've got a book at home about locks. If I had enough time, I know I could spring this lock; or I could make a key to fit it."

Ionia turned away and leaned against the wall. Tilting her head, she stared at the stars in the deep sky where night had already come. She did not want to see Jason fuss with the lock anymore. She did not believe he could break it. If it were an ordinary lock, maybe he could; maybe then all that Jason knew from his books would help. But this lock was not an ordinary lock. It was her father's lock. That meant not only that it might be magic—she did not know about magic or remote control—but that it was her father's will. She dared Jason to break *that*.

"If I had time," Jason repeated, "I know I could do it."

No one encouraged him. Fred, losing interest in what he could not understand, wandered away to watch Lion digging for an old bone. Ionia continued to concentrate on the stars. Jason stepped back from the gate to survey the wall. As he did, he caught sight of Lion making the dirt fly past Fred's feet, and an idea came to him.

"What is Lion doing, Fred?" asked Jason.

"He's digging," answered Fred, pleased to be able to tell Jason something.

"Ah ha!" said Jason.

Ionia lowered her head and looked at him. Seeing that he had caught her attention, Jason repeated himself.

"Ah ha!"

He waited, but neither Ionia nor Fred asked him, "Ah ha what?" so he went on.

"I have just had a brilliant idea," he informed them. "If we can't go through the gate or over the wall, I propose we go under it."

"Under it?" wondered Fred. "How, Jason?"

"Elementary. Even Lion could tell us how. What's Lion doing?"

"Digging," said Fred, surprised to be asked again.

"Exactly. And if Lion can, so can we, right under the wall and out the other side."

Jason paused, waiting for someone to acclaim his idea. Fred looked from Lion to the wall. Then he crouched down and began, experimentally, to scratch at the dirt with his fingers. Ionia returned to the sky.

"Well, isn't it a good idea?" demanded Jason.

"If we had time," said Ionia without looking at him.

"Children!" called Grammar. "Come wash your hands at once!"

The children and Lion ran for the kitchen door. There was Grammar, waiting, one hand on her hip; in the other hand she held a gigantic soup ladle, as if she meant to scoop them out of the night.

🌿🌿🌿

The soup was asparagus. For awhile the only sounds in the dining room were of sipping or slurping. No one could think of a safe course of conversation for all seven to follow. Adam and Eva had already caught up on each other's work during drinks. The children, except Jason, were accustomed to keeping silence when grown-ups were present, and Jason was preoccupied with thoughts he knew better than to mention. Grammar was busy watching Ionia and Fred to make sure they were minding their manners in front of the Brookes. She had already kicked Fred twice because he was dunking his roll in his soup and making a mess. Adam found the tension of having Eva on one side and Lilith on the other for the first time since Twelfth Night more intense than he had anticipated, so he gave his full attention to the soup. It was Eva, unused to such silence during meals, who came to her social senses first.

"This soup is delicious," she said. "It must be homemade."

"It is," replied Grammar. "And not only homemade but homegrown. My own asparagus. But as for the seasoning, you may thank Lilith."

Eva thought she saw Adam start. Out of the corner of her eye, she noticed Jason hesitate, his spoon in midair, and then resolve to go on eating. Remembering Ursula Underwood's previous suspicions of poison, Eva smiled at Lilith, who sat across from her.

"A highly successful collaboration, I would say, wouldn't you Adam?" she asked, turning towards him.

"Indeed" was all he said.

Since Adam would take no more responsibility for the conversation, Eva turned to Ursula Underwood again.

"Do you grow other vegetables besides asparagus, Mrs. Underwood?"

"Oh yes," said Grammar. "I've already put in my peas and beets and lettuce. I've got some tomato plants in the kitchen, which I've started from seed. I'll wait until there's no danger from frost before I put them out. Are you interested in gardening, Mrs. Brooke?"

"I'm afraid I don't know much about it, Mrs. Underwood. I've never had a garden, at least not since I was a little girl. I've thought of growing herbs in a window box, but my apartment doesn't get much light. Are there some kinds of herbs which don't need much, Lilith? You must know all about growing herbs."

Lilith shook her head.

"In my country we do not have gardens. I have heard stories of the Garden, but I had never seen a garden until I saw Ursula's. My people do not grow herbs or vegetables or flowers; they grow themselves, and we gather them. I do not know why they grow; that is their mystery. I do know that some grow in light and some grow in the shadow of hill or rock or inside caves, and some grow in the far forests, and we journey there to gather them along with mushrooms and toadstools."

"You mean your people don't have any agriculture?" wondered Jason. "You don't keep any livestock?"

Lilith looked puzzled.

"I mean you don't grow food or raise animals for milk and eggs?" he translated.

"We are wild," Lilith explained, "so the wilderness feeds us. It is only tame creatures who must be fed by human beings, and only human beings who must make their own food. That is because they ate the forbidden food."

Adam cleared his throat.

"Excuse me," he said.

All eyes had been fixed on Lilith. They now moved reluctantly towards Adam.

"If no one objects, I think we had better leave stories for bedtime and botany to the schools where there are those qualified to teach it."

Everyone did object. Jason had dozens of questions he wanted to ask Ionia's mother about the vegetation of the Empty Land that no botany teacher could answer. Ionia and Fred felt that anytime was the best time for a story. Grammar, in spite of herself, was curious about the habits, dietary and otherwise, of the Creature and her kind. Eva simply wanted Lilith to go on speaking. Lilith's voice had made her recall the dream she had forgotten or never quite remembered. Moreover, Eva felt that Adam was being rude but she dared not tell him so in his own house where she was a guest. Nor did anyone else oppose him openly.

"Very well, then," continued Adam, "since no one objects to a change of subject, Eva and I have a matter to discuss with you all."

Eva looked at Adam blankly. She had forgotten what the matter was.

"Will you tell them or shall I, Eva?"

"You, Adam," she said.

Everyone waited, Grammar on the edge of her seat; for the wild thought had torn through her mind that Adam had proposed marriage to Mrs. Eva Brooke and that she had accepted. It might make her son a bigamist, but all their troubles would be over.

"It's just this," said Adam, settling back in his chair, enjoying the suspense he had created, "Eva and I would like to attend the World Conference of Professors and Practitioners of Ancient and Magical Arts. As it turns out, I am to be one of the speakers. The conference takes place the week after school is over. Whether or not Eva may go depends on whether or not Jason Brooke may stay here. So I put it to you, Mother, as you are in charge of operating this household."

Grammar felt let down. Was it only a matter as simple at that? She moved back from the edge of her seat and took a spoonful of tepid soup before answering.

"Can Jason stay here?" whispered Fred. "Can he?"

"Of course Jason may stay here that week," answered Grammar, addressing Fred instead of the whole company.

From their diagonal corners of the table, Ionia and Jason exchanged a brief look of understanding.

"May he not, Lilith?" Grammar added; for it occurred to her that Adam had snubbed his wife, if that's what he chose to call her.

"Jason, Son of Eva, is always welcome," said Lilith, bowing her head towards Jason.

Ionia was pleased to see that Jason bowed his head in return.

"Very well," said Adam. "That's settled then. Mother, this soup has grown cold. You might consider serving the next course."

Without a word, Grammar rose to clear the table. To Adam's surprise, Lilith rose to help her.

28
 Darkness and Dawn

WHEN Adam Underwood returned from taking Eva Brooke and Jason to the station, all the windows of the house were dark except the kitchen's. Through those, as he walked up the path, he could see his mother washing dishes. She had already locked the front door, he discovered when he tried to turn the knob. She might, at least, have waited until he got back. Reaching into his pocket for the keys, he wondered why she bothered to lock the doors at all. No one could possibly get in through the gates or over the wall. Did she lock the doors to keep Her out or the children in? Or was it simply an old, unbreakable habit?

Once inside the house, he wandered towards the kitchen, not because he wanted to ask his mother why she locked the doors, but because he had a vague hope that he might find Her there. He would have liked to see her under the harsh kitchen light performing some dull task. Eva's presence had not had the desired effect: Eva had imparted no ordinariness to Lilith; she had lent her no substance. On the contrary, the solidity of Eva's presence exaggerated the elusive quality of Lilith's.

For some time after Adam entered the kitchen, his mother refused to acknowledge him and continued to scowl at the pot she was scouring. Only after she had rinsed the pot and balanced it in the dish rack did she speak.

"What do you want?" she asked reaching for a dish towel.

Adam hesitated. He did not know what he wanted. That was why he was here in the kitchen watching his mother wipe the pots. What was it he wanted? He thought of Lilith rising to clear the table. He wanted to know what his mother knew; he wanted to know if she knew what he did not, but he did not know how to ask.

"Where is She?" he said at last, failing in his attempt to make his voice sound off-hand.

"Whom do you mean?" asked his mother, succeeding where he had failed.

Adam saw no point in responding to her evasiveness.

"If you mean Lilith," she continued, "why don't you say so? Why are you so afraid to say her name? Why are you so afraid?"

Adam felt his face redden. His mother's observations stung him. He knew she was a sharp old lady, but he had always thought her oblivious to nuance. Her perception of him humiliated him, but almost before he could recognize his shame, it turned to anger.

"Where is Lilith?" he said in a loud voice. "Where is my wife?"

"I sent her away," answered his mother inspecting the bottom of the pot. "She's not very good with dishes. The other day she broke three."

Adam suddenly felt jealous of their commonplace intercourse.

"How long has she been helping you in the house?"

"You're awfully interested in her all of a sudden," she commented as she bent to put away the pot, then, straightening up, she faced him. "Why now, when you haven't spoken to her nor hardly looked at her these two months past? What do you want?"

Adam stared at his mother as she stood by the sink glaring at him. It occurred to him that his mother was trying to protect Her. Though he was angry at his mother's interference, the idea of her protecting Lilith made him want to laugh. It was as if a Scottish terrier were trying to protect a wolf.

"Where is she now?" he persisted.

His mother sighed, turned back to the sink, and pulled out the plug. Adam sensed that her bristling fur had flattened; she knew she was beaten.

"She looked exhausted after you left," she said as she watched the water drain. "I hope she went outside to sleep."

"Where exactly does she sleep?"

Again his mother ignored him as she took an unnecessary length of time to wipe the sink and to polish the faucet and fixtures. At last she rinsed out her rag and draped it over the dish rack to dry.

"She is your wife," said his mother untying her apron, "or so you claim. If you don't know, who am I to tell you where she sleeps?"

She brushed past him and hung her apron in the closet.

"Good night, Adam," she switched off the kitchen lights. "I'll leave the hall light on. Remember to turn it out when you come up."

Left alone in the dark kitchen, Adam stood still trying to determine what it was that he wanted. It was not, he knew, to wander upstairs to bed or to his study turning out the hall light after him as his mother had told him to do. Calling on his radar sense to guide him around the table and chairs, he crossed the kitchen to the back door. It was locked, but after some fumbling he found the skeleton key that opened it hanging on a nail beside the door. Unlocking the door and leaving it open behind him, he stepped outside.

The yard was still; the night was still; he stood still on the back step, but he knew what he wanted. He had known all along; it was only a matter of admitting it to himself: he wanted Her. He always had; he always would. Eva's presence had not lessened his desire; she had not made neutral Lilith's effect. Her power over him was unbroken. When he tried to find her, she eluded him. When he tried to forget her, she haunted him. He could neither possess her nor exorcise her, yet he would never let her go. If he was to be her prisoner, then she must be his. He had married her, whether she recognized the legal bond or not. He had his rights, and tonight he would claim them. He would know her in that way at least, even if he had to force her. If she fought him, so much the better. His desire for her that night was something savage, and he would satisfy it.

Determined, he left the back step and entered the darkness. Wandering about the yard, he felt less sure of himself. He could only see the shapes of the house and the wall, the branches of the trees against the sky. Everything else was formless. He wondered how he would find her, whether he would see her eyes glowing in the dark as they sometimes did. It unnerved him to think of her hidden somewhere, watching him with her animal eyes. She had the advantage over him in this night world; night was natural to her as it could never be to him. He was almost ready to give up, out of mortal fear of the unseen, when he saw Her.

Her arms and legs, her face and neck, were so white that even the darkness could not obscure them. Gradually he made out that she was leaning against a tree and looking towards the gate. Although he felt sure she must be aware of his presence, she did not acknowledge it; she did not move at all. He paused, wishing to still his trembling before he went further. Yet he must not wait long or surely she would disappear.

"Lilith."

At the sound of her name she slowly turned her face towards him. Even in the darkness, especially in the darkness, her beauty was apparent, for it was stark and unearthly as the moon's. Cautiously, he began to move towards her. She made no motion to run away, yet the leaves in the trees began to rustle, though no breeze stirred them. He advanced steadily, and she watched him steadily, her eyes faintly glowing. When he was near enough, he reached out his hands for her. She did not resist, but as he closed his hands on her waist, he felt that she was trembling, just as the animals he used to trap had trembled. As if she were one of them, he lifted her and carried her back to the house.

Later that night, Ionia woke from a sound sleep. In response to some unknown summons, she slipped out of bed, went to her round window, and curled herself in it. The window was open; there was nothing between herself and the night. The air that touched her face and her bare arms and legs was chilly but not so cold that it deadened the scents in the air; rather the coolness clarified them. Ionia could smell the wet grass, the lily of the valley, the lilac. She thought of her mother and how, waking or sleeping, she must be breathing the same scents. Ionia peered down into the yard hoping that she might see her mother, though her mother did not usually sleep where she might be seen from the windows, but the yard was too dark. Anything might be there, or nothing.

Ionia looked out at the hills and the sky, idly wishing that the walls might be made to disappear as easily as the glass of the window. And yet, now that there was even a little hope, Ionia wondered if she really wanted her mother to escape. It was comforting to wake in the night and know that her mother was near, and that in the morning she could go outside and find her, see her, touch her, know, for certain, that she was there. And now there was hope. Her father was going away, and Jason was coming with his books on locks, his plans for digging a tunnel. Hope was unsettling; she had grown accustomed to hopelessness, almost comfortable with it. Without hope, at least everything was certain. Her father had the power; her father kept the key. They would all go on, captives together, and her mother would always be there. If her mother was free, nothing was certain, except that she would go away again, and Ionia would have to choose once more, whether or not to go with her. Whichever way she chose, it seemed to Ionia, she would lose.

Absorbed in conflicting feelings, Ionia did not at once notice a strange sound drifting up from the yard. When she did, she imagined for a moment that it was the wind, but the trees were still. The sound rose and fell becoming more than a sigh, almost a song, except it had no tune. It rose and fell, rose and fell, over and over, its rhythm like that of waves breaking on a shore. Ionia could not name the sound, but gradually she realized that her cheeks were wet. She had been crying without knowing it, without knowing why. All she knew was that she had to find her mother.

Without hesitation, Ionia uncurled herself from the window, left her room, and tiptoed down the hall to the stairs. Though dawn was near, the house was still dark, but it did not occur to Ionia to be afraid. Guided by the need to be near her mother, she could not stumble. Swiftly and certainly, she made her way down the stairs, across the hall, through the dining room to the kitchen. The back door stood ajar; a little light crept in across the floor. Ionia did not stop to wonder why the door was open. The sound was stronger, nearer. Ionia walked towards the light and stepped out barefoot into the dawn.

On the back steps she paused. There, a few feet away, was her mother. She sat on the ground with her knees drawn up against her chest, rocking herself in time with the sound she was making. Her head was tilted back, as if she were looking at the sky, but her eyes were closed. The ends of her hair dragged back and forth over the grass as she rocked.

Ionia watched, awed by the sight of her mother's aloneness. She felt unsure of how to approach her, of whether or not she could reach her, for she sensed that her mother was more than alone in the empty yard in the early morning: she was alone in a place Ionia had never been. Even if she could reach her in that unknown place, what could she offer her mother? Maybe her mother didn't want her there; maybe that place was private. It might be best just to go away quietly and pretend she had not seen. But Ionia could not pretend, at least not to herself. She was a witness, whether she was wanted or not, and she could not walk away.

Softly Ionia stepped onto the lawn. Although her whole attention was directed towards her mother, she was acutely aware of the dampness of the grass, the smell of the earth, the sound of the birds waking, the growing light. These were not distractions; rather, it was as if she were gathering them into herself so that she might be possessed of some strength greater than her own. As she neared her mother, she lost all uncertainty and self-consciousness. Kneeling beside her mother, she reached out her arms and encircled her shoulders. For a moment her mother stiffened; then she relaxed and leaned against Ionia. Ionia began to rock her mother as her mother had rocked herself. In silence they rocked together while the gray world took on its colors at the touch of light.

Then, without warning, her mother drew herself apart and opened her eyes. Ionia sat back and watched her mother's face. The light brought it no color but only showed the lines and shadows, making them deep and distinct. For the first time Ionia wondered if her mother might be very old. She had never thought of her mother as having an age at all. Even before her mother had come back, in Ionia's mind, her mother had been her mother, someone unchanging and eternal.

"Ionia," said her mother without turning towards her, "I am dying."

"No," whispered Ionia, and she reached out her hand as if to stop her.

Her mother caught her hand and held it.

"But I thought," began Ionia, struggling against panic for words, "but I thought you couldn't. I thought your people, our people couldn't. . . ."

"Yes, Ionia," said her mother, still staring straight ahead, "we are of an immortal race. The Grand Mother is immortal, though the men who fathered us were not. We, her daughters, are made immortal by the rites of the water of life. But I am cut off from the water, Ionia, and some things there are which the water cannot heal. Captivity will kill me; I am dying of it. I have no choice.

But if I did, I would choose to die. It is considered dishonorable among my people, your people, Ionia, to suffer a captive existence."

Ionia turned her face away from her mother and looked at the wall. The sun had just risen high enough so that the glass along the top of the wall glittered. Ionia recalled with shame how a little while ago she had wished her mother might never be free so that she could keep her here forever where she felt safe with Grammar and Fred. She had not thought of her mother dying. She had not thought it possible.

"No," she repeated.

"Accept it, Ionia."

Her mother's voice was stern, emotionless, as if she felt nothing, not even despair. Despair was all Ionia could feel; or rather not feel. Despair was not a feeling; it was nothing, hard, blank nothing, like the wall at which she stared.

Then Ionia remembered.

"What if you were free again?" asked Ionia, turning towards her.

"What is the use of wondering that?"

"Jason is coming," said Ionia slowly, "the week my father's going away. Jason says he can spring the lock; or if that doesn't work, we can dig a tunnel. He's coming the week after school gets out. It's not very long until then," she pleaded. "Can you; I mean you won't. . . ?"

Her mother, at last, turned towards her.

"I do not think I will die until the Great Dance begins, the Great Dance of Summer. I cannot live if I lose my place in the dance. Will Jason, Son of Eva, come before then?"

"Yes," said Ionia.

She and her mother gazed at one another, agreeing to hope.

29

 Misguided Counsel

THE question is," began Jason, "how far can we trust your grandmother?"

Neither Ionia nor Fred answered Jason right away, and in the Secret Counsel Chamber the sound of rain on the eaves and of Lion's panting seemed unnaturally loud. The storm, which had begun earlier that afternoon, had done nothing to alleviate the stuffiness of what Jason could not help perceiving as a small crawl space rather than the counsel chamber Fred and Ionia insisted it was.

"I don't think that is the question," said Ionia breaking the silence. "We can't hide what we're doing for long. It would be better to tell Grammar tonight at dinner and get her to help."

"But that's just the point," persisted Jason. "Would she help?"

"She wants our mother to go away," said Fred, who was holding Lion's paw because Lion was afraid of thunderstorms. "I heard her say she does lots of times."

"Ah," said Jason, "but would she be willing to get her hands dirty?"

"No," said Fred decidedly, "Grammar doesn't like dirt."

"She got her hands dirty on Twelfth Night," Ionia reminded him.

"Ah," repeated Jason, "but that was different."

"I don't see how," objected Ionia.

"As different as can be," Jason went on. "She didn't actually do anything then! I mean she didn't plan anything. All she did was to set up a potentially disastrous situation. She didn't know what was going to happen. It's different if she deliberately lets your mother go while she has been left in charge."

"Do you mean," said Ionia slowly, "you think Grammar's afraid of my father?"

"She is not," said Fred. "Once she threw a butter dish at him."

"Either that," continued Jason, "or she'll believe she must be loyal to him. She is his mother." Jason concluded as if that settled the matter.

"But she likes my mother," protested Ionia.

"Really?" Jason was skeptical. "Has she ever said so?"

"No," admitted Ionia, "she never says things like that about liking people. But she and my mother are together all day long. My mother told me. They work in the garden together, and Grammar even lets her help with the house sometimes."

"Well then," said Jason, "if your grandmother likes your mother so much that's all the more reason why she wouldn't want to let her go."

"No, it's not, Jason," said Ionia sharply. "Not when you really like someone." Then feeling helpless to explain what she meant, she went on. "Besides, Jason, Grammar's got to know if we start digging."

Fred had forgotten about digging the tunnel under the wall. So that's what Jason meant by dirty hands.

"But Ionia," said Jason, "don't you understand? I doubt we'll have to dig. That's only a last resort. I told you, I've been studying about how to pick locks for a month now. I showed you the key I made for the science laboratory and the janitor's closet at school. Well, last weekend I made one that fits the University gate. I tell you, I can make a key to fit any lock. I've got a book about it."

"Are you sure this lock works that way?" asked Ionia. "By rules in a book, I mean?"

"It's got to," said Jason. "Everything works by some sort of rules. Look, Ionia, you're making the whole matter more complicated than it needs to be. I can make a key for that lock and let your mother out all without your grandmother knowing it."

"But Grammar knows everything," put in Fred. "She sees without looking."

"Not when she's asleep, I'll bet," countered Jason.

"Even you can't see in the dark, Jason," Ionia pointed out.

"True," conceded Jason. "I was not intending to try. My plan is to get up at four-thirty A.M.—I brought an alarm clock—and go outside. I'll put the blank in the lock and mark it. Then I'll spend the day filing the blank. Tomorrow night I'll let your mother out. Nothing could be simpler."

Jason waited for someone to acclaim his plan, but only the thunder answered. Jason was not superstitious enough to consider this a sign. He just hoped the storm would pass before morning. It would be difficult to mark a blank in the rain, and everything must go smoothly.

"So we'll do it my way?"

It was more a statement than a question.

That night Jason had a hard time falling asleep. After what felt like hours of trying first one position and then another, Jason gave up, got out of bed, and went to the window. The storm was over; a fresh wind blew away the clouds. There were stars—as soon as he had rescued Ionia's mother he was heading for the roof with his telescope—and the moon was waxing towards fullness. He had forgotten what time of the moon it was, but what could be more convenient? There would be just the right amount of light for the escape tomorrow night. Back in bed, Jason imagined the escape scene. He played it over and over. Each time he rehearsed it, the scene became more his scene, his role in it more central until, at last, self-satisfaction lulled him to sleep.

At dawn, Jason sat up in bed and shut off the alarm. He glanced over at the small lump on the other bed that was Fred. Incredibly enough, Fred still slept. Jason decided not to wake him; it would waste time and make noise. Time and silence were essential. Jason slipped out of bed and opened his suitcase. Concealed among his clothes were his lock-picking tools: assorted blank keys, a candle, matches, a file, and a book entitled: *The Inner Reality of Locks*. He tucked the equipment into his briefcase. Then he got dressed and tiptoed out of the room into the hall, which was still dark as night.

Beside Ionia's door, Jason paused, debating whether or not to summon her. She would not be as troublesome as Fred, but when he considered, he found no reason why she should come with him. In fact he wasn't sure he wanted her there at all. He didn't need her help, and she might make him nervous. This was the most delicate part of the operation; his hands must be perfectly steady. It would be better to work alone. Then, tomorrow night, when the success of his plan was sure, Ionia and Fred would come with him to witness it.

Decided, Jason continued down the hall, unaware that Ionia, moments later, had slipped out of her room and followed him on bare, silent feet. On the landing she caught up with him. Startled, he frowned at her but said nothing; nor did Ionia speak. In silence they went downstairs, hugging the bannister so that the stairs would not squeak. Without even a whispered conversation, they made their way to the kitchen where Jason opened the back door with the skeleton key Grammar thought she had hung out of Ionia's and Fred's reach.

"How come you didn't wake us up?" asked Ionia when they were outside.

"Ssh!" said Jason, although there was no longer need for such caution.

As they headed for the gates, Jason glanced anxiously around the yard. He had forgotten about Ionia's mother being outside. He hoped she wouldn't wake up and come to watch him, too.

"Where does your mother sleep, Ionia?" whispered Jason.

"I don't know exactly," she answered, "but I can go and find her."

"No!" said Jason; then, attempting to make his voice more casual, he added, "Let her rest. There's no point in her being here, too. I mean there's nothing either of you can do to help."

Ignoring Ionia as best he could, Jason set down his briefcase, opened it, and began to arrange his equipment on the ground before the gate. Then, with both hands, he touched the lock as the book had instructed him to do. According to the book, practiced hands, and his were surely that, should communicate to the mind much of the inner reality of the lock before experimentation with the blanks had even begun. Jason stood touching the lock for some time, unwilling to admit to himself that his brain had received no message from his fingers.

At last he gave up and turned his attention to the array of blank keys spread out on the ground. He studied them for awhile, then, with a pretense of scientific certainty, he selected one. All the while, Ionia watched him without a word, but instead of forgetting her presence, Jason became more and more acutely conscious of it. He wished she would go away, but he could not ask her to; he could not let her know that she unnerved him.

After testing all the blanks and setting aside several that seemed to fit, Jason lit the candle. Then he picked up one of the blanks and held it to the candle's flame until it was thoroughly blackened. Blowing out the candle and handing it to Ionia, he attempted to steady his hands. Ever so carefully he inserted the blank in the lock and then, as carefully, he withdrew it. He stared at the blank unbelieving. It showed no marks, no markings whatsoever.

"What's the matter?" asked Ionia.

"Nothing," mumbled Jason. "Hand me that candle."

He picked up another blank and went through the process all over again with the same lack of results. Though baffled, he would not give up. To give up would be to admit defeat, not only of his plan, but of the laws of science and logic. Systematically, he tried one blank after another, growing more and more frustrated as each one failed to reveal to him the inner reality of the lock.

By the time he was ready to test the last blank, his hands were shaking and he was appallingly close to tears. He wished he had never come to the Underwood's house at all. It was stupid of his mother to make him stay with people just because she was going away. He was old enough to take care of himself. Maybe he'd go home, right now before breakfast. He'd—but then he remembered that, of course, he couldn't go home. Like the others, he was trapped unless his plan succeeded. Hoping against hope, he withdrew the last blank from the lock.

Nothing.

"It doesn't make any sense!" he shouted, and he hurled the blank to the ground.

Jason turned away from the gate and away from Ionia. He could not face her, but as he turned he found himself face to face with Ionia's mother instead. She gazed at him calmly, steadily, a little curiously. How long had she been there? He had not heard her come up behind him. He wished she would stop staring at him. Under her gaze he felt helpless: helpless to move, helpless to speak, helpless to defend himself.

"My daughter tells me you are a springer of locks, Jason, Son of Eva."

Jason's face grew hot, and he lowered his eyes. Looking down at his feet, he noticed that his sneakers were wet with dew and that one lace was untied. He felt no impulse to tie it. What did it matter? What did anything matter now that his plan had failed?

"I can't spring this one," he said.

He continued to stare at the ground, wishing that she would question him so that he could explain to her the peculiarities of this lock, how it refused to obey the most basic mechanical laws, but she said nothing. He raised his eyes a little and looked at her bare feet in the dirt of the driveway. Then, curiosity overcoming caution, he lifted his eyes to her face. It had not changed: it showed no reproach, no disappointment, no anxiety. As he looked into her face, he began to feel some of its calm. He forgot all his excuses and explanations. He forgot his claim of expertise and his shame at failing to prove it. None of that mattered anymore. Only she mattered. He felt he would not mind any amount of dirt and sweat for her sake.

"We have another plan," he began.

Just then he was interrupted.

"You!" shouted an angry voice. "So this is how you repay my friendship! Plotting behind my back!"

Jason turned and saw Ionia's grandmother striding towards them, still in her nightgown, dragging Fred by the wrist with one hand, and pointing at Ionia's mother with the other.

"It's my fault," Jason called out. "No one's been plotting behind your back, except me."

Old Mrs. Underwood stopped before them and turned on Jason.

"Is that how your mother brought you up? To undermine a household that receives you as a guest?"

"My mother had nothing to do with this," said Jason. "The whole thing was my idea." He turned towards Ionia. "And I've made a mess of it."

30
 Certainty and Risk

FOR breakfast, Grammar served burnt toast, lumpy oatmeal, unsweetened grapefruit juice, sour milk, bitter coffee, and cold silence. She did not sit down with the children and Lilith but ate her breakfast standing up at the counter, keeping a vulture's eye on the table. As soon as anyone had finished his food, she swooped down and removed the remains. Then, noisily, she scraped, rinsed, and stacked the dishes.

At the table, everyone obeyed the law of silence, but now and then feet and knees encountered each other under the table, and elbows found a place to nestle in neighboring ribs. Glances were exchanged over the rims of juice glasses. After one such exchange, Jason broke the silence.

"Mrs. Underwood," said Jason, rising from his chair and carrying his milk to the sink, "I'm sorry about what happened. Ionia and Fred wanted to tell you about the plan last night. They said you ought to know. I see now that they were right. All of us here are agreed about the injustice of. . . ."

"I don't think all of us here are agreed about anything, young man," snapped Grammar.

Jason paused and looked at Ionia, who frowned and shook her head. He gathered his approach was wrong.

"I mean we all know that," he paused unsure of what to call Lilith, "that Ionia and Fred's mother wants to go back to her own country."

Jason looked at Lilith, but she gave him no sign. Why wouldn't she do anything to save herself? It didn't make sense.

"And we, I mean Ionia and Fred and I, want to help her. What we want to know is, will you help?"

Grammar didn't answer; she turned to the sink and began drawing dishwater.

"Will you hear our plan at least?"

"I suppose if you speak I can't help hearing," said Grammar without turning from the sink.

"Well," said Jason, "we thought that since we can't get through the gate, we'd dig a tunnel under the wall."

Grammar began to wash the dishes.

"First of all," Jason went on, "we need to know if there are any shovels."

"There are," said Grammar rinsing a dish. "Two of them. In the tool closet." She set the dish in the rack and reached for another.

"It's locked," said Grammar plunging the dish into the water. "I have the key."

"You mean," said Jason slowly, "you mean you won't open it?"

Grammar turned from the sink.

"What does it matter what I mean? If you want those shovels, I know you'll go behind my back to get them." She stopped and stared at each one of them in turn. "Now get out of here." Her voice was low, almost a growl. "Get out of my kitchen. All of you!"

Lilith rose first and led the way through the back door with Lion at her side. Ionia followed, then Jason. Fred sat still, after the others had gone, staring at Grammar. She glared at him until he, too, left the table. As she turned back to the sink, Fred paused by the door.

"I don't want my mother to go either," he said in a loud whisper.

Startled, Grammar whirled around, but Fred had disappeared. Shaking her head, she went to the table to clear away the rest of the dishes. All the briskness was gone from her movements, and she made no clatter. Now that the children had gone outside, her anger was subsiding to sadness. Back at the sink she drew more hot water and added another dash of soap. As she watched Fred wander past the window in search of the others, her eyes stung and her vision blurred. His gesture of sympathy had touched her, but Fred did not understand. No one did.

She did not, as Fred supposed, mistaking her feelings for his, want to keep Lilith here. She knew well enough that the Creature was unhappy. Had not she, Grammar, been opposed to her staying from the first? True, of late she had become fond of the Creature, but she could see that Lilith no more belonged in a house and a yard than a tidal wave belonged in a bathtub. Though the children adored their mother—to excess in Grammar's opinion—she was not a good influence on them. She undermined regularity and routine. She encouraged them in their wild ways, had them running barefoot in all weathers. She played with them in the dirt and told them endless stories of her own country.

One evening not long ago, Grammar had come upon the three of them during a storytelling. The children had been sitting on either side of their mother in grass that was already damp with dew. Their eyes were wide as they listened to the low voice that almost sang rather than spoke, enthralling not only the children, but the birds and the squirrels, the toads and the snakes, and even, against her will, Grammar herself. Grammar stood in the shadows and listened to the voice tell of the wild beasts of the wilderness, their fearlessness, their gentleness, how if moon and mood were right, you could meet a lion and stroke his mane. You could wrestle with wolves and run with deer. Then the voice told them of clear rock pools and underground rivers. It told of dirt houses built into the sides of hills and how the houses were lined with dried grasses and herbs and each house held a tiny pool of fresh water. They lived in the houses when it was cold winter. In the hot summer they slept inside the houses during the day, because by night they danced the Great Dance until dawn.

It was then that Grammar had interrupted, ordering the children upstairs for their baths. She could not bear the look in their eyes. They no longer saw what she saw. The world behind the wall, her world, was unmade by the visions that voice invoked. All the human comfort she could give, good food and hot baths, clean sheets and turned down beds, could never compete with the wild beasts and rock pools, midnight dancing and houses made of dirt. It was cruel, unthinking and cruel, of the Creature to fill the children's heads with fantasies and make them unhappy with what they had.

As Grammar dried the dishes and put them away, her anger revived. She would gladly have let Lilith go if she could have. The others had no right to think her cowardly or selfish. What enraged her was their plotting behind her back, plotting against her. What reason for secrecy could they have but that they meant to run off with Lilith and leave her alone? Now this show of including her in their plans. What difference did it make? If they dug a tunnel, what was to prevent the children from crawling out after their mother? Why should she help the children to leave her? For she would be left. She could not go chasing after them into the Empty Land. Even to climb the stairs winded her. She would fail after the first few hills, and they would leave her then. If she was to be left, she would rather be left in her own house. And supposing she could keep up with them, what would she do in a country of wild beasts and wild women who lived like animals, in holes in the ground?

No, she would not help them carry out this plot against her, though doubtless Mrs. Brooke's brat would break into that closet if he wanted to. Grammar reached into her pocket and felt for her keys. One by one she fingered them, knowing most of them by touch. There were dozens of keys, keys to all the closets and all the rooms in the house, save one. Only the key to the tower room and the key to the gate were missing. If she had that one, she would let Lilith out during the night when the others were sleeping. Then she would lock the gate and keep the children safe forever. Slamming the door to the cupboard so hard that the dishes rattled, Grammar stalked out of the kitchen and devoted the rest of the morning to violent housecleaning.

At noon, Grammar put away the vacuum cleaner, with which she had surreptitiously evacuated some spider's webs, violating the agreement she had made with Lilith to let them be. Since the weather was fine, she decided to make sandwiches and take them outside on a tray. Then she could come back inside, eat her lunch in peace, and take a long nap. The morning's upheaval had tired her.

When the tray was laden with a pitcher of milk, glasses, cheese, baloney, and peanut butter and jelly sandwiches—more peanut butter and jelly than any other kind, since Fred would eat nothing else and Lilith had developed, in her captivity, a passion for peanut butter—Grammar went out the back door and began to walk slowly around the house looking for the children and Lilith. The grass was over grown (perhaps she could set Jason to mowing it) and her feet made no sound. As she came up behind the little group sitting beneath a tree, no one heard her. Lion, who might have sensed the nearness of baloney, was asleep.

"I guess you know I could break into that closet tonight and get those shovels," Jason was saying.

Grammar paused to listen, never minding the heaviness of the tray.

"If we're going to dig a tunnel we need time, and. . . ."

"No," Lilith silenced Jason, "I will not go behind Ursula's back."

No one spoke for a moment.

"Won't you at least talk to her?" pleaded Jason. "Try to persuade her?"

"I will not force Ursula's hand."

"But I don't understand."

"What don't you understand, Jason, Son of Eva?"

"Well," he began, embarrassment evident in his voice, "you tried to force Ionia's father to let you go."

"Yes," admitted Lilith, "but I have learned a little since then about human beings."

"What?" asked Ionia.

"Just that they are not so different from my people; they, also, would be free."

She paused, and no one filled the silence until she spoke again.

"And I have learned something else: I am not afraid to die."

The sight of Fred's face hit Grammar harder than Lilith's words. As he turned to stare at his mother, Grammar saw on his face a look she had not seen since he was a very small child, hardly more than a baby, and she had, by accident, dropped him. There had been a moment before the tears and howls began when he had just looked at her in utter bewilderment. So he looked at his mother now, and Grammar could not bear it.

"Lunch," she announced, and her voice cracked on the word as if she had not spoken in a thousand years.

After lunch, alone in her private parlor, lying on the daybed with a light shawl covering her, Grammar found she could not sleep. She felt fidgety but could think of nothing to relieve the fidgets. She had played one game of cards, but she could not concentrate; nor did she wish to read her current mystery novel: the plot was too complicated and the characters too simple. Besides, she was bone tired and entitled to a nap. So she continued to lie on the daybed with her eyes firmly shut in her determination to have one.

But her attempts to lose consciousness were futile. She could not take her mind off what Lilith had said about dying nor could she escape the image of Fred's face when he had heard. Why did the Creature have no more sense than to speak of death before a child? But then, when had the Creature ever shown any sense, animal or human? There was no evidence that Lilith ever thought about what she said or did. She did not think; she simply was, and she could not or would not account for that being. Lilith's lack of responsibility irked Grammar. It made her own responsibility unbearably heavy, for it seemed Lilith had left everything up to her, even life and death.

Death, Grammar could no longer evade the word, and she let it reverberate in her mind. Death. She had not thought it would come to that. Though Lilith had warned her months ago, she had refused to believe that anyone could die, except of starvation, disease, old age, or accident. Even now, that the Creature could die of captivity seemed incredible. Maybe she was mad, or else feigning, playing on their sympathy. Sense she might lack but she had a kind of animal cunning. She had shown that at Twelfth Night.

Yet even as Grammar admitted the thought, she rejected it, ashamed of herself. The Creature had never, directly or indirectly, asked for sympathy. She had simply stated a truth, as she might have said: the grass is green or the sky is blue. And how could Grammar deny this truth? It was self-evident. In spite of air and light, exercise and quantities of peanut butter, the Creature had grown steadily paler and thinner, a wraith of the woman who had crossed the threshold that winter night, a shadow of the vibrant being whose very presence had made the house and all within it quiver with life. Yet how could it be? How could this existence, which Grammar herself had endured for years, destroy Lilith in a season?

Then Grammar remembered Lilith's other words.

"Human beings are not so different from my people: they, also, would be free."

Grammar sat up in bed and let the shawl fall from her. There was the difference between herself and Lilith, greater than the difference between their habits and their natures: she had chosen this existence; Lilith had been tricked and trapped. She had chosen to care for the children and put up with Adam. It did not matter that the gate was locked nor that the wall surrounded her. "We are all prisoners," Lilith had said. But that was not so. She, Grammar, was free; maybe not free to come and go, but free to do what she was meant to do, made to do. Was that what Lilith meant when she spoke of following the steps of the dance?

Grammar pushed her shawl aside, forgetting to fold it, and began to wander around the private parlor, as if activity, however random, might help her decide to act. For she must do something; that much was plain. She could not let Lilith die before the children's eyes. Yet how could she let Lilith take away her own reason for living? Grammar paused in her pacing. If only she could exact a promise from Lilith that she would not take the children with her; the children would obey if their mother ordered them to stay. Yes, that was it; she would make an agreement with Lilith, a fair exchange: her freedom for the children. The children did not mean to Lilith what they meant to her; Lilith had left them behind before, and the children needed a proper home and schooling. It was only right. . . .

Grammar's thoughts translated themselves into action at once. Forgetting to put on her shoes, she left her private parlor, hurried downstairs and out the back door. Only when her feet touched the grass did she realize that they were bare. Preoccupied as she was, she noted that it was a pleasant sensation.

She found the others constructing dirt houses in a yet unplanted portion of her vegetable garden. Reminded of the stories, Grammar's feelings toward Lilith hardened, and she resolved that tomorrow, without fail, she must plant the zucchini.

"Lilith," said Grammar, "I'd like a word with you—alone."

In spite of the frailness that damaged her beauty, Lilith was still graceful. She rose from the ground as if she were growing. The children turned to watch her. With a motion of her head, Grammar indicated to Lilith that she was to follow. She led her to a sheltered corner of the yard out of the sight and sound of the children.

"Lilith," began Grammar, "I have decided to open the tool closet and to help you in any way I can if you will promise me one thing."

"What is that, Ursula?"

"That you will not let the children go with you, either of them."

"I cannot promise that."

"Why not?" demanded Grammar. "If I do something for you it is only right that you do something for me."

"Is that another of your human laws, Ursula?"

Grammar did not answer. She did not know what to say. How had she ever hoped that Lilith would listen to reason? She was not a rational being.

"Fred will not come with me, Ursula," said Lilith more gently. "Though he was born of my body, he is not of my people. Ionia is, Ursula, as much as she is of your people. She must choose between them. I will not destroy her choice."

"What do you think you do when you tell her those pretty stories of your people!" exploded Grammar. "Their dirt houses and their midnight dancing?"

"I do no more than tell her the truth. You give her food, baths, clothing, and comfort. That is your truth, Ursula."

The two women looked long at one another.

"I am sorry, Ursula. I can make you no promises. If you help me, you will be taking a risk."

Then Lilith bent and kissed Grammar's forehead. Before Grammar could speak, Lilith was gone.

For some time Grammar remained motionless, as if her bare toes had sent down roots into the ground. Why could she not have been a tree, with no need to do, only to be? Slowly she began to make her way around the house towards the front door. To go inside by the back door she would have to walk past the children who were still playing in the garden. She didn't want to see them right now. All at once, she felt ashamed of her attempt to drive a bargain with Lilith, her attempt to buy the children. She had lived a long time. She was old enough to know that there were no bargains, no guarantees.

Wearily, Grammar climbed the front steps and reached out her hand to turn the knob. The door was locked. Of course. She had never unlocked it that morning. As she drew her key ring out of her pocket she wondered, for the first time, why she had locked it at all. She stared down at the keys in her hand. There must have been twenty at least. Why had she so many keys? What was she guarding? The children, she reminded herself. Then she asked aloud: "Guarding them against what?" From that unnatural woman came the old, automatic response, but it no longer held true. Lilith had lived within the walls for months. And perhaps it had never been true. Perhaps she had never guarded the children, but only herself, against their loss. Wasn't that exactly what Adam was doing?

Grammar singled out the front door key and saw that her hand was trembling. The parallel between herself and Adam had shaken her. For what did Adam guard: an unhappy creature who longed to be gone, and whom he would lose in the end in spite of locks and gates and walls. Loss it seemed was the only certainty.

Why not risk it?

At supper time when the children, Lilith, and Lion came into the kitchen, they saw that the door to the tool closet stood open, but there was no sign of supper, and Grammar was nowhere in sight. She had begun at the top of the house, unlocking the door to the attic, and working her way down to the bottom, where she was, at that moment, unlocking the door to what Fred called the dungeon.

31

☥ Digging ☥

THE next morning everyone rose at dawn. After a breakfast of banana pancakes, which Grammar prepared in honor of the occasion, they all filed out of the house. Lilith led the way, for she had spent hours last night pacing around and around the wall in order to determine where the ground would be best for digging. Jason carried one shovel, balancing it over his shoulder. Fred, with the other shovel, tried to imitate Jason, but the shovel was longer than Fred was tall. After losing his balance and dropping the shovel a number of times, Fred contented himself with dragging it behind him. Lion followed, sniffing curiously at the shovel. When they came to the spot Lilith had chosen, Grammar was relieved to see that it was not in any of her gardens or near any of her rose bushes. It was, in fact, the quiet corner where they had spoken yesterday, the northeast corner of the yard. Lilith proposed to tunnel east.

Everyone agreed that Jason ought to be the one to break the earth. They all stood around him in a circle and watched as he placed one foot on the shovel. Then, using his whole weight, he thrust the shovel into the earth. The earth yielded, and a crack spread for several inches on either side of the shovel. Then Jason removed his foot and leaned hack against the weight of the earth. Shifting the position of his arms, he lifted the first shovelful of dirt and let it fall to the side of the small hole he had made. Everyone cheered, then Fred said:

"Now let me!"

Jason's only response was to thrust the shovel into the ground again and again and again. The hole grew steadily deeper and the pile of dirt higher. Encouraged rather than tired, Jason thrust harder and harder. Then everyone heard a scraping sound.

"A rock," Jason explained, and with his shovel he began to probe its size and shape. "Ionia," he said after awhile, "get the other shovel and come round the other side of this rock."

Obediently, Ionia turned towards Fred, who was standing beside her, and grasped the shovel assuming he would let go of it, but instead of relaxing his grip, he tightened it.

"No, Ionia," he said, "I want to." And dragging the shovel, he ran around the other side of the hole. "I'll help you, Jason."

"No," said Jason, who was growing short of breath. "I need Ionia to do it." Fred remained planted by the hole, gripping the shovel, looking both stubborn and tearful. Grammar was about to intervene and explain to Fred that he wasn't old enough just as she wasn't young enough, when Lilith spoke.

"Let the man-child try his strength, Jason, Son of Eva."

Jason looked up at Lilith and saw that her face was as stern as her voice.

"All right," agreed Jason.

Fred managed to lift the shovel, and it fell by its own weight into the hole where it hit the rock.

"See if you can get it underneath the rock so we can both lift," instructed Jason.

Fred tried but he could not maneuver the shovel. He lost his balance and fell backwards, still holding the shovel so that it showered him with dirt. He would have cried out of humiliation and frustration, but Jason left his own shovel, picked up Fred's, and positioned it beneath the rock.

"Now Fred," he said, "pull back on the shovel with all your might."

Fred pulled and Jason pulled, but the rock would not budge. Fred began to grow tired; his arms and fingers ached, and still nothing happened. Helping was not as much fun as he thought it would be. Still he kept on until he found himself once more sitting on the ground. The handle of the shovel quivered above him. The shovel had remained firmly in the ground though he had fallen down. Slowly and with some dignity, Fred stood up.

"Ionia, you can help now," he announced, and he went to watch Lion who was digging his own hole some feet away.

After that morning the digging fell into a routine that filled the days. Jason, Ionia, and Lilith, who amazed everyone by being able to thrust the shovel into the ground with her bare feet, were the diggers. They relieved one another in shifts. One shift was the digging shift, another was the helping shift, which meant standing by with the other shovel in case of rocks, and, when the hole was deep enough, lifting out buckets of dirt, and the third shift was the resting shift. Jason, on his first rest break, made a schedule of these shifts, concerning their length and who was supposed to be on which one when. At regular intervals, according to some inner schedule of her own, Grammar carried fresh lemonade to the workers.

Fred was the only one who was not on a schedule and who had nothing in particular to do. For a while he helped Grammar whenever she made the lemonade. He would sit on a stool at the kitchen table and stir the lemonade with a long spoon. Then, one time, without asking, he tried to lift the whole tray, but it was too heavy, and before he could set it down, one of the glasses fell off and broke on the floor. After that Fred had decided he better stay clear of the kitchen.

So he wandered around the yard, sometimes following Lion, sometimes with Lion following him. Now and then he'd stop to watch the digging, and several times he tried to attach himself to the person on the rest shift. When it was Jason's turn to rest, Jason usually went upstairs to Fred's room. He'd lie on the cot facing the window and pretend to rest while Fred sat on the cot and watched him. After a few minutes, Jason would prop himself up on his elbow and peer out the window so that he could see the digging. Then he would get out pen and paper and make calculations about how long it would take to finish the tunnel. The only time he spoke was to ask Fred what he thought his father would do if he came back and found them digging the tunnel. Fred knew his father would lock them all in the dungeon.

When it was Ionia's turn to rest, she went to her own room and did not invite Fred to come with her, except once when she asked him to come with Lion and pose for a portrait. Fred, who didn't know what posing for a portrait meant, eagerly agreed and was disappointed to discover that all he had to do was to sit still while Ionia drew a picture of him. While he sat, he looked at the pictures she had taped to the wall. She didn't hide them anymore since Mrs. Brooke had given her the easel and Grammar knew about it. The pictures were not like the ones she used to draw: of things he had never seen. Instead they were pictures of things he might see any day: Grammar hanging out the laundry, Grammar washing dishes, Grammar with a broom. Then there were some of the garden: green lettuce leaves in brown dirt, beet and carrot tops. There was one of a squirrel scrambling up a tree, one of a bird flying over the wall, pictures of the house from all sides, and lots of pictures of his mother, not faraway on a hill, but close up, just her face, sometimes only her eyes.

When Ionia finished his portrait, she hung it on the wall beside a picture of Grammar. Fred inspected it. He was doubtful about the boy in the picture; he knew he was bigger than that, but Lion did look just like Lion. Ionia promised that she would make him a picture of Lion that he could keep, but not now. Now, she said, she needed to be alone.

Fred understood that he was supposed to go away, and he went, with Lion padding after him, but he did not understand how anyone could need to be alone. Except for Lion he had had little company since the digging started, and he was tired of being alone. He remembered that when he was little, before he went to school, he had been alone most of the time, but he hadn't minded then. He had always had lots of things to do, especially with his zoo. Now he didn't have a zoo because his mother didn't like things to be in cages. He hadn't missed his zoo. It had been more fun to play with his mother. But now his mother didn't have time to play, and neither did Ionia or Jason. They all just kept digging and digging that hole so that his mother could go away again.

He couldn't tell anyone about the ache in his belly that had been there ever since his mother said that thing about dying. Jason was too busy to listen, and Ionia wanted to be alone. If he told Grammar about the ache, she would make him take medicine. He wanted to tell his mother, but when it was her turn to rest, she really did. She would walk away from the digging, find a patch of sun—or if it was hot, a patch of shade—curl up in it, just like Lion did, and go to sleep. Fred would crouch nearby, pulling up bits of grass and digging his nails into the dirt while he watched her.

It was just so that Grammar spied him, late in the second day of digging, as she was hanging the laundry on the clothesline. Immediately she resolved to find something for Fred to do. She did not like to see him brooding over his mother that way. With a clothespin still clenched in her teeth, she went to the tool closet and reached into the pocket of her garden apron for the packet of zucchini seeds she had begun to plant the day before. Then she picked up the bucket of fertilizer and made straight for Fred.

"Come along, young man," she said, the clothespin dropping from her mouth. "I have a job for you."

The clothespin bounced off Fred's head and landed beside him. He picked it up; then, glancing once more at his mother, he got to his feet and followed Grammar to the vegetable garden.

"Now," she said, "I am going to teach you how to plant zucchini."

"Is it magic?" Fred asked after watching her demonstration.

Feeling that it might insure his attentiveness and care, Grammar answered:

"Yes, it's a kind of magic. One day these tiny seeds will grow into big bushy plants with lots of zucchini on them. Do you remember eating zucchini last summer?"

Fred did, and he hadn't liked it. He was a little disappointed that this magic only made vegetables, but he would rather make vegetables than eat them.

"Now," said Grammar, "the next hill of seeds must be planted exactly the length of this stick from the others." She measured the length. "You plant these seeds, and I'll watch this time."

Slowly and accurately Fred repeated all the steps he had seen Grammar perform. Then, without being told, he measured with the stick and started another hill. Satisfied that she knew what he was doing, Grammar went back to her laundry, leaving the clothespin where Fred had dropped it between a row of beets and carrots.

Fred went on contentedly with his task, each time solemnly counting his seven seeds out loud, as if he were intoning a magic spell. So thoroughly absorbed was he that he did not notice when his mother came and seated herself at the edge of the garden.

"What are you doing, Man-Child, that makes you so serious?"

Fred looked up, holding a seventh seed in his hand, one that was to be planted in the very center of the circle.

"Magic," he replied, and he placed the seventh seed in the earth. "I am doing magic to make these seeds turn into zucchinis," he explained, covering the seeds with dirt and patting them.

"That is good magic," said his mother.

Fred measured the distance to the next hill, which brought him closer to her, and as he drew the magic circle, he went on:

"I will save some of these seeds and take them with me when I go to your country. Then I will plant them there, so your people can eat lots of zucchini."

Lilith remained silent while Fred counted out the seven seeds, knowing his mother was listening.

"Fred," the gentleness of her voice was touched with sternness, "I thought you understood that you cannot come with me."

A stubborn look came into Fred's face as he pressed the seeds into the ground.

"I am," he said dropping dirt onto the seeds.

"No, Fred. "

"How come?" he slapped the dirt that covered the seeds. "Ionia was going to go."

"I have told you before that we raise no man-children."

She had told him before, but he still could not imagine or understand a place where there were no boys, no beings like himself and Jason. Gripping a clump of dirt in his fist, he looked up at her in bewilderment.

"How come?"

"Because when the First Woman, the Grand Mother, for whom I am named, fled the Garden for the Wilderness, she fled mankind and his ways to live in freedom. There is no freedom among men and women. They are captive to one another."

His mother spoke in a singsong voice, and Fred sensed she wasn't seeing him anymore.

"In the Wilderness she gave birth to a woman-child, whom she had conceived by Adam. That was the beginning of our race. Since then we have grown slowly; most of us never know men or bear children. We are few in number, but that matters not for we do not die."

Fred had not understood most of her words, but the last phrase caught his attention, because of what she had said the other day about dying. She had spoken as if she could die, then, as if she would, almost as if she wanted to. When he was little and one of his toads died, Grammar had told him to stop crying. Everything and everyone died someday, she said, so he might as well get used to it.

The dirt Fred clutched in his hand was growing sticky. He unclenched his fist and buried his hand in the cool, dry dirt. Then he looked up at his mother. She was still staring as though she could not see him, and she had begun to rock back and forth.

"But Grammar says that everything dies," Fred shouted, as if she were too far away to hear him. "And you said you were going to die, too."

Fred could almost see his mother coming back from wherever she had been. And when she gazed down at him, it was with a look that made Fred drop his stick and run to her and bury his face in her lap. Rocking him as she had rocked herself, she spoke:

"I did not mean that we could not die, but that we do not, unless something or someone kills us."

Fred looked up from his mother's lap.

"You mean my father?" he whispered.

"He has taken away my freedom," she said, then added as if to herself, "and he has lost his own."

Fred did not know what his mother meant by that. His father was free. He could do anything he wanted to. He could open gates that even Jason couldn't open. He was about to ask his mother what she meant when a shout from Jason interrupted him.

"We've gotten to the right depth! We're starting to dig horizontally from the bottom of the hole!"

Fred sat up and drew back from his mother's lap, but Jason paid him no attention. He stood before Lilith, breathless from running around the house with his news.

"It's your turn to stand by," he told her, "but I'll stay on, too, to make sure Ionia knows what she's doing."

Jason turned and started back towards the digging.

"I think we'll break through to the other side tomorrow," he called over his shoulder, and he broke into a trot.

"Finish your magic, Man-Child," said Lilith turning to Fred. "Then come with me to behold this tunnel."

While his mother watched, Fred covered the ring of bright, colored pebbles. Patting the earth, he stood up. Then he carefully folded the packet that contained the remaining seeds.

"Here," he said handing her the packet. "Do you know how to do the magic?"

"I watched you very carefully."

"Then you take the seeds with you to your country and plant them when you get home."

As she rose from the ground, Lilith kissed Fred's forehead. Then the two of them walked side by side to the digging.

32

 ## A Saving Obsession

TOWARDS noon on the third day of digging, Ionia lay stretched out on her back beside the entrance to the tunnel. Because there remained only two full days until her father's return, they had all decided to work continuously even in the heat of the day and for some time after dark. At the moment, Ionia was taking her turn at the standing-by shift, which meant that when Jason had filled a bucket with dirt, she was supposed to haul it out of the hole, dump it, and hand it back to him. This process repeated itself every ten minutes or so.

Unlike Jason, to whom standing by meant leaning over the hole and shouting instructions to the digger, Ionia stayed quiet between times and stared at the sky. To Jason's bewilderment, she had not shared in his excitement over the digging. He did not understand that in order to endure the waiting Ionia had lulled herself into a state of perfect passivity. She had ceased to will the success of the plan and made herself merely an instrument of its carrying out. Though she worked as hard as Jason, she did not tire as easily, for she wasted no energy wishing. While she waited for the next bucketful of dirt, she thought of nothing but that the blue of the sky had softened with haze and that the pale daytime moon was almost full.

"Ionia!" Jason shouted.

She got up at once and leaned over the hole, ready to receive the bucket. But instead of the bucket, Jason himself appeared.

"We've run straight into the wall."

Ionia said nothing but moved back to let Jason climb out of the hole. Still silent, she waited while he threw himself down beside her.

"I knew the wall would extend several feet under the ground to give the whole structure stability," he continued, "but I didn't think it would go further than six feet."

"We'll have to dig deeper," she said.

"That's what I've been doing half of the morning," he shouted turning his frustration on her. "I didn't want to tell you until I was sure, so I just kept digging down next to the wall. Ionia, I dug another six feet, and I couldn't. . . ."

"Sure of what?" she interrupted.

"Sure that your father built the wall so far into the ground on purpose. I mean not just as a foundation but to prevent anyone digging a tunnel.

As she grasped the meaning of Jason's words, Ionia felt cold all over. Her father's foresight frightened her. Was there nothing he had not thought of long before they had?

"Time for lunch!"

Ionia and Jason turned to see Fred running towards them.

"Jason," said Fred, breathless, as he slid to a halt beside them, "can I go inside the tunnel?"

"Not now," said Jason, getting to his feet and brushing himself off. Something in Jason's voice warned Fred not to plead. In silence, the children walked around the house to where Lilith and Grammar waited for them with sandwiches and milk beneath a tree.

"Baloney for you as usual, Jason?" Grammar inquired.

Jason took the sandwich Mrs. Underwood offered him and sat down on the ground, but after one bite he found he could not eat. He laid the sandwich in his lap and stared at it, unconscious of Lion, some feet away, stalking the baloney. Ionia did not even attempt to eat but shook her head at the cheese sandwich her mother held out to her.

"All right," said Grammar, when she had finished her liverwurst sandwich and brushed the crumbs from her lap. "Out with it. You two look more like you've come from digging a grave than a tunnel."

Ionia dug her nails into her palm and hoped that Jason would speak.

"Well," said Jason, sitting up straight and assuming responsibility, "I'm afraid we have bad news. The wall extends into the ground much farther than we thought it did." He paused for a moment. "We don't know how far."

Jason glanced at Ionia's mother. Her face was calm, even peaceful. Had she not understood what he said? Should he explain? Just as he was about to go on, she spoke.

"Of course. Adam is no fool. He has built a perfect trap." She turned to look at Jason. "Never mind, Jason, Son of Eva. You have done your best, and it was well done."

Jason tried to sustain her gaze, but his eyes stung and he turned his face away. Fred, not fully understanding what the bad news meant, drew nearer his mother with an instinct to comfort and a need to be comforted. Ionia, numb with the cold that had overcome her by the tunnel, felt nothing. There was nothing left to feel.

"I should have known all along," muttered Grammar to herself. "And I, his own mother. Haven't I lived with his twisted mind longer than anyone else?" Then she raised her voice and addressed the others, "I only wonder why I didn't tell you before not to waste your time trying to dig under the wall. I could have saved you time and trouble."

No one answered or even looked at her. Grammar got to her feet and began to pace among them.

"But I tell you you're wrong to give up now," she went on. "Look here! We've got a mess on our hands and no amount of moping is going to tidy it up. Something has got to be done."

"Peace, Ursula," said Lilith. "Have done with hope. I would die with a little dignity."

"Dignity be damned!" shouted Grammar. "There's nothing dignified about dying, and if your people did it more often you'd know it. And I won't have you dying here: not in my house, not on my lawn. It's indecent!"

All at once, Lilith began to laugh. She laughed and laughed. The children, Grammar, and even Lion stared at her.

"Now then," said Grammar when Lilith's laughter had subsided, "let us be sensible. We are all overwrought. After lunch we will all take naps. On waking we shall spend the rest of the afternoon in solitary contemplation of the situation. Then at dinner we will meet to discuss our course of action."

Grammar bent to pick up the tray, but before she turned to walk away, she added:

"And no talking among yourselves. I won't have you scaring each other and devising such plans as a lunatic might to escape from an asylum."

Grammar took the tray into the house, emerging a moment later to enforce her orders.

A little while later, in her private parlor, Grammar lay on her daybed while she finished her latest mystery novel, *The Search*. She felt that reading might distract her and help her fall asleep. Then, when she woke, she could tackle the problem with a fresh mind.

The strangest thing of all—began the last paragraph—was that the answer had been there all along, so close that it might have tickled his nose and made him sneeze. How was it that it had taken him his whole life to find what he might have had at any moment? But that was a mystery greater than the one he had just solved.

Grammar closed the book and tossed it away. It was no mystery to her why it had taken Lord Digsby his whole life to find the answer. She had never encountered a more doltish hero. Mystery novels were not what they used to be. Sighing, she pulled her shawl closer about her, leaned back, and let sleep take her.

When Grammar woke, the light in the room had shifted, and she could tell it was late afternoon. Now she must think. No thoughts came to her. Instead an old familiar urge stole upon her. The urge to pick, pick, pick at the lock of the tower room.

"Stop that!" she told herself. "There's no time for such idleness!"

Try as she might, Grammar could not dispel the image of the tower room nor her urge to get inside it. Then, suddenly, she sat bolt upright.

"Why I've been as stupid and blind as Lord Digsby!"

Without losing another moment, Grammar made for the tower room. As she stood before the door and sniffed, the familiar odor greeted her. She wondered why she had not realized before that if there was an answer to how to open the gates without a key, it must be among his musty old books.

Tearing a pin from her hair, Grammar began to pick at the lock. She had been broken so long from this habit that it felt strange to indulge in it again. Picking the lock took her back to the days before Lilith had come. Her life then had been orderly, and she had made sure everyone else's was, too. Her only escape from routine had been picking the lock until that in itself had become routine. When she thought of them now, the days before Lilith seemed all the same, nothing to make one different from another. Since Lilith, almost everyday had been difficult or dangerous or different. As she stood picking the lock, Grammar admitted to herself for the first time how much she would miss Lilith: Lilith who had been both enemy and friend.

Grammar's hand trembled, and she raised it to brush away sudden tears. Then it occurred to her that she was wasting time picking the lock by this haphazard method. Sticking the pin back into her hair, she hurried downstairs to the dining room where she found Jason asleep with his head on the table and his mouth open so that he drooled on some pole-vaulting calculations he had made.

"Wake up, boy!" Grammar shook him. "I've got a lock for you to pick."

After dinner everyone except Lilith and Lion followed Jason upstairs to the tower room. Grammar stood beside Jason on the landing holding a flashlight; Ionia and Fred waited on the top two stairs. They all held their breath as Jason fitted the key he had fashioned into the lock and turned it. The door opened. They all let out their breath and breathed again. The smell was overpowering, worse than mold or mildew, Grammar thought. It was like the smell of something dead. She pinched her nose with her fingers and breathed through her mouth.

Stranger than the smell was the pale light that came from the room. Fred and Ionia, on the stairs, could see nothing but the glow. Jason, standing in the doorway, discerned that the light came from an object on the Professor's desk, a round object that seemed dark at the center though bright on the surface. There was something unnatural about that light, Jason thought. Then he realized what it was; it cast no shadows. Only Grammar knew what the object was.

"It's only his old crystal ball," she said as if she were dismissing some toy he ought to have outgrown. "Come on. We've got to ransack this room and take all the books downstairs. We can't search for spells among such smells."

Pleased with her rhyme, Grammar stepped into the room and set to work.

33

ᚨ By the Power of the Moon ᚨ

LIVER of toad, whisker of mouse, sweat of baboon, and baking soda," intoned Grammar as she sat bent over a book at the kitchen table.

"No, Ursula," called Lilith from the back steps, "I told you: there is to be no killing, not even of toads."

"This is a recipe for hair tonic," explained Grammar, fingering the ill-concealed bald spot at the back of her head. "But how on earth could I get hold of baboon sweat?"

Grammar fell silent and resumed her study of a book called *Common Household Spells.* The only sounds in the kitchen were those of pages turning, moths beating their wings against the light bulb, and a gentle snoring that came from Fred. He could not read well enough to search for spells so he had decided to look at a book about dragons and sea monsters that had lots of pictures. He had fallen asleep over a picture of a green dragon with its red mouth wide open.

"Lilith," called Grammar, "if you have nothing else to do, would you take this child up to bed?"

In answer, Lilith padded soundlessly into the kitchen, lifted Fred in her arms, and carried him out of the room with Lion following after.

"You two haven't found anything yet?" asked Grammar in a low voice.

Both Ionia and Jason shook their heads.

It was nearing midnight. Grammar, Ionia, and Jason had been pouring over spells for hours. They were all tired, and though the pile of books in the center of the table was not yet exhausted, they were all discouraged. Jason had been perusing the Professor's books on Alchemy in hopes of finding something on the dissolving of metals, but, predictably, most of the books were about the transformation of base metal into gold. The rest were about the philosophic and historic significance of that operation. Ionia had been looking through one book after another on magic, but they were mostly scholarly: *The Origins of Magic, The Age of Magic, Magic in the Middle Ages.* Few were practical. The only book resembling a how-to manual was the one Grammar had, and that was of little value except as a curiosity. Sighing, Grammar cast aside the book of household spells and took up another volume at random, resolved, like Ionia and Jason, to stay up all night if need be. Engrossed in their work, none of them noticed Lilith, on her way back from putting Fred to bed, pause in the doorway to watch them.

"I should put you all to bed," she said, just loudly enough for them to hear her.

"Nonsense," croaked Grammar, whose voice was as tired as the rest of her.

"I wish I could help you at least," said Lilith approaching the table, "but I do not understand the black squiggles that crawl across the white paper."

"It is our job to help. . . ." Jason's gallantry was lost in a yawn.

Lilith, standing beside Ionia, reached out and touched Jason's head in the barest caress. Then she began to go through the pile, feeling the size and shape of the books, exploring their texture with her fingertips, sometimes picking them up and smelling them. Grammar, Ionia, and Jason continued to read until Lilith interrupted them.

"What is this book?" she asked holding up a slender volume in purple-dyed leather. "It has a strange scent, different from the rest."

Lilith handed the book to Ionia.

"*Mysteries of the Moon,*" she read slowly, "*The Making and Unmaking of Magic.*"

Opening the book to the first page, Ionia began to read:

> *In ancient times, when man first walked with his feet touching earth and his face turned toward the sky, he knew the power of the moon and did homage to it. Even in modern times, scientists recognize the moon's effect on ocean tides, the birthing of animals, and it is generally supposed that at one time the menstrual cycles of women correlated with the cycle of the moon. Farmers still plant at the dark of the moon, and police expect more incidents of homicide when the moon is full. But the knowledge of how to call forth the moon's full power to raise the wind and the water, to move the dry land and set fire to the sky, has been long forgotten, except by a very few. . . .*

Jason closed Professor Higginbottom's treatise on the laws of alchemy. Grammar laid aside a book called *Alchemical Marriage: How to Transform Your Spouse.* Ionia read on and on until just before dawn.

At sunset the next day, Grammar, Fred, Ionia, Jason, and Lilith, all wearing life jackets, raincoats, and rubbers, climbed through a trap door in the attic onto the railed walkway on the roof. Lion, also wearing a life jacket, at Fred's insistence, had to be lifted, as he could not manage the ladder, and Fred would not leave him behind. None of them had ever been on the roof before—which Adam's father had built as an observation deck so that he could study the migratory habits of birds—because Grammar had never and did not now consider it a safe place to be. As a safety measure she had brought with her a clothesline. As soon as everyone was on the roof, she busied herself with tying each person to all the others. Then she tied the ends of the clothesline to the railing, leaving just enough slack to allow minimal freedom of movement.

"Now then," said Grammar satisfied that she had done all she could, "when is this moon supposed to rise?"

"Not for another half-hour," answered Jason a trifle sullenly; for he thought all this fuss with ropes and raincoats was silly. He had decided not to risk bringing his telescope, however. It was hard to believe that anything was really going to happen, but he supposed the occasion required of him a certain amount of scientific open-mindedness, and it was better to be on the safe side.

"We might as well have some tea and cakes while we're waiting," said Grammar.

Jerking them all slightly forward with her motion, Grammar knelt and opened a large wicker basket, which contained a thermos bottle, five cups and saucers, a platter of cupcakes, a jar of water, a jar of dirt, a lantern, kitchen matches, and a fan. When she had served each person, she told him to sit down. Soon they were all seated in a semi-circle around the basket, sipping tea and eating cake. Grammar and Jason were at either end. Lilith was in the middle, with Ionia on one side next to Jason, and Fred and Lion on the other next to Grammar. They all sat cross-legged with their knees just touching. No one spoke.

As she waited, Ionia laid down her cup of tea and let it grow cold. She forgot to finish her cake and let it crumble in her lap. She no longer felt the pressure of Jason's knee or her mother's. The roof and the railing faded, and she felt herself carried out on the cool air to the place where the moon would rise, to meet whatever would happen there. Unlike Jason, she had no doubts that something would happen. But she was not afraid, even if what would come meant the end of all things. She was ready for the end.

Then the sky behind the three trees brightened.

"It is time."

Her mother's voice seemed to come from everywhere, from inside herself, from beyond the trees. Yet it drew her back from wherever she had gone, and she found herself on the roof, behind the railing, tied between her mother and Jason. Everyone was standing except Grammar, who bent over the basket and lifted out the jar of dirt, which she handed to Lilith. Opening the jar, Lilith reached in her hand, took a handful of dirt, and put it into Ionia's cupped hands, replacing the jar. Grammar handed Lilith the lantern and the matches. When Lilith lit it, she passed it to Jason. Next Grammar gave Lilith the jar of water.

Lilith poured some water into one of the cups and handed it to Fred. Last, Grammar offered Lilith the fan. It was a dark green fan, decorated with pink elephants and roses, a relic of Grammar's dancing days. After holding it for a moment, Lilith handed it back to Grammar, and Grammar returned to her place.

Now all of them were standing facing the moon, which had risen halfway above the horizon. When the moon at last detached itself from the hill of the three trees, Lilith began to sing:

> Mysterious Moon,
> Raiser of wind
> Ruler of water
> Mirror of fire
> Mover of earth,
> We the captives
> of one man's magic
> make supplication
> to your Majesty.

Lilith went on singing, but Grammar could no longer understand her words. Soon the sound of her voice was lost in another sound: the sound of wind rising in the Empty Land and rushing towards them. Before it reached the roof, Grammar could see it rocking the three trees. They seemed closer than they ever had. She could see the shine of the moon on their leaves; she could hear their branches creaking. The rope at her waist tightened as she and the others prepared themselves to meet the onslaught of the wind. She clutched at her fan, but when the wind came, she yielded to it. After that she knew nothing of the others. Nothing, even, of her own body. Nothing but the wind.

When the wind passed, Fred still trembled with fear. He felt he could not hold the cup of water much longer, for it was growing heavier and heavier as the moon rose higher. The only thing that comforted him was the sound of his mother's voice. Soon that sound was drowned by a roaring sound louder than the sound of the wind. Then he saw a huge blackness, a wave of blackness, swallow the three trees as it rose with the moon higher and higher until it covered half the sky. The roaring grew louder, and the darkness came down, down, down to swallow the world. He tried to cry out to his mother, but his voice had disappeared. And then, so had he.

When the blackness receded, Jason was surprised to see that his lantern still burned, and even brighter than it had before; so did the stars, and the moon shone bright overhead. The night was still again except for the sound of singing, which Jason guessed must be Ionia's mother. He wondered if whatever had happened was all over. He was about to ask, when he became aware of an intensification of light. He could see the green of the leaves on the trees, and he could discern the various grasses and herbs of the Empty Land. The light was like no light of day, not even noonday. It was a hot, fierce light, like firelight or the light of molten iron. Then Jason saw that the light was coming from the stars, which were growing larger and brighter every second. Shrill whistling sounds, like the sound of firecrackers soaring in the air, deafened his ears, and he saw that the stars were moving, spinning round and round. The faster they spun, the hotter and brighter they became. It seemed to Jason that the earth could not stand such heat; at any moment it must ignite. Then Jason felt his own body melting in the heat, melting into light.

When the blaze died down, Ionia could still hear her mother's singing. The stars had resumed their usual size, but now she could see their colors more distinctly than she ever had before. Green, blue, red, purple, gold, white, they pierced the night; and the moon, now in the western sky, shed its light on the hills of the Empty Land, making them shimmer as if they were not earth but water. Frozen waves; for all was still: no sound, no motion, nothing but her mother's singing.

Then her mother's voice was joined by other voices, and beneath the three trees on the hill, a woman appeared, and then another and another until a whole band of women danced in a circle around and around the three trees. As the singing grew stronger and the dance wilder, the hills began to rise and fall, rise and fall, as if they, too, joined in the dance. One moment Ionia could see the women dancing beneath the trees; the next moment the whole hill would be gone. Each time the hill reappeared it seemed closer. Ionia could see the women's faces now; she could see the fierceness of their joy. Just when they were so near that Ionia felt she had but to reach out her hands to be swept along in the dance, she heard a great rumbling. The earth trembled, and she felt it open beneath her. The women vanished; the hills vanished; the sky vanished, and she felt herself falling, falling into a deep, warm darkness.

⚘ ⚘ ⚘

When Ionia opened her eyes, she saw a pale gray sky. Lying still, conscious of being cold and uncomfortable, she wondered where she was and how she happened to be sleeping outside. Then she remembered: they had all been on the roof; she had been holding dirt in her hands; her mother had sung the incantation, and then, and then—what had happened after that?

Ionia sat up suddenly and looked about her. There was Jason sleeping beside her in his raincoat and life jacket; his hand rested on the lantern, which had gone out. There was Fred, curled up with his arms around Lion; the cup lay on its side, empty. She looked down beside her and saw the dirt that had spilled from her own hands. Beyond Fred was Grammar, stretched out on her back; the elephant and rose fan obscured her face and quivered each time she drew a breath and let it out.

Ionia's mother was gone.

Pulling at the rope that was still around her waist, Ionia freed herself and tiptoed to the railing. The yard was still; everything was as usual, except for one thing: the gate had disappeared; no trace of it remained. The place where it had been was an empty space in the wall, which still stood as high and solid as ever. Ionia stared, seeing but unbelieving. Images of the night that had just passed returned to her. They were images of utter destruction, of the end of the world. How could any of them, any of this, the house, the wall, have survived unless it was all a dream they had dreamed, lying asleep on the roof under the full moon? Yet the gates were gone, and so was her mother.

Ionia lifted her eyes and looked out into the Empty Land. The sun was just rising behind the three trees, casting their shadows towards her. The shadows looked like arms reaching for her, and Ionia remembered the dance she had seen in the dream last night, if it was a dream. The memory of those faces brought home her loss to her. All the faces had reflected her mother's face.

Ionia clutched the railing and swallowed the sob that rose in her chest. She had never believed that this morning would come. She had thought last night that there would come an answer. She and her mother would be magically carried beyond the wall to her mother's country. Either that or the end would come, the end of all things. She had been ready for the end, she had been ready for anything but this: that life would just go on and on, as it had before, without her mother. Her mother had gone and not even said good-bye. Her mother had gone, and there was no end to anything. No end to the emptiness.

Ionia turned away from the railing wondering what she would do next, what she would ever do, and her eyes fell on the sleepers. They looked so funny lying asleep in their raincoats and life jackets among the teacups and cake crumbs that, in spite of her grief, Ionia almost laughed. In that moment she loved them, and she knew that they had loved her mother, too. It occurred to her that even if her mother had not left her, she could not leave them alone to face her father. Who knew what he might do to them? As she watched them sleeping, she resolved to stay with them, at least for a little while, and face whatever came of their common action.

But just now she wanted to be alone. She wanted to walk to the top of the hill of the three trees and look, even if only that one time, into her mother's country. And maybe when she was sure the others would be all right, she would journey, alone, into the Empty Land, and search for her mother's people.

As quietly as she could, Ionia lifted the trap door and climbed down into the attic. Then she went downstairs and left the house by the front door heading straight for the empty space. Just as she was about to walk beyond the wall for the first time, she heard a voice.

"Ionia!"

Ionia whirled around and saw her mother. Then she was in her mother's arms sobbing the tears she had stifled before.

"What is it, Ionia?" asked her mother when Ionia had quieted. "What is it that makes you tremble so?"

Ionia sensed that her mother was not just concerned but curious. She stepped back and looked at her.

"I thought you had gone," Ionia said.

"How could you think that I would leave without you when I have waited so long? Nor would I leave without saying good-bye to Ursula and the man-children."

"You were going to leave without saying good-bye before." Ionia reminded her.

"Before they had not given me back my life."

For a while neither Ionia nor her mother spoke but only looked at one another.

"Will you be ready when the time comes, Ionia? Have you chosen?"

It seemed to Ionia that in spite of all that had happened, nothing had changed since that first night she had spent with her mother. Her mother was still asking the same question, and she still did not know the answer. But she did know that there on the roof when she had turned and watched the others sleeping she had made a kind of promise.

"Mother, I. . . ."

She stopped.

"Speak, Ionia, do not be afraid."

"Mother, I can't go with you, not now, I mean not right away. . . ."

She paused hoping that her mother would prompt her or, better, say that she understood, but she made no response.

"I mean I can't leave the others alone to face my father. He'll be very angry. I don't know what he'll do to them. I have to know. I can't just leave them."

Ionia heard the pleading in her voice. She knew she wanted her mother to say: yes, you are right; that is best. But still, her mother remained silent.

"But when it's all over, unless he locks us up, then I could come to you. By myself. If you just tell me how to get there."

At last her mother spoke.

"I do not need to tell you, Ionia. If you wish to find us, you will know the way. The knowledge is within you, it has been always. And you are old enough and brave enough to come alone if you will. I do not say you are wrong to wait with Ursula and the man-children. I do not know right and wrong. But I must give you one warning, Ionia, child of two worlds. You do not yet know what you are. You are still trying to be two things. There will come a time when you must choose. Not now, perhaps. I do not know the time; nor is it for me to set it. But the time will come."

For a moment Ionia felt the old anger and confusion. Why must she choose? Why must she always be choosing? But as she looked at her mother, she grew calm. She felt sure that when the time came, if it came, she would know what to choose. Where her mother was, there she would be. It was just that, well, for a little while she had to do something else.

"I hope you don't think you're going anywhere before breakfast!"

Ionia and her mother turned and looked towards the roof to see Grammar, Lion, Fred, and Jason standing by the railing staring down at them.

Breakfast, of porridge and muffins, was a silent meal. No one felt able to speak of what had happened in the night. Each was absorbed in thoughts of his own. Jason wondered why whatever had happened had not happened to more than the gates. He gazed at his porridge and ate ponderously. Fred ate only a few bites of his muffin and then went to sit in his mother's lap. Grammar exercised all her will power to keep from exploding with one question. She stirred her porridge round and round without eating it. Now and then she stole a glance at Lilith and Ionia, who sat side by side at the table. Neither gave her any sign. Lilith rocked Fred, and Ionia sat still, not even pretending to eat her porridge. That hurt Grammar. Who knew when Ionia's next hot meal would be or if she would ever eat one again?

"Ionia," she said sharply, "if you're going on a journey, you must eat a good breakfast."

"I'm not going, Grammar."

Grammar gasped and dropped her spoon, but before she could question Ionia, Lilith put Fred from her lap and rose.

"It is time," she said. "Let us say good-bye at the empty space."

Lilith led the way out the back door. Single file, the rest followed her. At the opening, she turned to face them, and they gathered themselves about her.

"You who have braved deep magic for my sake—You who have given me my life. . . ."

Lilith did not finish. She knelt before them, but only for a moment. Soon the others were kneeling, too, and their arms were around her. No one stood up until Lilith did. Then she embraced Jason and Fred and Lion and Grammar and last Ionia. Standing back, she looked at each one of them in turn, and the look she gave was beyond words and embraces. At last she turned and began to walk away.

"Wait!" cried Ionia.

Lilith paused; Grammar's heart stopped.

"I will walk with you to the top of the hill." Lilith held out her hand to Ionia. Grammar, Jason, Fred, and Lion watched as the two walked together towards the hill. Beneath the three trees they embraced once more. Then Lilith disappeared beyond the hill. A moment later, Ionia turned and walked back down the hill alone.

BOOK FOUR

Summer
The Return of
the Wild Mother

34
Empty Space

IT was high noon when Adam Underwood and Eva Brooke turned off the main highway onto the narrow road that ran along the edge of the Empty Land to Adam's house. The sky was clear, and the sun, unveiled, was hot. The hills of the Empty Land lay bare and exposed beneath it, unprotected at noon day by the shadows they might have cast early or late. To relieve the heat inside the car, Eva rolled down her window all the way. She leaned her head on her arm and breathed the warm air, full of the scent of scorched herbs and berries, which rushed past her face and tangled the loose wisps of her hair.

Adam, in the driver's seat, had opened his window only halfway. He drove staring straight ahead at the familiar road as if he suspected it of inconsistency, some alteration made in his absence, meant to trick him. So he had driven since early that morning, looking neither to the right nor the left, not speaking to Eva. They had discovered last night, when they met at dinner for the first time in several days, that their opinions of the conference differed drastically. Eva had never disputed with him before, and he would not have minded that she had begun to now if her argument had not been so irrational, even religious. Something about the Garden of Eden, the apple of knowledge, the arrogance of wanting to become like God. She did not deserve a reasonable answer.

Adam looked over at Eva with her head cradled in her arms and the wind making her hair even more untidy than it usually was. She is a child, he told himself, and he softened towards her. Besides, he would be taking her to the station this afternoon, and he would have the whole summer to himself in which to do some serious research about the possibility of alchemical control over planetary movement. His findings might prove invaluable to the government in aiding space exploration. All he needed was silence and relative solitude to allow him full concentration on this project.

Suddenly self-conscious, Eva sat up and smoothed her hair. She glanced at Adam. He was looking at the road again, but she saw that his face had relaxed. She waited for a moment to see if he would turn towards her, however briefly, and exchange at least a look, but he did not. She turned her face away instead and joined him in staring at the road. She was sorry that they had quarreled last night, sorry that she had displeased him, but she saw no reason to recant. Perhaps, as Adam had claimed, her unfavorable impression of the conference was due to the fact that, unlike Adam, she knew no one there. She was unfamiliar with the writings of the various speakers. She was, as Adam had informed her, an outsider. Whether or not she was of the inner circle, she had, nonetheless, kept her eyes and ears open. It seemed to her that the professors and practitioners were not so much concerned with the ancient and magical arts as with their own specialized knowledge of them, and, through knowledge, their power. Nearly all the speakers had concluded: ". . .and if we can master the secrets of whatever art we can control. . . ."

"Eva."

Adam interrupted her thoughts and startled her with the first word that had been spoken on the journey.

"You have often asked me if you could take my children with you on a summer trip."

Eva turned to look at Adam, but he did not look back.

"I am prepared to accept the offer if it is still open."

"Yes, of course, Adam, but why. . . ."

"My wife needs a rest from them. So does my mother. And I need some undisturbed quiet in which to do my research."

"Yes, of course, Adam," she repeated.

Suspicious, after last night's disagreement, of sarcasm underlying her words, Adam turned to scrutinize Eva's face, but all he could see was the back of her head: the loose bun coming undone, strands of fine hair pasted to the back of her neck with sweat. He turned away again and thought of Lilith; how he would be alone with her at last as he had been in the beginning before the children came and ruined everything.

Eva stared out the side window, and the hills began to move as if they were made of water. Then swimming towards her she saw Fred's rickety grey farm. As discreetly as she could, she brushed the tears from her eyes and faced forward again. From the top of the hill, they could see the house and wall. Adam accelerated his speed and reached his right hand into his pocket feeling for the touchstone. Eva leaned forward slightly and clutched the seat with her hands as the car swerved sharply around the last bend before the gate. Then, without warning, Adam slammed on the brakes. Eva's head banged against the window shield, and, for a moment, she could not see. When the shock and the dizziness lessened, Eva realized that Adam had left the car. Lifting her eyes, she saw that he was standing with his back towards her in an empty space where the gates should have been.

Adam did not hear Eva get out of the car. He did not hear her running up behind him, panting for breath and calling his name. When she touched his arm, he scarcely felt it.

"Who has done this thing?" he whispered, and then he screamed, "Who has done this thing!"

The silence that followed was broken by the sound of the front door opening. A moment later Grammar, Jason, Ionia, Fred, and Lion appeared on the door step. Then, led by Grammar, they proceeded single file down the walk.

Eva glanced up at Adam. He remained perfectly still, giving no sign of what he would say or do. Eva tightened her grip on Adam's arm as if her touch might restrain him.

When Grammar was within ten feet of Adam, she stopped and the others grouped themselves around her. Eva looked at Jason, but he did not answer her look. Like the others he stared at Adam.

"Where is she?" asked Adam so softly that if they had not anticipated his words, they might have missed them.

"She's gone," answered Grammar in a voice that sounded unnaturally loud.

"And you let her go," he said, still quietly. "Didn't you?"

He began to walk towards Grammar.

"You were always against me. From the beginning."

With one swift motion he shook Eva from his arm.

"I know your tricks, your treachery. You let her go. . ."

With each word the volume of his voice increased.

". . .just like you let the others go. The animals. My animals. You had no right. They were mine."

He raised his hand as if to strike her.

"You meddling old woman! You fool!"

"Leave her alone!" shouted Ionia, and she sprang in front of him.

Adam lowered his arm and looked confused. Slowly he realized what had distracted him. He stared down at Ionia standing before him and saw Lilith's eyes staring back.

"It wasn't Grammar's fault. She didn't want to. We made her."

"Child!" cried Grammar, and she reached out her hand, but it was too late. Adam had already grasped Ionia by both shoulders.

"You," he breathed, "I should have known. You drove her away the first time. She never would have left me if it hadn't been for you and your brat of a little brother. Damn you both!"

Still holding onto Ionia with one hand, Adam grabbed Fred with the other. Then he turned and dragged them toward the empty space. Eva and Grammar screamed and tried to pull Ionia and Fred away from Adam. Lion attacked his legs. Jason attempted to loosen his grip, but Adam walked on impervious to resistance. When they were all beyond the wall, Adam hurled Ionia and Fred away from him. Before Eva and Grammar could rush to the children, he caught them by an arm each. The children remained where they had fallen, with Lion licking them, gasping for breath and staring at their father.

"Get out of my sight," Adam growled. "Get out of my sight or I'll kill you. Don't come back unless she's with you. Go! Now!"

Ionia and Fred scrambled to their feet and began to run hand in hand towards the hill of the three trees with Lion following close behind them. Jason hesitated, looking from his mother's face to the diminishing figures of Ionia and Fred. Then he turned to his mother and said softly:

"I can't let them go alone, Mother."

Before anything or anyone could stop him, Jason was racing after Ionia and Fred at full speed shouting their names. Eva lunged forward with all her might, but it did no good; she only fell at Adam's feet sobbing. On his other side, Grammar was pounding Adam with her free fist and cursing him. Adam stood still, as if unaware of the commotion on either side of him, while he watched Jason catch up with Ionia and Fred. On top of the hill Adam saw all three of them turn to look back once. Then they disappeared beyond the hill.

Suddenly Adam felt a pain he could not ignore in his left hand. Startled, he let go of Eva and lifted his hand to his face. Blood. Bitch, he thought, animal. Then he realized that Eva was running, stumbling every few feet in her high heels and narrow skirt, towards the hill. But it didn't matter anymore. Let her go. He looked down at his mother still pounding him with her fist and shouting words he could not understand. How absurd she was. They all were. Everything was. Adam let go of his mother so abruptly that she fell down and, in surprise, stopped squawking. Without even glancing at her, Adam turned away and walked back through the empty space.

By the time Eva had reached the bottom of the hill, she had left her shoes behind her, and her skirt and stockings were torn. Each short breath, still half a sob, tore at her lungs, and her side ached as if someone had smashed her ribs. Still she ran on and on, as in a nightmare, without seeming to go forward. She could scarcely see anymore; she only felt the steep incline of the hill. Then all at once the three trees were before her. She quickened her pace and reached out to clasp the trunk of one of the trees. Pausing for a moment to recover her breath, she wiped the tears and sweat from her eyes and gazed down into the Empty Land. There, standing before a small body of water, she saw the children and Lion. She waved her hand and cried out with joy:

"Wait! I'm coming, too!"

The children and Lion appeared neither to see her nor hear her. They stopped to drink from the water. And then they disappeared. Eva stood clutching the tree and staring at the empty space where Jason, Ionia, Fred, and Lion had been the moment before. The world turned dark and swirled around her. She was falling; falling into nothing.

"Mrs. Brooke! Mrs. Brooke!"

Eva struggled to open her eyes. Her lids were swollen as if encased in ice. She wondered vaguely if she had fallen asleep in a snowstorm and who it was that was trying to wake her.

"Mrs. Brooke."

She felt a warm hand touching her face, her forehead, her eyelids, melting the ice. She did not want to open her eyes yet. She wanted to be in the dark for a while where it was warm with the hand touching her.

"Mrs. Brooke, wake up. I can't carry you by myself, and I'm damned if I'll let him do it!"

She mustn't be a bother to anyone, Eva thought. She must not let people carry her around when she was perfectly well able to walk. With effort she opened her eyes and saw Ursula Underwood bending over her. Then she remembered.

"Mrs. Underwood," Eva murmured, "the children. . . ."

"Yes, I know," said Grammar in a voice that was strangely calm and soothing. "They've gone."

"But not just gone," Eva moaned, and she drew away from Grammar's touch and covered her eyes. "Disappeared. I saw them. . . ."

Eva sat up suddenly and looked out into the Empty Land.

"I saw them disappear," she repeated, turning to Grammar and begging her with her eyes to deny that it was possible.

"I know," said Grammar quietly.

"What do you mean!" shouted Eva, and she stared at Grammar in horror as if Grammar had somehow willed what had happened.

"I've got to find them," she whispered.

Gripping the tree, Eva rose to her feet and then backed away from Grammar. Before she could turn and run, Grammar laid hold of her arm.

"It's no use, Mrs. Brooke," Grammar pleaded. "It's no use your disappearing, too."

"You don't understand," Eva screamed, and she began to sob again as she struggled to free herself from Grammar's grip.

"I've lost my children, too," said Grammar sharply. "All of them. Now listen to me, Mrs. Brooke. We'll call the police, and they'll go over the whole area with helicopters. But it's my belief that if they really have disappeared, like you say, they've disappeared into Her country. Our best hope is that She'll find them and bring them back. But how can she if they have no place to come back to? She can't bring them here. You've got to stay, Mrs. Brooke, and be a home for them. They haven't any other now."

Grammar fell silent as she felt Eva yield. A moment later the two women were holding each other and weeping together beneath the three trees.

From the window in the tower room, Adam watched them. He guessed what had happened. He knew. But his sense of the wrong Grammar and the children had done him still outweighed his uneasiness about what he had done. After he had left Grammar he had gone straight to the tower room. It was as he suspected. They had broken in and meddled with his magic. His books were all back, piled in stacks on the floor. The culprits had made no attempt to hide the fact that they had gone through his books. He wondered which book had told them how to blast the gate; though it didn't really matter now. He had plenty of time to figure it out if he cared to. He could ask his mother. She was certainly not as innocent as Ionia pretended, but she need not fear him. His rage was spent. She would dry up and die without the children anyway. Meanwhile she could come or go as she pleased. It didn't matter anymore. Nothing mattered; She was gone.

She is gone. He tried the words out in his mind several times and even spoke them once. They sounded hollow, false. They failed to make him feel anything. They were words he had read in a book or heard in a play. Someone else's words. Not his. They didn't mean anything. Nothing did.

Through the window Adam saw Eva and his mother starting down the hill. The one supporting the other, they walked like the lame and the blind; slowly, stupidly. At the bottom of the hill, they stopped to search for something. Eva's shoes, no doubt. He ought to go down to meet them, Adam reflected. He was not a coward. He was not afraid to face them: a couple of hysterical women. He supposed he should offer Eva a ride and perhaps try to reassure her a little. The children would be all right. They were sure to find lots of roots and berries. He smiled at the fairytale cliché and turned away from the window.

When Eva saw Adam waiting in the empty space, she paused, not in fear, but in wonder. She knew she had never seen this man before. He was a stranger. Yet it would not have been accurate to say that she could see him now. She could not distinguish the features of his face, nor his hands, from the rest of his body. He was dark and insubstantial as a shadow.

"You must enter the shadow."

The words sounded in her mind without her knowing why or where they had come from. She drew apart from Grammar, and, in obedience, advanced towards the shadow. There was something she must say. She did not know what it was, but the need to communicate it was a power growing within her.

"Eva," said a voice from outside of her, "you mustn't take it so hard; you must try to understand. Be reasonable. . . ."

Eva recognized the voice. It seemed to come from the stranger, but that was impossible. It was a voice she remembered from a long time ago, though she did not remember whose voice it was. Not that it mattered now. No one would turn her back until she had said what she must.

"Yours is the power. Yours alone is the power," said the inside voice.

As Eva drew near him, Adam had to exert all his will to keep from backing away. Her eyes made him uneasy. They were not the gentle eyes of Eva Brooke. They were the eyes of some mad prophetess. She had gone mad. She did not see him. Adam glanced at his mother to see if she, too, realized that Eva had gone mad, but she just stood there watching quietly. Eva had stopped before him still staring with her unseeing eyes. Drawn by her intensity, Adam looked into her eyes again. For a moment he saw his reflection. And then nothing. Her eyes were endless, bottomless, black, and he was falling; falling down into them.

"Eva," he cried.

Then he heard her voice as if it came from inside of him or as if he were inside of her:

"You are evil."

When Adam returned to himself, Eva was walking away. She had almost reached the bend in the road.

"Wait!" he shouted. "I'll give you a ride."

He was about to run after her when a hand closed on his arm.

"Leave her alone, Adam," his mother commanded. Then she added more softly to herself, "She has lost her only son."

35

 Into the Empty Land

THE sun, though still bright, was beginning to set. Jason, Ionia, Fred, and Lion cast their shadows before them as they continued to walk on and on. Fred and Ionia had shed their shoes, though at Jason's insistence they carried them along. The ground, covered with wild thyme, felt soft and springy beneath their bare feet. The crushed herbs had a fragrant smell. Here and there grew patches of cloud berries, which Ionia and Fred picked and ate in passing. Jason, however, decided that they ought to have a store of berries, and so he had taken off his shirt and made it into a sack. As a result his back was beginning to ache with sunburn, and he was growing tired and thirsty. Yet he did not suggest that they stop for a rest. It would be best for them to keep walking while there was still light in hope of finding water. They had not had a drink since the one they had taken from the small lake just over the hill from Ionia's house.

That had been hours ago. Jason thought of that water and its peculiar earthy taste, which was due, Jason supposed, to the fact that the lake was fed by underground springs. It was dangerous to drink water from unknown sources, but they had no choice. He wondered now if that drink of water had not had some ill effect on his brain. Since then his memory had not seemed to be working properly. He knew that at some time, though he could not remember when or why, there had been a terrible fight and that Ionia's father had gone into a rage; but his memory of what had happened was like the memory of a dream: a series of disconnected images that had no particular meaning. Only one image was sharp and vivid: that of his mother's face. None of the other images seemed real; they stirred no response in him; but when he recalled the image of his mother, he experienced a sensation of loss equal in intensity to his present sense of adventure and his sense of responsibility.

For Jason had quietly assumed leadership. There had been no need of verbal agreement, and, indeed, none of them had spoken more than a word or two since the journey's beginning. His leadership was a natural fact as far as Jason was concerned. He was, after all, the oldest, and he knew more about navigation than the others. As long as the sky remained clear, he would know day or night in which direction they were going and which way they had come. He had more common sense than Ionia and Fred, too; that was certain. They would probably not have survived more than a few days without him.

As Jason contemplated it, his responsibility as leader began to weigh upon him. Jason glanced anxiously at Fred, who looked tired and a little frightened. Sometimes Fred held onto Ionia's hand, and he scarcely ever took his eyes off Lion, who kept bounding away, following scents or chasing rabbits. Earlier Fred had tried to prevent Lion from leaving his side, but Jason had convinced him that Lion must be allowed to hunt for his meat. "Lion likes vegetables and berries," Fred had protested, but after trying in vain to coax Lion to eat cloud berries, Fred had let Lion wander. When Lion was out of sight, Jason had noted, Fred often looked behind him with a puzzled expression on his face, as if he couldn't understand why they just kept going farther and farther away.

Ionia, however, never looked back. Although she knew nothing of navigation, Jason had an odd feeling whenever he looked at her that Ionia knew where she was going. He would have liked to question her, but the silence, like the pace of their footsteps, was difficult to break. So Jason walked on beside her, too intent on his thoughts to hear as Ionia did, that the faintest stir of air in the Empty Land sounded like the inside of a seashell.

Because the day had been clear and bright, the coming of night was sudden. One moment the hills towards which they walked glowed in the light; the next moment they were scarcely distinguishable from the sky. In the almost-dark the ground beneath the children's feet felt less sure. They could not anticipate the small dips and rises. Weary, hungry, light-headed, they felt as though they were walking on water, not earth. Yet Jason led them up one more hill in hope of finding water on the other side.

On top of the hill Jason paused, scanning the valley below for the least glimmer of reflected light and listening intently for the sound of moving water. Nothing reflected the pale light of the first stars, and the wind had risen, obscuring all sound but its own. Jason resolved to stop for the night at the base of the next hill. Maybe when the moon rose he would go in search of water. They continued down the hill. Every few feet Fred stumbled and then got up again sobbing quietly to himself.

"We'll stop here for the night," said Jason.

Jason's voice sounded strange to himself: small and ineffectual, swallowed up by the huge space around him, out of place in the emptiness. Yet its effect on Ionia, Fred, and Lion was immediate. Soon they were all sitting as close together as possible in a circle. Jason did not usually like physical contact, but now he welcomed it. Although he could not bring himself to do it, he felt he might even have liked to hold Ionia's hand. Instead he laid his shirt full of berries in the middle of the circle.

"We'd better eat," he said.

None of them spoke as they reached their hands into the pile and lifted berries to their mouths. Sometimes two hands touched. Then each hand withdrew to let the other go first. Soon the berries were all gone.

"I'm thirsty," said Fred.

It seemed more of a statement than a request, so no one replied.

"I'd like a drink of water," he added.

"There isn't any water," Jason explained.

Fred was silent for a moment, and then he asked:

"How come?"

"There just isn't any," said Jason helplessly. "We haven't found any yet."

"Are we going to?" persisted Fred.

"I don't know," answered Jason. "We ought to. This isn't a desert. Things grow here. Things that need water. We'll find some tomorrow."

Fred said nothing more. In the dark Jason could not tell whether or not he was reassured. Jason hoped that he would go to sleep soon, but in a little while Fred whispered:

"Are we lost?"

Jason did not know how to answer. In one sense, they were not lost. He knew that all day they had walked due east. He supposed that if they wanted to, they could retrace their steps all the way back to Ionia's house. Yet there was some reason, which Jason could not quite remember, why they could not do that. Oh yes, Ionia's father. That was it. In confusion Jason thought of that drink of water and the strange feeling that had come over him, almost of entering another world where what had happened before had no meaning. And if they could not go back, what difference did it make where they went? Did that not mean they were lost? or was "lost" now a concept without meaning? Jason was about to begin an elaborate explanation designed to evade the issue, when Ionia startled him by speaking for the first time in hours.

"No, Fred," she said in a sure voice, "we are not lost. We are going to our mother's country."

It was not only Ionia's speaking that surprised Jason, but the sound of her voice. Unlike his voice, which had become flat in the open, her voice had taken on several dimensions. It had greater tone, texture, vibrance. It was musical. Then Jason realized: it was like her mother's voice.

"Ionia," Jason asked in excitement, "do you really know how to get there?"

Ionia considered for awhile.

"I don't have a map in my head," she said at length. "It's a feeling. I mean, I think I'd know if we started to go the wrong way. I'm sure I would."

Jason didn't question her further. He was a little disappointed. He wished her knowledge was something more substantial than a feeling: detailed directions, say, that her mother had given her. Still, Ionia's feeling was all they had to guide them. He supposed he'd have to trust her.

"You'd better lead then," he said shortly. "And right now we'd better get to sleep."

Without speaking, they arranged themselves on the ground as comfortably as possible. Fred lay curled with his arms around Lion, his back against Ionia's back. Jason lay beside Lion, looking up at the sky, waiting for moonrise.

"Does Grammar know where we are, Ionia?" asked Fred in a sleep-heavy voice.

"I think so," said Ionia.

Soon Jason heard Fred's deep, regular breathing rising and falling with Lion's, and he knew Fred was asleep. He waited for Ionia's breathing to mingle with theirs, but if Ionia slept, she slept softly. Turning his full attention to the sky, Jason studied the stars while he waited for the moonlight. There was something about the stars that disturbed him. He recognized them; they stood in right relationship to one another, yet they seemed closer to the earth than usual, too close. That might be the effect of open space, he reminded himself. Then all at once Jason realized what was wrong: the stars were not in the right position for what he knew must be their latitude, or rather the season of the year. Then he was not sure what he meant. Was it time or space that had changed, or both? He must try to figure it out. North and south was latitude; east and west, the time of year. . . .

Against his will, Jason drifted off to sleep. When the moon failed to rise at its appointed time, Jason was none the wiser.

🐾

The next morning, Fred and Jason were awakened by cold drops of water splashing their faces. They opened their eyes to see Lion standing over them, his legs, belly, and chest soaking wet. Laughing, Fred reached up his arms and wrestled Lion to the ground, not minding in the least the smell or dampness of his fur. Jason sat up, half in excitement, half in alarm. Ionia was nowhere in sight, though wherever she had gone she had left her shoes and socks behind her. Struggling to his feet, Jason realized how stiff and sore he was. All his leg muscles and his feet ached. The cool morning air on his scorched back made him shiver. Jason looked up and scanned the sky. Clouds had blown in on the night wind, and though there was still plenty of blue sky between them, their undersides were dark. Jason scowled. It would be no fun to be out in the Empty Land during a storm.

"Come on," said Jason sharply to Fred, who was still rolling around on the ground with Lion. "We've got to find Ionia."

"Oh, Lion knows where she is," said Fred cheerfully as he scrambled to his feet with no apparent discomfort.

"Put your shoes on," commanded Jason, for it annoyed him to see Fred so free of the worries that weighed on him.

"But I want to go wading in the water like Lion did," protested Fred.

"We've got to find the water first," said Jason grimly, annoyed even more that Ionia had gone off by herself without telling him. It showed a want of consideration and sense on her part.

While Fred was putting on his shoes, Jason slipped into his shirt. It was sticky with the juice from the cloud berries, but it was better than no protection at all. Someone else's back could be burned today. Jason leaned over and picked up Ionia's shoes and socks and then motioned Fred to follow him up the hill. It was a steep one, and Jason hoped that from the top they would be able to see Ionia. When he reached the summit, all he could see was an infinite number of hill tops. The valleys, except for the one immediately below, were invisible.

"Damn!" shouted Jason.

As if in reaction to his voice, Lion suddenly took off down the hill.

"Look!" said Fred, "Lion's leading us!"

Without waiting for Jason's permission, Fred ran after Lion, leaving Jason no alternative but to follow. Instead of leading them in a relentlessly straight line, as Jason had the day before, Lion led them around the hills, but at such a pace that Jason lost both his breath and his sense of direction before long. He was beginning to feel that he could run no further when they came into sight of a lake, like the one from which they had taken a drink yesterday, only smaller. Jason stumbled to a halt. Then he caught Fred, who had fallen behind in the race, and pulled Fred down beside him, covering Fred's mouth with his hand.

Wading at the water's edge were two large animals which Jason took to be wolves. On the far side of the lake stood a group of tall, long-legged animals, which, except for the nearness of predators, Jason would have sworn were deer. Surrounded by these animals, not ten feet's distance from the wolves, was Ionia, immersed to her waist in the water. Lion trotted towards her without any apparent fear of the wolves. At the sound of his approach, Ionia turned, then waved as she saw Jason and Fred, beckoning them to join her.

Fred started to run, but Jason restrained him, forcing him to proceed at his own cautious pace. They must be careful not to startle these wild animals who might turn dangerous if alarmed. Ionia was a fool to go among them. It was one thing for her to risk her own life, but now she was risking theirs as well; for, of course, they must rescue her.

As Fred and Jason crept along their way, a breeze raced past them and carried their scent to the deer, who lifted their heads from drinking to sniff the wind before they bounded away, disappearing quickly beyond the next hill. The wolves, who had also caught the strange scent, took their time. Slowly turning their heads, they gazed at Jason and Fred with faintly glowing eyes. Jason stiffened, waiting for the attack. The wolves, after taking one more drink, turned in the direction the deer had taken and loped away at a leisurely pace, as if to give their prey a good head start.

"Come on!" Ionia laughed. "What are you afraid of?"

Fred broke loose from Jason's grip and skipped joyfully towards the water, but Jason remained where he was, feeling himself grow red with anger and shame. Ionia had called him a coward. How could he have known that the wolves would run away? How could he have known that the wolves would not attack her? He had been frightened for her, and she accused him of being frightened for himself. Nothing made sense in this place: not the stars, not the animals, not Ionia, not himself. He did not belong here. He should never have come. Ionia did not need him. It was her country. Jason dug the toe of his shoe furiously into the ground, tearing up the carpet of herbs to get at the dirt.

"Jason."

Reluctantly he looked up. Ionia was walking towards him without any clothes on. Jason had never seen a girl naked before. Somehow he resisted the impulse to turn and run. Ionia took his hand.

"Come on, Jason," she said, and he let her lead him to the water's edge.

As soon as Jason's lips touched the water, he realized how thirsty he was. He drank for a long time. The water had the same earthy taste as that other water, only this time Jason did not wonder about the water source. He did not care. When he had finished drinking, he sat back and watched Ionia and Fred playing together in the water some feet away from him, laughing and splashing each other as they might have in a bathtub at home. He was aware, as he watched them, of feeling closer to them and at the same time more detached from them than he had the day before, the moment before. Somehow they had changed from being his responsibilities into being his companions.

The sun rose above a cloud and shone down on Jason's back. He began to sweat, and the sweat mingled with the cloud berry juice, making him uncomfortable. He took off his shirt and dunked it in the water, kneading it and squeezing it in an attempt to wash it. Then he laid it on the ground beside him to dry. Cupping one hand, he lifted as much water as he could and splashed it on his back. He repeated the motion again and again, feeling not only the stickiness but also the pain of his sunburn dissolve. His splashing became more abandoned, and soon his pants were soaked. Hesitating a moment and glancing at Ionia and Fred, who were still absorbed in their play, Jason stood up and stripped himself naked. Then he ran into the cool water, his feet springing against the smooth rocks until he could no longer touch bottom, and his whole body was submerged.

By the time they had finished bathing and breakfasting on more cloud berries that grew nearby, it was midmorning. They were all eager to go on. Jason had tried to devise a method of carrying water in his shoes but had succeeded only in making his shoes very soggy. As a result, Jason went barefoot, too. Fred and Ionia wanted to leave their clothes behind, but Jason persuaded them that this would be a foolish thing to do. What if they wanted to go back, he pointed out.

"Go back where?" Ionia asked, but she put her clothes on.

When they were all ready, shoes and socks in hand, it was Jason's turn to question.

"Where are we going?" he asked as politely as possible.

Fred, Jason, and Lion all watched Ionia, waiting for her answer. She stood still, eyes closed, concentrating. Then, opening her eyes, she turned towards the northeast.

"That way," she said, and she started to walk.

"Ionia," Jason spoke before the steadiness of their pace prevented him, "why were those deer and those wolves drinking from the water at the same time? Why did they only run from Fred and me and not you and Lion? And why," he paused, still embarrassed about his own response, "weren't you afraid?"

"I don't know, Jason," she answered. "You'll have to ask my mother when we get there."

"When are we going to get there, Ionia?" asked Fred, who was already lagging behind a little.

"I don't know."

They walked on in silence, as they had the day before, deeper into the Empty Land.

36
Beyond the Wall

LATE that afternoon Grammar stood alone in her private parlor trying to decide what to take with her. She had already packed a large wheeled suitcase full of clothes, towels, and bed linen. Now with an empty carpet bag in hand, she glanced over her book shelves. She had read most of the mystery novels there more than once. They were not worth their weight. Let them rot with the rest of the house. She was quite sure the house would rot after she was gone. She had given it one last thorough cleaning that morning, not for the sake of its one remaining inhabitant, but as a tribute to the house itself and to the way of life she was leaving. Not that she would miss that life much; there was nothing left to miss. Still, she had a respect for ceremony and decorum. It would not do to leave behind her a dirty house. The house was now as clean as it had ever been, except for the spiders' webs. But spiders' webs, she reminded herself sternly, were not dirt but design.

Turning away from the book shelf, Grammar crossed the room to her work closet, which had been unlocked since the day she had relinquished the shovels to the children. Inside the closet were skeins of yarn and stacks of pattern books, which she began, indiscriminately, to stuff into her carpet hag. Then, suddenly, she stopped. With Fred and Ionia gone, the yarn was useless. She might as well leave it to the moths. But no, she must not allow herself to think that way. The children would come back. Of course they would, no doubt having outgrown all their old clothes. Resolutely, Grammar packed the rest of the yarn. Then she closed the door to her work closet. The room was dim around her. Was there nothing more that she needed? Slowly she paced the room once more, pausing by the daybed to pick up her shawl. Opening the drawer in the table beside the daybed, she drew out her sewing kit—that she must take to keep herself in repair!—and her favorite deck of cards. These she placed in a silk-lined inner pocket of the carpet bag where she had already stowed Fred's spotty cow and some drawings of Ionia's. Now she was ready.

Closing the door to her private parlor behind her, forever, as she told herself, Grammar stood uncertainly in the hallway. She would have liked to go to the attic to rummage among her old things. There were some she would have liked to take with her, the pink dancing gown, for instance. The other day when she had been looking for the fan, she had found some old photograph albums. But no, she did not want those. She did not want pictures of Adam as he had been as a little boy. Nor did she want to walk past the present Adam on her way to the attic. She could hear him moving about the tower room, as he had been all day, putting his precious books back in order, no doubt trying to find out how they blasted his blasted gates. Grammar smiled to herself grimly, but the smile hurt her face. She would like to blast him—but no, it wouldn't make any difference now. She only wanted to have nothing more to do with him. She would not spend another night in this house. To be alone with him made her flesh creep. Hearing a creak on the tower stairs, Grammar turned and fled down the hall.

When she went in search of him, a little while later, to tell him of her decision, she found him seated at his accustomed place at the table.

"Is dinner going to happen?" he inquired.

"I haven't the slightest idea. I don't work here anymore. I'm leaving."

Grammar waited for a reaction to her announcement, but Adam's face revealed nothing as he gazed at her silently. She was about to speak again or turn away before his gaze immobilized her when he released her himself.

"Very well," he said quietly. "When?"

"Right now. There is a train that leaves for the city in an hour. I may miss it, but in that case I shall spend the night on a bench at the station."

"Is my company so loathsome to you?"

This time it was she who remained silent.

"You shall not spend the night on a bench," he said, rising from the table. "I shall drive you to the station. Where are your things?"

"Upstairs," she answered. "Just outside my door."

Grammar moved aside and did not look at Adam as he walked past her out of the room. She had not expected so little resistance from him nor so much courtesy. But then, she did not know what she had expected. She did not understand him.

He remained mysterious to her as he always had from the very day he was born. What would it be like for him left alone in this empty place, she wondered, and, for the first time since she had made her decision to leave, she worried. It was too late now for her to change her mind, however, too late for regrets. If she was leaving him, it was his own fault. Let him learn to get his own dinner.

Suddenly the idea of Adam alone in her kitchen alarmed her. As if to warn it of the coming invasion, she hurried across the dining room into what had once been her exclusive domain. She did not need to turn the lights on to see the kitchen. She knew it with her eyes closed: every crack in the wall, every lump in the linoleum, every cupboard and closet and all their contents. In a moment she could have laid hands on the least toothpick, the obscurest spice. The kitchen was hers. She had created its order, an order which would be incomprehensible to Adam. He would have to create his own order, but he would not. She knew. He would allow disorder: dishes unwashed, floor unswept, mold and mildew creeping into the cabinets, ants in armies crawling across the counters, mice feasting in broad daylight at the table—Grammar opened her eyes. She must not think of what would happen. It was not her kitchen any more. Hardening herself, Grammar left the kitchen by way of the back door and went to have one more look at her vegetable garden.

The light of day was almost gone. Grammar inspected her garden by touch as well as by sight. Pinching one of the pods, she felt that the peas were ready. The beans would be along soon. She must remind Adam to pick the peas. No sense their going to waste, and she hadn't time to pick them now herself. The corn had been neglected these past few days and would need weeding if it was to grow, although she didn't suppose she could expect Adam to tend to that, and the tomatoes would soon need stringing up. The zucchini she and Fred had planted was sprouting and would, in another week or two, require thinning. Some of the lettuce and spinach had already gone to seed, but the spring cabbages were just perfect at this very moment. She ought to take a head with her. Crouching down, she cupped both her hands beneath a large, firm cabbage and lifted it roots and all from the earth.

"Mother," Adam called, "are you ready?"

"Yes," she answered, "I'm ready."

Tucking the cabbage under her arm, Grammar walked around the house to where Adam was sitting in the car.

On the way to the station, neither of them spoke. Grammar watched out the window for Fred's precious farm, but when they passed it the farm seemed no more than a blur of light in the darkness. Daylight distinctions had disappeared. Night had erased all the boundaries. The world looked large, too large. Grammar felt lost in it. She had not been beyond the wall in almost seven years.

"I suppose you've made plans as to where you're going once you reach the city," Adam said as they drove into the station parking lot.

"I shall go to Mrs. Brooke if she'll have me. If not, I'll find a hotel."

"You have money, then?"

"Yes, some your father left me."

Grammar opened her door before Adam could get out and open it for her. She walked ahead with the cabbage and the carpet bag. Adam followed with the suitcase.

"Adam," she said as they stood on the platform, "the peas are ready to be picked. The beans will be, too, in a couple of days."

"Thank you," he replied gravely. "I will try to remember."

Encouraged, Grammar went on. "If you think of it, you might weed the corn and string the tomatoes, and in a couple of weeks thin the zucchini."

"I shall probably not think of it," Adam warned. "I am engaged at the moment in some serious research."

"Never mind then," Grammar sighed. "Good-bye, Adam."

"Good-bye, Mother. Let me know if you need anything."

"Yes," she said, and she turned away.

Albert, the conductor, stared curiously at the little old lady with the cabbage and the carpet bag struggling to maneuver a large suitcase down the aisle.

"Here, I'll take that, Ma'am," he swung the suitcase onto his shoulders.

"You are kind, Sir."

Soon Albert had the woman installed in a seat towards the front of the car across the aisle from where he had laid his briefcase. The woman kept glancing at the suitcase on the rack above her as if would either fall on her head or disappear altogether. She clutched the carpet bag at her side, and the cabbage sat in her lap.

There was something familiar about the woman, Albert considered as he handed her the one way ticket she requested. As he counted out the change, an image juxtaposed itself: this woman in a white cook's cap and apron, quite tipsy. Yes, that was it; she was Underwood's cook. Something fishy must be going on out there. Yesterday that nice Mrs. Brooke had ridden the train and in such a state that he had gotten off the train with her and found her a taxi. He had failed, however, to get a word out of her about what had happened.

"Excuse me, Ma'am," he ventured as he handed her the change, "but didn't you used to work at Professor Underwood's establishment?"

The woman eyed him with obvious suspicion.

"I did," she said at length.

The woman was hardly forthcoming. He ought to sit down and mind his own business, but he couldn't. His mind filled with images of Her: slashing her ball gown with a dagger, dancing naked on tabletops in the torchlight, reaching out her hand to him, Albert.

"Pardon me, Ma'am," he tried again, "it may be none of my business, but would you mind telling me how her Majes—I mean how Mrs. Underwood is?"

"Which Mrs. Underwood do you mean?"

"I didn't know there was more than one!" Albert's eyebrows rose.

"Professor Underwood has a mother as well as a wife."

"Oh," Albert was somewhat disappointed to discover that Underwood was not a bigamist. "I mean his wife."

"She is well," said the woman, "so far as I know."

"And the children?" Albert persisted.

The woman turned and stared, not at him, but as if she were seeing a ghost. Albert felt the creepies go up his back. Something was wrong all right. This woman was behaving like a character in one of the Gothic novels Esther was always reading. The demented housekeeper. Underwood's ex-cook. Unnerved, Albert sat down and made no further attempt to question the woman.

As soon as the train reached the station, the woman stood up on tiptoe, straining to reach her suitcase. Fearful that she would pull it down on her head, Albert jumped up and lifted it off the rack.

"You mustn't try to carry this suitcase by yourself," he said kindly. "Come along now, and I'll find you a taxi."

Without waiting for the woman's assent, Albert took the woman's arm with his free hand and escorted her and her cabbage and carpet bag off the train, out of the station, and into the street.

"Where are you going?" he asked as he hailed a taxi.

He listened in surprise as she gave Mrs. Brooke's address.

"You have been very kind," she concluded, "and there is one more favor I'd like to ask of you."

"Certainly," said Albert, seeing her hesitate.

"If you ever see Mrs. Underwood and the children, I wonder if you would tell them for me that I am at Mrs. Brooke's and that we are waiting for them."

"Of course I will," promised Albert helping her into the taxi. "But what is your name?"

"Mrs. Underwood," replied the woman.

"Oh, I beg your pardon, Ma'am. I thought. . . ."

"It's all right," Mrs. Underwood said. "You were correct."

🌱🌿🌱

As the taxi twisted through the streets of the city, Grammar leaned back against the seat and closed her eyes so that she would not have to see all the lights and the people and the confusion. She had not realized until that moment how tired she was. Dead tired. She wondered, indeed, why she was not dead. What she had been through these past few days and weeks was enough to kill any respectable woman of a certain age. She had a right to be dead.

The taxi stopped. Grammar woke in confusion. Without knowing where she was or even wondering why she was there, Grammar got out of the cab and climbed some steps and then some stairs. She gave some strange man (was it the train conductor?) some money she had been clutching in her hands. She saw the man uncrumple it, look at it, shake his head, then turn away. She was standing alone with her luggage on a second floor landing facing a door with a number two nailed on it. The appropriate thing to do would be to knock, she supposed. So she did. A moment later the door opened, and Mrs. Brooke stood before her. In one glance Grammar took in the fact that Mrs. Brooke had not changed her clothes nor washed her face since the day before. Probably she had not eaten.

"Here I am, Mrs. Brooke," announced Grammar, handing Eva the cabbage.

"Ursula," said Eva, using Grammar's given name for the first time, "I'm so glad you've come."

And it was a good thing she had, Grammar thought, as she helped Eva carry her suitcase inside. There was no doubt about it: Eva Brooke needed her.

37
Solitary Splendor

ADAM put down his fork and poured himself another glass of
wine. The omelette had been a failure; the eggs were runny and the cheese,
unmelted. He suspected the milk with which he had mixed the eggs of being
sour. Moreover, the omelette had refused to fold. It had been a mess in the pan
and then a mess on his plate. He could not eat it. Nor did he want the rest of
the salad. The dressing was delicious; he had spent twenty minutes looking for
the ingredients, but he had neglected to wash the lettuce. His first bite of salad
had included a large slug, which he had narrowly escaped swallowing.

Adam took another sip of wine. The wine at least was good: dry and delicate,
all smoothness, with nothing harsh about it, nothing to jar him. It flowed into
him as though it were not a separate element. Lowering his glass, Adam looked
at his food with disgust. He did not want the eggs and the slug near him. With
a sudden, violent motion, Adam hurled the plate from him. It spun down the
length of the table and crashed onto the floor. Adam reached for the candle, by
whose light he had meant to dine, and pulled it nearer, drawing the darkness
closer about him. He stared into the glass, seeing his reflection in the wine. Then
he lifted the glass and drank once more.

The silence of the house surrounded him. Each tiny sound—the sputtering
of the candle, the mechanical chorus of the night insects—only served to accen-
tuate the silence. Adam listened. All at once it seemed to him that there was
something alive in the room with him, hiding itself in the darkness. He could
hear the sound of heavy breathing, as though the thing, whatever it was, were
sleeping. Unconsciously, he held his breath. The sound stopped. He breathed
again and knew the thing was himself.

Adam's face flushed at the idea of having frightened himself. He drained the
glass. If he was startled by the sound of his own breathing, it was no wonder,
he considered, as he poured himself another glass of wine. He had not heard
that sound in years. For years, it seemed to him, he had scarcely breathed, as
though he were a child tiptoeing past a graveyard, only not the dead but the
living had suffocated him: all the people who had constantly surrounded him
in his house, in his work, at the conference, and everywhere Eva Brooke. Eva

Brooke hovering about him like some moth about a light bulb. Eva Brooke, following him, unbidden, like a stray dog. Like a dog, but at last she had turned vicious.

Adam lifted his left hand and examined it by candlelight. The flesh looked a little puffy and had a purplish tinge. Mixed with the dried blood there was a yellowish substance, which he supposed was pus. If the bite was not better in a day or two he would have to see a doctor. He could say a dog had bitten him, and it would be the truth. His mother was welcome to Eva Brooke; Eva Brooke was welcome to his mother. They deserved each other. He was glad they were gone from him. No doubt they thought they punished him with their absence. No doubt they thought he needed them, but they were wrong. He did not need anyone. He welcomed solitude. Solitude was the highest state in which man could exist. Alone, man was his most god-like. Adam lifted his glass in a silent toast and drank to himself.

The wine was warm inside his empty stomach, and the warmth crept through the rest of his body like a woman's caress; only no woman had ever touched him that way. No woman's hands could reach inside him. No woman had ever touched more than his skin, the bare surface of his being. No woman had ever known him. Adam thought of Lilith or tried to, but her image was a blur. He could not keep the features of her face in focus; he had forgotten them. She was only a shadow against the sky, a dream figure. He tried to recall some word, some look, some gesture that would make her memory real to him, that would make the ten years of wooing, waiting, suffering mean something. Worse than any pain or grief was the discovery that she meant nothing to him now that she had gone. Yet, she had run away before, and he had spent six years attempting to lure her back. Six years wasted on a woman who had never touched him, whom he had never touched. She had tricked him; she must have tricked him into believing she was real when she was nothing more than water and air, a little dirt made substantial by his imagination. Now he was undeceived. He knew she was nothing. His desire had been to possess nothing. Impossible, but perhaps it had been the very impossibility that had driven him.

Adam finished his glass of wine and reached for the bottle to refill it. Only dregs were left. Adam watched the particles of cork and the small impurities floating at the bottom of his glass. They looked as though they were tiny organisms swimming about in his wine by their own power. Against his will, Adam thought of the slug crawling on the lettuce leaf. His gorge rose and then fell again. As if it were bitter medicine, Adam lifted the glass and gulped the rest of the wine. Lowering the glass, he stared at the candle. Its flame seemed less steady than before, perhaps because the candle had burned so low, but the flickering was almost rhythmic. The motion of the flame became a dance in the darkness. Then the darkness joined the dance swirling around the light. Adam, his hand still clutching the fragile stem of the wine glass, felt himself to be the only fixed point, the center of all movement. Then his eyes closed, and his solidity gave way. He floated out among the moving shapes, insubstantial as the air.

Adam woke in the dark, uncertain of where he was or why, certain only that his head ached, and his neck was stiff. Groping, he knocked over his wine glass. Then he remembered, and he began to perceive the shape of the dining room chairs and table, visible in the moonlight that shone through the window. Exploring further, he encountered the candle; the wick had been drowned in wax. It was no use lighting it again. Shamed that he had fallen asleep at the table, Adam rose abruptly, then sank into his chair once more, overcome with dizziness. Steadying himself, he got up more slowly and proceeded cautiously to the door. There he paused to switch on the hall lights. For a moment they blinded him, and he stood blinking in the doorway. Then out of the corner of his eye, he caught sight of his reflection in the long dining room window. Half-reluctant, half-curious, he turned to face it. Staring back at him was a dishevelled middle-aged man with bags under his eyes. The man lifted his arm and disappeared as the lights went out. In the dark, Adam turned and made his way across the hall and up the stairs to his bedroom.

As he undressed, Adam stood before the window and stared out. Moonlight flooded the empty space. He would have to see about having a new gate installed, Adam reflected. What was the use of a wall without a gate? But then, what use was the wall at all? There was only himself now to lock in or out. He was through with Her. Let her go and never come back. It did not matter anymore. He was through with them, all of them: Eva, his mother. He hesitated when he thought of the children. They had always seemed irrelevant to him except in relation to Her. How could he be through with what he had never begun? In any case he would not miss them, for what he had not known he could not miss. What he had lost was not worth lamenting. His life would be much simpler now that they were all gone.

Adam lifted his eyes and looked at the waning moon. There was something female about its lopsided shape. It looked like a pregnant woman's womb. But even more female, Adam thought, was the visible darkness of the moon in shadow. Drawing the curtains against the moon, Adam left his clothes where they had fallen and went in search of his pajamas.

The next morning, Adam slept late while the sun rose higher and burned hotter. He woke drenched in sweat and twisted up in his bed clothes. His sweat had an unpleasant alcoholic odor. Disentangling himself from the sheets, Adam got out of bed, lifted the shade, and opened the window, but the air afforded him no relief. It was warm, humid, stagnant. The sky, though blue, was hazy, and the edges of everything, even as short a distance away as the wall, looked blurred. Adam frowned in disapproval of the day, then turned away from the window, deciding on a course of action. He would shower, breakfast, and then settle down immediately to his work. External conditions could not prevail over internal discipline.

Refreshed by his shower, dressed in clean clothes, Adam descended the stairs. He hummed to himself as he crossed the hall. When he entered the dining room, he did not notice the empty bottle, the burnt-out candle, or the glass lying on its side. He walked on, cheerfully unaware of his surroundings until something shattered beneath his foot. Looking down he saw the broken pieces of a plate, the splattered remains of an omelette, some scattered leaves of lettuce. His automatic reaction was anger: why hadn't someone cleaned it up? Why had it been left there for him to step on?

"Mother!" he shouted.

A faint echo was the only response. Adam was shaken, not because he suddenly found himself alone, but because he had forgotten he was. Carefully, he removed his feet from the debris and tiptoed to the kitchen trying not to leave tracks behind him. He grabbed the first thing he could find, which happened to be a clean dish towel, and wiped his shoes. Tossing the towel in the direction of the sink, he went to the kitchen closet where he supposed he would find a broom.

After sweeping the carpet, then rubbing it with a damp cloth, Adam felt hot and sticky again. His left hand was throbbing from the effort of holding the dust pan. Hungry and cross, he went to look in the refrigerator for the makings of breakfast. He had used the last of the eggs last night, not that he wanted eggs again. There was no bread. All he could find in the way of fruit was one greenish-looking orange. Slamming the refrigerator door, he stalked to the pantry in search of cereal, but he found only oatmeal, boxes and boxes of raw oatmeal. The idea of hot cereal on a hot day did not appeal to him. He decided that coffee would suffice him. Locating the coffee, however, was another matter. He concluded that his mother must have deliberately sabotaged the kitchen just as she had deliberately gone off without leaving a shopping list. As he hunted through cupboard after cupboard, he found some relief in cursing her.

It was not until midafternoon that Adam finally climbed the stairs to the tower room. He had spent the remainder of the morning organizing the kitchen to suit his own purposes. Then he had gone shopping. He had not simply left a list with the grocer as he usually did, because there was no list. In order to know what he needed, he had to pace up and down the aisles himself. It had been a disagreeable experience to search through a supermarket surrounded by mothers with screaming babies who pushed him aside, as he stood pondering a shelf, to grab what they wanted. He had laid in enough supplies to withstand a siege, however, so he hoped he would not have to repeat the experience soon.

It was with a sense of relief that he entered the tower room. Here were his proper surroundings: his books, his rocks, his papers, his relics. The tower room was a mirror of his mind, an outward expression of an inward state. Here he was most at home. Here he was perfectly self-contained. With a sigh of satisfaction, Adam sank into his chair, then propping his elbows on the desk, he rested his head in his hands. The crystal ball lay quiet before him; it needed darkness to make it shine. All that appeared in it now was the reflection of his face upside down. Adam pushed the crystal ball aside. He would not need it anymore. No more nights wasted in trying to make contact with Her. He had more important things to do. Unlocking a drawer of his desk, Adam took out a copy of a manuscript written by a contemporary of Aristotle's. It was the first known tract on alchemical control of planetary movement. The one he would write this summer would probably be the last. He meant it to be a definitive study.

For the substance of the sun is of gold, and the moon's substance of silver.
The gold and silver found on earth are cold and dead, but the gold and silver
of the sun and moon are living. . . .

Adam read, but he found it difficult to concentrate. Of course, the man's theory was nonsense, but it was designed to explain facts, real results of certain experiments. That was the meat of this man's subject, and Adam wished he would not take so long to present it. What Adam needed was a clue as to how to begin his own experiments.

In influencing the motion of any heavenly body, it is necessary that the four
earthly elements be symbolically represented during the incantation. . . .

A combination of Aristotle and more hocus pocus and mumbo jumbo. It was all old hat to Adam. Would he never discover anything new? Would he never be able to claim anything for his very own? Lilith, she had been the secret knowledge that was to have given him power, the fruit of his most daring venture: that summer spent in the Empty Land. He might never have returned from the Empty Land. He had risked his life. But for what? To possess knowledge that no other man possessed? Well, he had failed. He possessed nothing but volumes of other men's knowledge that anyone literate might also possess. He possessed nothing of his own. He never had.

Adam slammed shut the ancient treatise, and the dust flew in his face, making him sneeze. For the first time, he noticed the unpleasant odor that pervaded the room. The room had been left shut up too long in this summer heat, he thought, or a rat might have died in the walls. He had spoken to his mother about fumigating the house a long time ago, but apparently she had done nothing about it. He'd have to see to it himself. The whole place was in want of repair.

Decisively, Adam rose from the desk and went to open the window. The sky was darker than it had been, he noted; the haze had turned to thunderclouds. A breeze that swayed the three trees on the hill swept through the window and rustled the papers on his desk. The rain would come soon. As he began to turn away from the window, he caught sight of his mother's vegetable garden, and he remembered the peas. Fresh peas would go nicely with the steak he had purchased for his dinner, and he had better pick them right away before the storm. Feeling like a school boy released for recess, Adam left the tower room, not bothering to close the window or lock the door behind him.

Outside, Adam stood uncertainly before the garden, holding an empty paper bag. He did not know where the peas grew or even what peas looked like when they were not lying on a plate. From his present perspective, his mother's garden looked vast and confusing. He supposed he would have to explore. He began to walk slowly up and down the rows of the garden just as earlier he had walked the aisles of the supermarket shelves. All he could see in that light were leaves: red leaves, feathery leaves, round leaves, pointed ones, leaves like fans. The only leaves he recognized were lettuce leaves. Then he spied what he knew to be a bean. That might mean that the peas were close by. He stepped over the row of beans and squatted down by the next row of vegetables. Beneath the leaves, he found pods. He picked one, opened it, and discovered that there were peas inside. His discovery pleased him immensely; he felt as though he might have invented the arrangement of peas in pods. Smiling to himself, he moved down the row, bending over the plants, picking pods, and dropping them into the bag, taking care not to get his pants dirty. When he had picked a little less than half the row, the rain started to fall. Considering that he had more than enough peas for dinner, Adam stood up and hurried to the house.

After dinner, Adam sat back and stared out the long dining room window. Flashes of lightning illuminated the wall and yard for split seconds. The thunder crashes that followed obscured even the sound of the pounding rain and of the wind that rattled and seemed to rock the house. The storm had increased in violence all afternoon. Adam had enjoyed it, as he had sat in the kitchen scooping peas from their pods and into a pot and as he cooked his dinner over flames that seemed brighter for the darkness outside. The storm suited his situation. If he was to live alone, it was best to live alone in a large, empty house surrounded by a furious storm. Solitary splendor sustained him throughout the afternoon.

Now the splendor was beginning to pale. The steak and the peas had both been a little tough. An upstairs shutter had come loose and crashed down into the yard, but there was something else causing him a vague feeling of unease. His mind approached, then retreated from whatever it was, unsure that it wanted to know. It was something he had done or left undone that could not be repaired. Was it his treatise? No, he had all summer for that. What then?

Adam looked away from the window. Lightning flashed again, revealing the expanse of the empty table, and then he knew: it was the children. They were out in this storm, most likely. It troubled him, though he didn't know why it should. What was done was done. He hadn't worried when he threw them out; what good would his worrying do now? And what was it, precisely, that was troubling him? His conscience? Or his concern for the children? Even now, they scarcely seemed real to him. He could hardly believe he had children. Yet his reason assured him that he had. So far as he knew, they were out in this storm surrounded by open space, likely targets for lightning. The girl and the boy, Ionia and Fred, his son and his daughter. His flesh. Why had he never thought of them that way before? Of all that he might have called his own, they, at least, had been right there within his reach. Why had he never laid a hand on them to claim them, then? They were beyond his reach now.

Or were they?

Adam rose from the table so suddenly that he knocked his chair over. Walking swiftly, he left the dining room and headed for the tower room. When he entered, he found the curtains flapping and the rain pelting in through the open window making a puddle on the floor. The crystal ball was glowing, its light illuminating the tower room as the lightning illuminated the night beyond, only more steadily. Adam closed the window and drew the curtains. Then he sat at his desk and reached for the crystal ball. Pressing his fingertips to his temples, he gazed into it, entering deeper and deeper into the darkness at its center until its fiery edges receded from his sight. In the darkness he waited for the images to come, but nothing happened. He felt himself to be alone, in that halfway world where he had so often waited when he tried to reach Her. He willed her image to appear now. He willed communication to be established, that he might tell her the children were lost in the Empty Land. He willed the image of the children to appear. He willed some means to tell them that they might return, but there was not the faintest glimmering, not the slightest vibration to indicate that he had broken through to that world. The darkness was a dead darkness, a solid darkness, solid as a wall, dead as an end. His connections had been severed. He felt himself begin to surface from the darkness when something drew him down again.

He waited, full of expectancy, and slowly the darkness began to take shape. He saw a figure, a woman's figure. At first he thought it was Her, but the figure was too heavy, too bent. The woman was leaning against something, a desk. Her face was buried in her hands. Suddenly, as if in response to something, she looked up.

Then Adam saw: the woman was Eva.

"Eva!" he cried. "Eva!"

For a moment it seemed that she saw him, too. Then her image dissolved. The darkness reformed in his own image. He had never seen himself inside the darkness before. Frightened, he willed to surface, but his own eyes held him captive. He screamed a soundless nightmare scream, and the image disappeared. Swimming frantically through the darkness, as if some monster of the deep pursued him, Adam found himself alone in the tower room once more.

38

 How Do You Know?

ON the leeward side of a hill, Ionia, Fred, Jason, and Lion lay huddled together for warmth. Though the hill provided some protection from the wind, nothing could keep them from the rain or dry the damp ground beneath them. The comfort of their own bodies was scant: cold, wet, tired, and hungry as they were after trudging through the storm for hours, searching for shelter. Night had come, and they had found nothing, so they had dropped with exhaustion, asleep as soon as they lay down, in spite of the pelting rain. Sleep was their only shelter. As they slept, they did not hear the sound of heavy, steady steps shaking the earth, plodding towards them.

When Fred opened his eyes the next morning, he saw two long, furry brown legs standing inches away from his face. He was so surprised he closed his eyes to see if the legs would still be there when he opened them again. They were, and when he looked between the legs, he saw more legs beyond, lots and lots of legs all brown and shaggy, standing still and close as tree trunks in a forest. Carefully, so as not to disturb the legs nearest him, Fred rolled over onto his back, and found himself looking up at the underside of whatever animal belonged to the legs. Hanging directly over him was an udder swollen with milk. Fred reached up and explored it with his fingers. The animal stirred uneasily and stepped on Lion's tail, causing him to wake with a yelp. Suddenly, there was sound and movement all around. The other beasts began to paw the ground. One of them gave a long, low bellow, which the rest answered in chorus.

"What's going on around here?" demanded Jason in a sleepy voice.

"Cows," whispered Fred, and then he shouted joyfully, "Cows!" and he scrambled out from underneath the cow, brushing his head against its warm belly. In a few moments Fred, Ionia, Jason, and Lion were standing side by side staring at the cows, who grouped themselves around the children in a circle and stared back. Jason counted seventeen altogether; five of those were calves.

"It's a wonder they didn't trample us last night," commented Jason.

"They wouldn't have stepped on us," Ionia defended them. "They knew we were there."

"Why do they look so surprised to see us, then?"

"They're not surprised. They're just curious. Don't complain, Jason. They kept the rain off us last night."

Jason looked down and discovered that his clothes were indeed dryer than they had been when he had gone to sleep.

"Well, do we have to stand here staring all day to show our gratitude?" demanded Jason.

Glancing at the sky, he saw that the storm had swept itself away, leaving behind a clean blue sky.

"Let's get going," he said impatiently; for the silent contemplation of the cows made him uncomfortable.

Ionia ignored Jason as she took a step towards one of the cows. Reaching out her hand, she touched the cow gently just between its eyes. As if in response to Ionia's touch, the cow bent its legs and lowered itself to the ground. In a moment, all the other cows did the same.

"Ionia, what did you do?" asked Jason.

Ionia did not answer. Instead she knelt before the first cow and, laying her hands on either flank, raised the cow to its feet again. When all the cows were standing once more, Ionia nodded her head, and, one by one, the cows turned away and began to graze on the grass and the herbs, except for the calves, who drank their mothers' milk. Fred followed after one of the nursing cows and crouched down to watch the feeding, so entranced that he did not even mind when Lion dashed off to look for breakfast.

"Ionia," began Jason, who was still studying her instead of the cows, "I don't understand."

"I don't either," she said.

"How do you know what to do?" he went on. "Did your mother tell you?"

"I don't know because my mother told me anything," said Ionia slowly, "but I think I know because of my mother."

"Is it like birds knowing how to build nests? Is it instinct?"

"I suppose so," said Ionia vaguely. "Jason, I think we should follow the cows today."

"Follow them! But how can we? Cows never go anywhere. They just eat all day."

"You're thinking of tame cows," said Ionia. "Of course, they can't go anywhere. They're fenced in."

"And wild cows are different, I suppose?" asked Jason skeptically.

"Yes," said Ionia with assurance. "They're just having their breakfast now. Wait and see."

"Speaking of breakfast, I'd like to see some of that."

Jason looked around. There was not even a patch of cloud berries near.

"I wish Lion would share some of his meat," said Jason, catching sight of Lion trotting towards them with the remains of a rabbit in his jaws. "He's doing better than the rest of us. We can't live on cloud berries forever."

"Maybe we won't have to," said Ionia thoughtfully, and she walked away from Jason towards the cows.

The calf Fred had been watching had finished its feeding and was now playing a game of tag with Fred. Ionia approached the mother and, stroking her behind the ear, spoke to her in a low voice. In a few moments, Ionia turned and called out to Fred.

"Would you like a drink of milk?"

Fred paused in his play and skipped back to where Ionia stood beside the cow, with the calf following after him.

"She says you may have a drink," Ionia told him.

"I don't have a cup," said Fred shyly.

"Neither does the calf. Come on. I'll show you how to drink."

Jason, watching from some distance, saw Ionia and Fred crouch down beneath the cow and take her tits into their mouths. The cow stood perfectly still, apparently unalarmed by the proceedings. Jason did not share the cow's calm. He did not like this latest manifestation of Ionia's instinct. He supposed he would be invited to drink next, and he didn't know if he could do it. Yet it made sense; he could not deny that it made sense. How he wished he had brought a canteen.

"Jason," called Ionia after awhile, "do you want some?"

Jason held back for a moment and then decisively took a step forward, resolving firmly, as he went, to regard the whole thing as a scientific experiment.

"How do you do it?" asked Jason grimly as he knelt beside the cow.

"It's like sucking your thumb," explained Fred happily.

"I have never sucked my thumb in my life," said Jason coldly.

"Well, try it now," suggested Ionia.

With an expression of distaste, Jason inserted his thumb into his mouth.

"Don't just hold it there," said Ionia impatiently, "suck it!"

Reluctantly, Jason obeyed. To his surprise, he found the sucking motion natural. It was as if he had known all his life how to do it.

"Now try it with the tit," instructed Ionia.

Jason took the tit into his mouth; it was larger and stiffer than his thumb. With determination he began to suck, yet he was so surprised when the first milk gushed into his mouth that he almost choked on it. Soon sucking and swallowing became one continuous motion. Jason was too absorbed in what he was doing to feel disgust. All he knew was the warmth of the cow's body and the warmth of the milk entering his own body, the first nourishing food he had had in three days.

By the time Jason had finished drinking, the rest of the cows had begun to move on at a surprisingly swift pace. Fred and the calf were among them.

"Come on," said Ionia to Jason and the cow, "we'd better run a little to catch up."

All day the children kept pace with the cows. Sustained by the warm, fresh milk and by more cloud berries they found along the way, the children felt happier than they had since the journey's beginning. Fred did not ask even once when they were going to get there. Although the cows' course was somewhat devious, due to the fact that the cows preferred walking around the hills to climbing over them, Jason had to admit that Ionia was right: the wild cows seemed to have a definite direction and purpose.

By late afternoon the children were hot, tired, and discouraged. The wonder of wandering with the cows had worn off. The seeming endlessness of their journey had become oppressive. It was hard to remember the journey's beginning, difficult to believe in its end. Both seemed unreal. The only reality was one step following another through a land so empty it was impossible not to feel lost. Fred walked with his head down, taking some comfort in his shadow. Ionia scanned the hilltops. It was Jason who saw.

"Look!" He took Ionia's arm and pointed. "There's a hut built into the side of that hill!"

Letting go Ionia's arm, Jason went to investigate. Lion bounded after him, stopping here and there to sniff the ground in excitement. Fred and Ionia followed, too intrigued by the discovery to mind that the cows went on walking without them.

The entrance to the hut was an open space that faced south; there was no door. Jason stood in the space staring down into the hut; for the floor was lower than the ground outside. In the center of the hut was a small pool, the size of a bathtub, only round.

"I want to see, too," said Fred, who was trying to peer around Jason.

Jason walked down some stone steps. Soon all three children and Lion were standing inside the hive-shaped hut. The walls were covered with leaves and grasses, which looked as though they ought to be growing outside instead of underground. Jason touched the walls. Beneath the grass and leaves he could feel a network of roots, which, he concluded, must be the support of the structure. There were no beams anywhere, just a stone fireplace and chimney built into the north side of the hut. Jason crouched beside Ionia and Fred, who had sat down beside the water, and he saw that the pool, with its bottom of smooth stones, was an exact replica of the small lakes they had encountered. He wondered about the drainage system.

"Who lives here, Ionia?" whispered Fred.

Ionia did not answer. She stared into the water, which reflected the afternoon sunlight slanting in through the door. Suddenly the door darkened. The water reflected a woman's figure.

Ionia turned and saw her mother.

Before Ionia could speak, Fred cried out and flung himself on his mother. Lion, with as much joy, alternately barked and licked Lilith's feet. Jason stood by, uprooting grass with his foot as he dug it into the dirt floor, his mind crowded with questions, his tongue tied with awkwardness.

For Ionia, to gaze into her mother's eyes was like taking a long drink of water when she was thirsty. Fred had stolen from her the impulse to rush into her mother's arms, and she was content, for the moment, just to look; or almost content. There was something about her mother's face that disturbed her. It was not that she had changed—though she had; she was well and strong again as Ionia had first seen her, as Ionia had dreamed of her—it was her expression. Ionia could not tell whether her mother was glad or anxious or surprised. She longed for a welcome, some sign, some reassurance that she had done right.

It was Fred, overcome by his natural curiosity, who broke the silence.

"Who lives in this house, Mother?" he asked, leaving his mother's arms to look around again. "It's a funny house. Why are there grass and leaves growing inside, and why is the bathtub in the middle of the house? Who's going to take a bath?"

His mother laughed. "I live in this house, Man-Child. How clever of you to find my own place in all this space."

"Jason was the one who saw the house," said Ionia.

"Ionia led us here," added Jason. "I mean she knew which way we should go. She knew we should follow the cows."

"Yes," Lilith acknowledged Jason; then she turned to Ionia again. "I have known for some time that you were coming."

"How did you know?" asked Jason, unable to contain his questions any longer. "And how did Ionia know which way to come, and how did she know about the cows? How do people know things in this country?"

"That, Jason, Son of Eva, is something I would not tell you if I could."

The sternness of her voice more than her words silenced Jason and quenched, momentarily, his other questions. Fred, however, still had one pressing concern.

"But, Mother, you never told me, who is going to take a bath?"

"Fred, Grandson of Ursula, as you prove yourself to be, that is not a bathtub; it is a fresh water pool, fed by an underground stream. I drink from it. Sometimes I do what you would call bathe in it. In winter I watch the reflection of the fire in it. You will play in it as much as you like. But come outside now while it's light. I want to teach you how to dig wild root vegetables and to cut sod to dry for the fire."

"Are all the lakes and pools in the country fed by underground streams?" Jason started up again as they followed Lilith outside.

"Yes."

"Do they all come from the same source? I mean are they all tributaries and capillaries of one river?"

Jason saw Lilith hesitate but did not perceive her hesitation as a warning.

"Why do the streams all run underground? Why do the lakes and pools all have stone bottoms? Why. . . ."

"You ask too many questions, Jason, Son of Eva," said Lilith walking swiftly towards a patch of Jerusalem artichoke.

"What I mean is," said Jason thinking to make himself more clear, "are the lakes man-made?"

"Man-made?" Lilith looked him full in the face, then repeated, "Man-made?" That put an end to Jason's questions for awhile.

When Lilith had set Fred to digging artichokes and Jason to cutting sod with a knife made of antlers, she took Ionia's hand and led her away from the others. In silence they walked to the top of the nearest hill. There they sat down close together, and after a time Ionia's mother spoke.

"This is your country, Ionia, if you choose it."

Ionia said nothing but gazed out over the hills that seemed golden in the sun-lit haze; the pools that lay between the hills seemed not pools of water but pools of light.

"The wilderness is for the wild," her mother spoke again.

Ionia felt herself drifting, dreaming on that haze, dissolving in those pools.

"How came you to bring the man-children with you?"

Her mother's question jarred her.

"I, they," she faltered, "I didn't bring them. They came themselves."

She felt her mother looking at her, but she could not look back.

"Jason just came. I didn't ask him to. And Fred, I couldn't leave Fred."

She turned to appeal to her mother.

"I do not know, Ionia. I have told you before, my people do not know right and wrong. We have our laws, but they are not like human laws. I must tell the Grand Mother. She will decide what to do."

Ionia looked away from her mother. Perhaps it was only because the sun was near setting that the hills looked dimmer and the water had lost its shine. All Ionia knew was that nothing was as she had imagined it would be when she got to her mother's country. She had thought when she got there everything would be all right, simple. She had come such a long way.

It wasn't fair.

39

 # In His Own Trap

"**E**AT a little more of your broccoli, Eva Brooke," ordered Ursula Underwood, "and at least another bite of your lamb chop."

Eva Brooke obeyed while Ursula Underwood stopped eating her own dinner to watch. When Eva had dutifully eaten a little more and taken another bite, she laid down her fork and looked at Ursula Underwood silently and a little sullenly.

"It's that letter that's upset you," Ursula Underwood accused. "Bother the man. And you were just beginning to behave yourself sensibly again."

"I don't know what you mean by sensible behavior," protested Eva. "How can there be such a thing under the circumstances?"

"There is always such a thing as sensible behavior," returned Ursula. As if to illustrate her point, she speared a spear of broccoli and dipped it into the cheese sauce she had persuaded Eva to concoct that afternoon.

"Will you tell me again exactly what he said?" asked Ursula when she had finished chewing and swallowing.

"You can read the letter if you want to."

"You mean you haven't torn it up and thrown it away?"

"What would be the use of that?"

"No use," admitted Ursula, "except that it might relieve your feelings a little."

"Nothing can relieve them."

Eva rose from the table and went to get the letter, while Ursula looked after her anxiously. In the little time they had lived together, they had arranged their housekeeping so efficiently. They took turns cooking and washing dishes. They went marketing together. They shared household expenses and chores. They even had an emotional economy: Eva grieved; Grammar worried, as much about Eva as about the children.

"Here," said Eva returning to the kitchen. "Read it."

Dropping the letter on the table, Eva began to clear the dishes. Without bothering to wipe her fingers first, Ursula picked up the letter.

Dear Eva,

After several days of solitary contemplation, I have come to the conclusion that my action concerning the children was unwise, unwarranted, and unfortunate. I have nothing to say in defense of myself except that I acted under the influence of certain violent and uncontrollable emotions.

I have, as you know, notified the police that the children are missing. They are conducting a careful search of the area. That the police have not yet found the children means nothing. I have conclusive evidence that the Empty Land exists in a separate space accessible only to a very few. I am confident that the children will find refuge in that country with my estranged wife and that we will hear from them by some means or another in the near future.

Until then, I beg you to forgive me, and I remain your friend.

Adam Underwood

P.S. Tell my mother, if she's with you, that I am sorry for what I did. She has sent me no address.

For awhile after she had finished reading, Ursula Underwood stared at the letter. To her knowledge, Adam had never admitted that he was wrong in his life, not that this admission could make up for that wrong. Punishments fitted crimes; apologies were too small.

"The letter was posted the morning after the storm."

Eva's voice was toneless, but as Eva briskly stacked the dishes and ran the water, Ursula sensed that she was not only anxious but angry.

"What do you intend to do about the letter?" asked Ursula, turning to look at Eva's back.

"I don't know. What would you do?"

Ursula considered for a moment.

"Either I would ignore it," she said slowly, "or I would tell him to go to hell."

Ursula was shocked by the strength of her own words, but Eva made no response. She began to wash the dishes.

"Leave the dishes for a while," said Ursula. "Let's go out to the ice-cream parlor for dessert," a suggestion which, coming from Grammar, would have amazed and delighted Fred.

"You go if you want to, Ursula. I'm not hungry. Besides, I'd like to be alone for a little while."

"You're alone too much," said Ursula, getting up to dry the dishes. "It's not good for you."

"I don't care what's good for me."

They finished cleaning the kitchen in silence.

Later that evening, Ursula Underwood sat by herself at the kitchen table playing solitaire, losing one game after another, because she was too distracted to cheat. By the time she had played her fifth round, she had decided, once again, that solitaire was a pointless game. There was no adversary but chance. To lose was not to be defeated but merely frustrated. It was like turning a corner and discovering a dead end or opening a door to go out and finding oneself in a closet. How she did wish that Eva would come out and play gin-rummy.

Rapping her cards against the table, Ursula stared at the closed door to Jason's room. It would have been better if Eva had allowed her to sleep in Jason's room instead of giving up her own. She would not have minded sleeping among Jason's collections. She had told Eva so, but Eva would not hear of any other arrangement, and she had moved her things into Jason's room at once. There she spent hours of each day. She ought not to grieve so much, Ursula thought. Why, she behaved as though the children were dead. Ursula wished she could persuade Eva of her conviction that they were not, but it was difficult to justify that conviction, even to herself.

Her intuitive certainty had something to do with Ionia's drawings, which hung over the desk in Eva's room. Each morning Ursula woke to find herself confronted with them. At first the pictures upset her because they reminded her, not only of Ionia, but of the ways in which she had failed the child; for it seemed that Eva had been much closer to Ionia than had she, Ionia's own grandmother, who had raised her. After a while she had stopped reproaching herself and started studying the pictures. There were many of the child's mother, and though Ursula had never seen or tried to imagine Lilith's country, if she had, she felt it might have looked very much like the world of these pictures. Gradually she had begun to find comfort in the pictures, for they made Lilith and her country seem real. Ursula considered, as she absentmindedly dealt herself another game of solitaire, that whatever he had done wrong, Adam was right about one thing: the children had found their way into that world, and Lilith would look after them. There might well be some word soon, especially if Adam, with his crystal ball, could. . . .

But she dared not voice that hope even to herself, much less to Eva. It sometimes seemed to Ursula that the more she hoped, the more hopeless Eva became. It had come to the point where they could no longer share their loss, because they did not experience it in the same way. That grieved Ursula. She had come to comfort Eva, as well as to seek comfort, and instead, Eva had withdrawn to an extent Ursula would not have thought possible for one who had been so open and naive, almost childlike, before. Ursula did not know how to approach Eva. Every approach seemed to lead to a dead end, a closed door.

As Ursula picked up her first card, she glared at Jason's door, as if it were to blame, as if only the door stood between them.

Behind the door, Eva sat at Jason's desk. Before her was a blank sheet of paper; beside it lay Adam's letter. In her hand she held a pen, but she made no motion to write with it. She continued to stare at the paper as if waiting for it to suggest something, for her mind was as empty as the page.

It ought to be simple, she told herself. He had made a request. She had but to answer yes or no. Yes, she would forgive him; or, no, she would not. But forgive whom? Who was he? That was the question she could not answer: the man who had been her friend for five years, who had given structure and meaning to her life? Or the man who had cast out his children, who had lost her, her son? She could not seem to think of these two men as one man. Yet to think of them as separate was to be unsure of which was the real man. That was just the trouble: she did not know anymore what was real and what was not.

As she gazed at the paper, she tried to recall other images of Adam: Adam lecturing in a crowded hall, Adam smiling at her across a table in the Pearls and Swine, Adam walking beside her down a street, Adam drinking coffee in her kitchen, but even her memory had altered. No matter how she tried to picture him, his eyes were always the same: cold, black, empty, like nothing, nothingness itself, as they had looked while he waited for her in the empty space, drawing her into their darkness and emptiness, into that awful moment when she had known him and not known him, as if, in all of five years, that moment had contained their only real contact.

That moment had drained her of everything. She did not know how she had managed to get home that day. She did not know how she managed to get up every morning. Every motion seemed empty of meaning. If not for Ursula Underwood, she supposed she might never have moved again. She knew she ought to be grateful, but she could not feel gratitude; she could not feel anything. Ursula Underwood thought she wanted to be left alone to grieve. If only she could grieve! She had never yet wept. Nothing relieved the emptiness. Ursula kept trying to tell her that the children were not dead, but Ursula hadn't seen the children disappear into nothing. If she had, she, too, might have found it difficult to believe in their existence. She, too, might have found herself paralyzed, unable to mourn, unable to hope. In this state of suspension, she felt that she had not only lost Jason but her memories of him, her feelings for him. That was why she wanted to be in his room: in the absence of feeling, she might at least be surrounded by facts of him, artifacts of a life she had given, nourished, witnessed, from which she had been so suddenly cut off.

Still unable to respond to Adam's letter, Eva stood up and began to wander around Jason's room as if she were exploring it. She paused before the glass case. His collections had collected dust. Opening the door, she reached in, picked up an antique doorknob, and dusted it with the hem of her dress. Tomorrow, she decided, she would dust the rest of the objects. Turning from the case, she headed towards Jason's map of the stars. On her way across the room, she tripped over a loose flap of linoleum. Bending over to see if she could smooth it down, she found a key which she supposed must unlock the drawers of Jason's desk. She hesitated for a moment, then tucked the key back under the flap, resolving not to violate any secrets he had seen fit to keep from her. After she had stared at the stars for a time, she found herself walking towards Jason's clothes closet. There she buried her face in his shirts and tried to breathe his scent, but the shirts he had left behind were clean, and, before Eva could stop her, Ursula had washed the clothes he wore at the Underwoods', insisting that they were dreadfully dirty.

Pressing further into the closet, Eva stumbled over some shoes and fell against the wall. The secret panel Jason had constructed sprung open, and Eva found herself on the floor gazing at a cardboard model of the Underwood house. Not only was it an exact replica, perfect, so far as she could tell, in proportion and shape, but the gate, here, was also missing. That Jason might make a model of the house was in itself no wonder, but to see the empty space in the small scale wall had an uncanny effect on Eva. As she wondered at it, against her will she began to relive that day. She saw Adam's face distorted with anger. She saw the violence with which he flung his children from him. She saw the pleading, fleeting look Jason gave her before he turned and ran after Ionia and Fred. She felt the grip of Adam's hand on her arm; she felt her teeth sink into his flesh. Then she was stumbling blindly, wildly after the children. She heard herself cry out to them. She saw them disappear.

"No!" she cried out.

As if to escape the vision, she scrambled out of the closet. Without hesitating, she crossed the room to the desk. Still standing up, she wrote one sentence on the empty page. Then she folded the paper, stuffed it into the envelope, which she sealed and addressed. For a moment she stared at what she had done. At last she sank into the chair, laid down her head, and began to weep.

Ursula Underwood, alarmed by the cry from the closet, had been standing by the door listening. Crouching down, her knees crackling so that they might have given her away, Ursula peered through the keyhole. What she saw removed her reticence. Without knocking, she opened the door and went to Eva. Lifting Eva's head so that she could cradle it, Ursula held Eva and rocked her.

Adam Underwood could not concentrate on his work.

Exasperated, he slammed shut Volume One of the complete works of Bacon, and, with one motion of his arm, he swept the desk clean of books, papers, rocks, pens, bones. The crystal ball, which had been poised at the edge of the desk, flew across the room and crashed in the fireplace. Adam did not even turn to look. Instead he stared for a moment at the empty space he had created. Then he reached for his wastebasket and searched through it, uncrumpling a dozen discarded beginnings of his treatise before he found the piece of paper he wanted. Spreading it out before him on the desk, he read:

I will never forgive you.

The words were as stark and uncompromising, as devoid of ambiguity as before. He did not know what he had hoped to gain by reading them again. Perhaps the discovery of some overtone or undertone he had missed or that the invisible ink with which she had written the rest of the letter might have appeared, but there was nothing more. She had not even signed the note. She not only refused to forgive but to give anything at all. No explanation, no word about his mother, no acknowledgment of his apology, except this blunt refusal to accept it. Really, after five years of friendship, he deserved better than this from her. Perhaps that was why he wanted to reread the letter: to persuade himself that if Eva was going to behave in this childish way, she was not worthy of his notice. He had made his move towards reconciliation; if she would not meet him half way, then let her be. It need not affect him one way or another.

Yet it did affect him. That was what upset him most: that he should be upset. Obviously Eva Brooke had not recovered her senses. The Eva Brooke he knew could never have written such a note. He was right to be concerned for her mental health, but beyond that why should anything she said upset him? He would have been willing to help her if she had asked. Hadn't he extended his friendship to her? But she would not have it. She had slammed the door in his face. Well, it was her loss.

Resolving to think no more of the matter, Adam got up to inspect the damage he had done. The crystal ball had shattered into a thousand tiny pieces; it could never be repaired. One of the last crystal balls in the world was now nothing but broken glass. Now that was something that ought to upset him. That crystal ball had been his prize possession. He had gone to great trouble and expense to get his hands on it, and now it was gone forever. He crouched and fingered the broken pieces in an attempt to sense his loss, yet his anxiety and agitation refused to focus on the fragile remains of his prize possession. After a few moments he admitted to himself the astonishing fact that he just did not care about the crystal ball.

Adam stood up suddenly, and the blood drained from his head. The room seemed darker, and he felt dizzy. With a sense of relief, he realized that he was very tired. Fatigue had been his whole trouble. All he needed was an afternoon nap, and he would be himself again. He would regain his perspective. Averting his eyes from the desk, Adam turned and left the tower room.

When he had drawn the shades and removed his shoes, Adam lay down on the bed and closed his eyes. Sleep enfolded him as if it were the arms of some woman who had waited for him. As he yielded to sleep, he felt as though he were being held and rocked, an infant once more, not separate from all he saw and sensed. Slowly the warm darkness that rocked him gave way to light. Looking up, he saw Eva's face bending over him, as large as the moon's face and as bright. She was looking down at him and her eyes seemed liquid. He could see his own face reflected in her eyes, a thousand times tinier than her face, as if he were looking at his face through the wrong end of a telescope. Gradually his face grew larger, and as it grew larger, it grew younger and younger, until it was the face of a baby. Yet he knew the infant was himself and that, somehow, Eva was his mother. She was smiling at him, and her lips were moving. Sounds came through them, but he could no more understand their meaning than he could have known the meaning of the wind's sound or the water's. He only knew that her voice was infinitely soft, unspeakably tender. It acted on him like a lullaby. He closed his eyes, and the warm darkness enveloped him once more. He pressed himself closer to the body that held him. For a moment he knew perfect contentment, perfect union with another. Then it was gone.

Darkness surrounded him still, but without warmth, without softness, without sound. All he knew was that he was alone, alone as he never had been before, alone without knowing where he was or even that he was. He dared not move for fear he would find out that he was not, or that there was nothing beyond whatever was himself. So he stood still, waiting for something to be. After an undetermined span of time, a gleam of light distinguished itself from the darkness. As the light grew brighter he saw that it came from the rising moon. With relief, he realized where he was: in his own yard, surrounded by his own walls, standing before his own gate. He lifted his own hand and looked at it in the moonlight. Satisfied with himself and his surroundings, Adam turned and began to walk up the path to the house. Suddenly he stopped midstep and stared. There was no house. Slowly he turned in a complete circle. There was nothing: no car, no trees, no gardens, no grass, no other living thing; only himself.

In terror, he ran towards the gates. Attempting to open them, he found they were locked. He reached into his pocket for the touchstone and discovered that he was naked. He looked down at his body. His flesh was as white as a frog's belly. It was repulsive to him as the flesh of a corpse might have been. He looked up at the moon. For a moment he thought he saw Eva's face in the moon looking down at him as it had before. He cried out her name. Then the vision passed, and the moon appeared again as what it was: a cold, empty ball spinning in space with no light of its own, only a mockery of light. He wished the moon would go away so that he could be in the dark again. He could not bear the sight of himself naked in its false light, but the moon would not move. There was no escape from himself. In desperation he turned to the gates and began to pound on them screaming: "Let me out! Let me out!"

Adam woke, drenched in sweat, panting for breath, pounding the bedroom wall with his fists. When he knew, at last, that he was awake and lying on his own bed in his own room, he stopped. For a long while he lay rigid, trying to control his breathing. When it had quieted, he drew his knees against his chest and held them there with his arms. He did not move again until the bedroom was almost dark. Then, slowly, he uncurled himself and let his feet slip to the floor. Lifting the window shade, he looked out, glad, for the first time, to see the empty space. Lifting his eyes, he looked at the three trees. The last light of day was touching the tips of their branches. The sky behind them was deepening to night. He waited until the first stars appeared; then he left the room and went downstairs to see about supper.

But when he entered the kitchen, he knew he did not want to eat. There was an ache in his stomach that came from something besides hunger. Standing in the kitchen, he felt at a loss for what to do. He wanted to be occupied. He wanted one activity to follow another. He wanted his life to make sense. But as he stood still in the dim, unlit kitchen, he knew that his life didn't make sense. Possibly it never had.

Then he remembered that he had not yet swept away the remains of the crystal ball. Grateful for an immediate task, he went to the cleaning closet, found a dustpan and broom, and headed upstairs again.

There was only just enough light in the tower room for Adam to see what he was doing. The broken pieces did not shine; there was magic only in a whole crystal ball. When he dumped the pieces into the waste basket, they sounded no different than broken pieces of a bottle or a light bulb might have. Laying down the dustpan and brush, he began to pick up his books and papers, stacking them to one side or the other of his desk. Where he used to keep his crystal ball, Eva's note still lay. In the half-light, it seemed to gleam as if it had taken on the properties of the crystal ball.

When his work was done, Adam turned to leave the tower room, but at the door he hesitated. He dreaded wandering through the empty house without purpose or direction. He did not want to eat; he did not want to sleep; he did not want to read; he did not know what to do next. Slowly he turned towards the desk, drawn there by the note. It seemed the only object in his house, the only point in his life that had meaning, however terrible its meaning was. As he stood before his desk, he knew all at once what he must do next, first, before anything he ever did would have meaning.

He sank down into his chair. There was not enought light for him to read the note. Instead he picked it up and pressed it against his eyes. Deliberately he made himself remember what he had seen in Eva's eyes the day he had cast his children out. He looked into her eyes again and saw his own emptiness. Then, for the first time in his life as a man, he broke down and wept.

40
The Dance

THE last light of day still lingered at the edges of the earth when the great fire was lit. From miles around, solitary figures glided, silent as their own shadows, over and down the hills towards its light, each coming from her own place in the Empty Land. As the women drew nearer the center of their common life, they would raise an arm in silent greeting or call one another by name. Then two or three might walk together the rest of the way to the great fire.

Ionia, standing close by her mother, watched each woman as she entered the circle of light. There was one woman with hair like fire, another with hair the color of clouds or ashes, yet another with hair like light itself. Their skins were of many different shades, too. At first it was only by hair and skin color that Ionia could distinguish one woman from another. In that light all their eyes were bright, all their bodies naked, and all seemed ageless in the human sense of the word. After she had looked at them for awhile standing side by side, she began to realize that they differed from one another in shape and stance in much the way trees did. They aged, too, like trees. Some might have been older than others by thousands of years, but they showed their age as strength instead of weakness. As they stood perfectly still, waiting for whatever was going to happen, they might have been trees growing silently together in a forest.

Then, as if the softest breeze had stirred their leaves, a subtle movement began among them. Although she did not know its source, Ionia sensed the excitement. Two women drew apart to make an opening in the circle. A woman entered the space, and the circle closed behind her once again. Ionia felt an impulse to kneel, as she had read in storybooks you should in the presence of majesty. Without being told, Ionia knew that here was the First Woman.

The other women remained standing as this woman proceeded slowly around the circle, wordlessly greeting each one. On her head she wore a crown of dark leaves, like the crown she and her mother had made for the snow woman. Her white hair, like the snow woman's, fell to her knees. It contrasted with the smooth darkness of her skin like the moon with the night sky. She was taller than the other women and thicker of limb and waist, not because she was fat, but because she was massive.

Ionia trembled as the First Woman drew near where she and her mother were standing. Afraid to look at her now that she was so close, Ionia lowered her eyes. Holding her breath, she waited for the First Woman to pass by. She did not. Staring down, Ionia could see the First Woman's feet planted in front of Ionia so firmly that they might have been the roots of a tree.

"Lilith, ninth to bear my name, show me your child, the youngest of our race."

The First Woman's voice was like her mother's, only stronger. If her mother's voice had been a river, this woman's voice would have been the sea.

"Grand Mother of all, here is my daughter, Ionia."

Her mother pressed her forward.

"Look at me, youngest daughter," the Grand Mother commanded.

Ionia raised her head and looked into the Grand Mother's face. Perhaps because they were in shadow, Ionia had difficulty distinguishing her features. The Grand Mother's face seemed as cold and remote as the stars.

"Come into the firelight that I may see you better."

Her mother stayed behind as Ionia followed the Grand Mother. When they were near enough the fire to feel its heat, the Grand Mother stopped and turned towards Ionia. Taking Ionia's face in her hands, she gazed at her. The Grand Mother's hands were cool and smooth as water. Ionia stared into eyes that kept changing from green to gold as they reflected the dance of the flames. After a time Ionia lost all sense of herself. She had fallen into those eyes; she was drowning in them.

"Why have you waited so long to come to us, Daughter?"

The necessity of answering the Grand Mother's question recalled Ionia to herself. She became aware once more of her surroundings, of the women standing in a silent circle around the fire, of her mother among them, of the Grand Mother who had let go her face as she stood back, watching, waiting for an answer.

"I could not come sooner."

Ionia was surprised that her voice showed none of the fear she felt.

"You could have come with your mother when she returned to us. You could have come with her when she first came to you."

Ionia felt herself flush with heat that had nothing to do with the fire.

"I couldn't just leave my little brother and my grandmother. I couldn't. . . ."

"Your Grand Mother?" interrupted the Grand Mother. "Ah yes, of course, your human grandmother."

The Grand Mother paused. Ionia was unsure of whether she ought to say something more. But she did not like to seem as though she were making excuses. So she waited for the Grand Mother to speak again.

"You have brought two man-children into our country."

Ionia hesitated, wishing she could explain that she hadn't meant to, that she couldn't help it.

"Yes," she said at last.

"You know that it is against our law."

"I know that only women live here."

"Why did you bring them with you?"

"I, they," began Ionia, "I mean none of us can go home again."

The Grand Mother's gaze seemed to intensify.

"What do you mean by home, Daughter?"

Ionia remained silent, for she could not think of an answer.

"Do you mean that you did not come here of your own free will?"

Ionia felt confused. Surely she had chosen to come, and yet. . . .

"I wanted to come here," she said. "I have always wanted to come here since before I can remember, since before I knew there was here, but," she paused, "I also had to come here, and I couldn't leave my brother."

"You chose and you did not choose."

It seemed a statement rather than a question, so Ionia said nothing but looked steadily at the Grand Mother, unable to tell from her expression any more than she would have been able to tell from looking at the face of a mountain whether she had met with approval of disapproval, love or wrath.

"Daughter," said the Grand Mother after a silence, "have you become a human being?"

There was her mother's question again, asked in a different way.

"I don't know what you mean."

The Grand Mother regarded her for a moment.

"No, you do not," she said at last. "Where there is not choice, there is confusion. But there is yet a little time for confusion. When that time draws to an end, you will choose; you will know. Tonight," she said, raising her voice so that she addressed the whole company, "Ionia, daughter of the ninth Lilith, youngest of our race, must enter the Dance!"

Inside the hut, a mile or so away, Jason was still awake when the music began. He could hear the singing voices drifting towards the hut on the night air; he could feel the beating drums and the pounding feet through the earth beneath him. The music made his blood race with excitement and fear. He knew he would never sleep. He did not understand how Fred could, except perhaps because Fred had fallen asleep right after supper with his arms around Lion and his head in his mother's lap while she sang him a lullaby. Fred had not seen Ionia and his mother get up and steal out of the hut without a word about where they were going or when they would be back. But Jason had, and he resented it. All day Ionia's mother had refused to answer any questions about the other inhabitants of her country, their system of government, whether or not he and Ionia and Fred would be presented to the ruler. This lack of information did not appear to distress Ionia and Fred, but it disconcerted Jason. As he lay awake alone in the little dirt hut, listening to that eerie music, Jason began to feel homesick, though he didn't know what he was feeling. He only knew that he was thinking about his mother and wondering why he had left her. She needed him more than Ionia and Fred did. They had each other, and now they had their own mother. His mother didn't have anyone now that he was gone. He wondered if he'd ever see her again.

Brushing a sudden tear away as quickly as it had come, Jason sat up. He refused to lie awake and be miserable while Ionia was out having some sort of adventure. It wasn't fair. She might at least have told him where she was going, but it was obvious she didn't care, didn't trust him after all this time. Or maybe she hadn't known where she was going either. She had slept beside him every night until now. It made him nervous to have her gone. Who knew what might be happening to her among her mother's people? They might even be sacrificing her to some god, or rather goddess. As the drums beat stronger and wilder, Jason decided that it was his duty to see where Ionia had gone. Softly, so as not to wake Fred, Jason crept out of the hut.

The night was dark and moonless. The afternoon haze had thickened to clouds and covered the stars. Outside the hut, Jason turned slowly in a circle searching for some guiding light. In one direction he saw an orange glow on the horizon. Sure that it was too late for the glow to belong to the sun, Jason began to walk in that direction. The night air was chilly. He would have liked to hug himself with his arms for warmth, but he needed to hold both arms out for balance. The darkness was so deep, it was difficult to believe that anything, his own body or the ground on which he walked, had substance. Once he thought of turning back, but then he realized it would be of no use. He would never find the hut again except by miracle or accident. He had to go forward. The light in the distance was all that kept him from being utterly lost, but for a long time the light did not seem to be getting any nearer, nor the music any louder. He kept trudging on and on, over and down one hill after another. It worried him that he had come so far from the hut. What if he could not find his way back, even by daylight? What if no one ever found him? But then again what if they did? That, too, was an uncomfortable thought. He might well be trespassing on some secret, sacred ground. If daylight discovered him in a place he ought not to be, there was nowhere in that bare, open country to hide. He was beginning to think he should stop where he was before he saw anything he shouldn't. Then he reminded himself that the forbidden sight might be something terrible happening to Ionia, and he resolved to go on.

At the top of the next hill, Jason found that the music had grown stronger and the light brighter. Jason hesitated. His hands trembled, and his knees felt weak, but he forced himself to go on down the hill and up another. Then, looking down, he saw the great fire. Silhouetted against its light, so that they looked like the shadows they cast, were women circling round and round the fire, sometimes with their hands joined, sometimes not. All the women had long hair that whirled around them as they danced.

Lying with his belly touching the ground, Jason watched the dance, straining his eyes for a glimpse of Ionia among the dancers. He had almost given up and was debating descending the hill to search for her when he caught sight of a childish figure, smaller and slimmer than the others and with short-cropped hair. He knew it was Ionia. She danced with the rest of the women, equal to them, Jason thought, in grace and skill. As he watched Ionia move in the dance, her arms outstretched, her hands clasping the hands of the women on either side of her, Jason understood that he could not go near her now; she did not need him. Yet that thought did not rankle as much as it once might have. He had never known Ionia except in relation to himself, whether that relationship was antagonistic or tolerant. Now, for the first time, he accepted that there was an Ionia he could never know. So he lay still, content to watch her when she was within sight and to wait for her when she was not. Before Ionia had circled the fire three times, Jason, wearied by his night journey and hypnotized by the dance of the flames, had fallen asleep.

When dawn came, the beating drums and the singing voices hushed. The dance ended in silence. The Grand Mother paced a circle sprinkling each woman with ashes from the great fire. When the Grand Mother had finished, she turned and walked toward the sunrise. At the top of the first hill, she stood still for a moment, her figure small and black against the immensity of the brightening sky, but powerful nonetheless. Turning towards them, the Grand Mother raised her arm, then disappeared beyond the hill. While a few women remained to bury the live embers of the great fire, the rest made their various ways to their own places in the Empty Land.

Ionia walked up a hill between her mother and a woman her mother had introduced as her grandmother, Istar. It overwhelmed Ionia, who was exhausted from dancing all night long, to realize, as she was only just beginning to, that she not only had a grandmother, but a great grandmother, a great, great grandmother, a great, great, great grandmother, all living, all proceeding back, she could not guess how many generations, to the Grand Mother. She stole a look at the woman walking beside her, the woman who was her mother's mother. She was the woman Ionia had noticed earlier with the flame-like hair. Ionia now saw that she had fire-colored eyes to match her hair. She resembled Ionia's mother only in the shape of her face and features. Then Ionia's grandmother caught her looking at her and stared back.

"She has your eyes, Lilith," commented Istar, "but where did she get that dull brown hair?"

"From her human grandmother, I think," answered Lilith. "But I do not find it dull; not everyone can be a walking torch, Mother."

"Hhmph," sniffed Ionia's wild grandmother.

The three walked on in silence until Istar nearly tripped over Jason's sleeping body.

"Oh, look!" she cried. "What is it!"

"It's Jason!" exclaimed Ionia.

"Jason," repeated Istar. "What is Jason? Oh, you mean this is one of the man-children! How exciting! I have never seen one before!"

"Surely, Mother, you must have seen a man," Lilith pointed out.

"That was many hundreds of years ago, Lilith," her mother reminded her, as she bent to examine Jason. "And I have never seen a half-grown one. May I take its garments off?"

At that moment, Jason woke. Looking up, he saw two fierce orange eyes staring down at him out of a face framed with hair that looked too hot to touch. He knew, at once, that it was all over. The wild women had discovered him and they were going to tear him to bits.

"Let him be, Mother, you're frightening him."

Jason turned his head and saw, to his relief, that Ionia and her mother were standing close by. No one else seemed to be near.

"I only wanted to look," protested Istar, rising to her full height. "After all, it seems he's been spying on us."

"Have you, Jason?" asked Lilith sternly.

"I was not spying," said Jason with as much dignity as he could muster, and he stood up to face his accusers. "I was just looking for Ionia. I was worried about her."

"Worried," wondered Istar. "What is that?"

"It is something that often happens to human beings," explained Lilith.

"I didn't know where you had gone," said Jason, turning towards Ionia. "I didn't know what they would do to you. I didn't know if you were coming back."

"I'm sorry, Jason," said Ionia half-touched, half-annoyed by Jason's anxiety. "I didn't know you were still awake or I would have told you it was all right."

And he should have known, Ionia thought to herself, that her mother would never do anything to harm her.

"Child," said Ionia's grandmother, taking Ionia's face into her hands, "I do not understand. It must be the influence of that unfortunate brown-haired human grandmother of yours. Why, in the name of the Grand Mother of all, do you hold yourself accountable to this man-child? This is not even the little brother, is it?"

Ionia hesitated. Jason had certainly placed her in an awkward position, yet he meant well.

"Jason is my friend," she said.

"What is friend?" asked Istar, letting go of Ionia and turning helplessly to Lilith.

"It is a word we do not have, Mother. We are all bound by one blood, the blood of the Grand Mother. Friendship is what binds human beings together."

"Are they not all of one blood, too?"

"Yes," said Lilith, "but they don't know that they are. But come. Ionia is half asleep. Let us go to my hut, and you can see my man-child, the one to whom I gave birth. Some things about him I think you will not find unpleasing, Mother."

"I still cannot believe you did that, Lilith," said Istar. "I must see with my own eyes this terrible deed that has brought such shame upon us both."

Lilith and her mother walked ahead. Jason and Ionia trailed behind. Now and then, Ionia stumbled, and Jason helped her up. After a while he kept hold of her all the time. Ionia, her eyes half-closed, let him lead her. They walked in silence as Ionia was too tired to speak, but Lilith and Istar talked as they walked, unaware that Jason could hear them.

"He has seen the Dance that no man may see. He must be brought before the Grand Mother, Lilith."

"No, Mother."

"But it is the law."

"It has never been enforced before."

"There has never been cause."

"But the law means death."

"Well, and so it does."

"I will not do it. I will not take him before the Grand Mother. Nor will I allow you to do it. I cannot."

"I fear you are becoming a man-lover, Lilith."

"There you are wrong, Mother. I have no cause to love men. I have suffered more at the hands of one man than you could ever imagine, you with your one night of mating in the moonlight, leaving the man before day so that he never knew whether or not you were a dream."

"And your man, Lilith, does he know that you are not a dream?"

"He tried to imprison me. He. . . ."

"That is exactly what I mean."

The two women were silent for a moment.

"Well, Lilith," said Istar, "if you have suffered, it is no more than you deserve for following a man into his own country. Never did I raise you for such folly. And I still do not understand why you would spare this man-child."

"It is true, as you say, Mother. I brought my suffering on myself. But this man-child, whom you would hand over to death, helped to save my life. He braved deep magic to do it. I owe him his life. It is a matter of honor. Honor among our people and among human beings has the same meaning. It is the law above the law."

"Honor," repeated Istar. "Yes, I see. I did not know there was a question of honor."

The women fell silent. Jason, following behind, felt weak with relief and warm with gratitude. As they walked on he became aware, for the first time, of how sweet the morning air of the Empty Land smelled. For the first time, the shapes and the shadows of the hills pleased him; the open space exhilarated him. All at once he felt so glad he wanted to shout, but he kept quiet and only held Ionia's hand a little tighter than before.

41
🕺 Vegetable Life 🕺

ONLY after Eva Brooke had finished one cup of coffee and poured herself another was she able to understand the note Ursula Underwood had left for her on the kitchen table.

Gone for the day. Back by supper. Remember the melon. Bottom shelf. Don't worry.

Love,
Ursula

Eva glanced at the clock on the kitchen wall. It was only just past eight now. Ursula must have gotten up very early and left very quietly. For some reason she had not wished to discuss where she was going, or why, and so it was obvious where she had gone. Half-annoyed, half-amused, Eva smiled to herself at Ursula's attempt to be secretive. Then she remembered the melon and went to fetch it from the bottom shelf of the refrigerator where Ursula said it would be. Even before she cut it open, Eva could smell that the melon was perfectly ripe. As she sliced herself a piece, she recalled Ursula at the open-air market pinching and sniffing and finally pronouncing that this melon would be just right in a day or two. Eva also recalled that she had wondered how Ursula could take an interest in such things as the ripeness of melons or the bargains to be found in an open-air market, for it had been Ursula's idea to go to the market. Eva had only gone at Ursula's insistence, and because she knew that Ursula could not find her way around the city alone. Eva recalled that she had resented being dragged along and that she had gone silently, even sullenly. While Ursula had haggled over the price of this and that, she had stood by, telling herself that Ursula had not been so deeply injured by her loss as she, Eva, had.

As she sat down to eat the melon that Ursula had picked, Eva felt ashamed of her assumptions. As if in penance, she made herself eat the melon slowly, savoring each bite, inhaling the fragrance as well as tasting the fruit. When she had scraped the melon to the rind, she sat back and stared at it, aware that for the first time in a month, she had been absorbed in something besides her grief; not that the grief had gone away, but, for a moment, it had become a part of her life, not the whole of it. It was less the arid emptiness, the desert that it had been, and more a live part of who she was.

Alone in the apartment with Ursula and her bustling, clucking, caretaking gone, Eva felt that she understood Ursula a little better. Her insistence that life go on, no matter what, which had, until now, seemed unfeeling to Eva, began to seem valiant. Eva realized how much she had been depending on Ursula, how she had turned over to Ursula all the details of daily life, how without Ursula she could not have afforded continual grieving, brooding, aching, at times almost non-being. She saw that even worse than forcing Ursula to be the one to cope, she had made her grief a private grief. She had shut Ursula out: Ursula who had suffered her own loss, Ursula who had come to comfort her in her time of need, in the time of their mutual need, but Eva had done no comforting. She saw that now. She had offered no help, no support. No wonder Ursula had slipped out of the house without waking her, without saying where she was going. She had made it impossible for Ursula to speak with her.

Well, it was not too late to make amends. Ursula would be back for supper. Eva read the note again and smiled, this time with affection. Putting the note in the pocket of her bathrobe, Eva got up, washed her cup and plate, then went to Jason's room to dress. Half the summer was gone, and she had made no preparation for her fall courses; nor had she begun research for the article she meant to write: *The Fairytale and Daily Life: How Heroism is Required of Us All*. She resolved to spend the morning in the library and the afternoon in the kitchen preparing a small feast. Ursula would no doubt come home hungry from her mysterious journey.

A little while later, Ursula Underwood stepped off the train at the Empty Land station. She was both thankful and disappointed that the conductor handing her down was not that nosy man (quite literally the man had a beak) who seemed to know all about everyone. She would have liked to question him, but she was just as glad not to have him question her. After she had disembarked, she stood on the platform watching the train reload to make sure Adam was not among the passengers. He was not. The train pulled out of the station, and Ursula Underwood found herself alone on a warm summer morning at the edge of the Empty Land. The silence, after weeks of city noise, soothed her. She realized that she missed her life at the old house, however lonely it had been. She thought of her vegetable garden and her flower beds with longing and anxiety as she started on her pilgrimage to the house.

Her apprehension about the inevitable meeting with Adam dulled her pleasure in the fine morning. When she had left, she had believed it was forever, that she would never see Adam again, never even want to see him. Gradually her curiosity had gotten the better of her. It had started with that note, wondering what had prompted him to write it. True, it was stiff, formal, even arrogant, and altogether inadequate, but it indicated some change of heart, or at least change of mind. Grammar had allowed herself one dangerous hope: if Adam had decided that what he had done was wrong, might he not have done something to remedy it? She had left early that morning for fear of sharing the hope with Eva and then having to dash it.

At last Grammar stood in the empty space. Her heart pounded and her hands trembled as she peered into the yard. She had prepared herself for an overgrown lawn, loose shingles and shutters, and unswept walk. But the lawn was new-mown, the house in better repair than when she had left, and the walk might have been swept that morning. Adam must have hired a caretaker. Cautiously, she entered the yard, searching the windows of the house for a sign of life. Then she stood still again and listened. Somewhere someone was raking—or was it digging? She turned and tiptoed in the direction of the sound.

In the south yard, standing in her vegetable garden, hoeing the corn, was Adam. His back was towards her, so he did not see her hesitate, unsure of whether to call out to him or approach him silently. She was still poised midstep when Adam finished his row and turned, unknowingly, in her direction.

When he saw her, he stared. Then, dropping the hoe, he left the garden, advanced a few steps, and stopped.

"Mother?" he asked, as if he were not sure.

"Adam?" she answered with the same uncertainty, and she ventured towards him a few steps, pausing within feet of him.

For several moments, which seemed longer than they were, Ursula and Adam looked at each other awkwardly, each resisting the impulse to look away. Neither knew what to say to the other. Ursula was used to Adam's quick sarcasm; she knew how to respond to that with a sharp retort, but, to this obviously embarrassed man standing before her, she did not know how to speak. As for Adam, it seemed to him more than a month since he had spoken with another human being. The language he had spoken then and for most of his life seemed old, a useless, a dead language; but he had not yet learned a new one. And here was his mother standing before him. It was for him to speak; or else how could she know that everything had changed?

"How are you, Mother?" he asked, and he came forward to take her hand.

"I came here to find out how you are, Adam," she said, allowing her hand to rest in his.

"Well, you have come a long way to learn that. You must be thirsty."

"Yes," she said, "I am."

"Come and have a drink. Then we will talk."

Ursula walked beside Adam as he headed for the back door, half-curious, half-afraid to see the kitchen. When she entered her old domain, she discovered that it was clean, not as orderly as the kitchen she had kept, but not the ruin she had expected. Adam saw her eyes roving over every surface, searching every corner, attempting to penetrate cabinets and cupboards, and he smiled.

"I had to rearrange it a little, Mother, so that I could find things. Will you have lemonade or iced tea?"

"Iced tea, please. You've done very well, Adam," she said judiciously.

Adam said nothing as he poured her a glass of tea.

"Sit down, Mother," he invited, handing her a glass, "or would you rather go to the living room?"

"The kitchen has always been good enough for me," she said, settling herself on a stool. "You needn't treat me like a guest just because I don't live here anymore."

"Of course not, Mother. I'm sorry."

Adam poured himself a glass and sat down in a chair. From her perch, Ursula surveyed him suspiciously as she sipped her tea. Something was wrong or at any rate different. He had never been so polite or considerate. She was not sure she trusted the change, if it was a change and not just another production put on for her benefit, another part he was playing to win her sympathy. Adam was a man who could not live without sympathy, and he had lost Eva's.

Adam felt her scrutiny and smarted under it. Her silence accused him, and he longed to defend himself. Each time he felt he must speak and insist that the change she saw was real, he stopped himself. The essence of his change lay in the realization that he had no defense. To defend himself would only belittle, if not belie, the change. If she could not believe in it, he could not blame her. He deserved disbelief.

"The house and grounds," she said at last, "they are so beautifully kept up. I wonder how you manage it with all the important work you have to do. Or have you hired someone?"

Adam blushed as he thought of his treatise, ashes scattered in the garden now, and remembered how recently it had been all important.

"No, Mother," he said, "I haven't hired anyone. I have lots of time to work outside. You see, I've abandoned my research."

"For good?" she asked incredulously.

"I think it's for good," he said. "If you mean forever. I wouldn't care to predict. There's nothing wrong with taking a scholarly interest in one's subject;

in fact, that's part of my job, but, well, what I was after with this alchemical control of planetary movement was getting my name into government circles."

Ursula could scarcely believe what she was hearing. She stared at Adam with her mouth open as he continued.

"But it's no good getting alchemy mixed up in space research. It's much less harmful and much more useful to look at alchemy from an historical-philosophical perspective. It has its place there."

He paused to clear his throat and looked up again, almost laughing aloud at his mother's expression.

"I know it seems an extraordinary change in my outlook, Mother, but I have come to believe that there are more important things than scholarship. Gardening, for example."

His tone of voice had become eager, almost pleading. He waited for an answer from her, but she had hardly listened to his last words.

"Have you given up magic, too?" she asked slowly.

"What, exactly, do you mean by magic?"

"Well, your crystal ball. . . ."

"The crystal ball is broken," he said. "But it doesn't matter. Magic doesn't mean anything to me any more."

"Oh!" she cried. "Oh. . . ."

"Mother, what's the matter?" asked Adam, half-rising from his chair.

"It's nothing, Adam," she said recovering herself. "Sit down. It's just that I, I thought, I hoped that maybe you had been able to find out something about the children."

Her voice trembled and she turned her face away. Adam understood in a way he had not before how the suffering for his wrong extended far beyond himself.

"I tried, Mother," he said, "but I couldn't get through. I'm sorry. I. . . ."

At a loss for words, he reached out a hand to touch hers, then withdrew it, feeling he could not comfort a sorrow that he had inflicted and which, even now, he could not fully understand. Her grief was a mystery to him. Humbled by the sight of it, he turned his own face away.

"I'd like to have a look at the garden," his mother said after what seemed like a long time.

"Of course," said Adam getting to his feet, "I'm glad you came today. I've been having trouble stringing up the tomatoes. I don't know how to do it, you see."

"Oh, that's easy," she said. "Come. I'll help you."

Grammar and Adam spent the morning in the garden stringing up tomatoes, then picking zucchini from wildly prolific plants. Ursula stuffed four or five into her carpet bag, along with some beets and carrots and a plump, perfect eggplant. The rest she and Adam carried to the kitchen.

After lunch, which consisted of a perfect cheese omelette and a green salad prepared by Adam, Ursula went to the dungeon to search for her canning equipment while Adam washed the dishes. Returning triumphant, Ursula proceeded to give Adam lessons on how to can vegetables. So they spent the afternoon as they had the morning, thoroughly absorbed in what they were doing, speaking little except about what was immediately before them. By the end of the afternoon, they were hot and tired, but feeling closer to one another than they had in decades.

"You'll stay for supper, of course?" inquired Adam as they cleaned up after the canning operations.

"Supper? Is it getting that late? No, Adam, I'm sorry. I can't stay. I told Eva I'd be back for supper. She'll be worried if I'm not. If you'll just drive me to the station."

"I'll drive you to the city, Mother."

"But, Adam," she protested, "you know you don't like to drive to the city."

"That's just because of the parking. I won't be parking tonight." He paused. "I doubt Eva wants to see me."

He spoke stiffly, and for a moment his mother caught a glimpse of the old Adam.

"Well, you can hardly blame her," she said.

"I don't blame her."

On the way to the city, the camaraderie they had experienced while engaged in a common activity gave way to constraint. There was no subject they could raise that would not be painful. Each kept silent out of consideration for the other, while each wished the other would speak. As the car moved through the dusk away from the darkness of the Empty Land towards the city lights, Ursula kept stealing looks at Adam's face. It might have been the fading day or simply that he was older than she had remembered, but it seemed to her that his face wore an expression she had never seen there before. She tried to think of what it was, and the word that came into her mind was sadness. When they entered the city limits and began winding their way towards Eva's street, Grammar's need to speak overcame her reluctance.

"Are you all right out there by yourself, Adam?"

"Well, Mother," he answered lightly, "haven't you seen that for yourself?"

"That's not what I mean, Adam. I know you can manage. I mean are you all right alone?"

While they waited at a stop light, Adam turned to look at her.

"Is anyone?" he asked.

The light changed, and they drove on, silent once more. After a time, Adam asked:

"Is Eva all right?"

"She's taken it very hard, Adam," said Ursula, "but she'll live."

"Is there anything I can do?"

Ursula didn't answer for a moment. They turned onto Eva's street.

"Stop here," she commanded. "I can walk the rest of the way. I don't want her to see your car."

Adam obeyed and pulled the car to the side of the street, leaving the engine running.

"Is it that bad?" he asked.

Ursula could hear the pain in his voice; she turned and saw it in his face.

"Yes, I'm afraid it is, Adam. There's nothing you can do now. Not now. Just give her. . .give her time."

"I would give her anything."

Ursula looked at him sharply. For the first time that day she was growing angry.

"Adam Underwood, do you realize how you've treated that woman, how you've used her for five years while she worshipped you like a blind. . . ."

"Fool," Adam finished for her. "Well, I've been a blind fool, too, Mother. Dreaming day and night for years of the Other One when she was nothing but a fantasy, a sickness of my own brain, while Eva, all the time Eva. . . ."

"No, Adam," Ursula cut him off. "Don't speak of Her that way. She may have addled your brains. I don't deny that. But your brain didn't make Her. Lilith was real, Adam, as real as I am. You just couldn't see her, because you were always trying to make her into something she wasn't. You never saw anyone, not me, not the children, not Eva, not anyone but yourself. . . ."

Ursula stopped when she saw Adam cover his face with his hands.

"I'm sorry, Adam," she said, lightly touching his arm. "What does it matter now?"

"It matters, Mother," he said lowering his hands, and turning to look at her. "It all matters. But you are wrong about one thing," he paused. "I never saw myself either."

They stared at one another for a moment.

"I must be going, Adam. It's late."

Ursula made a motion to open the car door, but Adam quickly got out of the car. She waited until he opened it for her.

"Will I see you again?" he asked as they stood facing one another under a street lamp.

"Yes, of course, Adam," she said briskly, "and I'll write to you, but don't write to me at Eva's address. I'll get a box of my own and let you know the number."

"But Mother, that's absurd that I can't even. . . ." He stopped himself. "Very well, Mother. I understand."

"Good-bye, Adam," she said holding out her hand.

"Good-bye, Mother," he returned. "Thank you for coming today."

They lingered hand in hand, feeling as embarrassed at parting as they had that morning in greeting. Then, without warning, Ursula stood on tiptoe and kissed Adam fiercely on the cheek. Shouldering her carpet bag, she turned and stalked down the street.

Adam watched her go. His cheek burned as though he had been slapped instead of kissed. When he had seen her disappear into Eva's building, he got into the car and backed out of the street, now and then touching the place where the kiss had been planted as if he expected something to grow there.

Inside the building, Grammar climbed the stairs to Eva's apartment feeling suddenly very tired. Her carpet bag felt as though it were filled with rocks instead of vegetables. She dreaded facing a silent or questioning Eva. She could not share the good news of the change in Adam or the bad news of no news about the children. She wondered what Eva had done all day or if she had started supper.

When she stepped into the apartment, she almost found herself thinking she had somehow opened the wrong door. In the living room was a table set for two covered with a white cloth. In the center of the table was a vase of flowers; on either side of the flowers, candles burned.

"Welcome home, Ursula."

Ursula looked up. Eva stood in the doorway to the kitchen, smiling.

42

Time

$\mathbf{W}$HAT are you doing, Jason?" asked Fred curiously.

It was early morning in the Empty Land, and the sun that day, a large, listless red ball instead of the brightest morning star, was half-risen above the horizon. The small fire, over which the breakfast drink of milk and honey and herbs was heating, appeared brighter than the sun. While he and Fred waited for Ionia and her mother to return, Jason had absorbed himself in carefully moving pebbles one by one from one shoe to another. His brows were drawn together in concentration, and his lips formed silent words. He did not answer Fred's question.

"Why are you playing with those pebbles?" persisted Fred.

"Quiet," said Jason abruptly. "Counting."

Fred fell obediently silent and contented himself with watching Jason. He had not known until this morning when he had seen Jason remove the pebbles from a small hole covered with a rock that Jason even had the pebbles. He wondered what they were for and if Jason would let him play with them later while he went on his expedition. Fred could think of things to do with the pebbles besides moving them from one shoe to another.

"Sixty-three," Jason announced, as he dropped the last pebble into his shoe.

"Is sixty-three pebbles a lot of pebbles, Jason?"

"Lots of days," said Jason. "The pebbles are for days."

Fred peered into the pebble-filled shoe.

"I don't see the days, Jason, where are they?"

"Gone," said Jason. "Past. We've been in the Empty Land sixty-three days, Fred."

"Is that a long, long time?"

The question perplexed Jason. It was the one he had meant to answer that morning when he had set about counting the pebbles he had collected each day. He had succeeded in discovering that they had been in this country for two months and a day. It was the interpretation of that information that was so difficult. The ordering of time he had always taken for granted did not exist here. There were no hours or minutes. The days did not have names; nothing distinguished one day from another. The moon went through its phases, but no one spoke of months. He supposed sixty-three days might not be a long time in itself or measured against all time or even a lifetime, but it seemed to Jason a very long time not to know what was going to happen next, or why anything happened at all. For Ionia it might be different, and perhaps Fred did not care, but Jason knew he was living in a no man's land, literally. It seemed to him that something ought to be decided by someone, but he did not know what or who ought to make the decision. He disliked living in a state of suspension—which was what he had begun to call the Empty Land in his mind. He wished he could speak to Ionia about what was to become of them, but she was part of the problem. He only saw her at breakfast and supper. Then she was not alone. Both she and her mother seemed to avoid the subject of future or past. The present Ionia was one he did not understand. They had no common ground. She slept while he explored, and while he slept, she danced. The way she looked when she returned in the morning worried him. It was not just that she had grown pale from lack of sun, it was something about her eyes that bothered him. They had that look they used to have in the old days when he teased her, a vacant look, as if no one lived behind them.

Suddenly Jason became aware of Ionia and her mother approaching the fire, and he recalled himself from his preoccupation and focused on the present. He discovered that Fred, grown tired of waiting for a response from him, had dumped the pebbles on the ground and was playing with them.

"Hey!" said Jason sharply. "Leave those alone. I don't want to lose any of them."

"I'm not losing them," protested Fred, "I'm making a mountain with them."

"What is the matter here that is more important than the milk which you have allowed to boil over?"

Fred and Jason looked up and saw Lilith standing over them. Ionia crouched by the fire and removed the pot of boiling milk.

"I'm making a mountain with Jason's sixty-three pebbles, I mean days, and I'm not losing any of them," said Fred all in one breath.

Lilith knelt beside Fred and put one arm around him, while with her other hand she reached out to touch Fred's mountain. She looked questioningly at Jason.

"I was using the pebbles to keep count of the days," he explained.

"Why should you want to count them?" wondered Lilith.

"To keep track of time, of course."

"Ah," murmured Lilith, "I had forgotten. Time has a meaning for human beings."

"Don't your people have any idea of time at all?" demanded Jason. Ionia, who was pouring milk, felt her hands tremble. She spilled a little of the milk and scalded her feet.

"Not in the way human beings do. You think of time as having a beginning and an end; for you it does. For us time runs in circles, like the circles of Dance. We watch the cycles of the moon and the changing of the seasons to know when to perform our rites. But as to counting the days and nights, how can we count that which for us is without number?"

Ionia handed Fred and her mother their bowls of milk. Then she held Jason's out to him. He did not notice her gesture. His head was bent, and he was scowling at his knee.

"Jason," she said.

He looked up, and, for a moment, he transferred his scowl to her. Taking the milk, he quickly looked away. Ionia sat back and lifted her own bowl. Although she stared down into the milk, which faintly reflected the morning sky, she did not drink. She had been startled by Jason's report that sixty-three days had passed. It was not the length of time that disturbed her as much as the fact that she had forgotten time while Jason had carefully kept track of it. To her the sixty some nights seemed one night, the Dance one continuous dance. The days between the dance did not always seem real to her; they were recurring dreams within a dream. Often she was aware of Jason watching her, wanting something from her, but, after a night of the Dance, she had nothing left to give. She was empty.

Sometimes she missed the companionship they had known on the journey, the companionship that came of sharing everything. Now they shared nothing but meals. Even if it had not been forbidden her to speak of the Dance, how could she have described to them what happened to her when she danced; how when she moved, her body was not hers anymore but belonged instead to that motion, that power that was the Dance? Jason might have seen the dance from the outside that night, but he didn't know; he couldn't know. She and Fred and Jason might occupy the same space, but she had entered another time, or rather timelessness, while they remained in time, counting the days and waiting.

As she glanced from her untouched milk to watch Jason unmaking Fred's mountain, it dawned on Ionia that Jason was waiting for her. The sense of his waiting drew her back, momentarily, into his time. She felt the weight of his waiting. Suddenly she became angry and impatient. She wanted to shout: "Go away! Leave me alone! Who asked you to wait! Who asked you to come in the first place!" Instead she just rose abruptly, spilling her milk.

"I'm going to sleep," she announced.

Without waiting for a response from anyone, she entered the hut. There she lay awake for a time, listening to the voices of the others.

"Jason, can I please play with the pebbles while you're away today?"

Ionia remembered that Jason did go off everyday, but she had no idea where he went or what he did. She had never asked; he had never told.

"Well, all right. Just make sure you don't lose any."

"How can he lose what is already lost?" Ionia heard her mother ask as she drifted into sleep.

ᚠᚤᚢ

Fred sighed as he stared after Jason's retreating figure. His mother had already joined Ionia in the hut. He sighed not so much out of sadness as out of habit. After sixty-three days, he was used to being left alone: by his mother and Ionia, who slept most of the day; by Lion, who spent much of his time hunting; by Jason, who went exploring. At first he had accompanied Jason on his expeditions, but Jason went too far, too fast; or sometimes Jason squatted down and looked too long at something Fred could not see. Most days Fred stayed just outside the hut, sometimes patting the sod his mother and Jason had chopped, helping it to dry, sometimes picking berries, or digging vegetables, or tending the zucchini his mother had planted with the seeds he had given her. But most of the time he played in the dirt where he constructed railroads, farms, and houses. Today he had the pebbles. They would be useful, not only for making mountains, but for building walls. Probably the orange-haired lady wouldn't like his walls anymore than she did his railroads.

The orange-haired lady, whose hair was the same color as his, was Fred's secret, and she was why Fred did not mind so much being left by the others. She came nearly every afternoon to play with him, but she had made him swear not to tell anyone or else, she said, she would swallow him alive. At first he had been afraid of her; she looked fierce with her orange eyes, and once she had taken his clothes off to see what he looked like underneath. But after awhile he had gotten used to her. She was also fun. She didn't like his dirt constructions and sometimes stomped on them, but she would play for hours a game called: "Catch it! Catch it!" in which they took turns chasing each other. When they were both tired, they would sit down, lean back against the hillside, and tell each other stories. She told him stories about all the animals in the Empty Land, and he told her stories about the place she called "man-country," though he had tried to explain to her that ladies lived there, too. The stories she liked best were the stories about school and how horrible it was. He soon discovered that stories about Grammar upset her so much that she pinched him. He guessed that was because *she* wanted to be his grandmother. That's who she said she was, but he did not believe her. Grammar was his grandmother. Defiantly, Fred began to build his miniature wall.

A mile or so away from the hut, Jason continued his explorations. Their purpose was his secret. He had confided in no one, and though Fred had sometimes accompanied him, Jason had never explained to Fred the object of his quest. The quest was all that sustained him. He was afraid that if he disclosed his purpose, he would be prevented from pursuing it. What he wanted was to discover the source of the water that ran through the Empty Land. The water, he felt sure, was the source of the wild women's power.

He had made experiments, such as bathing a cut finger in the water or soaking a dried or decayed vegetable, and he had determined that the water had healing, perhaps even life-renewing, properties. That the wild women somehow controlled the water seemed almost certain. Why else would the wild cows come to give their milk or the deer donate their antlers for tools? How else was it possible for the wild women to dwell safely, without protection, among carnivorous animals of all kinds. Not only were they unharmed, Jason had seen for himself the homage the cows gave Ionia. Also, Jason suspected that the water was the secret to the wild women's immortality. He owed it to science and to mankind to learn what he could about this water and to share his knowledge with the human world, if he ever returned to it.

Yet in sixty-odd days, he had made little progress in his quest. Although he had discovered pool after pool, the connecting channels were all underground. He dared not disturb the earth. He always felt that he was somehow being watched and that if he ever did anything wrong, retribution would come swiftly. The Empty Land might appear to be empty of all but scattered animal life, but he knew it was not. Every now and then, he would pass another hut like Lilith's. The idea that some strange wild woman was sleeping inside made him uneasy. He would tiptoe past these dwellings holding his breath as he went. His sense of being secretly, silently watched inhibited him from proceeding as directly and scientifically as he would have liked. Usually he returned to the hut in the evening feeling that he had done nothing but wander around all day in circles.

That night in the circle of light surrounding the great fire, Ionia stood between her mother and her grandmother, Istar, as the Grand Mother made her customary procession past each woman. When she came to Ionia, she stopped as she had not since the night Ionia first entered the Dance. As she had then,

Ionia stared down at the Grand Mother's feet, but for some reason she was even more frightened tonight.

"Look at me, youngest daughter."

Ionia obeyed.

"Do you know the answer to the question yet?"

Ionia at once felt the old resistance and confusion.

"Are you wild or are you human?" came the Grand Mother's voice. In it she heard her own mother's voice asking the question over and over.

"I still don't understand what it means." Ionia spoke at last.

"It means, child, that you must choose. You cannot belong to my people and to the people of the man-children, whom you have unlawfully led into our country and whom I suffer to remain here only while I wait for you. I am weary of waiting. The time has come. At the full moon, we perform the sacred water rite, the rite that will make you finally and forever one of our race. For this rite, the Dance is a preparation, an emptying that you may be filled. The moon is half now. Before it is full, you must choose. You cannot be human and not human."

The Grand Mother continued to gaze at her. Ionia, once more, felt that she was being drawn into those eyes and drowning in them.

"But what is being human?" Ionia demanded.

"To be human is to know that you will die."

The Grand Mother turned away. The music began. The Dance went on.

43

 Adam and Eva

WHAT did you do on your vacation?" asked Esther Sharp of Margery Pierce, as she dusted the stacked trays.

"I went to the beach," Margery stretched her arms and closed her eyes as if she were still in the sun. "And what did you do, Mrs. Sharp?"

"What did I do?" mimicked Esther, annoyed with Margery for flaunting her tan. "She asks me that and I'm a married woman."

Esther liked to throw her marital status in Margery's face, unaware that Margery could have cared less.

"What's that got to do with anything?" Margery wanted to know.

"Albert didn't get any time off, so how was I supposed to go anywhere?" Esther began to slam the trays down on top of one another.

"Too bad," said Margery, reaching into her bag for her mascara.

"A few items of interest did come my way, however."

Esther paused, waiting for a response from Margery. None came.

"But as I would not want to injure anyone's reputation or character, perhaps I should keep them to myself."

"Yes, perhaps you should," agreed Margery.

"Put that paint away!" Esther was exasperated. "Don't you know any better than to make your face up in public!"

Margery looked up, startled, but said nothing as she obeyed.

"Suppose He saw you. Not that he's any better than he should be, but I guess he knows the difference between what a lady is and isn't."

"Who and what are you talking about?" demanded Margery.

"Well!" Esther triumphed. "I thought we had decided that that was none of your business."

With a flourish of her dust rag, Esther stacked the last tray, then swept away to the kitchen, leaving Margery to suffer, as she supposed, in suspense.

Margery waited a few moments after Esther had gone; then she took out her nail file. Business was slow, and she did not see why she should not occupy herself in some useful fashion between customers. While she filed her nails, she tried not to wonder what Mrs. Sharp would not, but wanted to, talk about. She had already guessed, however, whose reputation and character Mrs. Sharp was pretending to protect, so when she saw Professor Underwood enter the cafeteria, she put away her nail file and regarded him curiously.

He went to get a cup of coffee and a french roll as usual. From the back she could not tell much, except that he was less strikingly dressed. He was not wearing his white suit, as he often did in warm weather; nor his pinstripe one. The jacket and pants were gray, and she wasn't sure they matched. When he turned towards her, she was even more surprised to see that he wasn't wearing a tie. She had never seen Professor Underwood without a tie before. She supposed the informality must be due to the fact that the term had not yet officially opened.

"Well, you look as though you've had a good summer."

Margery looked up at him, embarrassed to realize that she had been staring at his shirt. She saw that he was smiling at her as he laid down his coffee and roll and reached for his wallet. There was something different about his smile, but she could not figure out what it was.

"Yes, I have," she said returning the smile. "I hope you have, too, Professor Underwood."

Then she realized what it was; he was smiling with his mouth instead of his teeth. The effect was to soften the smile; it was not so dazzling. There was something different about his eyes, too.

"It has been a quiet summer," he said, handing her a bill. "I have spent most of it gardening."

He had never offered any information about himself before; she did not know what to say in response; so she said nothing as she made change. Stealing another look at him as she handed him the change, she thought that he did not look as though he had had a quiet summer. He did not look well rested. He looked tired. Then she knew what was different about his eyes. All the glitter had gone out of them. They did not seem so dangerous, did not make her feel penetrated, known to the bone. Yet somehow she liked their expression better, and she felt that for the first time he was seeing her, Margery, not secrets that she didn't even know she had.

"Have a good day," said Margery earnestly.

"That is what you must do also," he replied, and, still smiling, he nodded and turned away.

Mrs. Sharp, who had been watching furtively from the kitchen doorway, approached Margery.

"Do you see what I mean?" she asked in a confidential tone.

"I don't know what you mean," returned Margery. "And I see nothing—except maybe," she spoke softly as if to herself alone, "that he is a little older."

Margery turned back to the cash register and scrutinized her own reflection as if she expected to find the change mirrored there.

When Adam Underwood finished his coffee and roll, he left the cafeteria and headed for the library. The day was sultry, so he removed his jacket and carried it over his arm. As he passed the building where Eva had her office, he paused and looked up at her window. It was open. Most likely that meant she was inside her office. It would be easy enough to find out. In his mind Adam entered the building and ran up the three flights of stairs to Eva's office and stood knocking at Eva's door. After that his imagination failed him. He had no idea what her face would look like when she saw him. He felt a strong desire to find out, but it was overcome by his mother's conviction that any contact with him would be harmful to Eva and by his own realization that he had been imposing on her for five years. His whole relationship with her had been one huge imposition. Now it was over, and he did not know how to initiate a new relationship without similarly imposing. So he hesitated beneath her window for some time, hoping that she might just chance to look out and chance to see him, but she did not. At last he went on. With each step, a strange, heavy feeling in the bottom of his stomach grew heavier.

Eva, unaware that anyone had been waiting beneath her window, had just finished reading the final draft of her article and had sealed it in an envelope addressed to a scholarly periodical. She stared with some satisfaction at the finished product lying on her desk. Then she stood up, stretched herself, and went to the window. There were still few people on campus, so her eyes were drawn to the retreating figure of a man. She drew in her breath and clutched the window sill, because, for a moment, she thought the man was Adam. The back of the head, the rhythm of the walk were so similar. Then she reassured herself that she had been mistaken. This man was in his shirt sleeves. Adam would never appear in public dressed like that.

Without looking at the man again, Eva turned from the window towards her desk. When she picked up the envelope, she found that her hands were trembling. She felt annoyed with herself for being so affected by a glimpse of a man who was not even Adam. How would it be when she really saw him? As if preparing herself for the meeting, she smoothed her hair and skirt, composed her face, clenched her hands until they stopped trembling, tucked the article under her arm, and left her office. Looking neither to the right nor the left, she walked briskly out of the campus to the Post Office where she launched her article by first-class mail.

As soon as the article left her hands, Eva felt lost again. Leaving the Post Office, she wandered back towards campus, not knowing what she would do when she got there. For more than a month the article had kept her occupied. She had felt heroic while writing it. For that time she had been able to believe that she was at the dark center of her own fairytales, struggling, enduring, and that some day her bravery would be rewarded.

As Eva entered the gates, she knew that that was rubbish. There was no ordering of human existence except the arbitrary order human beings themselves created, like the order of academic life. Suddenly she felt estranged from that order which she had always taken for granted. The idea of time rushing by marked by such artificial events as lectures and term exams appalled her. It had been different when she had had Jason. Then time had been measured by his growing; it had an organic meaning. Now time meant nothing, went nowhere, and she went with it. There in the midst of the quiet campus, she wanted to shout, "No!" But no one would have understood or even heard if she had. Instead she just stopped and stood dead still, as if with her very immobility she could resist time.

It was just so that Adam saw her when he emerged from the library. He paused on the steps and stared at her, aware, at some level of his being, that he had never seen her before. He did not know why she happened to be standing still in the middle of the campus; he did not even wonder. What struck him was her bearing; it seemed defiant and strong. He had always thought of her as being ridiculously weak and pliant. Because of that, he realized, he had never been sure what she looked like. As often as he had walked down the street with her, he had never noticed that she was a tall, well-built woman. The people who walked past her motionless figure seemed puny by comparison. He was beginning to feel uncomfortably small himself, and he was wondering if he should not slip away before she happened to see him. Now that he had witnessed her majestic stillness, approaching her seemed even more impossible than knocking on her door had earlier.

Then she began to walk again. In movement she lost her majesty. Her feet dragged; her head bowed; her shoulders drooped. She looked tired and discouraged. For an instant Adam forgot all about himself. Before he had time to remember, he was running after her, without any idea of what he meant to say or do. It didn't matter anymore. He didn't matter anymore.

Eva heard the sound of running feet but paid no attention. When she became aware of someone breathing heavily and walking beside her, she paused. Looking up, she found herself face to face with Adam, but not Adam as she had ever seen him before. His hair was dishevelled; his mouth hung open; beads of sweat stood on his forehead. She was not prepared for this Adam. She stared at him for a moment or two in confusion; then she turned away and kept walking. He walked beside her without attempting to speak. She did not look up again, but she could see his hand opening and closing slowly. It was not an angry motion or a grasping one; rather it was rhythmic, as if he did it to soothe himself. They continued to walk in silence all the way across campus until they reached a small gate. Then both hesitated as if they were two birds balancing on a branch preparing for flight.

"Eva."

She turned towards him.

"What do you want?" she demanded.

The harshness of her tone surprised both of them. Eva could see its effect in his face. She wanted to look away before the nakedness of his face aroused her pity. She would not be manipulated anymore.

"Which way are you going?" he asked.

"What is it that you want?" she repeated.

Her tone was gentler, but her face was stern. All the anger and confusion had gone out of it. She looked at him steadily, calmly, even politely, while she waited for an answer. Her composure discomforted him more than anything else could have. He did not know what to say to her. He did not know the answer to her question, yet it seemed the answer was vitally important. He tried to think; he searched his mind, but it was empty of answers.

"I don't know," he said at last.

He looked at her helplessly as though begging her to tell him the answer, yet hopelessly, as though he expected nothing from her. His eyes, which had once seemed so penetrating, now made her think of the eyes of a blind man. She suddenly felt as though she were standing outside of his darkness watching him search for someone he could not see. Her composure crumbled, her eyes filled with tears, and she turned her face away.

"Eva, I'm sorry," Adam cried out. "I'm so sorry."

"Yes," she said, glancing at him swiftly, "you are."

Without another word, she turned and walked away as fast as she could without running.

Adam stood watching her until she was out of sight.

"I wanted to see you," he said at last. "I love you. "

At dinner that night, Ursula noticed that Eva seemed preoccupied. She spoke even less than usual, and she only toyed with her spaghetti. She had not been so incommunicative in more than a month. Ursula's suspicions and anxieties were aroused, but she had learned not to interrogate Eva. So she chattered on and on about the flea market she had gone to that afternoon, fully aware that Eva was not listening, while she watched for some sign that Eva was ready to speak. Silence would only put Eva on her guard. The trick was to catch her off guard, and so at the end of her monologue, Ursula casually dropped a question.

"What did you do today, Eva?"

"I finished my article and mailed it to a periodical."

"Ah," said Ursula, "and when will they publish it?"

"Probably never," said Eva smiling. "Not every article that's submitted gets published."

"But they ought to publish what you write," said Ursula staunchly.

"They ought to publish this article," Eva agreed. "It was inspired by you, Ursula."

"By me?"

"Yes, it's called: *The Fairytale and Daily Life: How Heroism is Required of Us All.*"

"Daily life is no fairytale," said Ursula gruffly, to cover up how pleased she was.

"No," said Eva, "maybe not. But that only makes the heroism more heroic."

"I hope you're not calling me a hero," Ursula protested.

"Yes, Ursula, I am."

This last remark rendered Ursula speechless. She concentrated on winding her spaghetti round her fork. During the silence that followed, Eva discovered that she wanted to speak.

"I saw Adam today."

It was the first time his name had been spoken by either of them in the presence of the other.

Grammar stopped winding her spaghetti; it slowly slipped from the fork which she held in midair. Eva went on without looking at Ursula.

"He ran after me. I asked him what he wanted. He didn't know."

She spoke slowly, carefully, as if she were reciting three steps of a magic formula. Then she suddenly turned towards Ursula.

"What does he want?" she demanded. "You saw him yourself. What does he want?"

Ursula laid down her fork. "He's changed, is he not?"

"Perhaps."

"I know," said Ursula. "I didn't believe it at first either, but he's changed."

"It is too late."

"Are we to decide that?"

Eva did not answer.

"What is it he wants?" she repeated softly, as if asking only herself.

"I don't know," said Ursula standing up to clear the table, "but I think only you can give it to him."

Eva shook her head. "I have changed, too, Ursula. I have changed, too."

That night the image of Adam's face kept Eva awake, and when she slept, it disturbed her dreams. In one dream she was standing again on the hill of the three trees looking down on the pool where the children had disappeared.

"Come pluck the fruit of your labor," spoke a voice, not her own, yet within her.

Jason, she thought. Of course. He was the fruit of her labor, and the way to Jason must be through the water. Slowly, solemnly, joyfully, Eva approached the pool. She stooped to drink. Then, suddenly, she froze.

Lying still under the water was Adam's naked body. She stared in horror, supposing that he must have drowned. But then, somehow, it seemed to her that he was only sleeping. Her fear ebbed away. She noticed that his face seemed older than she ever remembered it, full of lines and shadows she had never seen there before. There was a sadness in his face that touched her. In his seeming sleep he looked so vulnerable. She reached out her hand with an impulse to caress and then withdrew it, for his face began to change. The shadows and lines dissolved. His face grew younger, harder, emptier. She recognized it as the face she had known. Then it grew younger still and softer. She had not seen this face before. As she wondered at it, his body began to change, too, growing smaller, smoother, suppler. She glimpsed for a moment a child that looked very much like Fred. Then even the child dissolved. In the water she saw a tiny infant. Somehow his wrinkled face looked as tired and sad as the face of the older man. She reached into the water and drew the baby out. Then she unbuttoned her shirt and put him to her breast. The baby opened his eyes, and she knew he was Adam; she felt that he knew her, too. She started to sing softly, not words but sounds like wind and moving water.

When Eva woke the next morning, she found that her eyes were swollen and her cheeks stiff with salt.

44

🕺 Ionia Chooses 🕺

WHERE is Ionia?" demanded Jason as he looked up and
saw Lilith approaching the breakfast fire alone.

"She wanted to be by herself for awhile," explained Lilith seating herself
cross-legged before the fire.

"When is she coming back?" asked Fred worried.

"When she has chosen," answered Lilith. "The moon is full tomorrow night."

"But how can anyone make a choice like that!" shouted Jason, exploding
with the anger and anxiety he had tried to keep hidden from Ionia. "How could
anyone, who didn't have to, choose to die?"

"You are supposing, Jason, Son of Eva, that to choose to die means to choose
not to live."

"What else could it mean," began Jason.

"I don't want Ionia to die," broke in Fred, "or Lion or Jason or Grammar or
me."

"We don't have any choice in the matter, Fred," said Jason flatly. "We have
to die whether we like it or not."

"I do not know," said Lilith slowly, "but from what I have seen of them,
human beings choose between life and death everyday. It is my people who
have no choice."

🌿🙌

Weary from one more night of giving herself to the Dance, Ionia wandered
through the Empty Land, conscious, at that moment, only of a great sense of
relief at being alone. The days and nights since the Grand Mother's ultimatum
had been difficult. No one would speak of her decision, but everyone watched
her: Jason, Fred, her mother, all her grandmothers and great grandmothers, and
worst of all, the Grand Mother herself. Everyone, human and wild, waited to
see what she would choose to be. She was tired of all their watching and
waiting, their passive scrutiny of her confusion. Inwardly she rebelled against
the choice she was compelled to make. As she went her way alone, she wondered if that might be the answer: to be neither wild nor human but simply

alone, forever alone, with nothing to choose and nothing to lose. Yet alone, unless she were wild, she would not live out one winter in the Empty Land. She could not be both; she could not be neither. She had to choose. But how could she made a choice like that? It wasn't fair. Out of frustration and exhaustion, Ionia began to sob.

Blinded by her tears, Ionia did not realize, until she stumbled into it, that she was approaching one of the lakes. Finding herself there, she knelt and splashed her face and body with water. Then, her sobs quieted, she took a long drink. When she had quenched her thirst, she felt calmer and more alert. She stepped back from the water and looked around her. It was a cloudless, windless day. Its stillness seemed to Ionia a waiting stillness. The sky was such a delicate blue that it looked fragile, as though it might shatter. The near-full moon, setting in the morning sky, seemed transparent. Without consciously deciding what to do, Ionia climbed the closest hill and sat down on its summit.

The Empty Land spread out before her. Never had it seemed so vast and unending. Yet she knew it had an end. Had she not lived all her life at the edge of the Empty Land? But then perhaps the hill of the three trees was only the Empty Land's beginning, and the rest of it went on and on forever. Forever. Forever was a frightening idea. She could not imagine it. Everything else she knew had an end. School ended; roads ended; sleep ended; Fred's zoo animals ended. Days and nights ended. Seasons and years ended, although they began again. Maybe that's what forever was: beginning again and again and again, just as the Dance kept going round and around and around. Maybe her mother and her grandmother and great grandmother and her great, great grandmother and the Grand Mother never wondered about forever; they were forever. Maybe only people who couldn't imagine forever tried to. Yet, if she chose, she could be forever, too; she did not have to die. She could become one of her mother's people and live forever and ever, without an end, only a beginning.

Ionia closed her eyes and tried to picture herself as a full member of the Grand Mother's race, growing to be wild and beautiful like her mother, never aging, except in strength and grace, living by the rhythm and rule of the Dance while days, nights, seasons, years passed in endless succession. It seemed to Ionia that her endless life would also be endlessly certain and secure. There would be no more doubt or indecision ever again, and no more sense of not belonging. When she compared such a life to human life in which the only certainty was death, the decision seemed simple. There was nowhere in the human world that she belonged now and no way of knowing what would become of her if she went back. Death was an uncertain certainty. Death was even more difficult to imagine than forever. No one could tell her, from the inside, what it was like or what happened afterwards or whether anything happened at all. If she did not know what forever was, at least she knew her mother, and she knew what it was like to be alive. Maybe that was all she needed to know about forever; that she would spend it with her mother, never to be lost from her again. Back in the human world she had been ready to die for her mother. Now all she had to do was live.

Suddenly sure of her choice, Ionia scrambled to her feet and started down the hill, anxious to tell someone of her decision. To tell someone would make it final. She would run to the hut and tell her mother. Her mother should know first. She would run to the hut and tell her mother. Run to the hut and wake her mother. The words repeated themselves rhythmically in Ionia's mind as she ran. Run to the hut. Tell Mother. Run to the hut. Wake Mother. She tried to picture her mother's face when she told her she would be her daughter forever. Run to the hut. But she could not imagine her mother's response. Wake Mother. The image that formed in her mind was of an expressionless face. Run to the hut. Tell Mother. The harder she tried to force the face into smiles, the blanker the face became. Run hut. Wake Mother. At last the features became indistinct, and the image was a blur. Run wake. Run tell. Then slowly the face took form again. Run. The image this time was not her mother's face but Fred's. Tell. His expression was plainly one of bewilderment.

Out of breath and blinded with sweat, Ionia stumbled to a halt and lay panting in the hollow of a hill. She had forgotten about Fred. Fred would be outside the hut playing. She had forgotten about having to tell Fred. And later Jason. They wouldn't say anything, she knew. They would not begrudge her ever-lasting life. Fred wouldn't even understand, but he would sense somehow that he was being left behind. He would look at her like a sad puppy who does not understand why he is being punished but does not protest. Jason would not look at her at all. He would look away. He would never look her in the face again but would treat her in that strange, distant manner he had used of late, which made her feel as though she belonged to a different species than he did. And, if she chose to become one of her mother's people, she would.

As her breathing quieted and her mind cleared, Ionia knew that she had not decided yet, because she had not honestly reckoned her loss. If she became one of her mother's people, she would lose Jason and Fred; that was certain. Even if the Grand Mother allowed them to remain in the Empty Land, which was unlikely, she would have to watch them change and grow old and die while she remained forever unchanged. But they would not stay. They would go away, and she would never know what had become of them. Only one day she would know that they must be dead. One day no one she knew would be alive on earth. At this thought, a feeling of loneliness overcame Ionia. She wondered, if she stayed in the Empty Land, whether she would always be lonely. She wished she could ask her mother, but her mother might not know. Her mother had never been human or even part human. Her mother had nothing and no one to miss. But she missed Jason and Fred already, and, if she went away, she would miss her mother. Why did she have to make a choice like that between two different ways of being miserable? No one else had to make such decisions. She wished for a moment that none of them had ever come to the Empty Land. Then, for the first time, it occurred to her to wonder why they had come.

Why had they? Ionia tried to remember. Her memory of what had happened was unclear, but she was able to see images. She saw her father's face, white with rage. She felt his grip on her arm as he dragged her through the empty space and hurled her to the ground. She saw Mrs. Brooke crying and heard Grammar screaming. Then suddenly she was running, instinctively, joyfully, towards the hill of the three trees, leaving all the noise and confusion behind. Fred had hold of her hand and wouldn't let go so she dragged him along, but Fred hadn't mattered as much as she had told her mother and the Grand Mother he had. Nothing had mattered except that she was going to her mother's country at last. Then Jason had caught up with them. She remembered him panting beside her. She remembered that she had not wanted him. Why had he followed, she wondered, but she did not ask him, and soon she had ceased to wonder at anything.

Now she wondered again, for, all at once, the answer seemed important. It was important to know why Jason had followed when he had no reason to. He had not lost his mother or his home, and yet he had left both to follow her into the Empty Land, into unknown danger, possible death, with the chance that he might never see his mother again. Why? Because of her? Because of Fred? Because he cared what happened to them? For the first time Ionia understood that Jason had made a decision, too, but in making it he had not thought of himself but of them. Maybe that was why he made his decision in an instant while hers was taking her whole life. She had been thinking of no one but herself since they had entered the Empty Land. She had never once thanked Jason. She had never stopped to consider what he had given up for her sake. Nor had she considered what Jason's sacrifice cost his mother; nor what her mindless dash into the Empty Land cost Grammar.

All at once, Ionia began to cry; she wasn't sure why; her feelings were so strong and mixed. She wept for a long while until she was empty of tears. Then, exhausted by the Dance and the decision, she fell into a deep, dreamless sleep.

When she awoke, hours later, with the afternoon sun in her eyes, Ionia knew at once that everything was different. She was different. She was decided. She rose from the ground and walked neither slowly nor swiftly in the direction of the hut.

When she arrived, Jason and Fred were outside building the supper fire. As they did not, at once, see her, she paused, wishing to see them before she approached them. As she watched Jason, bare to the waist, chopping sod with a bone knife, Ionia noticed that Jason was strong, though she had always thought of him as being weak. Fred, she realized, eyeing the short legs of his pants, and the short waist of his shirt, must have grown. They had both been growing and changing without her knowing it. Standing up to fetch another square of sod, Fred caught sight of her.

"Ionia!" he shouted. "I don't want you to die!"

He ran towards her and nearly knocked her over as he threw his arms around her to give her a fierce hug.

"I'm not going to die yet," she said, holding Fred tightly but looking beyond him towards Jason who was standing, holding the bone knife in midair, and staring.

"But you are going to die?" Jason asked incredulously, dropping the knife and taking a couple of steps towards her.

"Someday, Jason," she said, "the same as you will."

"But, Ionia," he protested, "you have a choice! Do you mean you want to die?"

"I don't want to die any more than you do, Jason, or you do, Fred," she released herself from Fred's embrace, "but I will die when I have to, because I am a human being."

As she spoke, Ionia became aware of her mother standing in the entrance to the hut. Lifting her eyes so that she looked directly into her mother's eyes, Ionia repeated:

"I am a human being."

Whether it was pain or rage or grief that momentarily touched her mother's face, Ionia was never certain. The expression was gone almost as quickly as it had come, and her mother's face was as beautiful and still and unknowable as ever.

The next morning the children rose early. The milk was simmering over the fire when Lilith returned from the Dance. She did not speak as she seated herself before the fire, but she looked at each child in turn, her eyes resting last and longest on Ionia. It was Jason who broke the silence.

"We have decided to try to go back to our own country to live with my mother."

"Yes," said Lilith, still looking at Ionia, "that is a good plan."

Ionia looked steadily back. She did not regret her choice, but she had never loved her mother so much before.

"But we're not sure how to get back," Jason went on. "We were hoping you could tell us."

"If you will wait until tomorrow, I will take you myself."

Fred squealed with delight. Jason blinked with surprise. Ionia turned her face away and swallowed hard, torn between joy at being with her mother for a few more days and desire to get the parting over.

"I would like to see your mother again, Jason, Son of Eva. I did not get a chance to say good-bye to her or to thank her for what her son has done for me and my children."

Jason blushed with pleasure; then he blushed with embarrassment as he remembered, for the first time in months, that Ionia's mother was naked. He did not know how to tell her.

"If you come back with us to my mother's apartment, you would have to. . . ," he paused and cleared his throat. "You might need some clothes."

Lilith threw back her head and laughed.

"Do not worry, Jason, Son of Eva. I still have the black garment of Ursula's, which I saved because it made me remember her."

🌱🌱🌱

The following morning, Lilith, the children, and Lion set out on their journey, casting their strange, tattered shadows before them as they walked. Ionia was determined not to look back. Jason looked eagerly forward. Fred, holding his mother's hand and letting her lead him while he turned his head, was the only one who saw Istar, standing on a hilltop, watching them walk away, her orange hair looking, in that early light, like a spark that had fallen from the rising sun.

45

 ## The Human Mother

URSULA Underwood had taken it upon herself to wash and
mend Eva Brooke's winter wardrobe. Eva had protested at first, insisting that
she ought to care for her own clothes and that Ursula was to be her friend and
companion, not a maid-of-all-work. Ursula had not listened to Eva's protests,
however; for she could tell from the condition in which Eva kept her clothes that
she did not care for them. Eva seemed not to mind or even to notice when a
lining had torn or a hem had come loose or a button was missing, and as long
as her clothes did not have a discernible odor, she saw no point in washing
them. The trouble was that Eva Brooke had no appreciation of the underlying
principles of cleanliness and tidiness. Ursula Underwood had, and so that
afternoon she had taken over the kitchen for her operations. There were sweaters soaking in the sink and sweaters spread out on the counters to dry. Sitting
on the chair in a wicker basket was a pile of mending to be done, on the table
a stack of ironing. Hanging in the window, blocking the breeze, were woolens
that needed airing. As she alternately washed and ironed, Ursula perspired; for
although the autumn term would begin in a week and a half, it was nonetheless
a hot summer afternoon.

Ursula did not mind the strenuousness of her efforts, however. While she
was absorbed and uncomfortable, she did not think about other things, worri-
some things, which had been slowly undermining her strength of mind, her
sense of purpose. The children had been gone for months now. She had tried
all summer not to think in terms of time, but with summer's end approaching,
time was becoming more and more difficult to forget. When autumn began, her
summer formula for comfort and hope would be useless. Against her will, she
would be haunted by images of cold, hungry children, and if winter passed
without their return, there would be no hope left by spring. Life without hope
was something she was not yet capable of contemplating. So she worked with
a will while she could, grateful for Eva's disgraceful disregard of her clothes,
for the heat, for her own sweat, for anything that could postpone the nightmare
of nothingness.

Eva Brooke, sitting at Jason's desk, allegedly composing an opening lecture for one of her courses but actually watching the curtains float on the breeze, was having less luck escaping the nightmare, perhaps because she had never tried to escape it. The imminent opening of the autumn term had made Eva realize the passage of time also, but she had never had any hope. For her there had been no summer comfort. She knew the children were not coming back. She was reconciled to that reality as Ursula was not. In the future she, Eva, would have to be the strong one. She could return some of the support Ursula had given her; for she knew she would never fall apart again as she had earlier in the summer. She would fulfill all her functions; her performance would be adequate; outwardly she would appear to be the same person she always had been. If there was nothing behind the visible structure of her life, no one but she would be the wiser.

At least that was what Eva told herself over and over again until most of the time, especially during the daytime, she believed it. Yet there were other times—in the morning before she got out of bed; at night before she went to sleep or when she woke suddenly from troubled dreams; or at odd moments like this one, when she forgot her official function and stared instead at windblown curtains—when she wondered if she were right to be so resigned, not to the loss of the children, but to the emptiness of her life.

Since the day they had encountered one another outside the library, Eva had not seen Adam, but there had been another letter from him; of all things, a love letter. It had made her so angry that, after reading it once, she had crumpled it into a ball and prepared to throw it into a wastebasket. Then, against her will, for something stronger than her will had compelled her to do it, she had stuffed it into a drawer of her desk instead. A few days later, also against her will, she took it out and read it again. That time the letter touched her as she had feared it would. She knew he was telling her the truth. What convinced her was that he asked nothing of her, not even forgiveness, and he made no excuses for himself. He was not trying to win her sympathy or relieve his guilt. The letter was not written for gain. It was a simple statement of feeling. He had not even asked for an answer. Nor had she given him one. She had folded the letter and put it away without telling Ursula about it. Then she had tried to forget it. It had come too late. The loss of the children was a void between them, and out of that void nothing could be created.

Eva shook her head as she looked at the empty page, with the afternoon light slanting across it, that should have been filled with lecture notes. She had accomplished nothing, and yet she was tired. Rising from the desk, she stretched herself and went to stand in the window. As the kitchen window was open also, Eva could hear Ursula moving about. As she thought of Ursula's outrage at the condition of her clothes, she smiled. Her one concern in refusing to be reconciled with Adam had been that she might prevent Ursula from returning to keep house for him if she wanted to. She had told Ursula once that she must feel free to go to him, but Ursula had seemed offended at the very idea. It was then that Eva had realized that the bond between herself and Ursula was stronger than the bond of blood. They were both women who had lost their children. They would go on living with each other, if not for each other, until one of them died. They could not fill each other's emptiness, but they would keep each other from becoming lost in the emptiness. And that, decided Eva, was all she could reasonably expect from the rest of her life.

Having perfected her resignation once more, Eva experienced the sense of bitter peacefulness that came as a reward. Closing her eyes, she leaned against the window frame. The sun poured down on her face; the breeze played with the loose strands of her hair as she listened to the late afternoon sounds: Ursula wringing one more of her sweaters, rush hour traffic congesting the streets, doors slamming, dogs barking, children playing ball. A world of noise and commotion creating a contrast to the dead quiet within her.

Then Eva heard a sound that did not belong to the city afternoon: the sound of one voice singing, softer than any of the sounds that surrounded it, yet stronger. As the voice continued to sing, it unmade all other sounds, leaving silence in its wake. Eva trembled as she listened but did not open her eyes. Surely the voice she heard was a dream voice that had somehow invaded the daytime. But the voice kept growing clearer, stronger, more insistent. At last Eva opened her eyes and looked down into the street. When she saw, she clutched the windowsill for support and shouted.

"Ursula!"

Alarmed, Ursula dropped the iron, forgetting to set it on its end, and she hurried towards Jason's room. As she put her hand on the knob, Eva opened the door from the other side, and the two women collided, breathless.

"Ursula! It's them, the children, hurry!"

Ursula stared at Eva, fearful that the woman had at last lost her wits, but Eva dragged her through the front door, and then so swiftly down the stairs that Ursula nearly lost her balance as well as her breath. Then, through the glass doors, Ursula saw. As one force, the two women burst through the doors. On the steps there was such joyous commotion as had never been known in that neighborhood.

It took some time for the three women, the three children and the one dog to get back up the stairs in that condition. They filed into the apartment still breathless and wordless. It was Jason who recovered himself first.

"Mother," he said, "is something burning?"

Then Grammar shrieked, "The iron!" and still holding Fred by the hand, she made for the kitchen. "Eva," she moaned, "I've ruined your best skirt."

Then Eva began to laugh so hard that her son had to hold her up.

In a little while, everyone had crowded into the kitchen. Fred sat on Grammar's sparse lap. Lion stood under the table noisily lapping water. Jason sat beside his mother, allowing her to keep hold of his hand. Ionia sat on her other side opposite Fred and Grammar. All the mending, ironing, and airing woolens had ended up in an undifferentiated heap in one corner of the kitchen. The damp and soaking sweaters had been dumped into the bathtub to provide counter space for the making of lemonade. This office Grammar had taken on herself in an attempt to stop crying, but it hadn't worked. A quantity of salt water had fallen into the lemonade everyone was sipping, and though her sobs had quieted, Grammar now had the hiccups, which Fred thought very funny. Every time she hiccupped, he laughed, but there was evidence of tears on his face as there was on everyone's but Lilith's. As the human beings hiccupped and laughed and cried, Lilith watched with her head cocked to one side.

"I would have brought them back sooner if I'd known," said Lilith to Grammar and Eva, "but I did not know. I do not know about worrying and missing."

"None of us really knew," said Jason turning towards his mother. "It's the strangest thing, Mother. Something happened to my memory while I was there. I couldn't remember what happened here; or not clearly, only fragments." He reddened as he remembered how vividly he had recalled his mother's face; perhaps sometime he would tell her, but not now, before the others. "Nothing was connected. Now that we're back I can't remember much about what happened there. Can you, Ionia?"

Ionia did not answer; she felt that what had happened to her was not the same as what had happened to Jason, but she did not wish to speak of it; she could not, yet. She turned to look at her mother, who looked back at her. Jason was diverted from his question by his mother's account of their disappearance.

"So that's what happened," murmured Jason. "So that's why the stars were in a different place. It must have had something to do with the water. I wonder what?"

"Well, there's to be no further investigation," broke in Grammar between hiccups. "Is that understood? You're all to stay here where you belong."

Grammar spoke firmly, but the look she sent Ionia was a questioning look.

"Yes," said Ionia, "we're all staying here."

"Ionia," cried Grammar, her voice breaking and her face crumpling once again, "I've missed you so much."

Grammar stretched out an arm, and Ionia went to her, kneeling beside her and laying her head in what remained of Grammar's lap. Grammar put an arm around Ionia's shoulder while Fred patted her head as if she were Lion.

For a time no one spoke.

"Eva," said Grammar at last, "we have got to let Adam know the children are back; or at least I've got to."

As inevitable as Grammar's statement was, Eva felt startled. She had not yet considered how the children's return might affect him—them, herself and him. About the last she did not know what to think or how she felt.

"Yes," she said slowly, "he must know. He might want the children with him again."

Grammar felt Fred stiffen. Ionia lifted her head. Jason glanced at Lilith in the window. She had not moved, but she had the look of a deer waiting for the hunter's scent on the wind.

"But we can't," said Ionia, getting to her feet and looking from Mrs. Brooke to Grammar. "We can't go back to him. He said we couldn't unless we brought my mother with us, and we can't! We won't!"

"Child," said Grammar, "in the history of mankind many men have said many foolish and wicked things, and afterwards they were sorry. Your father is a changed man. You would not know him; not that you did before."

"But you can't send them back to him," broke in Jason; then he turned to his mother. "I told Fred and Ionia they could stay here and live with us. They can, can't they?"

"Of course Ionia and Fred are always welcome here, but. . . ."

"But the point is not," interrupted Grammar, "where anyone is going to live—we can settle that later—but that Adam should know what has happened. He is your father," she reminded Ionia and Fred.

Ionia and Fred stared at Grammar, finding the change in her attitude as mysterious as any change she hinted of in their father.

"What is this change you speak of, Ursula?"

Lilith slipped from the windowsill and approached the table.

"Well," began Grammar, "for one thing, he's forgotten you. He hardly believes in your existence. I had all I could do to persuade him you were not simply his own sick fancy."

"So it is as Istar said," murmured Lilith. "He never knew whether or not I was a dream."

"And since he gave you up," continued Grammar, "gave up all hope and interest in getting you back, that is, he has become an altogether more agreeable and sensible man. He has even taken up gardening, and I must say the garden is doing very nicely."

"You have seen him? And you are sure this change is not another trick?" Lilith asked warily. "You are sure it is real?"

"Yes," said Eva, before Grammar could answer, and she blushed as everyone turned to look at her.

There was an awkward silence as everyone waited for Eva to say something more, but she could not bring herself to speak of the letter; not now, not to all of them. She only blushed deeper as she thought of it.

"Well," said Grammar, eyeing Eva with more suspicion than surprise, "it is getting late, near suppertime. I suggest that some of us bathe,"—she gave each of the children a severe look, for although she had to admit that they all looked stronger and healthier than they ever had, they were dreadfully dirty—"while others of us cook. Then we will all go early to bed. We can decide what to do in the morning. Since Adam will refuse to have a telephone, there's no way we can let him know tonight unless we go there ourselves. And I think you've had enough traveling for one day."

So saying, Grammar went to get the sweaters out of the bathtub so that the children might get into it.

Late that night, the happy confusion of baths, supper, and bedding-down over, the apartment was silent; even the sounds of the city night had stilled. In Jason's room, Jason and Fred slept on the mattress and box springs with Lion on the floor beside them. Ionia and Grammar shared the big bed in Eva's room. Eva had taken the couch in the living room, but though she had lain still for a long time, she had not slept. The life she had thought was lost, not just Jason's but her own, had returned from the dead. Resurrection would not let her rest.

At last she rose, unable to lie still any longer, and went to the kitchen. In the doorway she paused. There was Lilith, sitting, as she had before, on the window sill, framed by what moonlight managed to filter down between the buildings. Eva had known that she might find Lilith there, since Lilith had not left; nor had she said when she would. Yet her presence, just then, was overwhelming, as if the moon itself sat in the window. This was the Lilith of Eva's dreams, and she seemed too large, too strange, too wild for the small apartment, just as the new life Eva felt within herself seemed to be straining at the bounds of her body. Then Lilith turned to look at Eva. Though Lilith's face was in shadow, Eva found or felt her eyes. She crossed the kitchen and sat in the chair closest to the window. For a time the two women shared the silence, waiting for the words that would come.

"Eva."

"Lilith."

They named each other.

"Eva, do you know what you will do?"

Until that moment she had not known.

"Lilith, I will go to Adam. I will be his wife."

"You would go freely?"

"Yes."

"He would honor your freedom?"

"Yes."

"Then let it be so."

Again they were silent.

"Eva," spoke Lilith from the silence, "my children, both of them, are human. I am wild. They need a human mother. Will you be the human mother?"

"Lilith, I will be the human mother, but they will not forget the wild mother."

"Let them remember."

Silence fell around their words, and Eva and Lilith sat together until dawn.

The getting of breakfast was a busy, bustling affair with Grammar attempting to scramble eggs and fry bacon, while Eva mixed biscuits, and the children squeezed orange juice. At last everyone sat down to more breakfast than he could eat. The eggs were a bit dry, the biscuits underdone, and the children had forgotten to strain the seeds from the orange juice, but no one complained. For a few minutes everyone ate busily; then Grammar took it upon herself to open the discussion.

"Well, what's to be done?"

The question was general, but Grammar looked at Eva, and so did everyone else.

"Well," began Eva, "I think we should all go to see Adam as soon as we can."

"You will go, too?" asked Grammar.

"Yes," said Eva.

"And she will go as a bride."

Four mouths fell open as four heads turned to stare at Lilith, then at Eva.

"Eva," said Grammar, "I think, especially for the children's sake, that you ought to explain what Lilith has said since you do not seem inclined to contradict it."

"Well," she said, looking at the children, "as Grammar told you yesterday, your father, Ionia and Fred, has changed," she paused. "He's changed towards me, too."

"Too bad you haven't changed towards him," muttered Jason, not meaning his mother to hear.

"But I have," she said. "You don't know. You weren't here. It's all different. . . ."

She felt helpless and flustered.

"If you think your mother's being too soft on him, you're mistaken, young man," said Grammar to Jason. "She's not like she used to be. She's been very severe with my son. It's news to me, too, that she's changed her mind. If she has, I suppose there's some reason."

Grammar turned again towards Eva.

"There is something I haven't told you, Ursula. I received a letter from Adam some time ago. It convinced me of his change, especially of his change towards me, but I never answered it. I never meant to. When the children were gone, when I thought they weren't coming back. . .well, it seemed no use for Adam and me to. . .well, now it's all different. The children are back! You're back! Don't you see?"

The children still looked bewildered.

"Will you mind having me for a mother?"

They shook their heads. Fred grinned. Jason thought to himself that for Ionia and Fred this change was no bad deal. But for him—he could hardly bear to finish the thought. And yet, and yet. . .to have unlimited access to that roof, to be able to use the telescope every night. . . .

"Well, if that's how things stand," said Grammar, beginning to beam, "then we have a busy morning ahead of us."

And she got up at once to clear the breakfast dishes away.

46

 To the Garden

LATE that afternoon, weary from bending and picking a whole row of tomatoes, Adam Underwood stood up. With his free hand, he rubbed the small of his back. With the other hand, he held a basket full of perfectly ripe tomatoes. It pleased him that the garden, which he had nurtured if not planted, should be so prolific, but it also depressed him; he did not know what to do with the abundance of produce. Sighing, Adam carried the heavy basket to the kitchen and set it just inside the door. He was too tired to do anything about the tomatoes at present, and it was too early to think of picking corn for supper. The afternoon sun, now that he was not laboring beneath it, felt good. He decided that he would go sit on the newly acquired garden bench and soak some of it in. He moved the bench closer to the wall. Then he sat down, closing his eyes, and leaned back, letting the wall support him.

As he sat resting in the sun with the palms of his hands spread over his knees, the feeling again overcame him, as it had so often in these past few weeks, that he was a very old man. Maybe he felt that way because the pattern of his future days and years was set. No great change would come to him. He had no hope of winning Eva. He had only written to her because it seemed to him that a truth so long unrecognized should at last be acknowledged. That the truth no longer had the power to move her saddened him, but he could not blame Eva. No, he did not blame her at all. Only sometimes the expanse of emptiness that was the rest of his life appalled him. To think of it made him tired, so tired. . .Adam's head rolled to one side. His mouth fell open. He slept.

Back in the city a strange party made its way to the train station, causing everyone it passed to stop and stare. Two women led the way. Both had loose hair that fell to the waist. One woman wore a green gown and she had flowers strewn in her smooth hair. The other woman wore black tatters that matched her tangled black hair, and her feet were bare. Behind the two women followed an older woman who clutched the hand of a ragged but well-scrubbed little boy.

Beside the boy trotted a large, golden dog. An older boy and girl followed these three. Like the small boy, the girl was ragged.

When Albert Sharp, the train conductor, saw the two women entering the car, he first rubbed his eyes in disbelief. Then, when the vision did not disappear, he fell to his knees; for he knew, at last, it was She.

"Mrs. Underwood!" he cried, kissing Lilith's hands. "Albert Sharp at your command."

"Rise," ordered Lilith. "And I am not Mrs. Underwood. Here is Adam Underwood's bride."

"Mrs. Brooke?" said Albert. "I don't understand. . . ."

"It is not necessary that you should understand," said Lilith, "only that you should rejoice."

Lilith sat down in a window seat and drew Eva down beside her. Across the aisle sat Grammar and Fred; behind them, Jason and Ionia.

"I am in charge of finances," said Grammar. "How much for six one way fares, uh, six and a half," she amended, glancing at Lion who stood uncertainly in the aisle.

"Not a cent," declared Albert. "It's on me. Er—a wedding gift," he gestured in Eva's direction. Then, leaning closer to Grammar he whispered, "Is everything all right?"

"All is well," she answered. "All is very well." Reaching across the aisle to touch Eva's arm, Grammar asked, "Shall we bring this gentleman along as a witness?"

"By all means," Eva agreed. "Let us have Mr. Sharp as a witness."

"But where is your friend with the green legs?" Lilith asked.

"I have no idea, Mrs. Under—I mean, Your Majesty, but I'll do my best to serve."

Bowing at the waist and tipping his hat, Albert left the wedding party and proceeded down the aisle, fulfilling, as best he could, in his state of bewildered ecstasy, his duties as a train conductor.

When they arrived at the house, they discovered Adam in the yard asleep on the bench. Without waking him, they gathered about him in a semicircle. Eva and Lilith stood before him. To one side stood Grammar, Ionia and Fred, and Lion; to the other, Jason and Albert. As he stared at the sleeping man, Albert felt his hostility dissolve. The magnificent and terrible Professor Underwood was, after all, only a human being, one who slept with his mouth open and drooled slightly. Albert felt some pity for him. He would not like to wake from an afternoon nap to find seven people staring at him. He was about to suggest that Professor Underwood might like some time alone to prepare himself for the ceremony, when She spoke.

"Adam, awake and behold your bride."

Adam opened his eyes and saw Eva standing before him with the light of the sun behind her. He spoke no word and made no gesture for fear she might disappear. Surely she was a vision; for the voice which had commanded him was a dream voice, speaking from inside himself. The longer he looked the less sure he was. If the woman before him was a dream, then the dream was more substantial than the reality had ever been. Never before had she seemed so radiant and so real. Perhaps it was partly her hair. He had never seen it loose before. He would have liked to touch it, but he dared not. He continued to gaze and would have gone on gazing if the vision had not spoken.

"Adam, our children have come back to us. Don't you see them?"

Only then did Adam become aware that he and Eva were not alone. There were his children, standing with his mother. There was Eva's son, standing beside her, hardly a child anymore. How was it they had returned alive?

He could not see Lilith.

He half-rose to his feet to greet the children. Then he fell to his knees instead and lifted his palms as if he were a starving man begging for bread.

"Forgive" was all he said.

"All is forgiven," said Eva taking Adam's hands and raising him to his feet.

"I have come to be your wife and the mother of our children, if you will have me."

For a moment Adam stared at Eva in astonishment. Then he said, "I will."

Keeping hold of one of Adam's hands, Eva went to stand beside Adam in the presence of the others.

The evening shadows lengthened, and one voice began to sing. Any of them could have said whose voice it was if they had wondered, but they did not. The voice seemed to come from nowhere and everywhere, disembodied as the shadows, drawing no attention to itself but focusing all attention on the man and the woman.

Although no words were spoken, Albert knew he was witnessing a marriage. He had, for a moment, forgotten the identity of the man and the woman, but it did not matter. Even those who had long known the man and the woman shared in his awed detachment.

Then the singing stopped.

No one knew that that was what had happened. They only knew that suddenly they were themselves again. Adam turned to kiss Eva. Then he addressed the whole company.

"There must be a wedding feast. Mother, children, whoever you are in the hat! I'm so glad you've come. The garden. I don't know what to do with it! So many vegetables! Come, you must all help me harvest the corn!"

In the gladness of going to the garden to pick corn, no one but Ionia noticed that Lilith was gone. Unseen, she slipped away from the others and ran to the empty space. There she paused. She could see her mother standing beneath the three trees, a small black figure against the purple of the evening sky. Her mother must have seen her, too, for she raised one arm. Ionia raised hers in answer. Then her mother disappeared beyond the hill.

Slowly lowering her arm, Ionia caught sight of a small black heap lying on the ground some feet away. She rushed to the spot. Crouching, she picked up the tattered black dress and cradled it in her arms. Then burying her face in it she began to weep, rocking herself, back and forth, back and forth.

It was just so that Jason found her. Without a word he sat down and waited for her to finish crying. He had, in a sense, lost his mother, too, that day. He would have cried if he could have, but he couldn't. Besides it wasn't right to cry over something that made his mother so happy. And it wasn't as if he'd never see his mother again. He felt bad for Ionia but could think of nothing to say to comfort her.

"Well," he began feebly when she had stopped crying, "I guess you're my sister now."

"I guess you're my brother now," she returned, and, in spite of herself, she smiled a stiff, salt-encrusted smile.

"Come on, then," said Jason.

Jason stood up and, offering Ionia a hand, helped her to her feet. Ionia, still holding the tattered dress, let Jason lead her back to the garden.

After Words

After Words 1979 - 1993

Ionia,
fourteen years ago I left you
mourning for your Mother,
allowing yourself to be led
where I needed you to go.
I still see your wild
mother's borrowed black
dress, shed
like the skin of a snake,
while She, bright, sinuous
as the bare hills,
glides free—or maybe
She flies with the wild geese,
still calling to you
as summer ends again
and again.

"How can I make that choice?"
you kept asking.
"Why do I have to?"
Choose: between Garden and
Wilderness. Choose:
between human bonds
and boundless hills.
Why did I make you choose?
Ionia, I only know
I have never stopped asking myself,
and your question echoes
in all my stories.

Listen, Ionia:
Don't let me have the last word.
Question authority.
Question the author.
But no, I see
you can't be bothered
with after words. You're busy.
You've turned your back to me
to face a wild expanse
of empty paper.
You draw the hill first,
then the trees,
then the moon,
and last the woman dancing.
Only this time, Ionia,
the woman is you.

Elizabeth Cunningham
with thanks to Megan